"In despair there are the most intense enjoyments, especially when one is very acutely conscious of the hopelessness of one's position."

------ Fedor Dostoevsky

THE GALACTIC ISLAND

PARISH V. DAMONE

Cadmus Publishing
www.cadmuspublishing.com

Phantom Press Publishing LLC

"EXPRESSION IS EVERYTHING" ™

Aknowledgements

I first give honor to God.

To my mother Brenda McClendon Pitts, a breast cancer survivor and my biggest hero. Thank you, mama, for all the sacrifices you've made so I could have an opportunity to chase my dreams – I couldn't have done this without you. To my dad William James Pitts, a great father and a man of God. Thank you, pop, for believing in me even when the chips were down. Well, look what the Lord has done for us now! God is good.

To my kids and grandkids – Brandon, Samantha, Brittney, Jamal, Unique', Sebastian, Devontae, Elexus, Darrius, Chloey, and Jacie – I love you more than words can ever express. This book is my gift to each of you. Especially Brittney, who inspired me to write a Black fantasy novel featuring characters she could more easily identify with growing up. Brittney's love affair with this story is the reason why "The Galactic Island" holds such a special place in my heart. Hey, Rootie! We did it sweetheart!

To Avis, who has always been like a sister to me, thank you for the love and encouragement you've given me all these years. You've made a lasting impression in the lives of me and my family. I thank God for you each and every day.

To all my friends and family back home and to my extended family at Second Missionary Baptist Church in Morgan City, Louisiana, I thank you for your continued prayers and for the encouraging sentiments you've shared with my mom and pop regarding the injustice of my wrongful incarceration. God bless you all, and I pray that you or your loved ones never have to go through what me and my family has for the past 20 years, and counting.

To my good friends and fellow authors Verone Johnson (author of "Crescent City Tales") and Curtis Ray Davis II (author of "Slave State: Evidence of Apartheid in America"), a sincere thanks for allowing me to contribute to your literary works, and for mentioning me in your books. May God continue to nurture our talents and give our voices the power to move nations.

To my dear friend Norman, who has always kept his word no matter what obstacles stood in the way. A truer friend cannot be found. Thank you, buddy, for checking on my family and being the brother I never had growing up. It's okay that you're white, I forgive you. (LOL)

To my fellow abolitionist, Calvin, much thanks and admiration goes out to you, my brother. You and I have seen what many have not, and even fewer have engaged in the struggle as we have. But be of good spirit young soldier, I will stand with you in solidarity to my dying breath.

So, in loving memory of our late, great teacher and friend Rebecca L. Hensley, I say to you: onward and upward, my brother. Onward and upward we must go until all of our people are free.

A WORD FROM THE AUTHOR

I have coined the following definition of the word "Phantom" to include the exceptional men and women who impact society despite having suffered a social death due to incarceration. Whenever referring to an incarcerated citizen who fits the description below, the first letter of the word Phantom is always capitalized.

Phantom: any person who is no longer part of society because of incarceration, yet possesses the uncanny ability to deliver--with great impact---remarkable stories, experiences, and ideas that positively affect those living beyond the confines of his or her penal environment.

I, myself, am a Phantom. My dreams and freedoms have been deferred for reasons I may never fully understand, still, I am grateful for the gifts that God has blessed me with---especially the gift of writing. Throughout history, Phantoms have made significant contributions to society via literature. For example, the apostle Paul wrote the book of Ephesians and the book of Philippians while imprisoned in Rome. He, along with many others, has unequivocally proved that even though Phantoms are physically denied freedom, our words and thoughts cannot be confined by the iron bars that guard our dungeons. It must be stated that the human spirit knows no boundaries, and neither does the ingenuity of those who never give up. The fact that you're reading this right now is proof that my words have found you even from here inside the "belly of the beast".

This incredible novel, The Galactic Island, was initially written as gift to my family, but the phenomenal success of the book has made it a gift to the entire world. I never expected that so many people would discover and enjoy the magical experience of reading this adorable story. A story that has captured the hearts and minds of countless fans and has broken through long-standing barriers to become a huge hit with the toughest critics in the business.

I have poured every ounce of my imagination into these pages, combining fact and fiction to create a "virtual reality" that is as real as the mind allows one to believe. And if you are one of the amazing few who can decipher the hidden messages in this book, a remarkable secret will be revealed to you.

Good luck and happy hunting!

--- Parish V. Damone

"I was taught to strive not because there was any guarantees of success, but because the act of surviving is in itself the only way to keep faith with life."

------Madeline Albright

DEDICATION

I dedicate this book to the "Phantoms" around the world. Those who have put down the sword and picked up the pen, and have given rise to an era of world-renowned writers who reside behind prison walls. Expression – whether verbal, written, or otherwise – is the most endearing of all human traits. It is what separates us from other forms of life on this planet. It is who we are. Expression is everything.

Phantom Press Publishing LLC
"EXPRESSION IS EVERYTHING" ™

$+ \mathrm{x} +$

"Been a loved child all my life so I am unafraid… a genius –
gentle and tender – I write you poetry and short stories, because
I know you love to hear me think."
    ------Jill Scott

Table of Contents

"Those who have quitted the world, and those who are not yet arrived in it, are as remote from each other, as the utmost stretch of moral imagination can conceive. What possible obligation... what rule or principle can be laid down, that two nonentities, the one out of existence, and the other not in, ... that the one should control the other to the end of time?"

------Thomas Paine

"When the world has judged you through tainted windows, the Great Redeemer will let his love shine brightly on you for all the world to see."

------Victor Damone McClendon

KEY OF ADWAH

Note: The Key of Adwah was created exclusively for The Galactic Island. It is a key for deciphering the encryptions found throughout the story

"That which is God within us opens like a thousand blossoms of purest starlight, we float from this world to the next and back again, like children playing a game we taught ourselves a billion years ago."

------Aberjhani

CHAPTER 1

THE BEGINNING OF THE END

Hello, may I speak to Brenda LeCour, please?" said the man on the phone.

"This is she," my mother replied.

"Mrs. LeCour, my name is Charles Hampton. I'm the Regional Director of Operations for Global Oil and Refineries International, the company that employs your son, Cartrell. Ma'am, I'm afraid I have bad news."

A sharp pain stung my mother's heart and for a brief moment she could not find her voice.

"Mrs. LeCour? Ma'am are you still there?"

With tears welling up in the corners of her eyes, my mother answered, "Yes, I'm here. Has something happened to my son? Is he alright?"

There was an awkward silence as Mr. Hampton searched his thoughts for the right words to explain the reason for his call. Then, in a baritone voice that sent chills down my mother's arms he began relaying the solemn news. "Ma'am, I'm sorry to report that Cartrell has been involved in an offshore disaster, the worst in our company's one-hundred-year history. More than two-hundred people were on the rig when the tragedy occurred, and so far we haven't located any survivors." There was another uncomfortable pause, then Mr. Hampton spoke the words that no mother wants to hear, "Your son Cartrell Damone LeCour has been reported missing."

Dead silence.

My mother suddenly dropped the phone and started screaming at the top of her lungs. The tragic news of my disappearance caused her to become so hysterical that she began pounding her fists hard against the wall, knocking down several photographs and breaking the huge mirror that hung next to the dining room table. "Lord have mercy, Jesus! Not my baby! Not my Trell!" She screamed. "Take me Lord, not my baby!" Completely distraught, she collapsed onto the sofa in the living room and sobbed uncontrollably.

Mr. Hampton waited patiently while my mother expressed her grief. He had gained a great appreciation for the heartache she was feeling, because hers wasn't the first heart he had broken that night. Mr. Hampton had spoken to several other grieving parents prior to calling my mother, and all of them had responded the same way that she did. Eventually, after she had time to calm down, my mother returned to the phone and asked Mr. Hampton to tell her what had happened. The gracious gentleman kindly obliged her.

"Ma'am, what we've discovered so far is that a series of explosions tore through the rig and ruptured the main line, which caused the entire platform to collapse into the ocean near Marker 124. That's about three hundred miles due south of Morgan City in the Gulf of Mexico. Several dozen search and rescue crews have been deployed to the location where the rig went down but none have reported finding any survivors as of yet."

My mother's sobs grew louder, prompting Mr. Hampton to pause for a moment to collect himself. Little did she know, he too had suffered a personal loss. His own son, Charles Hampton Jr., was also on the rig when it went down.

"Ma'am, there's a dangerous storm headed toward the Gulf, and it is expected to make landfall before morning," said Mr. Hampton after regaining his composure. "It means that we only have a few more hours before the Coast Guard shuts us down. I promise you, Mrs. LeCour, we're doing everything in our power to locate your son. In the meantime, here's my phone number. If there's anything your family needs, just give me a call." The Regional Director of Operations for the largest oil company in the world gave my mother his personal phone number, and she was grateful.

"Thank you, sir. I know in my heart that you are a good man, and you will do everything possible to find Trell and bring him back home to me." My mother said while fighting back tears.

"I certainly will, ma'am. You have my word."

As soon as the call ended so did my mother's resolve. She immediately fell to her knees and let out a primordial scream that could be heard throughout the projects. Her harrowing cries were all too familiar to the residents of the Calliope, many mothers had made similar outbursts when finding out their child had been taken either by the criminal justice system or by the violence in our neighborhood. My mother wasn't the first to suffer the loss of a child in the projects and she would not be the last.

People from blocks away came running to see what had happened at 5128 Rocheblade Street and found my mother lying on the floor with her heart completely broken. Several women from the neighborhood tried to comfort her but it was no use... she was inconsolable. The gentle soul who had raised me as best she could laid her weary head against the wall and screamed until her voice went hoarse and her eyes had no more tears left to cry. I'm sorry Mama.

The tragic incident that Mr. Hampton spoke about on the phone took place aboard the superstructure called Deepwater Leviathan---the largest drilling platform on earth. Throughout the rig's construction, massive protests led by environmental groups took place outside of the company's regional headquarters in Algiers, which sits directly across the Mississippi River from Downtown New Orleans. There were also reports that multiple threats by extremists looking to sabotage the company's most valuable assets were being posted online alluding to an attack on Mardi Gras Day, the same day of the incident. But none of us who were stationed on the Leviathan believed anything bad was going to happen---unfortunately, we were wrong.

"Attention all hands! Attention all hands! This is not a drill! I repeat! This is not a drill!"

Sirens blasted.

Whistles blew.

Bells rang.

It was absolute pandemonium.

The initial explosion collapsed the lower section of the rig, instantly killing several welders who had been working overtime to make sure the construction would be completed on schedule. Thankfully, I was occupying one of the portable restrooms on the top deck at the time. But the explosions kept coming one after another until finally the entire platform went up in flames. Once the main line was ruptured, a cataclysmic chain reaction caused a mega-blast that was so powerful it sent the mighty Leviathan crashing down into the crystal clear waters of the Gulf. The tiny restroom---with me still inside of it---was blown off the top deck and went sailing across the night sky like a shooting star. As it soared over the ocean my whole life flashed before my eyes. I saw myself as a kid again playing basketball in the schoolyard with some friends of mine back in elementary...The coolest girl in the whole school came over and kissed me right on the lips. Her name was Darlene and I remembered tasting the bubble-gum-flavored lip gloss she was wearing and thinking to myself--- Oh shit! I'm kissing a real girl! My friends were all laughing at me, but I didn't care because I was experiencing my first kiss. Man, I was in heaven...

My nostalgic stroll down memory lane abruptly ended when I saw thick, yellow smoke pouring into the cabin from the burning plastic that the "Pot O' Gold" restroom was made of. I immediately placed my face next to the small openings near the top of the restroom and took a deep breath. The caustic fumes were causing an unexpected giddiness to settle in my gut, and without warning, I burst into a fit of laughter like never before. I was laughing so hard that I almost fainted from lack oxygen. I mean there I was flying over the ocean inside of a flaming toilet seemingly about to die of smoke inhalation and for the life of me, I couldn't seem to get my shit together. Then low and behold out of the yellow smoke came this magnificent angel holding a golden scroll.Holy shit!

The six-winged seraph was glowing like the sun, so I shielded my face while he pointed to the markings on the scroll and instructed me to study them closely. Beneath each hieroglyphic symbol was either a word, an alphabet, or rudiments---prefixes, suffixes, syllables, and so forth---used to create other words in the English language. The table of symbols appeared rudimentary at first, but upon closer inspection I discovered just how ingenious the layout really was. The number of ways the symbols could be used to send and receive coded messages was limitless.

As long as the participants were savvy enough to understand the relationship between the rudiments and their counterparts, the levels of encryption could not be measured. The cool part about it was that the symbols were interchangeable, and could be used to create holograms and "super encryptions" similar to how geeks and nerds who called themselves "trolls" did with computer coding when the Internet was first created. I turned my attention back to the angel and asked him what was I supposed to be looking at, and this is what he said:

"You have been chosen to go on a great journey from which you may never return. And while on this journey, you will discover your true self---you are not who you think you are."

The angel spoke in an ancient dialect that pre-dated earth by more than a trillion years, yet I understood every word he said.

And it troubled me beyond measure. The angel's enchanted voice began to energize the symbols on the scroll, causing them to take on a star-like quality that made them shine brightly inside the tiny restroom. I watched him summon several of the glowing symbols out of the scroll and divide them into separate rows. A luminous message was formed in midair and the only way to decipher it was with the golden scroll which the angel called the "Key of Adwah". The message was this:

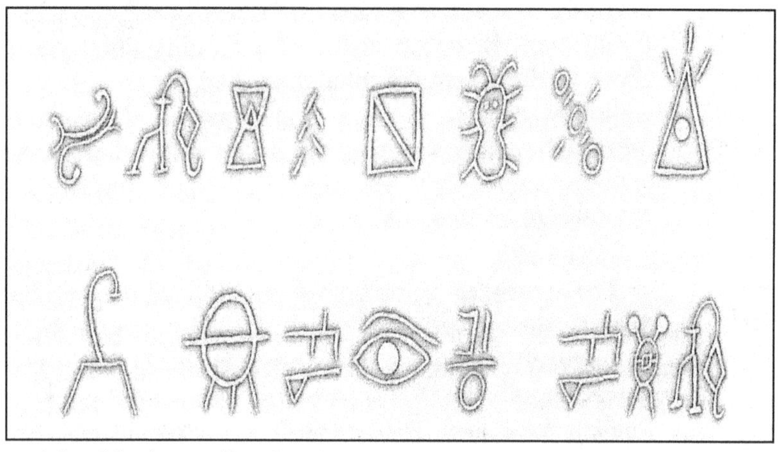

The blazing toilet finally splashed down off the coast of an uncharted island where a mysterious figure watched in disbelief. The curious onlooker wondered what kind of spacecraft had just plunged into the deep blue sea.

Note to reader: Use the Key of Adwah at the front of the book or refer to the Translation Table at the back of the book to decipher encrypted messages throughout the story.

"The old world is dying, and the new world struggles to be born... now is the time of monsters."
------ Antonio Gramsci

CHAPTER 2

A RUDE AWAKENING

The thunderous sound of the crashing surf abruptly awakened me from my slumber, thrusting me unexpectedly into a world that was not my own. I looked to my left and I saw a magnificent cove whose shimmering beaches were littered with bright stones that had been washed upon the sand by the rolling tide. Twinkling like diamonds, the glistening rocks added beauty and style to a radiant white sand oasis and illuminated the gateway to a mysterious realm whose secrets I had not yet discovered. To my right I saw a giant cliff standing more than a thousand feet tall. It was partially surrounded by an eerie forest that was filled with frightful looking trees of every kind. Their knotted trunks and scary branches made them look like hideous monsters frozen by a witch's spell. Many questions went through my mind as I stood horrified staring at the formidable landscape in front of me:

Where am I?

How did I get here?

How the hell am I going to get back home?

Adding to the anxiety of being stranded on a mysterious island was the vast ocean directly out front---its endless horizon stretching as far as the eye could see, its rolling tide creating huge swells so tall that they seemed to have mixed with the melancholy sky before tumbling wildly onto the crystalline sands beneath my feet. It was like a scene from a romantic movie. Not the kind where the guy kisses the girl and then rides off into the sunset, but the Shakespearian kind where everyone dies in the end.

From the moment I arrived on the island I sensed that something was oddly different about me, I felt like I was living someone else's life. The cherished memories I once owned were now just a collage of broken images scattered across the surface of my thoughts like pieces of stained glass shattered from the windows of a grand cathedral. Significant portions of my life were suddenly missing from my mind, replaced by false memories belonging to someone with a dark and mysterious past. I soon began experiencing powerful delusions that produced frightening images inside my head---witches, demons, dragons, giant sea monsters.

I was hoping to be reconciled to my true self when out of nowhere came an eerie feeling that sent chills down my spine. I turned and noticed a strange creature watching me from the forest. I couldn't see the animal outright, but I could feel its piercing glare through the shadows.

"I know you're there!" I shouted, "Might as well come out where I can see you!" The eerie silence that followed was more terrifying than the thing hiding in the woods. A sharp pain lodged itself in the pit of my stomach confirming that I was in imminent danger. My fear was palpable, and it set my heart to pounding hard against my chest. Then suddenly, a ferocious beast emerged from the shadowy woods with blazing speed and came running toward me. I tumbled out of the way then got to my feet and ran as fast as I could in the direction of the giant cliff. As fate would have it, the mysterious creature lost its footing and went sliding down into a gully that had been covered with overlapping brush, giving me just enough time to make it to my destination unscathed.I began climbing the cliff with all my might hoping the creature would give up its chase and head back into the woods. The ascent up the steep wall was exhausting, but I made it over the initial ridge and spotted a small ledge hidden behind a group of large vines. As I headed toward the obscure landing, a tremendous howl burst from the throat of the creature and scared the shit out of me.

"What the hell was that?" I said while looking back over my shoulder trying to determine which direction the sound had come from. The high-pitched howling continued for several minutes echoing loudly above the forest and through the valleys to my west. I scanned the woods with my eyes but all I saw was shifting shadows and ghostly phantoms playing havoc with my mind, appearing out of nowhere and then vanishing as quickly as they had come. The nightmare that unfolded before my eyes was all the motivation I needed to haul my ass up the cliff a lot faster. But after several long minutes of strenuous climbing, there wasn't any strength left in my arms or my legs. Even worse, huge blisters had started forming on the palm of my hands, prompting me to inspect the rest of my body for injuries. Only then did I discover the bruises on my knees and elbows which had come from brushing them up against the sharp rocks that lined the walls of the cliff. Despite it all, I made a daring attempt to reach the ledge before dark only to discover that I would not make it there in time---nightfall rushed in with a vengeance and before I knew it, the evening was fully dressed.

A magnificent full moon lit the night sky, and its silvery beams bathed the forest in an eerie incandescent light, allowing me to see the creature, clearly, for the first time. The strange animal moved like a man but stood more than 9 feet tall with long "ape-like" arms and glowing red eyes that peered out from the giant head of a wolf. Ropes of matted hair hung down from the creature's enormous head like Rastafarian dreadlocks, swinging wildly as the beast scoured the edge of the woods trying to pick up my scent. Its face was wolfishly long, with jaws hinged near the back of its skull, allowing it to open its dagger-lined maws disturbingly wide like the legendary werewolves of cinema. At first I had a hard time believing that any of this shit was real, but I soon realized I was in for a rude awakening.

After failing to pick up my scent the mysterious wolf-creature circled the base of the cliff and then disappeared into the depths of the forest where the moonlight could not reach. I patiently waited for several minutes and didn't move a muscle. I wanted to give the creature plenty of time to leave the area before resuming my trek toward the tiny ledge. And just when I thought it was safe to continue, a female creature with huge wings swooped down out of the night sky and drug me to the ledge herself. She appeared to be some type of forest nymph with phenomenal strength, and she slammed me against the wall of the cliff with tremendous force.

"Stay where you are and do not move!" the fairy warned. "The Dark Forest hides many secrets and if you wish to stay alive then pay close attention to what I'm about to show you." With the tip of one of her giant wings, the powerful fairy directed my attention toward a conspicuous-looking bush sitting in the middle of the woods.

"What do you see?", said the nymph while continuing to press my body against the wall.

"I see a bunch of colorful flowers covering an odd-looking bush, neither of which should be growing in these creepy woods." I said based on my knowledge of horticulture.

"Look closer!", demanded the nymph. "The forest is full of illusions, and things are often not what they seem." I took a closer look at the bush and discovered it wasn't a bush at all.

What the fuck?!

I couldn't believe it; the weird bush was a clever disguise being worn by the wolf-creature! The beast had planned to ambush me the moment I left the safety of the ledge. "Well, I'll be damned! This motherfucker got some shit with him," I said to the nymph.

"Do you see that? There's a whole goddamn floral arrangement growing right out of its back!"The strange animal had curled it-self into a ball, turning its body into an artificial bush with bright colored flowers on it: trilliums, Dutchman's breeches, wild gera-niums, hyacinth and roses of every size and color---pink, yellow, blue, white, purple, you name it. The only real plants were the trees and the Ophiopogon japonicus, also known as "Monkey Grass."

In a surprising move, the wolf-creature started replacing all the delicate flowers it had been using as camouflage with ones that were more robust. The beast was attempting to emulate the indigenous plants inside the Dark Forest, it was as though the wolf-creature had overheard me telling the fairy that the other flowers didn't belong there. The shit was getting way too weird for me.

"Hey, lady!" I said to the nymph. "Let go of me and get your heavy ass off this ledge before you make us fall!"

"Hold your voice down!", chided the nymph in a whispery hush. "I'm here to warn you about an ancient leviathan that is coming to destroy our world. The beast will stop at noth----"

"Wait a minute!" I interrupted, "Are you talking about the weirdo over there with the flowers growing out of its back?"

"No, that's not what I'm referring to, and there's no time to explain." she said while loosening the strangle hold she had on my neck. "Remain here until morning, and the moment the sun comes up I want you to travel as quickly as you can back to the area where you first arrived on the island. I'll be there to protect you."

"Protect me? Protect me from what?" I said to the mysterious nymph whose face I couldn't see because my head was still being pressed against the wall face-first.

"Never mind that," she said in a condescending sort of way. "All that matters right now is that you heed my instructions."

"Say, lil' mama, I don't know who you think you're talking to but I ain't him, alright. So you need to watch your tone. Besides, how do I know you ain't tryna set me up to get killed or something?" I said while tilting my head slightly, but not enough to see the fairy's face.

"I have no reason to harm you," said the nymph with noticeable ire in her voice. "Besides, if I was here to kill you, little human, you'd already be dead. It is forbidden for my kind to interfere with the natural order of things here on the island," said the fairy. "But I did so because I believe you are here for a very special purpose, and therefore, deserve to be spared a horrible fate. The Dark Forest is very much alive, and it is listening to every word we speak, so keep quiet and stay alert or you won't live to see morning."

Then the nymph leaned closer to my ear and whispered, "And all of this will have been for nothing."

And just like that, the mysterious fairy released me from her grasp and disappeared into the pitch black sky leaving me all alone with no one to keep me company except for the weirdo wearing the ugly coat with the flowers on it. I was bewildered and exhausted after the encounter with the nymph, so I leaned back against the side of the cliff and spent the rest of the evening in deep thought and complete silence. Partly because there was no one else to talk to, but mostly because I was afraid that the Dark Forest was listening to my every breath.

At first light, I made my way down the cliff and returned to the area where I had first arrived on the island. There was no sign of the elusive nymph who had accosted me the night before, but I did detect a familiar scent in the ocean breeze:

The sweet smell of jasmines.

I was standing in a tropical paradise and yet I had never been so afraid. The island's beauty seemed to be hiding something, a terrible secret of some kind. And while I gazed out at the tumbling surf something told me to look up at the sky.

"This can't be real," I said while staring at the scary anomaly up above. "What the fuck is this place?" The sky had become as black as soot, and the Dark Forest---oh, my god---it had become the most frightening thing of all. An unusual chill lingered in the air above the acrid sea, a dreadful warning that a deadly storm was soon coming that would bring an end to life on earth---Judgment Day was here at last.

Powerful lightning bolts entered my body and ripped my flesh apart, leaving deep gashes in my Black skin like the wounds on a slave's back from the lashes of his master's whip. The apocalyptic hurricane that appeared on the horizon was an unnatural event, a diabolical testament to the coming of the Beast! I looked and I saw armies of biblical monsters spewing from the dark clouds that were forming above the ocean. They were setting out to terrorize the four corners of the earth. And while fiery hailstones rained down from the heavens, I watched the world burn and saw the souls of men being cast into lakes of fire... and it felt very real.

The horrific vision left me badly shaken, so I quickly ran into the forest hoping to get as far away from the ocean as possible. My goal for the day was to find shelter, and hopefully some peace of mind. But I soon found out that navigating the dense forest would not be easy, there were thick vines and deep ravines everywhere. Plus there was something very weird about the woods that I couldn't quite put my finger on. Then it hit me!Oh, shit! That's it!

The reason I hadn't ventured into the woods before was because I didn't want to deal with all the bugs and creepy animals I might run across. But the whole time I'd been traipsing through the forest, to my surprise, I hadn't come across a single living thing---no bugs, no birds, no bears, no bunny rabbits, no anything. Well, except for the weird coconut grove that had all sorts of strange fruit growing on trees that were anything but organic. The coconuts themselves came in a variety of fluorescent blues, pinks, greens, and yellows. Even the ground was peculiar looking, it appeared to be covered with pink and yellow carpet because of the thousands of mushrooms that stretched from one end of the grove to the other. The weird fungi were able to produce harmonious music by harnessing the wind and then forcing it through their tiny pores in the form of beautiful sounds that were pleasing to the ear. When the mushrooms "sang", it was like the voices of angels performing for a gospel choir in the presence of God Almighty.

But not all of the mushrooms were musically inclined. There was an insidious bunch of red ones that stood apart from the rest and refused to sing for anyone. They were the same mushrooms that gave off a tantalizing aroma which somehow reminded me of my mother's delicious home cooking. I can't believe I remember this but um...Every Sunday morning our home would be filled with a scrumptious bouquet of mouth-watering aromas thanks to Mama's Creole cooking. I can still see her wearing her favorite dress, the one with the large sunflowers on it, making her way back and forth between the stove and refrigerator humming the gospel hymn "At the Cross Where I First Saw the Light".

My siblings and I could hear Mama's raggedy ol' slippers making that funny clapping noise as she slid her feet across the kitchen's linoleum floor. We would giggle and laugh, and Mama would hear us and smile. We knew that the sound of her clapping slippers could only mean one thing, that Mama was in the kitchen whipping up a delicious meal for the family. So all of us would jump out of bed and start straightening up our rooms to show Mama how much we appreciated her. And when we were finished cleaning up, she'd have a special treat waiting for us, usually in the form of something sweet to eat.

After church, the whole family would get together for a glorious feast featuring some of the South's finest home cooking. Mama's delectable meals included her delicious Southern fried chicken, mashed potatoes and country gravy, sweet peas, seasoned "dirty" rice dressing, crawfish étouffée, potato salad, honey baked ham, mustard greens, cornbread, buttermilk biscuits, pecan candy, apple pie, pineapple turnovers, strawberry cake made from scratch, and homemade ice cream. Damn, I miss my mama.

The red mushrooms definitely stoked my memories but there was too much weird shit going on, so I wasn't about to complicate things further by experimenting with a bunch of strange plants. Besides, I had more important shit to deal with---like staying alive.

GEMINI

"Then I saw another beast, coming out of the earth. He had two horns like a lamb, but he spoke like a dragon."

— Revelation 13:11

CHAPTER 3

A TALE OF TWO DRAGONS

My excursion into the Dark Forest led me to a huge valley where I discovered a shimmering stream that wound its way across the island like a giant python. The source of the stream appeared to be a series of magnificent waterfalls towering in the distance. Whatever lay beyond the falls was a guarded secret, and the wily brook offered no clues to the mystery surrounding its origin. "The Dark Forest hides many secrets," I remembered the words spoken by the nymph, "...things are often not what they seem."

I soon witnessed a fascinating event taking place on the surface of the stream. Colorful water jets were shooting high in the air like liquid fireworks, creating a dazzling spectacle that cast a whimsical reflection on the stream's glassy surface. I stood on the bank gazing at the wondrous event, and when there came a break in the action, I knelt down next to the stream and took a sip of cool, refreshing water. Immediately there was a strange sensation in the pit of my stomach and my vision went blurry.

"Oh, no! There must be something in the water! " I said as a tinge of panic entered my voice. I assumed the water must have contained hallucinogens that caused me to see bizarre things right out of a fairy tale. Because there I was face-to-face with a gorgeous mermaid who was staring at me from beneath the surface of the stream.

"Wow! You have the most beautiful eyes I've ever seen!" I said to the object of my hallucination. "I gotta hand it to myself, I sure know how to fantasize."

Her eyes sparkled like blue sapphires, and they appeared to be studying me for a future purpose, one that only the mermaid had knowledge of. I studied her as well: She had skin like African mahogany---a lush, reddish-brown color---and it covered her voluptuous body like smooth caramel poured slowly atop rich, dark chocolate. Her hair was long and shiny like silk, but it was the color of pure sunshine---golden-yellow with sparkling highlights that twinkled and glistened beneath the shimmering water. She also had little white seashells intricately woven into her micro braids, an exotic touch that made the ebony sea goddess look like she was straight out the hood. I had never imagined a Black mermaid before, and this one was more gorgeous than any I had seen in books and movies. She was blessed with luscious Afrocentric lips that pouted naturally, and when she licked them---oh, my god!---I nearly fell right over the bank into water.

I tried to play it off like I wanted to get wet on purpose, but then it occurred to me that I was putting on for an imaginary mermaid who appeared as a result of me drinking the hallucinogenic water from the stream. "Man, I'm trippin'!" I said as I closed my eyes hoping it would help bring me back to my senses. "I can't believe I convinced myself that I actually saw a damn mermaid."

When I opened my eyes the mermaid was nowhere in sight, she had vanished without a trace, and I was left standing there alone and disheartened by the whole ordeal. "That's just great" I said while wiping the tears from my face. I leaned over and stared into the water only to see my own reflection staring back at me with an expression I did not recognize---it was a convoluted mixture of sadness, anguish, and bewilderment. The reality of knowing that I was truly alone on the island stirred my emotions deeply, I could suddenly feel a painful stinging deep in my soul like the bite from a venomous cobra. And as the gates to my wounded heart were slowly unchained, a single teardrop fell from my eye and exploded on the surface of the water.

Soon more tears followed, turning the world around me into a sleepy Louisiana bayou after a midsummer's rain... misty... quiet... deserted. And when I closed my eyes a second time, the broken memories of an obscure past flooded my mind and began tumbling around like colorful fragments inside of a child's kaleidoscope, creating symmetrical faces of people I didn't remember. But then, in the middle of all the chaos, there appeared one face I did recognize---it was the smiling face of the mermaid who stole my heart with a single glance.

While walking along the banks of the stream still thinking about the gorgeous mermaid, a sudden disturbance in the water caught my attention. I turned and I saw a long, cylindrical-shaped creature gliding beneath the water's surface heading in the direction of the ocean with blazing speed. I immediately ran after the creature hoping to get a better look at it before it reached the bay, but it was swimming so fast that by the time I made it to the mouth of the stream where the water empties into the ocean, the creature had already vanished into the deep blue sea. I stood at the edge of the bank gazing out over the ocean hoping to see something... anything. But there was no sign of the elusive creature anywhere, and darkness was creeping toward the island like a vampire lusting to feed. I turned around and started to head back into the forest when all of a sudden a loud splashing sound came from the direction of the bay. I hurried back to the edge of the bank and- Holy shit!

A magnificent beast emerged from the shallows with great fanfare. It was joined by another beast that looked identical to it in every way.

"You've gotta be fuckin' kidding me! Those things look like real dragons!" It was true, the creatures out in the bay were the real deal and they were tumbling around like a couple of lion cubs, each one trying to gain a physical advantage over the other. The dragons were the size of a sea lion but had a head like a T.rex with two horns and mouth full of long sharp teeth. The beasts were about fifteen feet from where I was standing, and I still couldn't distinguish one from the other. So I named the dragons "Gemini."

The twin dragons were covered with multi-faceted scales that sparkled like brilliant jewels in the mauve sunlight, giving off stunning hues of purple, green, and gold reflections. Although their vibrant colors reminded me of Mardi Gras in New Orleans, the obnoxious dragons didn't embody the spirit of Carnival one bit. In fact, I wish I'd never met the slimy bastards in the first place. I mean, there I was jumping up and down on the beach screaming my head off trying to get their attention, when finally I realized that the dragons were purposely ignoring me. Well, you know I wasn't going to put up with that shit.

"Hey, Gemini!" I shouted from the beach, "I know you see me over here hollering at ch'all! If that's how y'all wanna play it, then you know what---FUCK Y'ALL! I don't need this shit! In fact, both you can kiss my Black---what the?---Ahhhhh! It burns! It burns!"

I couldn't believe it! One of those filthy weasels sprayed me right in the face with steaming, hot dragon piss! And my damn mouth was open, too!

"Why you nasty son-of-a-bitch!" I yelled from the beach, "I saw which one of you motherfuckers did that shit and I'mma 'bout to kick yo' ass, bitch!"

I went charging out into the ocean ready to settle the score with the dragon that had pissed in my face, but unfortunately, vengeance would have to wait. I suddenly discovered that Gemini weren't the only menace lurking in the shallows, the twin dragons were accompanied by a horde of vicious little bastards that had been hiding amongst the coral waiting for me to venture into the

water. The little sea vermin looked like aquatic pit bulls on ste-
roids, and apparently they loved the taste of "dark meat" because
one of them swam right up and bit the living daylights out of me.
It was the most excruciating pain I ever experienced in my life.
I immediately started screaming and went running back towards
the beach holding my left butt cheek where I had been bitten, not
even realizing that the stupid little sea mongrel was still dangling
from my behind. Talk about embarrassing.

And to add insult to injury, Gemini stood there laughing their
asses off while I struggled to pry the sea-mutt's sharp teeth out
of my throbbing butt cheek. I didn't know whether I should be
happy that the dragons finally acknowledged me or angry because they had hurt my feelings. Actually, the choice wasn't hard
at all:

"YOU LOWDOWN, ROTTEN MOTHERFUCKERS!
YOU THINK THIS SHIT IS FUNNY? WAIT TILL I GET MY
HANDS ON YOU BITCHES! I AIN'T SCARED OF YOU
MOTHERFUCKERS! LET ME TELL YOU ONE GOD-
DAMN THING, I'LL BLOW UP THIS WHOLE MOTHER-
FUCKIN' ISLAND, YA HEARD ME! KING---KONG----
AIN'T---GOT---SHIT---ON---ME!"

Gemini simply ignored me and kept right on playing as though
nothing had happened. I admit, the dragons got the best of me
that day---but payback is a motherfucker!

CHAPTER 4

FOOTPRINTS IN THE SAND

Cussing out the indigenous wildlife wasn't my idea of a good time, and Gemini had taught me a valuable lesson---if you can't take the heat, then stay the hell outta the kitchen. I vowed right then and there not to go near the beach for a while. I used the time away from the dragons to build a camp high in the mountains overlooking the Dark Forest where the wolf-creature had lurked during the night of the full moon. It provided security and solace and gave me a much-needed reprieve from the chaos down in the forest. Now, in the quietness of my thoughts I was able to reflect on my life more clearly, and the once distorted images inside my mind gave way to memories that were a lot less dramatic:

It was Carnival time in New Orleans and the French Quarter was buzzing with excitement. Cajun Cuisine, lavish parades, extravagant masquerade parties---it was all part of the ambience and mystique of the Big Easy during this wonderful time of the year. You could feel the magic in the air and see the look of enchantment on the faces of out-of-towners who had traveled from far and near to experience Carnival for themselves. The Crescent City to them was like a mystic realm where indigenous musicians dressed in gilded rags stood outside neon-lit nightclubs along Bourbon Street playing Dixieland, Cajun, country, zydeco, and jazz music year round. A perpetual dreamscape filled with people laughing and drinking and greeting each other saying "laissez les bons temps rouler (let the good times roll)".

Every year around this time the crowds pour into the French Quarter and people can be seen striking curious poses in front of the immaculate castle known as St. Louis Cathedral, the pinnacle of a glorious kingdom called Jackson Square. Bewitched by the sweet, delicious taste of powdered beignets at Café du Monde, starry-eyed patrons are left grinning ear-to-ear with traces of the sugary treat all over their faces. And the moment they're convinced that life can't get any better, here comes the second line parade with its magical sounds that make them move to the rhythm of New Orleans.

Imagine a spicy gumbo of syncopated notes and infectious beats being conjured out of musical instruments by mysterious figures dressed in Indian costumes that are so elaborate it takes an entire year to make a single outfit. They call themselves Mardi Gras "Indians", and every Carnival season they travel from different parts of the city to challenge one another to a battle of style and dress. Thousands of people line the streets of New Orleans to watch them promenade through the crowds wearing their colorful wardrobes made almost entirely out of feathers--- it's a campy spectacle not even the most exquisite peacock could match.

Every "tribe" has a "Big Chief" who is ceremoniously celebrated by high-stepping drum majors who are decked out in tailored suits with sashes and cummerbunds that complement the twirling umbrellas they carry. And no second line is complete without the "spy boys" who tote flaming torches and stay on the lookout for challengers from rival tribes ready to do battle. You can hear them from blocks away chanting, "Hey pocky way! Oon-nah-nay! Hey pocky way! Oon-nah-nay!" And then the ladies chime in singing:"My spy boy and yo spy boy, sit'n by the fi-ya! My spy boy told yo spy boy I'm gonna set yo' flag on fi-ya! Talk'n bout--- Hey-nah! Hey-nah! Iko! Iko! Un-dey!"

I clearly remember the French Quarter where people were standing on high balconies lined with wrought iron railings whose regal designs were reminiscent of the Bourbons, a French royal family that became an absolute monarchy spawning a system of government that practiced extreme conservatism, except when it came to issuing out aristocratic privileges to themselves and their friends. The life of a Bourbon was like a nonstop party. Where do you think "Bourbon Street" got its name from?

In reality though, most people in New Orleans have never experienced anything close to what the Bourbons and their friends had. Especially those who lived in the Calliope. If it wasn't for the grace of God and my mother's prayers, I would have never made it out of the projects alive. Mama used to always say to me, "Don't let your environment be an excuse to fail, you can be whatever you want to be if you put your mind to it."

Her wisdom and unwavering love inspired me to do my best at everything I tried. And because of Mama, when most of my peers started carrying guns and dealing drugs in our community, I chose to focus my attention on my studies and earned a scholarship to Southern University in Baton Rouge where I became a star-member of the greatest marching band in the world and graduated magna cum laude from the university's school of engineering. Even though I now find myself stranded on this godforsaken island with seemingly no way of returning home, I am not afraid because God is with me. I feel His presence and the presence of His angels all around me. They have come because of my mother's prayers and on behalf of those who truly love me.

The island turned out to be much larger than I assumed it would be, and there were vast areas I couldn't explore because the terrain was too treacherous to cross on foot. So after what seemed like weeks of exploration I wound up right back where I started---the beach.

Believe it or not, I was actually glad to be back in familiar territory. The alabaster sands and tall, sinuous palm trees swaying in the ocean breeze brought a little comfort to my soul despite all the weirdness that came with being in this strange paradise.

The palm trees, for instance, were able to change colors like a chameleon, constantly altering their appearance to blend in with the ever changing landscape. Viewing these magnificent plants from the ocean was like watching an artist paint a picture that would never dry.

Another odd thing about this place was the sweet smell of jasmine that always seemed to be present on the beach and no place else. The fact that I had not seen any jasmine growing on the island meant that this was another unsolved mystery to go along with the rest of the weird shit I'd come across since arriving here. This area of the beach near the bay, in particular, was like the Bermuda Triangle when it came to strange occurrences. It was the only place on the entire island where I discovered loads of buried treasure. I'm talking everything from rubies to emeralds to diamonds the size of coconuts. I assumed that it was all fake, but then I discovered a bag that had washed upon the beach, and it was filled with gold coins and an ancient map showing the location of even more treasure near the bay. At that point, I decided to name the area "Bling! Bling! Lagoon".

As I celebrated the authenticity of my riches by doing cartwheels on the beach, something in the sand caught my attention and I immediately stood still.

"I must be dreaming," I said to myself. "Those weren't there a few minutes ago." I stared for a solid minute before gathering up enough nerve to go investigate. And what I found was a set of footprints in the sand.

They had been made by a person of small stature, perhaps a woman, and they led in the direction of the Dark Forest. Immediately, that little voice inside my head started screaming, "Don't go into the forest! It's much too dangerous!" But it was imperative that I found out who the footprints belonged to, so I entered the Dark Forest. Intending to get to the bottom of this mystery even if it meant placing myself in harm's way.

I soon noticed something very strange. The footprints were growing in size, and the distance between each print was much farther apart than before. Not only that, the impressions now being left in the ground suggested that whoever made them had put on at least a couple hundred pounds since leaving the beach. Then I made the most frightening discovery of all. The mysterious footprints that led me into the forest were no longer those belonging to a human. They now belonged to a massive beast that moved on all fours... like a wolf.HOWL-L-L-L!!! HOWL-L-L-L!!!

A terrifying symphony of howls rang out in the distance.

The ominous high-pitched wailing was a deadly serenade from a mysterious boogieman that hunts during the full moon. I had made a terrible mistake allowing myself to be lured into the woods so close to dark... nightfall came without warning and once again the moon was full and bright.

After the last fleeting glimmer of daylight was choked from the sky, darkness rushed in and turned the once tropical paradise into a virtual "house of horrors". I could suddenly hear trees being torn from their roots and tossed aside like small twigs. Some unseen monster with phenomenal strength was drawing closer and closer. It was the same as my earlier encounter, except now I was without the protection of being high up on the ledge. The footprints, it seemed, were used to lure me into a deadly trap.But a trap set by whom? I wondered.

Moments later, the ferocious wolf-creature emerged from the pitch-black forest and stood in front of me snarling and growling and gnashing its teeth. The beast was thirsting for blood, I could see it in its eyes and smell it in its horrid breath which kept hitting me in the face like a sledgehammer.

The creature's awful stench was being driven my way by a frigid north wind, it smelled like a rotting corps had been laid at my feet. I took a step back and suddenly I came under attack! Blow after powerful blow, the beast imposed its will upon me, and though I fought back with everything I had, I was no match for its raw, animalistic strength. With the ferocity of a lion, the monstrous beast lunged at me and sunk its sharp teeth into my neck with tremendous force crushing down on my larynx to the point where I couldn't breathe---I thought for sure I was a goner.

Then, out of nowhere, the nymph with the huge wings came swooping down from the night sky and grabbed the wolf-creature from behind, nearly breaking its neck as she yanked the creature off of me. The powerful nymph carried the beast high in the sky and disappeared into the pitch black night. Moments later, the night sky lit up as bright as day as long streaks of lightning stretched across the heavens and booming thunder echoed loudly overhead. The atmospheric anomaly lit the forest and exposed a second wolf-creature hiding in the shadows.

"Oh, shit! Not again!" I said after spotting the beast making its approach.

Lightning struck nearby and I saw that the second wolf-creature's jaundice-yellow eyes were somewhat reptilian in nature, the beast was apparently a hybrid. I looked at its mouth and noticed that there was some sort of liquid dripping from its jaws, and it was glowing in the dark. It made me think of deep water jellyfish that produced light from within their translucent bodies. The creature's DNA contained genetic markers from a variety of animals I assumed. Especially after I saw what it did next.

Although the wolf-creature was as large and burly as a full-grown grizzly, it was remarkably swift and agile. I witnessed the beast leap across a forty-foot ravine in a single bound on its approach to my position. Fortunately, the earth beneath its feet gave way and the beast was forced to alter its route. Then right after that, all hell broke loose on the island and chaos reigned supreme. Giant plumes of charcoal-colored fumes started rising from the earth like demons conjured from the depths of hell. They were accompanied by tall columns of blistering hot steam that was pouring into the sky through huge fissures that had opened up in the ground all around me. I felt like I was watching the Apocalypse!

I began my daring escape by fleeing into the woods running top speed with no fear of skidding down steep hills covered with thickets of thorny briers, sharp rocks, or deadly pitfalls. I had made up my mind that I was either going to get free---or die trying.

After nearly an hour of traipsing through the thick woods wrestling vines and crossing rugged terrain, I collapsed to my knees from complete exhaustion. The thought of being eaten alive was my motivation for pushing as hard as I did, but my body had reached its breaking point and I was forced to stop and rest till morning.

The next day when the sun came up, I found myself lying underneath the hanging branches of a giant weeping willow. Its sweeping pedals were gently brushing against my bare chest, sprinkling me with soothing beads of morning dew. I tried to sit up, but my body was still hurting in places I didn't even know were there. Not only that, the bite I suffered from the wolf-creature seemed to be changing me somehow. I felt really strange, not quite myself... different.

CHAPTER 5

BEYOND THE GREAT WATERFALLS

While sitting underneath the giant willow tending to my wounds, I noticed a small clearing to my left that was covered with a gazillion white clovers. The little flowers were swaying back and forth in the spring-like breeze that was blowing across the dancing meadow. And as the swirling gusts swept over the field, a group of clovers took flight like tiny drones on a mission for freedom. I stood and cheered them on because I too wanted to sail away with the wind. After watching the clovers' aerial departure, my attention was drawn to the other side of the clearing where I saw a mysterious figure dart behind a huge log sitting at the edge of the woods. I prepared to defend myself to the death, no more running. So I reached down and picked up a long limb that had been broken off one of the trees nearby. Rubbing one end against a rough stone, I fashioned the branch into a formidable weapon that could easily puncture a lung or gouge out an eye in the heat of battle. I was ready for war!

"Stop hiding in the shadows like a little bitch!" I yelled, "C'mon! Let's do this!" My initial fear had been replaced by an overwhelming desire to control my own fate. Instead of waiting to be attacked by whatever was lurking behind the log, I decided to strike first. "Here! See how you like the feel of this!" I taunted as I hurled the sharpened tree limb at the log with the accuracy of a Zulu warrior. My makeshift spear struck the log with so much force huge pieces of bark went flying in every direction and out popped the figure who had been hiding out of sight.

"Oh, my god! It can't be!" I said when spotting the familiar face that peered out from behind the log. "I thought you were just an illusion!"

The mysterious figure turned out to be the gorgeous mermaid from the stream, and she was standing there staring at me with the same curious look that she had while watching me from beneath the water. She was now in the form of a woman, and she appeared even more beautiful than before. Still wet from being in the water, her voluptuous body was glistening in the early morning sunlight. The ebony mermaid was a sight to behold, and get this, she was completely naked.

"Hi, my name is Azoria," she said with a beaming smile. "I've been watching you from the forest." The first thing I noticed (besides that she was nude) was the freshly picked jasmine sticking out of her hair and I thought to myself:So that's where the sweet scent of jasmine has been coming from all this time.

"There is something I must tell you," said the gorgeous sea nymph. "You are not safe here. There is a terrible beast looking to destroy you. The leviathan is coming!" Azoria's voice was like the sound of Jazz: cool, sexy, sultry. But her message was just the opposite.

"We don't have much time, " she insisted. "You must come with me to the Great Waterfalls where you'll be safe from the beast." I was still in disbelief at the whole situation."Are you listening to me?" Azoria asked, and then waited on my response.

"I uh... I mean, you um... Wow! You're so damn gorgeous!" And there it was. I sounded like a complete jerk.

Azoria scowled, then she turned and started heading in the direction of the towering waterfalls in the distance. Curious as to why she felt I was in danger, I followed close behind and began pressing her for answers.

"Hey, Azoria! Is it likely that the leviathan was killed during the anomaly last night?" Noticing how incredibly naive I was about the current situation, Azoria turned and said to me quite bluntly, "If you wish to live beyond this day then you must come with me to the Great Waterfalls. Because if you choose otherwise, then I am afraid there's nothing I can do to save you. The Demon That Never Sleeps will surely have his way with you, and all will be lost."

She again headed toward the falls, and when I looked back in the direction we had just come from, I sensed that someone---or something---was following us. "Azoria, wait up! I'm coming with you!" I screamed out loud as if my life depended on her hearing my voice.

The mermaid was in superb physical shape and she moved quickly ahead of me through the forest. The only way I could keep track of her was by following the alluring scent given off by the jasmine worn in her hair. It led me to the base of a gigantic waterfall where Azoria had entered the water and transformed back into a magnificent mermaid. She then beckoned me to join her.

"Jump in!," she said. "The water's fine."

"Girl, you're crazy as hell if you think I'm 'bout to jump in that water. Ain't no damn way I'm going in there."

"What's the matter?" Azoria asked, "Are you afraid?"

"Hell no! I'm not afraid of anything!" I said to protect my pride. The reason I didn't want to jump in the water was because I never learned to swim. I had already taken a chance going after Gemini, but it was only because I knew the water near the beach was shallow. Besides, I was completely out of my mind at the time. This situation was totally different, I had no idea how deep the water would be once I jumped in. So to prevent Azoria from knowing my secret, I came up with the perfect excuse as to why I didn't want to get in the water.

"I have asthma!" I said as if providing the winning answer in a trivia contest. "It prevents me from being able to hold my breath for very long, so I'll keep walking in this direction until I find another spot to cross over to the other side."

Azoria stared at me with her arms folded---she wasn't buying it. Then, with a performance that could have earned her an Academy Award, she feigned a look of sheer terror at seeing something in the forest behind me. Acting on instincts alone, I leaped off the edge of the bank and entered the water with a huge splash. And just like that, my little secret was out of the bag.

"Help! I can't swim!" I screamed just before the currents pulled me under. It seemed the harder I struggled to reach the surface the deeper I sank beneath the water. I felt my arms and legs getting tired as fatigue set in, and my hopes of reaching the surface again quickly faded. I relaxed a minute and just let my body drift with the current, then eventually I stopped struggling altogether. The feeling was like being in one of those dreams where you're falling in slow motion, and everything is peaceful and quiet.

In the sereneness of my fall I began reflecting on my life. I had always dreamed of someday traveling the world and discovering new places, of striking it rich and vacationing on an exotic tropical island without a care in the world, moving my family out of the projects and into a nice neighborhood with white picket fences and cobblestone sidewalks.What a weird sense of humor life has...

I tried one last time for a breath of air, but the stream's frigid water rushed into my mouth and filled my lungs like an evil spirit, forcing what little oxygen there was left to escape through my nostrils and head toward the surface in a flurry of tiny bubbles. I felt death closing in, tugging at my gentle soul trying to get me to surrender. And just moments before I would succumb to a watery grave, Azoria's smiling face appeared next to me in the murky depths. She gently pressed her soft lips to my mouth and gave me a kiss, but this was no ordinary show of affection---this was something magical. The moment she kissed me everything changed, I was no longer concerned about death or dying. All I thought about was kissing Azoria. And when the kiss finally ended, Azoria spoke only one word: "Breathe!"

I immediately took a deep breath and found that my lungs were getting oxygen from the water as though I was standing on dry land.

"Wow! This is awesome!" I blurted while huge, wobbly bubbles burst from my mouth and raced toward the surface. At first I thought Azoria had turned me into a merman. But when I turned my head and looked behind me to see if I had grown a tail, there was nothing there... and Azoria started laughing at me for being so naive. Again.

The beautiful sea nymph took me by the hand and led me toward the Great Waterfalls. While we swam together beneath the surface it felt as though me and Azoria were the only two people alive. We were like the "Adam and Eve" of the deep blue sea.

"I feel like I just died and woke up in heaven next to an angel." I said to Azoria.Little did I know how close to the truth that statement would soon turn out to be.

Beyond the Great Waterfalls laid a series of passageways leading to an underwater labyrinth of grand proportions. This intricate network of tunnels and caves was hidden beneath miles of brightly colored coral and dancing seaweed that seemed to stretch endlessly across the ocean floor. Though the complexity of the maze was as daunting as it gets, Azoria was able to navigate her way through it with ease. She propelled us through winding corridors while avoiding sunken debris and made breakneck turns at speeds that even the fastest dolphin could not have matched. While Azoria sped along the ocean bottom, the underwater scenery flew by me in a collage of alternating colors from green to blue to yellow to pink to red to purple, and every color in between. I wanted desperately to know where Azoria was taking me in such a hurry, but I found it virtually impossible to maintain any bearings whatsoever.

"Slow down, Azoria! I'm getting seasick over here!" I pleaded. "Where are we going in such a rush?" By us being underwater, I was pretty sure that Azoria didn't hear me. But then all of a sudden her voice spoke to me saying, "We're going to the kingdom of Anog. You'll be safe there." Holy shit! What just happened?!

It was like having a clear, conscious thought. Azoria's voice could be heard inside my mind as if she was speaking out loud. Then I thought, "Oh, no! That means she can hear what I'm thinking too!"

My mind suddenly flashed back to the moment when I first saw her standing naked in the forest. The harder I tried not to think about it the more I did. And Azoria didn't waste any time, she got on my ass right away.

"That's quite an imagination you have," said Azoria while cutting her eyes at me and flashing a coy grin. "I especially liked the part where you and I were lying naked on the beach romantically staring into each other's eyes. That was um... interesting."

"C'mon, Azoria! That's not fair, you're embarrassing me."

"Perhaps you should be embarrassed. Those were very shameful thoughts considering the fact that you had them even before the two of us had been properly introduced. Don't you agree?"

I could see where this was going, and I wasn't about to play her little game. My best move was to not say anything at all, so I stood there and just smiled.

"You think you're pretty clever, don't you?" said Azoria with a smile of her own. "You obviously don't have a clue how telepathy actually works, so allow me to enlighten you."

"Go ahead. I'm listening." I said while still brandishing a toothy smile, aka, my defense mechanism.

"Telepathy is a common form of communication and many ocean creatures use it in one way or another." Azoria explained, "It'll soon become second nature and you won't even realize you're using it. My telepathic abilities only work underwater, so whatever was on your mind back in the forest is still your dirty little secret. I'm only aware of the thoughts you reflected upon while here beneath the water." I was suspicious of Azoria's lukewarm explanation. The entire time she was talking there was this sneaky smirk on her face, which meant she was definitely up to something. And I had every intention of finding out what it was. Let the games begin!

"Azoria, why are you standing over there with that huge grin on your face like you just won the lottery or something?" I said while trying my best to decipher her cryptic smile. "Yeah, I'll admit you have a nice body but don't play yourself, lil' mama. You ain't all that!" I was lying through my teeth trying to wipe that devilish grin off of her face. "So if you think I felt some kind of way about you back in the forest when I first saw you naked, then you got it twisted, ya heard me. I've seen plenty of naked broads way finer than you."

"Are you sure about that?" said Azoria as she approached me still grinning like the Joker. "Have you forgotten about the part where we're covered in coconut oil, and you start eating grapes right out of my----"

"HOLD UP! WAIT!" I immediately interrupted. "I thought you said that your telepathy only works underwater! I didn't reflect back on THAT part!"

"Oh my god! I can't believe you actually fell for that." Azoria said while laughing her head off. "I've never met anyone as gullible as you---hey, would you like to purchase a dairy farm in the middle of Anog? I have one, you know."

"Kiss my ass, Azoria!" I said over my hurt feelings, but Azoria was laughing so hard she didn't even hear me. It's cool, I let her have her little moment. But as soon as she calmed down again, I gave her a dose of her own medicine.

"Okay smartass, we'll just see who's gullible the next time I catch you without that fish tail of yours."

"What's that supposed to mean?", she asked.

"Come over here and I'll show you." I said with a slick grin of my own.

Azoria approached me and I immediately began projecting hardcore pornographic images into her mind of the two of us doing all kinds of wild shit in bed.

"That's disgusting!", she screamed. "Oh my god! You are soooooo nasty!"

I felt totally vindicated after paying Azoria back for embarrassing me earlier. She was still blushing as I stood ncxt to her smiling like an amphibious Cheshire cat.Ahhh! Sweet, sweet revenge.

✦ 38 ✦

✦ 39 ✦

"I've learned that people will forget what you said, people will forget what you did, but people will never forget how you made them feel."---Maya Angelou

CHAPTER 6

A Brush with Death

The closer we came to reaching Anog the deeper we descended into the abyss, and I could now feel the ocean's pressure pushing hard against my skin. We were travelling at depths far beyond the range of any manmade vessel, so I felt it was imperative to remind my guide that I wasn't fully equipped for this sort of thing.

"Azoria, I hope you realize that I'm not a fish."

"How can you be so sure?" she said while looking at me out the corner of her eye. "You look pretty fishy to me."

"That's not funny, Azoria," I complained. "That's not funny at all."

"Come here, I want to show you something." Azoria motioned for me to join her, and when I came near she gently placed her hand next to my chin and directed my attention toward a small group of whales swimming nearby.

"Wow! You've got to be kidding me! Are those things real?" I was completely amazed at how close we were able to get to the whales. I could almost reach out and touch them as they went gliding by in total silence. But of course, you know me. I had to turn the tranquil affair into a full-blown National Geographic event.

I started pretending that I was the famous French oceanic explorer Jacques Cousteau on an expedition to film a new documentary about the migration of whales. "Ah! This vixen of the sea---how should I say---she is magnifique!" I said with a very bad French accent, «Voules-vous bien m'y emmener, je ne sais quoi!» None of what I said made any sense because I don't speak a lick of French.

"Run that by me again," said Azoria looking confused and a bit agitated by my performance.

"I was telling you about my new documentary on the migration of whales, thank you very much." I chided with a snobbish attitude as though I was upset because she couldn't understand "French".

"What documentary? What are you talking about?" she asked. "On second thought, never mind. I don't even want to know! You are so weird." Azoria stood with her arms folded while I moved in to get a better camera angle.

Words could not describe the immense beauty and grace of these magnificent animals. A sense of great trust was imparted to me as I entered into their close-knit society. I was deeply humbled by the experience and felt privileged to be with them as we travelled through the sullen depths like one big family. The ocean's beautiful scenery provided the perfect backdrop for capturing the majestic creatures on film. And just as I was about to shoot my award-winning video, here comes Azoria who totally wigs out and starts yelling at me: "That's it, we're leaving! Now get your ass back over here!" Azoria snatched me away from the whales so fast that I almost got whiplash.

"Hey, Azoria! Don't come snatching on me like you're my mama or something!" I shouted in a ghetto-like fashion that infuriated her even more, and that's when Azoria went all the way "ghetto".

"Let me tell you something you lil' hardheaded son-of-a-bitch! If you don't start showing me some respect, I'mma beat the black off yo' ass!" Azoria growled through gritted teeth and with clinched fists ready to swing.

"Girl, you better chill out before I smack you upside the head! I don't play that shit; you better ask somebody! It's best you go sit yo' ass down somewhere, ya heard me!"

The next thing I remembered was waking up with two black eyes and a lump on the side of my head. I suspected that I'd gotten my ass whipped but I didn't ask questions because I didn't want to give Azoria the satisfaction of telling me what had happened. So I kept my mouth shut and continued rubbing the sore spot where I'd been kicked in the ass.

After swimming in silence for a while, I decided to offer Azoria an apology for getting so carried away with the whole Jacques Cousteau thing. But just as I was about to speak, something in the distance caught my eye. As the huge object slowly came into focus my mind started reeling with all kinds of thoughts of what it might be. Then I saw it!Holy shit! It's a pirate ship!

Visions of gold coins and chests filled with jewels of every kind immediately came to mind.

"Azoria, do you see that?!" I asked the mermaid, who looked at me and said nothing in return. She was obviously still fuming over the incident with the whales, so I figured I'd give her a little more time to cool off.

Once a fierce sight on the open seas, the rotting vessel now lay paralyzed at the bottom of the ocean in ghostly ruins. And though she still bared her teeth in the form of huge cannons that lined her facing side, the tattered ship would fight no more. Atop the ship's cracked and dilapidated mast was an eerie Jolly Roger still waving in the ocean current, a sure sign that pirates had once upon a time walked her seafaring decks.

"Azoria, can we go and explore the pirate ship? I promise I won't get carried away this time. C'mon, Azoria! There still could be treasure on board!"

"It is not safe to tarry in these waters," said Azoria in a raspy voice that made her words sound all the more scarier. "There are many unseen eyes watching us, and most belong to creatures that would love to have us for dinner. Not as guests but as the main course." And just like that the ocean became a very scary place.

"How far is it to Anog?" I asked with a tinge of anxiety in my voice. "Shouldn't we be there by now?"

"Shhhh! Be quiet! We're being followed!" Azoria's highly-developed senses had alerted her to an ominous predator lurking nearby.

"Wh-wh-what's happening?" I said while stuttering for the first time in my life, "Wh-wh-who's following us?"

"Not who, but what!" said Azoria as she pointed toward two figures that were headed straight for us.

"What are they?!" I asked.

"Killers!" she replied. "Take my hand and do not let go!"

I reached out my hand to Azoria and immediately we took off like a torpedo zooming through the water in a zigzag sort of way that made me super-nauseous. She was swimming even faster than before, and still, the huge silhouettes in the distance were gaining on us.

"Swim faster, Azoria!" I shouted, "They're catching up to us!" As the mermaid increased her speed, the centrifugal force produced by her powerful tail caused me to lose my grip, and then the unthinkable happened.

"Azoria, I can't hang on! My hand is slipping!" The moment I slipped from Azoria's grasp I was sucked into a whirling current where I spun around and around until finally coming face-to-face with a couple of real monsters.SH-SH-SHAAARRKKKS!

Two gigantic Great White sharks were coming toward me with blazing speed. Each shark was at least thirty-five feet in length and had distinct markings on its back like symbols. I kept thinking about how ridiculous it was for a guy like me to get eaten by a shark. Where I'm from, we know not to get our asses in the water if there's even the slightest possibility of sharks being around. How many inner city Blacks have you known to be killed by a Great White shark?Exactly.

What I initially noticed about the sharks that scared me the most were their eyes. The Great Whites' eyes were cold, black, lifeless circles incapable of expressing any type of emotion. No sorrow, no joy, no love, no pain, and certainly no remorse. But that's not what makes the Great White shark so fearsome, the reason for that is because these animals possess some of the most powerful "jaws" on the planet. Ones that come fully equipped with rows and rows of razor sharp teeth. Great White sharks never sleep and never stop swimming, their sole purpose in nature is to hunt, eat, and make baby sharks---that's it. They are nature's perfect killing machines. In fact, evolution has not saw fit to alter them in any way for several hundred million years. And now these monsters of the deep were coming after me.

I managed to dodge the initial attack and watched the sharks swim off in the opposite direction, hoping that they would keep on going. But in the blink of an eye the huge animals made a U-turn and came speeding right at me again. This time it was a brutal assault laced with savagery and mayhem. All I could do was watch in horror as the sea around me turned crimson with blood. Amid chunks of shredded flesh and broken cartilage I spotted the alluring face of the mermaid who had once again come to my rescue. For you see, the second attack wasn't committed by the sharks, it was committed upon them, by Azoria. She had driven a spear-shaped object deep into the abdomen of the first shark, spilling its intestines and spewing a large cloud of crimson into the water. Her aqua-blue eyes now turned bright red with fury; Azoria delighted in the mayhem she was causing, and the blood-soaked ocean seemed to excite her to no end. The mermaid had undergone a terrifying transformation which left her with an arsenal of deadly weaponry built right into her DNA. Huge fangs that curled inward like those of a pit viper sprang up inside her mouth, and at the tips of her fingers were six-inch claws capable of cutting through solid steel like a hot knife through butter.

There was so much blood in the water that I couldn't see anything in front of me; I knew the other shark was somewhere out there lurking in the distance waiting on the perfect opportunity for an attack... and I was right.

"Watch out! The other shark is right behind you!" Azoria's voice rang out in the deep, and as I turned around to face the shark---WHOP! WHOP! SLASH! It was all over.

Azoria stared at me in silence trying to make sense of what just happened. Apparently, when I spun around to face the oncoming predator, a sharp object struck the giant fish and sliced it in half. That sharp object turned out to be my new tail. I had become something other than human. A new kind of hybrid that Azoria found quite appealing. Now it was she who had become captivated by me.

"H-H-How did you do that?" she asked. "W-W-What are you?"

"I don't know," I said. "All I remember was turning around, and then the next thing I knew there was blood everywhere and the shark was dead." Azoria stood there gawking at me in disbelief.

"Why are you staring at me like that?" I asked.

"Like what? I wasn't staring at you." But Azoria was staring at me, and she was blushing like a Catholic nun on Bourbon Street.

"I um... you um... I mean what makes you think that I was staring only at you? I stare at lots of things." She was starting to sound like a little schoolgirl experiencing her first crush. I was actually flattered to see her besotted by my good looks. I smiled a gentle smile hoping that it would let her know that the feeling was mutual.

We continued on our way toward Anog and soon reached the outskirts of the glorious kingdom. Though I was anxious to discover what secrets lay beyond the huge gates in the distance, nothing could have prepared me for what was about to happen next.

AZURA

CHAPTER 7

SOLILOQUY OF THE DRAGON

The kingdom of Anog was a magnificent paradise located far beneath the ocean's surface. It was filled with huge, colorful structures and teeming with millions of tropical fish of all shapes and sizes.

"This is my home," said Azoria. "Come, there is much I want to show you."

We entered the kingdom through a series of elaborate gates made of giant coral that had been infused with gold and other precious metals. The mammoth gates were works of architectural genius and were decorated with beautiful seashells of every kind. Each gate weighed more than a hundred tons but was easily moved with a slight touch of the hand. The mystery behind their amazing design made me think about the Great Pyramids in Egypt, because they too were feats of remarkable engineering. I began to wonder if Azoria's people were in some way related to the early "dark-skinned" Egyptians who built the pyramids. Even the great historian Herodotus mentioned the black skins and wooly hair of the Egyptians of his time. Azoria showed me where to place my hand, and like magic, the gigantic gates slowly swung open.

Once inside the kingdom, I noticed a towering statue standing in the middle of the courtyard. "Azoria, who is that a statue of?" I asked while pointing to the golden marvel that bore a striking resemblance to the legendary "King Triton".

"The statue was made in honor of our most celebrated warrior." Azoria boasted.

"I'm sure he was a great warrior and all, but why's his statue so big?" I said while straining my neck to see the top of the huge monument.

"What do you mean?" said Azoria. "The statue is in every way identical to the King." I first looked over at Azoria, then back at the statue.

"But that would mean that he---" Before I could finish my thought, a legion of ferocious mer-warriors approached us from every direction and we were completely surrounded.

"It's the Imperial Guard!" Azoria said, "Whatever you do, don't make any sudden movements and do not say anything. It is forbidden for you to speak to them unless spoken to. Now stand still and let me do the talking."

The mer-warriors' faces were partially hidden behind shiny plates made of platinum, only their glowing red eyes were visible through the masks they wore. Each warrior carried a long, splendor spear and a huge shield that was emblazoned with a royal crest representing the Kingdom of Anog. They were indeed the "Spartans" of the deep.

"Greetings Princess Azoria," said the leader of the Guard as he and the rest of the King's Imperial Guard bowed their heads to show respect and obedience to Azoria. "Shall I inform the King of your return?"

"Yes, you may." Azoria said in an authoritative tone of voice that took me by surprise. "You may also inform him that I am coming to visit with him shortly, and that I will be accompanied by a guest." Azoria was speaking in a manner that I had not heard her speak before, her voice sounded very refined and quite regal. She was speaking as if she was royalty.

"Yes, Your Highness, as you wish." Again the leader of the Guard bowed his head in respect, but not before giving me a menacing glare that sent chills down my hybrid spine. It was a look of extreme disapproval. I wanted to say something, but I knew that Azoria would flip out if I did. So I just chilled and played it cool for the sake of not having to deal with her wrath. She has quite a temper that girl.

The Imperial Guard faded back into the murky depths like ghostly phantoms, leaving me with a burning question to ask the um... princess.

"Azoria, what's up with the royalty bit?"

"What do you mean?" she said with a coy smile.

"You know exactly what I'm talking about. Why did the clown with the spear address you as 'Princess Azoria'?"

"I suggest that you not refer to General Salazar by any name other than that which was given to him by the King. Anog's mer-warriors, each and every one of them, are born killers! They are lethal from birth, and they will stop at nothing if provoked!"

The fierce mer-warriors scared me half to death, but I didn't want Azoria to know just how frightened I was, so once the warriors left, I started talking cash shit.

"I don't give a damn about them being born killers, so what?! That don't scare me. In fact, I wish one of them bitches would've said something crazy to me, especially that General Salazar dude, I'dda punched him right in the---"

"Oh look!" Azoria shouted while pointing directly behind me. "The general must have heard you, he's coming back!" I almost shit on myself. Thankfully Azoria was just fooling around again. Her ass was standing there laughing like it was the funniest thing she'd ever seen.

"Girl, you need to stop playing so damn much!" I chided. "You could've made me hurt myself."

She kept on laughing for a while, but once she calmed down again I continued interrogating her about the conversation she had with the leader of the Imperial Guard.

"Like I was saying, what's up with the whole royalty bit---Princess?" There was a brief silence, and then the mysterious mermaid began revealing her true identity to me.

"The kingdom of Anog is comprised of six hundred twenty-three sectors and each is governed by an augur. The augurs are very powerful wizards, and when one of them lives to be a thousand years old, he or she becomes what is known as a Great Elder. No one in the kingdom is allowed to question a Great Elder's wisdom or authority. No one except the King of course."

Azoria paused to see if I was following the conversation, but she didn't have to worry, I was listening to her every word.

"Our king is a great and powerful ruler who is wise beyond measure. His bravery is legendary among our people, which is why he is the subject of many songs and stories told to children during bedtime. In fact, the statue that you saw in the courtyard was built in his honor. King Claudius is the reason that our kind still exists, he's our leader, our hero, our king. And um... he's my father."

I stood silent, staring out into the distance trying to wrap my mind around what Azoria said about her father being the King.

"So let me get this straight. Your daddy is the ruler of this kingdom, right? So that means that you really are a princess!"

"Yes, I'm a princess, so what?" said Azoria.

"What do you mean, 'so what?' This is a really big deal." I said in response to how nonchalant Azoria was being about the whole thing.

"You should have told me from the start that you were the King's daughter. I can't believe I've fallen in love with a real prin---" Before I could catch myself, I had revealed something very private to Azoria. And I could tell by the expression on her face that she was shocked to hear of it.

"What did you just say?" asked Azoria with a broad smile that showed every tooth in her head. "I didn't catch that last part; you mind repeating it for me?"

"Never mind what you thought you heard; you're just trying to change the subject. Why didn't you tell me who you were when we first met?"

"I don't see what difference it makes, just because I'm a princess doesn't mean that anything has to change between us."

"Are you crazy?! This changes everything!"

Azoria didn't understand why I was making a big deal out of the fact that she was royalty. I figured that me being from the projects and her being from of a royal family would mean that we would always be worlds apart.

"Azoria, I'm not royalty, you know. I'm just a kid from the 'gutta'. Aren't you like, betrothed to some prince guy from another kingdom or something?"

Out of everything I had just said to her, Azoria's only response was, "What's the 'gutta'?" Sweet Jesus!

"Azoria, will you please pay attention?! I'm lecturing over here! And another thing, what were you doing running around in the forest in the first place? Don't princesses have more important things to do than spy on people?"

"I wasn't spying on you!" shouted the princess. "I went into the forest only to protect you!"

"Protect me?" I asked. "Protect me from what?"

Azoria ignored me as though I had inquired about something forbidden for her to speak of. So I quickly rephrased the question.

"Why did I need protecting?" Azoria slowly looked up at me with those mesmerizing blue eyes of hers and I became like putty in her hands. She was so damn gorgeous it was ridiculous... and she knew it.

Speaking in a soft, sensuous voice she said, "I have protected you since the moment you arrived in our world. You came to us from the heavens like a magnificent shooting star, soaring across the sky inside a brilliant ball of fire before entering the ocean with a tremendous splash. I immediately rushed over to where you had landed but..." Azoria's words suddenly trailed off, leaving a deafening silence.

"Azoria, please tell me what happened when you got there? I want to know." At first she looked away, but then she changed her mind and decided to honor my request.

"When you entered the ocean a spectacular rainbow was formed in the water's mist. I followed the rainbow until I had reached its end, and there in the water was the person who stands before me." A long silence hung in the air before Azoria spoke again. I could sense that she was having trouble choosing the right words to say what needed to be said. "Can't you see? I couldn't just leave you that way, I had to do something!" said Azoria, now sounding a little distressed. "I didn't have any other choice."

She wasn't making sense to me, so I tried again to get to the bottom of this mystery.

"Azoria, did I miss something?" I said in desperation of wanting to know how I ended up in her world with portions of my memory missing.

"When I approached the area where your capsule went down, you were lying on your back and you weren't breathing. The only way to save you was to share my Quintess." Azoria then stared at me as if I was supposed to know what she was talking about, but I didn't have a clue. The only thing that relatively lined up with what she was describing was--- "Wait a minute! Did sharing your Quintess with me have anything to do with sex?" I said, and then immediately felt stupid for asking.

Azoria laughed out loud and said, "No, silly! What I shared with you is much more intimate than that."

"What could be more intimate than the 'horizontal shuffle'?" I said in the most euphemistic way I could think of.

"The horizontal what?" asked Azoria amid a slew of giggles. "Oh my god! You are so----" Azoria couldn't stop laughing, and I stood there wondering how could she not take this seriously.

"What I shared with you---fool!---was a very precious gift that only royal members of my kind possess," she finally stated but in a matter-of-fact kind of way. "The Quintess, which is also called the Fifth Element, allows a mer-person to become one with another being. It can only be used once, and even then there are strict rules that must be followed:

1.) Never use the Quintess for evil.

2.) Always protect the sanctity of the vessel that carries the Quintess.

3.) Forever keep sacred the Quintessence (Also called the Reckoning).

The magic of the Quintess is so pure and so powerful it even has dominion over death!" said Azoria with the charm of a sorceress.

Placing her hand next to my face while looking deep into my eyes, Azoria leaned toward me and whispered, "So you see, that which I have given you can never be taken back. It is the very essence of who I am---it is my Fifth Element. The sharing of the Quintess is by far the greatest gift that one can bestow on another. Never take its power for granted, it has already saved you more than once."

What in the world is Azoria talking about? I said to myself, forgetting that she could read my thoughts and hear everything I was thinking.

"What I'm saying is that we are forever joined. You are no longer just a human, and I am no longer simply a mermaid. We've become something other than what we were. Something new and extraordinary."

It was as if someone had suddenly come along and switched on a light inside my brain, everything started to make perfect sense. The magic of the Quintess allowed me to breathe underwater and communicate telepathically with Azoria, it was also the reason she could leave the ocean and walk on dry land in human form. It was all due to Azoria's Quintess which essentially gave us the best of two worlds.

"After I rescued you from the ocean, I placed you on the shores of the Galactic Island where I thought you'd be safe." Azoria said in a somber voice heavily laced with empathy.

"The Galactic Island?" I said while trying to piece together all the clues in my head. "So you were the one who brought me there? Why is it called the Galactic Island?"

"The name 'Galactic' is in reference to the island's immense size---galactic means enormous. You have no idea how vast the island really is because I made sure you remained in a relatively small area. Do you recall meeting the fairy who warned you about the forest?"

"Yes, of course. How could I ever forget her? Are you telling me that she was you?!"

"Like I said, I've been protecting you since the beginning of your arrival into our world. After sharing my Quintess with you, I began to discover new abilities that allowed me to do remarkable things, like take the form of other living beings. You were exposed to an even more powerful supernatural occurrence that took place during the mingling of our souls. It combined itself with the power of the Quintess and created its own energy field, which means that no one knows what you really are... your powers are virtually limitless."

I wasn't buying the fairy tale scenario Azoria was trying to sell me. Nevertheless, there was a lot of strange shit happening that didn't make sense, so who knows what could be true around here.

"Azoria, what about the footprints in the sand, was that you too?" Azoria just stared at me with a puzzled look on her face.

"What footprints?" she asked. And once again I could feel my mental stability coming into question.

"Never mind, it's nothing." I said, and then immediately changed the subject. "Why didn't you just bring me directly to Anog?"

"Well, as I just mentioned, the Galactic Island is quite vast, which makes it a good place to hide things that you want to stay hidden. I thought by bringing you there the leviathan would not find you. But I was wrong."

Azoria lowered her head as though she had failed me.

"What's wrong, Azoria? Why are looking so sad?" She didn't respond right away, so I was a little less intrusive on my next approach.

"Azoria, what exactly is this leviathan that you keep referring to? Is it some kind of animal or something? Because I saw a strange creature in the forest and----"

Azoria wasn't paying attention to anything I was saying, she had become lost in thought. She had to remind herself that I wasn't from her world and therefore had no knowledge of the beast she had been speaking about.

"I was referring to the Bringer of Death!" Again, she was speaking in a raspy voice that made her words sound extremely scary.

"The leviathan is the 'Father of All Wickedness', an ancient dragon who has plagued our world since the beginning of time." Her eyes were alit with fury, and as Azoria continued her soliloquy of the dragon, dark clouds gathered above the ocean like hordes of swirling demons summoned by the devil himself.

"Entire generations of my kind have perished at the hands of this merciless beast from the Underworld. His appetite for destruction is insatiable, the leviathan feeds on the souls of man and mer-people alike. All the dragon wants is to watch the world burn!" Azoria was becoming enraged; she was nearly in tears as she reached the conclusion of her story. "This beast was called Balthazar by the Great Elders of old, but to those living in my generation, he is known as Sapian---the red dragon."

"I had no idea, Azoria. I'm sorry to hear about the great suffering that was inflicted upon your people, but um... why would this 'Sapian' creature be looking for me?"

"Sapian knows that by destroying you, he destroys us all." Azoria was again speaking of things I did not understand because I had no knowledge of the history surrounding her kind. "Sapian already knows that you are not of this world, and the dragon will stop at noth---"

"Wait a minute!" I interrupted, "What do you mean, 'Sapian already knows that I'm not of this world?' How does the dragon know that?"

Looking up toward the surface, Azoria replied in a whisper, "He knows... everything."

As if this Sapian shit wasn't enough to worry about, I had a strange feeling that Azoria was still hiding something from me, and I wanted to know what it was.

"Azoria, do you mind if I ask you a question?"

"Of course not, what is it you wish to know?"

"Well, do you remember when you said I came into your world inside a brilliant ball of fire?"

"Yes, it was quite magnificent," said Azoria.

"Magnificent, huh? Well tell me this, how in the hell could I have survived such an event? It seems to me that you're not telling me the whole story there, princess. I demand that you tell me the truth."

"Since you insist, I will tell you all that you wish to know." My heart began to pound in anticipation of hearing what truly happened upon my arrival into Azoria's world. "The tremendous impact made when you entered the ocean was felt even here in Anog. No one knew what caused it except me, because I had disobeyed my father's orders---as I often did---and had ventured to the surface. I was swimming near the coast of the Galactic Island when you fell from the sky and..."

A sudden sadness befell the mermaid as she prepared to reveal what happened next. "I'm sorry to have to tell you this but um... you didn't actually *survive* the crash. The truth is----you died."

Azoria's words hit me like a ton of bricks, I couldn't fathom the meaning of what she had said. I mean, how could I have died in the crash when I was standing right there asking her what happened? Azoria was very forthcoming, and I really appreciated that she had the courage to tell me what I wanted to know.

"By the time I swam over to where you were, it was already too late... you showed no signs of life. In fact, you had no pulse, and you weren't breathing.

The capsule that brought you here was practically destroyed, but I did manage to salvage the main section. That's it over there." Azoria was pointing toward an odd-looking configuration that was standing not far from us. The mangled and twisted plastic that Azoria had brought to Anog formed a perfect semicircle on the ocean floor. It appeared to have three statuettes standing side-by-side facing inward with their heads bowed as if gazing down at something.

"What's wrong?" asked Azoria, "Why are you so quiet?"

Little did she know, the configuration of the silhouettes was very familiar to me. I had seen it many times as a young boy while riding through upscale neighborhoods with my family during Christmas season. I could suddenly hear the song "The Little Drummer Boy" playing softly in my mind... pah-rump. pum-pum-pum!

The configuration standing in Anog was almost identical to the ones on display on the front lawns of houses located in the Garden District where my family and I used to ride around looking at Christmas lights. Now, here at the bottom of the ocean was an eerie replica of the Nativity depicting the birth of Christ. As I moved closer to the figures, I noticed that the "three wise-men" were actually pieces of melted plastic. I could tell that the original color of the plastic was yellow, and on the back of one of the figures was an engraved placard with only part of a name. The rest had been destroyed by the searing flames that threatened to devour the entire capsule. The scorched letters read "***-*-G O * D". As in, "pot-o'-G O 1 D" portable restroom.

"You see, even your nameplate labeled you a god." Azoria said with a beaming smile on her face. I was so bewildered by everything that was going on, that I didn't even bother to tell her it was the name of a toilet.

Inside the semicircle of "wise-men" was a crater, and inside the crater was an impression of a man fitting my exact stature and build.

"The only reason you are here right now is because my Quintess brought you back from the other side," said Azoria.

"The other side of what?" I asked.

"The other side of death, silly. You've been resurrected... resurrected... resurrected." Azoria's words echoed inside my mind, and even though she was still talking, I didn't hear anything after the word "resurrected".

"Hold up! Did you just say that I was resurrected?"

"Yes, that's what I've been trying to tell y----", she started to explain but I cut her off.

"Listen, I don't know what kind of weird-ass voodoo you'd been practicing down here but I didn't volunteer to be turned into some kind of 'fishy' Frankenstein mer-monster! What the hell have you done to me?"

"Why are you so angry?" asked Azoria. "Being resurrected is a great priv---"

"Stop using that word!" I chided, "Can't you see how wrong this is?"

Azoria stood there with a look of indifference on her face, and it suddenly occurred to me that she really didn't know why I was upset. I had to remind myself that she wasn't from my world.

"Azoria, I'm sorry for yelling but this is very upsetting to me. In my world, people don't return from the grave. Once you're dead that's it, game over. There's no coming back."

"Geez! Living in your world must be awful," said Azoria in a sympathetic sort of way.

"Now why would you say that?" I asked.

"Well, it just seems to me that if someone you loved had only a single opportunity to live, then you both would be forced to exist in a state of constant anxiety hoping endlessly that death not call on either of you."

I thought about what she said, and then I responded saying, "It is because of that 'single opportunity' that we humans place such great value on life and true love. For the most part, you only get one shot at each."

Azoria shook her head acknowledging that she understood my position and she apologized for being so cavalier about bringing me back from the dead. I then decided to offer her an even more important perspective, one that dealt with religion. "Azoria, most people in my world believe in God, and we try to govern ourselves in accordance with His word. So whether things in our life are good or bad, we faithfully give thanks to our Lord and Savior Jesus Christ."

"Wow! That's very interesting!" said Azoria. "I wish to hear more about this Jesus of yours. He sounds like a wonderful king." Upon noticing how excited Azoria was to learn more about the teachings of Christ, I began telling her everything I remembered about the Bible. The way I was able to recite scripture and verse made me wonder if I was once a preacher. We covered the Bible from Genesis to Revelation, and Azoria was hanging on my every word. She was especially moved by my reenactment of the "Passion of Christ" where I demonstrated how Jesus was crucified and how He miraculously rose from the grave three days later. I believe it was then that she truly understood why I was initially upset at learning that I had been resurrected. To me, it was something that was associated with divinity and I was not worthy of such a thing.

There was one story in particular that drew her attention like no other. It was the story of Ezekiel the prophet."This Ezekiel, he reminds me of the Elders, and many of the things he speaks about are written in the prophecy."

"What prophecy?" I asked, but Azoria ignored me and looked the other way as if speaking about the prophecy was taboo.

"Um... tell me again what it says in the book of Revelation 12:12," said Azoria, obviously wanting to change the subject.

I searched my memory for the verse that Azoria wanted me to recite, and when it came to me, I said, "Woe to the earth and the sea, because the devil has gone down to you! He is filled with fury because he knows his time is short."

Azoria and I stared at each other because we were both think-ing the same thing... Could it be possible that Sapian is the same "Red Dragon" mentioned in Revelation? "That's impossible!" we said in unison.

Azoria was glad to see that I was feeling better, and to keep my mind off the resurrection she decided to ask me a burning question she'd been wanting to ask for quite some time.

"You mind if I ask you something?" said Azoria.

"No, go right ahead." I replied.

"In all the time that we've spent getting to know one anoth-er, do you realize that you have not mentioned your name even once?"

"I hadn't really thought about it, Azoria. But now that you mention it,..."

Holy shit! I couldn't believe it. After all this time Azoria didn't even know my name. But what was even more disturbing was the fact that neither did I.

"Azoria, you're not going to believe this! I can't remember my name!" She didn't seem at all surprised. In fact, the only thing Azoria said was:

"Titles are very important, you know. So if you don't remem-ber your old one then you should choose a new one."

"You mean just like that I'm supposed to just pick a new name out of the blue? What about my real name?"

"Well, if you can't remember it, then it serves no purpose. Let's choose a new one together, okay?"

"At least give me a minute to try and remember the name I've been called my entire life." I said out of frustration, causing Azo-ria to bite down on her lip in a coy, seductive way that made my heart melt. And once again I was like putty in her hands.

"Okay, fine. You can help me pick a new name if it'll make you happy. But nothing weird!"

The good news brought an immediate smile to Azoria's face and a round of applause. She was very excited about helping me select a suitable name to replace the one I had somehow forgotten. The naming process began with me reciting a few possible choices:

"What about Michael?" I asked, but Azoria immediately shook her head in disapproval.

"Well, how about Renaldo?" I said half-jokingly as the suggestion was met with extreme objection by the mermaid.

"Well then, what about Quincy,... Anthony,.... Brian,... Wayne,...?" Every name I came up with was rejected by the princess, except the name Victor. She really liked that one for some reason, but it didn't quite fit me. While judging name after name, Azoria would stick her finger down her throat and pretend to vomit in disgust. So after about the tenth name I reminded her that this whole thing was her idea to begin with.

"Hey, you're supposed to be helping me with this, remember?" I said to Azoria, who still had her finger in her mouth pretending to throw-up.

"I am helping, by not letting you make the wrong choice." It was exactly like something a woman would say.

"No, what I mean is---"

"I know exactly what you mean, and the choice has always been obvious to me." Azoria said with a smile. "According to the Great Prophecy, you are going to lead my people to the Promised Land. A glorious underwater kingdom called Atlantica."

"Azoria, you know I don't believe in any of that crap. Besides, what does that have to do with anything?"

"Whether you believe it or not you're the 'Chosen One'," said the princess. "Therefore, your title should reflect who you are."

"I don't get it. Are you suggesting that I call myself 'The Guy From The Galactic Island Who Finds The Promised Land'?"

"Don't be ridiculous," said Azoria. "I'm suggesting that you be called Theolonius D'Shawn Atlanticus---'the god who shows us the way to Atlantica'!"

"Hmm! I actually like the sound of that," I said in all sincerity. "D'Shawn, huh? Okay, I'll roll with that."

My mahogany princess put on a huge smile as she prepared to introduce my new title to the world.

"Very well then! From this day forth you will be known as D'Shawn, Lord of the Galactic Island."

It was exciting to hear Azoria pronounce my new name, she made it sound so dignified, so majestic, so royal.

"Wow! I don't know what to say, Azoria. Thank you." The princess smiled, then gave me a wink and a nod of approval.

We were now on our way to see her father, the King. And as we headed toward the immaculate castle in the distance I was reminded of a movie that I saw as a kid. It starred Sidney Portier and it was called "Guess Who's Coming to Dinner?". The film was about an interracial couple in love who went to visit the white parents of the girl during a time when such a relationship was socially unacceptable. Even though Azoria and I were Black, we came from two different worlds just like the couple in the movie. So I said to myself, "Her father is going to completely flip out when he gets a load of me!"

"From time to time an angel of the Lord would come down and stir up the waters."

---John 5:4

CHAPTER 8

A ROYAL PAIN

"ello, Princess Azoria," said a cute little mermaid when Azoria and I approached the main palace.

"Well hello yourself," said Azoria in a kind, motherly voice. "And what is your name?"

"My name is Chloey, and I live in the third sector near the Aquadome," said the mer-child with a gap-toothed smile.

"It's certainly nice to meet you, Chloey. You're such a doll." The little mermaid's smile got even broader at hearing Azoria compliment her appearance.

"Why thank you, Princess Azoria. You're not so bad looking yourself." Azoria chuckled at Chloey's choice of words.

"Chloey my dear, this is my friend D'Shawn. He is visiting our kingdom and I'm taking him to meet my father." The curious little mermaid stared at me, then quickly hid herself behind Azoria and covered her face like she was frightened.

"'What's the matter, sweetie?" asked Azoria. "Why are you hiding?"

Chloey immediately pointed and said, "He looks weird." She was right. I did look weird. Azoria hadn't thought about how my awkward appearance as a hybrid would make me stick out amongst those in her community. I remained distinguishably human even with the addition of my new tail.

"Oh, no! This is not good! " said Azoria. "I can't believe I didn't take into account how others might view you. What am I going to do now?" Azoria had become alarmed because the one thing her father despised above all, was humans. The shit was obviously about to hit the fan.

We entered the palace and nervously made our way toward the throne room. The moment of truth had finally come, and I could suddenly feel my heart pounding hard against my chest as Azoria and I knelt before her father, the King.

"Father, I bid thee good morning. I've come to speak to you about a very important matter," said Azoria, her voice quivering and her eyes nervously watching her father's expression. "This is D'Shawn, I met him on the Galactic Island, and he has come to---"

"SILENCE!", roared the King. "How dare you bring this despicable creature into my presence!" His voice was like booming thunder, it shook the entire kingdom and caused a wave of panic to wash over me like never before.

"And what is this?!" said the King after noticing my hybrid features. "Have you shared your Quintess with this beast?!" Azoria stood silent with her head down and her eyes closed hoping that her father's anger would soon cool. But as time went on, the King only became more enraged.

"Azoria, I have endured your callous behavior on many occasions. But today you have ventured beyond the boundaries of my tolerance! For this, you shall be made a pariah! An outcast never to return to Anog!" The King roared with great fury, "And this-this-thing! This abomination of yours must be destroyed at once! Summon the general of the Imperial Guard!"

"Father, wait!" cried Azoria as she went rushing toward the King. "I beg you! Please! You don't understand!"

"Foolish child, why have you brought such shame upon yourself? What possessed you to waste your precious Quintess on this despicable creature?"

"D'Shawn is not like other humans, father. He is a 'precious jewel' that was sent to us from the heavens above."

"Is that so?" said the King.

"Yes, father. I would have never brought him here if it wasn't of the utmost importance," said Azoria as she approached her father and began explaining to him why she brought me to Anog.

"D'Shawn fell from the sky in a brilliant ball of fire and landed in the ocean near the coast of the island. The only way I could save him was through resurrection." She now had the King's full attention. "Once I placed him on the Galactic Island the leviathan came looking for him."

"What?!", said the King. "Do you know what this means?!"

"Yes, father, I do," said the princess. "And that is why I have brought him to Anog." The wise king remembered what had been written in the prophecy about the savior who came down from heaven. The Great Prophecy predicted that one day a savior would descend from the heavens and do battle with the red dragon Sapian. This savior would not be from their world and would possess supernatural powers equaled only to that of a god. The prophecy also warned that legions of monsters would be sent forth by the beast to try and destroy the savior, because it too knows what is written.

The Great Elders believed that once the savior defeated the red dragon the prophecy would be fulfilled, and then the savior would lead the mer-people to an underwater paradise called Atlantica.

"Azoria my child, do you actually believe that this puny human is the one spoken about in the Great Prophecy?" asked the King. And with great confidence Azoria replied, "Yes, father. I truly believe that D'Shawn is 'the Chosen One'."

Azoria and her father were looking over their shoulder at me, still whispering amongst themselves, and I became very nervous.

"I wonder if the King is trying to decide which mantle he plans to display my head on."

I started easing my way toward the exit in anticipation of there being trouble, but then I heard Azoria call out to me:

"D'Shawn, come join us! I want you to meet my father!" said Azoria. "Come here, he wants to meet you!"

"Yeah, I'll be right over." I cautiously headed toward the King making sure to keep an eye on the deadly-sharp trident he kept next to his solid gold throne.

"Greetings, Your Highness." I said to the King. "I am honored to finally make your acquaintance."

"I am called Claudius, and I am the ruler of the kingdom in which you stand," said the King. "Welcome to Anog." I felt somewhat relieved after our introduction. I took it as a sign that the King wasn't going to kill me---at least not at the moment anyway---and I was welcomed to stay here with his daughter Azoria.

I guess some dreams do come true...

"My daughter tells me you're from the Galactic Island."

"Well Sire, I wouldn't exactly say I'm from the Galactic Island, I sort of ended up there."

"So then tell me D'Shawn, where are you from?" I was suddenly feeling nervous again about being there. My memory was spotty at best, but I was fairly certain that I knew where I came from. I first glanced over at Azoria, then back at the King.

"My home is in Louisiana. I'm from a city called New Orleans." Just then, the huge doors to my left burst open and in came Zenobia---the Queen.

"Azoria Angelica Sha' Nequa Jones, where in all the oceans have you been?" chided the Queen. "Your father and I have been worried sick about you."

"I'm fine mother. Come, there's someone I want you to meet." Turning her attention toward me, the Queen nearly fainted when she realized that a human was standing only a few feet away from her.

"Great Atlantica! What's a human doing in the palace? Claudius have you completely lost your mind?"

I looked at Azoria and said, "Didn't we just go through this?"

"SHUT UP, D'SHAWN!" both she and the King yelled in unison.

"Claudius, if the Elders get wind of this the entire kingdom will be cast into chaos. It would all but ruin the plans for the coronation---Azoria is to be made Empress soon and the guest list is nearly full."

The king nor Azoria had any real interest in the coronation, but they were both willing to endure the pompous ceremony for the sake of the Queen, who had her heart set on entertaining lots of guests at the palace. Thankfully my arrival had spared Azoria and her father from having to dress up and sit through a long, boring night of mingling with Zenobia's snobbish friends.

Azoria and her mother Zenobia could have passed for twins. The only obvious difference between them was that the Queen's eyes were emerald green, and Azoria's were ocean blue. I could definitely see where Azoria got her voluptuous figure from---she got it from her mama.

Queen Zenobia continued to question her daughter about me being in the palace, and I stood next to them smiling like I had just found a piece of candy in my pocket while the music of New Orleans rapper "Juvenile" played in my head:

"... A big fine woman'll make you smile when she pass you. Damn that girl fine! Her mama got ass too! ...Back that ass up!"

"What is he smiling about?" the Queen asked Azoria after noticing the droll expression I was wearing. But before her daughter could say anything, the Queen approached me and made her presence known.

"Wipe that ridiculous grin off your face right this instant!" I immediately sucked my lips inward forming an inverted pucker, but the harder I tried to look serious the more ridiculous my expression became. Finally, I tried to make conversation by complimenting the Queen's beautiful eyes using a broken Cajun French dialect that I had picked up from a pimp in my neighborhood.

«Bon jour, mes che le beaux yeux.» I blurted out in one long slurring sentence and finished it off with, "Oui, oui!"

"Is there something wrong with him?" the Queen asked Azoria.

"No, mother. He's just trying to impress you."

"Well make him stop. He's getting on my last nerve."

Suddenly, the leader of the Imperial Guard rushed into the room with a startling announcement. "Your Royal Highnesses!", he said as he greeted the King and the royal family. "I have received word from my lieutenants who were part of a scouting party. That there's trouble on the horizon, and I fear our kingdom will soon come under attack!"

"My goodness!" said Queen Zenobia. "Claudius, what are we going to do?!"

"How many are there?" asked the King.

"Sire! It's like nothing we've ever heard of before!" said the general.

"Yes, but how many are there?"

"All of our enemies have joined forces and are planning to attack us as one monstrous army... their numbers are in the millions."

The wise king began to contemplate what was happening, and soon he had reached his conclusion. "Our enemies have fallen under the spell of Sapian." Then Claudius looked over at me and said, "And I know why they have come."

The fierce mer-warrior suddenly noticed me in the room, and with blinding speed he took up his weapon and viciously attacked me. There was absolutely nothing I could do; he was too fast and too powerful. The leader of the King's army savagely stabbed me several times and as I went into shock, he brutally slashed my throat with his razor-like claws. I fell to the floor pleading to the general, asking him to stop the assault but the born killer was operating purely on instincts and had no intentions of stopping until I was dead.

"I'm not your enemy!" I yelled at him, "You're making a huge mistake!" The ferocious attack continued without cease, and out the corner of my eye I saw Azoria being restrained by her father and I faintly heard her cries for mercy in the distance.

"Please father! You must call off the general before it's too late!" But the King needed to know for certain that I was the savior mentioned in the Great Prophecy, so he did not intervene.

A miraculous event was about to take place before their very eyes. I became filled with a burning rage, and unlike what had happened during the shark attack, fear was not the motivating factor that triggered the metamorphosis. This time it was pure rage that caused the transformation to occur. Something inside of me was trying to break loose, I could feel it tearing away at my insides as it sent fiery acid coursing through my veins. The pain was excruciating at first but quickly subsided as my body adjusted to its new form. My dire situation had forced me to embrace the monster within me, and ultimately, I gave the beast permission to do its bidding.

Though the ferocious mer-warrior was still attacking me, my body no longer felt the pain being inflicted on it. An incredible metamorphosis caused me to grow to more than ten times my original size. I was suddenly thirsting for blood, and I wasn't going to be denied the pleasure of ripping my attacker to shreds.

I now stood towering over the puny warrior; I was bloodied but ready for war. My wounds quickly healed to perfection, and my arms and chest became a mass of bulging muscles. Tauntingly, I flashed my new razor sharp claws at the mer-warrior filling him with paralyzing fear. He could see that inside my mouth were several rows of jagged teeth accompanied by two enormous fangs dripping with poisonous venom.

My eyes had become lifeless circles, terrifying and empty, like those of the Great White shark. I felt a strange emptiness deep down in my soul, it was a gut wrenching feeling that left me hollow and ashamed. But the creature that had been created by the metamorphosis was incapable of reconciliation---woe be unto the soul that brought forth the beast! "You shall now become acquainted with a terror you've never known!" I roared in a thunderous voice that was not my own, "Prepare to die a most glorious death, for I am VENGEANCE!"

I began to savagely rip large pieces of flesh from the general's chest and back, toying with him like a rag doll until he begged for death to come and release him from his misery. Still, the beast that I became wouldn't let the mer-warrior off so easily. The way in which the general's head was detached from his body made me cringe, and yet I could not look away. Limb by limb, piece by piece the beast devoured the general until there were no traces of him left. The sheer power I displayed while defending myself against the warrior left a lasting impression upon the King. I took the weapon that belonged to the general and laid it in front of the throne, a trophy for my victory over the warrior who tried to kill me with it. Now that the threat of death no longer existed, I slowly returned to my earlier form as a hybrid with distinct human qualities. The royal family---the King, his wife, and their daughter---stood there staring at me in disbelief. They were in a state of shock, and I can't say that I blamed them.

"King Claudius, I humbly apologize for the trouble I've caused." I said while kneeling before the throne. "I do not yet understand this new power I possess. Azoria has tried to explain the essence of what I have become... She says I am like the wolf in the darkness, wild and swift. And that I am driven by a thirst which is both the curse and the gift. She met me as a man, weak and lame. But once bitten, I became something extraordinary that can never be tamed."

The king listened while I delivered my homily, for now he realized a savior had indeed arrived in Anog. One who possessed the supernatural powers mentioned in the Great Prophecy.

"My daughter was right about you, D'Shawn. You are the Chosen One." The mighty king bowed his head to me as a show of respect, and then he laid some heavy wisdom on my conscience.

"The power you possess is that of our long awaited savior, and with your great power comes great responsibility, D'Shawn. Your destiny is to lead our people to the Promised Land," said the King while resting his hand on my shoulder. I turned toward Azoria and I saw that she was not only honored to have me in her presence, she was also very grateful. I wasn't sure what being "the savior" was really about, but if it was important to Azoria then it was worth my effort. I graciously accepted my foreseen destiny as I addressed the King with my decision.

"Great and Noble King, I hereby accept the responsibility of leading your people to Atlantica. To this honorable endeavor I pledge my loyalty and my life."

The proud ruler of Anog instructed me to kneel, as was customary in the presence of royalty. But then unexpectedly, the King lightly tapped me on each shoulder with his golden trident and made a royal announcement:

"I now dub thee Sir D'Shawn, Royal Knight of Anog and Commander of the Imperial Guard and all its legions! Now rise and take your place as a prominent member of this royal court!"The members of the Grand Counsel had just taken their seats inside the Royal Atrium and had witnessed the ceremony performed by the King. My induction into the royal family was official. The powerful cabinet was made up of wizards from every sector of the kingdom---a grand assembly for a grand occasion.

"Greetings loyal subjects," said the King to the congregation. "It is with great honor and joy that I come before you on this glorious day. Today we celebrate the dawn of a new era in the history of our kind. Today is a day of days, for we have entered into the age of the Quintessence!"

Upon hearing the King's announcement Anog's most beguiling augur stood up from amongst the masses and said, "But Sire, how can you call this a glorious day knowing that our kingdom will soon come under siege by our enemies?"

"Judas, why am I not surprised that yours is the voice of skepticism?" said King Claudius as he glared at the conniving augur who governed sector nine.

"Your Highness, my concern is only for our many citizens who fear that war is coming," said Judas. "I meant no disrespect, my King. I beg thy forgiveness if I have offended thee." Judas quickly offered with downcast eyes and his head bowed low.

"Listen Judas and hear me well," said the King. "I say this to all of you out there! We are but one kingdom, and I am your king. I summoned you here today so that you can bear witness to a miracle!" King Claudius now had everyone on the edge of their seat, "Friends, worry not! For the prophecy is true! Just as it foretold of a great savior appearing from the heavens, I tell you, he has come!" King Claudius spoke with a vivacious tone as he prepared to introduce me to the Grand Counsel.

"The savior possesses supernatural strength unlike anything I've ever seen. I have witnessed it for myself, and I tell you, he is here! Here in Anog!"

"What is the savior's name, Sire?" asked someone from the crowd.

"His name is D'Shawn!", announced the King. "Sound the trumpets!"

While the trumpets brought forth their majestic fanfare, Zenobia and Azoria made their way to the balcony high above the crowd to listen to what I was about to say. Everyone was staring in amazement as I travelled down the center aisle of the Royal Atrium and headed toward the podium at the front of the crowd. The wizards---young and old---stood and bowed their heads as I passed them, and when I finally reached the podium I addressed the citizens of Anog as one of their own:

"My fellow citizens, I am honored to stand here before you as a brother-in-arms on this historic occasion. My name is Theolonius D'Shawn Atlanticus! Lord of the Galactic Island!" Never had an event such as this taken place in the history of the mer-people. It appeared that the present generation would be the first to witness the fulfillment of the Great Prophecy.

"I don't exactly know how I came to be here," I openly admitted, "but my coming has been foretold by the Great Elders of old---the original guardians of the Great Prophecy. It is in honor of their prediction that I pledge my solemn oath to each of you that I will lay down my life, if necessary, for the sake of ridding your world of the ancient dragon known as Sapian. I assure you that your children and their children after them will not know a world where tyranny and strife rule the day, neither will they live in the shadow of oppression nor feign loyalty in fear of annihilation at the hands of the red dragon.

Great brethren, let us go forth and avenge generations past, and make way for future generations to come. Together, we shall defeat the devil and his demons. Sapian's bloody reign of terror ends now! For I am D'Shawn, the savior! And I have come to fulfill the Great Prophecy!"

There was a brief silence, and then all at once the entire assembly burst into a boisterous celebration. The Great Elders, the augurs, and the many citizens of Anog who had secretly entered the atrium to hear me speak were now shouting and applauding with joy. Even the Queen was clapping in elation after hearing my promise to her people. The citizens of Anog formed a gigantic circle around me and began chanting my name in song. Though I bathed in the praise that was being poured out to me, I couldn't help but think about the statement King Claudius had made earlier when he mentioned something called the "Quintessence". Azoria too had spoken about it, saying that it was a guarded secret amongst her kind, a proverbial age where the powers of good will rise up and conquer the evils of her world... a day of reckoning. If this is true, then the fate of Azoria's world rests in my hands and I must not fail her. I must fulfill my destiny or die trying... may God be with us all.

Onward and upward until the war is won and our enemies are no more.

✦

"And I saw the beast, and the Kings of the earth, and their armies, gathered together to make war against him... and against his army."

---Revelation 19:19

CHAPTER 9

ATTACK OF THE KURNOOL

Now that I had taken over command of the Imperial Guard the enemies of Anog were in for one helluva fight. The beast known as Sapian had sent forth his armies of hideous monsters hoping to annihilate the King's military with maximum force, but I intended to leave all their asses floundering in a sea of blood. Our greatest opposition was a bloodthirsty colony of gigantic cephalopods known as the Kurnool. These horrid creatures were like genetically enhanced octopuses, and were the natural enemy of the mer-people. In each of their deadly tentacles was either a sword or a sharp harpoon. It was almost impossible to get near them without succumbing to an onslaught of deadly weaponry. The Kurnool had joined forces with some creatures called the Ghrammuth. They looked like giant crabs and had huge, jagged shells layered with dopamine---a neurotransmitter used in controlling muscle contractions and in learning, memory, and emotional processing. One scratch from the shell of a Ghrammuth causes terrifying delusions and horrific hallucinations that drive the victim to commit suicide. A disheartening way for any warrior to die.

When the fighting commenced, the ocean became a battleground, and the opposing forces became locked in mortal combat. Above the telepathic shouting and screaming, I heard the sounding of trumpets ringing in my head, and my mind quickly recalled the book of Revelation 8:8 where it says, When the second angel blew his trumpet, something like a great fiery mountain was thrown into the sea. A third of the sea turned to blood, a third of the living creatures in the sea died... The scripture gave me an idea which came to me like an epiphany from God.

"Fall back!" I commanded the mer-warriors. "Retreat to the center of the kingdom!" The leaders of each squadron of mer-warriors began delivering my message to retreat.

"General D'Shawn has ordered us to fall back and take cover!"

Legions upon legions of mer-warriors hunkered down near the center of Anog and it appeared that the battle would soon be lost, but nothing was as it seemed. In fact, everything was going according to plan. Using my newly discovered x-ray vision, I spotted a giant fault just beneath the ocean floor running adjacent to the kingdom. So when the last of the mer-warriors had reached the designated area inside the kingdom, I went forth through the gates of Anog alone and met head on with the Kurnool and their deadly allies: the Wutu (an aquatic species of stinging yellow jackets of the family Vespidae, having black and bright yellow bands), the Kaxapix (a species of giant starfish humanoids capable of producing ultrasonic sound waves that disrupt neurotransmissions to the brain), the Nehru (huge demonic sailfish of the family Istiphoridae, distinguished by a long, high dorsal fin, long pelvic fins, and a double keel on each side of the tail which is alit with hellfire), and of course the Ghrammuth (venomous decapod crustacean-like bottom feeders of the suborder Brachyuran, having eyes on stalks).

The monsters descended upon Anog by the millions, bearing down on the kingdom with a force never seen before. But even while facing what appeared to be certain death, the courageous mer-warriors did not cower or show any fear whatsoever. Their bravery empowered me to stand tall and face down the devil and all his minions.

"You who have come in search of me have instead wandered upon death!" I shouted after greeting the enemies of Anog with a loud and ferocious roar. "None of you will leave here alive!" While my thunderous voice stopped them dead in their tracks, the immense rage brewing within me triggered yet another metamorphosis, spawning a beast so powerful that even I was in fear of what I became.

The first to fall under my wrath was the overly aggressive Ghrammuth that came scurrying at me clacking their giant pinchers together as they mounted an attack----I was not impressed.

CRUuuUNCH! CRUuuUNCH! CRUuuUNCH!

The Ghrammuth had made a fatal mistake, and now tens of thousands of their crushed bodies littered the ocean floor like heaps of old jalopies piled up in a junkyard 20,000 leagues under the sea. The rest of Anog's enemies were not so eager. They halted their activity and muddled about until finally coming up with a different strategy. The new plan was to come at me collectively, showing a montage of attack formations hoping that in the fray and mayhem of battle that one of them could strike a death blow and deliver my dead body back to their master, the red dragon.

Within minutes I was completely covered in a swarming cloud of slashing weapons and stinging appendages. Though I put up a gallant fight, there was just too many of them to fend off... their strategy was working, and they could almost taste victory.

"The savior has fallen! Victory is ours!" I heard them yelling. But little did they know, the tables were about to turn in a major way.

The enemies of Anog began celebrating their apparent victory, but unfortunately for them, the celebration would be short-lived. They had no idea that I had lured them into a trap, and now they were right where I wanted them---directly atop the oceanic fault that I spotted with my x-ray vision. Without warning, the terrifying sea monster that I had become grew even larger, and when I slapped my gigantic tail against the ocean floor, the entire world trembled beneath me. The force was so tremendous that millions of geysers sprouted up from the deep and started spewing rivers of molten lava in every direction, killing every living creature within a third of the ocean. Neither the citizens of Anog nor the King's warriors were in harm's way. They had been saved from the lava flow because the moment that my giant tail struck the ocean floor it broke the fault line, completely raising the kingdom several thousand fathoms as the tectonic plates shifted in opposite directions---just like I planned it.

The bloodbath that was started by Sapian and his armies ended badly for them. But even as the enemies of Anog were burning to death in rivers of molten lava, the Kurnool continued hurling thousands of harpoons toward the citizens of Anog. What a bunch of evil bastards!

In response to their pure hatred of the mer-people, the metamorphosis unleashed The Wolf in the Darkness! An unpredictable super-predator that immediately went on a rampage killing everything in sight. None of the Kurnool were spared from the massacre, in fact, while the great earthquake swallowed up the rest of the leviathan's minions, I focused my wrath solely on the Kurnool. The brutal affair was pretty damn disgusting, yet I stood bathing in the blood-soaked ocean coddling the carnage of war and loving every moment of it. From the safety of the palace, the royal family witnessed the phenomenal strength and savagery I possessed, and in their minds there was no doubt that I was the "savior" who had come to them as promised by the Great Prophecy.

Though unseen, the red dragon had also witnessed my strength and cunning. And now for the first time ever, deep down in the cockles of his cold, black heart---the devil was afraid.

When there were no more enemies left to kill, I began sealing up the geysers so that the ocean could heal itself. I then returned to Anog to see what was left of the once great kingdom, and in her courtyard were all her citizens sitting with their heads bowed in silence as though praying.

"Azoria, what's going on?" I asked, "Why is everyone so quiet?"

"The citizens of Anog are paying homage to our glorious god, you, D'Shawn."

"What?!" I was shocked to hear such a thing. "Azoria, I'm not a god! Tell them to get up." It was at that moment I noticed that King Claudius and Queen Zenobia also had their heads bowed. Then, like a message from a dream, the words of the Great Prophecy came to me:....and because the savior is not of our world, he will possess supernatural power equaled only by that of a god.

I turned toward Azoria and said, "You mean to tell me that I'm now the ruler of Anog?" Azoria looked up at me and answered, "No, my lord,... you are now the ruler of our entire world."

She no longer spoke as my equal, I had become something more in her eyes.

"There are many kingdoms in our world, my lord, and Anog is relatively small compared to others. The greatest kingdom of all is called Abyssinia. It is home to more than seven hundred million of our kind," said the princess. "Abyssinia is also where the red dragon will seek his revenge for what has happened here in Anog. According to the prophecy, you must travel to Abyssinia if you are to defeat Sapian."

"Is there anything else I should know, Azoria?" I said in frustration after not being told this earlier.

"Only this, my lord: The ultimate battle between the forces of good and evil will begin in Abyssinia and will decide the fate of our world. That's why it is called The Reckoning."

"But wait a minute, Azoria! If the Reckoning starts in Abyssinia, then what was this?"

The princess looked out over the desolate wasteland that had been left in the wake of the Kurnool's attack on Anog and said, "My dear D'Shawn,... this was only a skirmish."

+ 83 +

CHAPTER 10

THE MUSHROOM INCIDENT

Your Highness, there is something I left on the island that I must return for," I said to King Claudius, who pondered my request before responding.

"Abyssinia is many days travel from here and we mustn't delay our departure any longer than absolutely necessary. The thing that you left back on the island, is it of great importance?"

"Oh, yes Sire. It is of the utmost importance... to me."

"Very well then. Azoria will escort you back to the Galactic Island where you can retrieve this thing of yours, then the two of you can rejoin the caravan to Abyssinia."

Word had begun spreading about the Reckoning, and about the savior who had arrived in Anog. Every mer-kingdom in existence was now joining together in one grand caravan headed to Abyssinia. Meanwhile, Azoria and I returned to the Galactic Island to retrieve the item I had left behind.

"D'Shawn, something is very wrong here," whispered Azoria. "Do you hear it?"

"Hear what?" I answered, "I don't hear anything."

"That's just it. There are no sounds of the forest, no sounds of... anything."

Azoria was right. The forest was totally silent. Not even the sound of wind blowing through the giant palms could be heard upon our return to the island. The dead silence became even more apparent when I realized that I could hear my own heartbeat pounding away inside my chest.

Azoria and I moved cautiously toward my camp, which was on the far side of the island. And as we crept through the eerie quietness, I began to question whether or not the item I had returned for was actually that important.

"Of course it is!" I told myself.

While walking through the forest on our way to the camp, Azoria began talking about the strange wolf-creature that roamed the woods whenever there's a full moon. She also brought up the subject of the bright flashes of lightning that lit up the sky just before we met.

"D'Shawn, besides you, there is only one other creature that inhabits the Galactic Island full-time. My people know very little about this creature except that it's able to divide itself into many separate entities at once. The Great Elders called it a Lycanthrope---it is a shape-shifter."

I had heard the word before, back when I was a small boy growing up in the Calliope. There was an old woman who ran a magic shop in the French Quarter and her name was "Mama Jo". All the kids from my neighborhood said she was a crazy old woman who put spells on people for money, they called her the "Voodoo Lady," and the strange thing was, she looked like a real witch!

Mama Jo would always tell us stories about haunted houses and magic potions, and though we enjoyed listening to her scary tales, my friends and I didn't believe in that sort of stuff. Mama Jo wore the same tattered black dress every day. It had a huge white broach shaped like a human skull pinned on the front of it and that thing scared the shit out of me. She claimed it had come from the island of New Guinea, and that it was a real shrunken head. Everyone knew that she practiced voodoo. Her favorite thing was cooking up a big pot of funky-smelling gumbo in a huge black kettle that hung over an open fire in the back of her shop. She would chant strange words while filling her bubbling brew with wild herbs, live animals, and the eye of a newt. No one would dare eat her gumbo, but during the summer when school was out, me and all the kids from the neighborhood would go to Mama Jo's magic shop for snow cones, candy apples, icy-cups, popcorn balls and praline candy---hers was the best in the city.

One day, me, "Boogie Black", "Lil Toochie", and "Uptown Slimm" went down to her shop on Bourbon Street and Mama Jo told us a story about a man who lived so deep in the bayous that no one hardly saw him. Well one fateful night, the man's young wife suddenly took ill and died, causing the man to become so distraught with grief that he decided to take her body to a voo-doo priest who lived deep in the swamps. The man was planning to ask the priest for a powerful potion that would bring back his young bride, but by the time the man found the small hut where the priest lived, his wife had already been deceased for more than 36 hours.

The priest tried to explain to the man that too much time had passed, and that the potion would not work. But the crazed, grief-stricken husband didn't want to hear it. He demanded the voodoo priest to perform the ritual on his dead wife anyway. When the witch doctor refused to do it, the man became enraged and grabbed the priest by the throat and tried to choked the life out of him. When that didn't work, he resulted to fire!

Pouring kerosene all over the priest and the cabin, the man went for his lighter and Whhhoooffhhhh!, the entire building went up in flames. Thick clouds of black smoke bellowed out of the tiny windows of the cabin, and from inside you could hear the muffled screams of the priest as the fire consumed his blistering body. But before he died, the old witch doctor cast one last spell. He placed a powerful curse on the man using a forbidden form of black magic, so that whenever there was a full moon over the bayous, the man would be forced to hunt for food... not as a man but as a Lycanthrope! The French word is loup-garou, which means werewolf.

A memory began to surface in my mind about a strange incident that made world news. Social media had become abuzz after a scary-looking creature was spotted in the bayous near the quaint little town of Morgan City. A man named Troy Boudreaux went missing after posting a video on YouTube of the bizarre creature standing near the ferryboat landing where he worked. The video showed what appeared to be a large wolf-like beast standing upright like a man, looking directly into the camera. The footage was shot in an area of Morgan City called Avoca Island, which was an uninhabited stretch of swampland that was accessible only during a certain time of day and only by the ferry. No one goes there except hunters and trappers looking for coons, snakes, and alligators.

As soon as the news broke, thousands of people flooded into the region looking to become famous for capturing or killing the creature. CNN and other news media outlets labeled the video "Werewolf on the Bayou". Now here I was in the same situation as Boudreaux.

"Azoria, you mean to tell me there's a werewolf running around on the island?"

"Calm down, D'Shawn. The Lycan only appears during the full moon, and you were usually at the camp on those nights, I tried to make sure of it."

"Man, I can't believe this shit. There's a real goddamn werewolf running around on the island." I complained. "And all this time, I thought it was just some weird creature with a bad temper and a fetish for wearing pretty flowers."

Finding out about the werewolf turned out to be just the tip of the iceberg, something even more shocking was about to be revealed to me.

"There is something else you should know, D'Shawn," said Azoria. "The creature is not just a werewolf; it is capable of dividing itself into many separate creatures all with the ability to act on their very own." I listened closely while Azoria continued to fill me in. "The explosion that lit up the sky that night was caused by the red dragon as he entered into our dimension. Sapian has obviously cast a spell on the Lycan, making it more powerful than before. Now, we can't be sure what to expect."

"Well that's just great, Azoria." I chided, "Thanks for the news flash. What the hell are we supposed to do now? We're in the middle of the forest and nightfall is just around the corner."

Azoria looked at me and smiled saying, "What does it matter, you are as powerful as a god now."

"That might be so," I replied. "But what about you?"

Azoria stared out into the distance as she realized she'd made a terrible mistake returning to the island.

"Hurry up, D'Shawn! Let's go get what we came for and then leave this place at once. C'mon! I'm serious!"

Now running, the princess and I made our way through the forest and found the camp just as I had left it. My most precious possession was still in the secret hiding place behind the large stone that sat next to the pallet that I had made to sleep on. I reached behind the stone and retrieved a thin object that fit in the palm of my hand.

"What's that?", asked Azoria. "Is it what we came back for?"

"Yes, it is." I said as I stared solemnly at the glowing screen in my hand, a smartphone with a screensaver photo of me standing with a group of people and we're all smiling. "I believe this is a picture of my family back in New Orleans."

"Is that your mother?", the princess asked.

"Yes, I believe so. And I think these are my sisters and brothers." I said while pointing to the young people in the photo.

"Wow! Your mother is quite beautiful," said Azoria. "You definitely have her eyes. I really would love to meet your family someday."

"I'm sure they'd love to meet you too, Azoria."

"D'Shawn, exactly how does one get to New Orleans?"

I looked out over the ocean as I had done many times before, and then solemnly said, "I wish I knew..."

The photo of my family was my prized possession and the only clue to my true identity. I tucked it away and turned to Azoria and said, "We'd better get moving, there's no telling what's in store for us when darkness falls."

We were now on our way to rejoin the caravan to Abyssinia, the ocean was quite a ways from the camp so time was of the essence.

"Will you hurry up, D'Shawn. You act like you've never had legs before," complained Azoria. "Hurry! It's getting late."

Azoria was in an exceptionally playful mood despite our situation. The mermaid princess looked vibrant and energetic as she skipped along through the forest ahead of me. She was young and beautiful and full of life. Everything she had ever dreamed of was happening at once, and unbeknownst to me, the princess was madly in love.

"D'Shawn, do you remember the night on the beach when you were running around naked singing weird songs and cussing at the ocean?" asked the princess with a puzzled look on her face. "Was that some sort of ritual or something?"

I thought back to the night in question and said, "No, it wasn't some ritual, and I really don't want to talk about the mushroom incident." I said to Azoria because I was still pretty embarrassed about the whole thing.

Azoria stared at me curiously for a moment and then asked, "Did you say mushroom incident?"

"Yep, and I also said I really don't want to talk about it."

"You didn't eat the little red ones did you?" Azoria asked despite me telling her I didn't want to talk about it, twice.

"Listen Azoria, can we just get to where we're going and hold the chatter?" She bit down on her lip to keep from laughing, but apparently it didn't help. She started laughing so hard that tears were coming down her face and she could hardly catch her breath.

"It wasn't that damn funny, Azoria. I could've been poisoned, you know." I pouted in an effort to quell her laughter, but she kept right on laughing it up. And when I thought about how ridiculous I must have looked running up and down the beach buck naked singing songs I had forgotten the lyrics to, I had to laugh myself. Thinking back...

It all started when I began finding these incredibly large eggs lying near the beach. I assumed they were ostrich eggs, but I hadn't actually seen any such animal on the island, and this was before I knew about the Lycan.

Finding one of the giant eggs meant that I wouldn't have to settle for coconuts and shellfish that day, and it also gave me a chance to show off my culinary genius. Speaking of which, that's what led to my dilemma in the first place. One morning after staving off the urge to go down by the ocean and cuss out the Gemini dragons, I ran across what had to be the largest egg I'd ever seen, this baby was the size of a Volkswagen!

But instead of questioning where it came from, the only thought on my mind was using the giant egg to create the world's largest omelet---and I wound up doing something incredibly foolish. So foolish in fact, that from this point on I'm simply going to refer to it as the "mushroom incident." It was supposed to be my tribute to Southern cuisine, my "belles-lettres" to Cajun cooking, my grand chef d' oeuvre (masterpiece)! But things went very badly.

Though the egg was ridiculously large, its color concerned me the most. All the other eggs I had found were basically the same: a soft shade of ecru sprinkled with white, black, and beige specks. But the Volkswagen egg was draped-up and dripped-out like a candy painted Escalade. Its oyster-pink finish and deep shine gave it the illusion of having a fresh paint job. In fact, when I placed my hand on the lustrous shell I was expecting to draw back a painted palm, but the egg's surface was dry and cool to the touch. I looked and I saw my reflection in the shine, and I thought to myself, "Man, I look a little rough around the edges, like I was out partying the last few nights. And what's this?" I stepped closer to my reflection and noticed there were leaves and twigs sticking out of my hair, I stepped even closer and saw that there was some sort of raspberry-colored mascara smeared on my eyelashes. Which I found to be very disconcerting. I stood for a moment trying to remember where I'd been the past few nights, but nothing came to mind, I drew a complete blank.

Meanwhile, I had to come up with a plan to get the giant egg back to the camp without breaking it. There were plenty of vines lying around on the ground, so I decided to tie a few of them together to make a harness. I then strapped the egg into the harness and made sure it was secure. Next, I used a makeshift sled to tow the egg through the forest and then lifted it up with a pulley system that would have made any Boy Scout jealous. Once I got the egg settled into the bed of straw I had prepared for it, I focused on the next task at hand, which was gathering the necessary ingredients to make the grandest omelet of all time.

I immediately returned to the forest and began foraging for the right herbs and spices to pull off my masterpiece. I soon came across a plethora of flavorful seasoning that was perfect for my mission. Things like green onions, wild garlic, parsley, peppers, bay leaf, cinnamon, and thyme were plentiful in the forest, I even came across a tree whose bark smelled and tasted like bacon. From the ocean I gathered the ingredients for the delicious stuffing that would fill my grand omelet: shrimp, oysters, clams, anchovies, and some salty seaweed.

Before returning to the camp with my collection of ingredients, I stopped by the beach and gathered some driftwood that was lying in the sand.

"These dried pieces of wood will be perfect for making a nice campfire." I thought to myself. "I'll just rub a couple of twigs together really fast until the friction generates enough heat to light the wood, and then, voila!"

The stage was set, and all the performers were in position as I sat next to the giant egg looking like an expert jeweler preparing to cut a priceless diamond. I then took a chisel made of stone and gently placed it dead center of the shell, and with one mighty blow the humongous egg split wide open. I quickly grabbed the large bowl I had prepared for the occasion and sat it beneath the cracked shell to collect the yolk as the egg's liquid soul came gushing out.

Once the bowl was full, I began whipping the yolk into a smooth, creamy batter and then poured it into a separate piece of cookware made of stone but shaped like a skillet. While the egg batter sizzled and popped inside the stone skillet, a sudden euphoria came over me and I felt extreme satisfaction for what I had accomplished. Even in the aftermath of the great debacle that you will soon hear about, I'm still proud of that moment. After the batter simmered a while, I took a huge spatula made from the shell of a giant clam and gently flipped the omelet over. Then, as soon as I started tossing in the seasoning and all the ingredients I had collected, my magnificent omelet came to life and produced a delectable Cajunesque aroma that was so familiar to me, I felt like I was back home in Louisiana... if but only for a moment.

Now that the stuffing had been added, the only thing left for me to do was fold the omelet in half and move the skillet away from the searing heat of the raging inferno fueled by the dried out driftwood---and here's how I screwed the whole thing up.

In the haste and excitement of making the ultimate omelet, I totally forgot to gather a key ingredient... mushrooms. The plan was to make a nice mushroom topping to go on top of the omelet, my royal masterpiece needed a crown, or it would fall short of its potential to rule supreme over every omelet in the universe. I was determined to complete the quest.

Knowing that the giant entrée would get cold soon, I quickly made my way back to the strange coconut grove where I had spotted the mushroom patch and grabbed the first 'shrooms I could get my hands on. Unfortunately, it turned out to be the red ones. Yeah, I heard the little voice in my head screaming, "What are you doing? You don't know if those things are safe to eat!"

Did I listen? Nope.

The moment I approached those little red bastards the air became filled with the tantalizing aroma of my mother's home cooking. No matter how weird it got, I was determined to get what I came for. I carefully reached down and snatched up a few of the red demons then headed back to the camp. But by the time I made it back, the omelet was nearly cold. So rather than making a mushroom gravy like I had planned, I decided to quickly sauté the mushrooms instead. First, I rekindled the fire and once I got it going again, I grabbed the skillet, lightly glazed it with coconut oil, and began waving it back and forth over the fire until the surface was good and hot.

When the mushrooms entered the hot coconut oil it caused a chemical reaction, and soon there were sparks shooting out of the skillet in every direction. The angry mushrooms started ramming themselves into the walls of the skillet in the same way that the velociraptors did in the movie "Jurassic Park" when they were testing the fences. The chaotic scene only lasted a brief moment, plenty enough time to scare the bejesus out of me. Once it was over, the tiny fungi lay idle in a puddle of pink protoplasmic gunk ready to be spread atop the omelet. After the deed was done, the insidious mushrooms begrudgingly clung to the spongy outer layer of the omelet in protest. Retribution was sure to come, but at that moment, I was enthralled in pursuit of happiness. I was, in fact, ready to make a complete pig of myself despite whatever consequences followed. So for the next hour or so, I sat there and scarfed down nearly eight pounds of frothy egg whites stuffed with seafood, herbs and spices, and topped off with a colony of angry mushrooms. Such mindless gluttony would levy a heavy toll, and I was about to discover the exact price.

It began with a feeling like being in the first seat on a roller coaster as it goes roaring down the tracks at top speed---my heart literally skipped a beat! I tried to stand, but unfortunately my legs were no longer under my command. I then tried to scream but even that was denied me. The ill-fated attempt to devour the mega-omelet left me stretched out on my stomach barking like a seal---the mushroom incident had officially begun.

After trying several times and failing, I finally managed to roll over onto my back. And as I lay there woefully looking up at the stars, I saw the entire universe begin to spin slowly to the right, then to the left, then back to the right again. After that came the pink elephants and yellow dolphins that kept appearing in my mind alongside the exotic belly dancer who had a tail like a lion! I wanted to stay calm, but sweat was already pouring down the side of my face and a wave of panic was rising inside of me.

"Oh, no!" I cried, "I think I'm going to be sick!" My intestinal bowels did something resembling a backwards somersault, sending me back down on my stomach barking like a seal again.

Ark! Ark! Ark!

The oscillating landscape was spinning out of control and I said to myself, "Why the hell did I eat those damn mushrooms?"

Malice filled my heart as I angrily glared at the last piece of the omelet still sitting inside the skillet wearing the mushrooms like one of those stylish hats that church ladies sport during Sunday service. The last of the omelet remained resentful toward me, poking out its tongue in a disrespectful manner that made my blood boil.

Suddenly out of nowhere I was struck with an overwhelming urge to get undressed. The next thing I knew, I was running down the beach with no clothes on singing Christmas carols at the top of my lungs. I couldn't exactly remember the words, but I loudly sang them, nonetheless. Something had gone terribly wrong, and before long, I completely freaked out and ran toward the ocean to get even with the Gemini dragons for what they did to me.

I stopped and took a fresh dump inside two coconut shells and mixed in a little urine to make it squishy, then I crept down to the edge of the water and surprised the dragons with my shitty coconut bombs. You should have seen the look on their faces. It was fucking hilarious! I had caught them with their mouths open and there was nothing they could do but stand there and look stupid with piles of shit splattered on their faces.

"I told y'all I was gonna get you back!" I yelled to the dragons while laughing my ass off on the beach. "Here's a little something to help you to always remember this night." I turned around, bent over, and then showed Gemini the "dark side" of the moon.

After getting my revenge, I dashed into the woods like a wild animal. Let me tell you, things really got weird after that. I can't recall everything that happened, but I do remember running naked through the forest not caring about life nor limb as I desperately tried to escape gravity...

Perhaps it was the trailing lights or the heat of the night against my bare skin. Or maybe it was the sallow moonlight shining down into the forest through jittery pockets of swirling clouds and shifting shadows---I don't know. But I truly enjoyed the exhilarating feeling of crisp leaves crunching beneath my feet as I went gallivanting through the woods, skipping and whistling and shaking my ass to the music playing in my head. I even made up lyrics to my own song: "Airplanes fly-ing. I've got jelly-beans and lollipops, baby. Gonna take me 'round the world and I ain't coming back todaaaay!"

It took nearly two weeks for the effects of the mushrooms to finally wear off, at the end of which I found myself perched high in the branches of a massive redwood covered head to toe in berry stains and wearing a "tutu" made with half-eaten banana peels. Even now, I sometimes have to resist the insatiable urge to impersonate Kanye West.

What the fuck is that about?

We were still on our way to rejoin the caravan to Abyssinia and Azoria was still laughing her head off about the mushroom incident, when all of a sudden, she froze dead in her tracks and had a look of sheer terror on her face.

"What is it, Azoria?" I asked, as I too felt that something was wrong. "What's the matter? What do you see?" The answer would soon become apparent. We had just reached the edge of the forest when darkness fell upon the island and the full moon appeared in the night sky directly above us.

"Oh, no!" Azoria cried, "We're too late!"

We immediately heard the sound of a thousand hooves galloping through the forest. Then, without warning, the unthinkable happened:

"Watch out!" I shouted hoping to alert the princess in time; but I was too late, fate had already chosen its victim.

From the shadowy woods came a flaming arrow straight and true. It had been shot with the force of a cannon and it struck the princess directly in the center of her chest. Azoria let out a horrible scream as the arrow's sharp tip pierced her body. She stood motionless---frozen with fear---unable to fathom what had just happened. She instinctively reached out her hand to me, but her fragile body collapsed onto the ground before I could get close enough to catch her in my arms. I looked and I saw her royal blood seeping into the soil beneath my feet, and that's when my universe began to crumble.

Lightning streaked across the black expanse overhead and then came a torrential downpour as even the heavens cried for Azoria.

"Nooooo! This can't be!" I yelled out, "What have you done?"

While several flaming arrows pierced my neck and back, I did not budge. Instead, I knelt down next to Azoria and wept for the fallen princess.

"My love, look what they've done to you," I bemoaned. "How could I have allowed this to happen? It's all my fault for wanting to return to the island." While holding Azoria's lifeless body in my arms, I became more and more enraged at those who were responsible for her death.

The Lycan had divided itself into legions of centaurs, these creatures were half-man and half-horse and were under a spell conjured by Sapian. Every centaur was armed with a giant bow and a sheath of flaming arrows. But none of that shit mattered, because the monstrous beast that emerged from the metamorphosis to avenge the death of Azoria was more ferocious than any animal that had ever lived---in fact, it could not be named.

One by one, two by two, three by three, I slaughtered the centaurs in a brutal fashion. Some of them I struck with blows so hard that their bodies went flying for miles out into the ocean. Some I disemboweled. Others I decapitated. And to the rest of them I did things that were much, much worse. All through the night the forest was filled with the sounds of a bloody massacre: the crushing of bones, the tearing of flesh, the screams of the dying. The carnage amassed like heaps of debris left behind in the aftermath of a raging hurricane. By the time morning came there wasn't a single living creature left on the island, the entire place was covered with the dead, mutilated bodies of the centaurs and there was blood everywhere.

Exhausted from taking my wrath out on the Lycan, I returned to my previous form and knelt down beside the person who meant the world to me.

"Azoria my love," I said while holding her in my arms one last time, "I'm so sorry that this happened to you. I don't know how I'm going to go on without you." I gently rocked Azoria back and forth, caressing her head and running my fingers through her golden braids of sunshine. Unable to cope with the loss of my soul mate, I wept throughout the morning and all through the day until light turned to dark and the moon was again full and bright in the night sky. I carefully lifted Azoria from the sand and carried her back into the ocean, but this time only I transformed into a mer-person. Azoria's body no longer responded to the aquatic world from which she came. The princess remained in human form and showed no signs of life.

Meanwhile, hundreds of ocean creatures lined up and started following the slain princess as if they were taking part in a New Orleans-style funeral procession. The farther into the ocean we went the more creatures joined the procession: stingrays, sea turtles, jellyfish, eels, whales, and dolphins. They had all come to mourn the princess.

As I was nearing the rendezvous point where we were supposed to meet up with the caravan, I began thinking about how King Claudius and Queen Zenobia would react to the news of their daughter's death, and I became sick to my stomach. I blamed myself for the horrible tragedy because it was me who had insisted on returning to the Galactic Island, and now the princess was dead. I remembered the times Azoria had protected me, and now when she needed protecting, I failed her miserably.

"I am completely heartbroken over this, Azoria. I wish there was a way to trade my life for yours, I would do it in a heartbeat."

Suddenly, Azoria's words echoed softly in my mind as I remembered what she had said to me a while back:

What I shared with you was a very precious gift that only royal members of my kind possess. The magic of the Quintess is so pure and so powerful that it even has dominion over death... it is the very essence of what I am... it is my fifth element.

"That's it!" I said to myself. "That's how I'll bring back Azoria!" King Claudius had made me a royal knight, which meant that I became royalty and now possessed a Quintess of my own. I would use it to resurrect the fallen princess.

Focusing my attention on Azoria, I began to feel a tingling in my chest. It quickly spread throughout my entire body and sent an electrical charge into the water, causing all the little creatures that had been following behind me to disperse in a frenzy, leaving streams of bubbles in their wake. My hands and arms began glowing with a bluish aura making me appear angel-like in the depths of the deep blue sea. The illuminating aura slowly enveloped Azoria's body, completely wrapping her in a soft blue blanket of light. I watched her wounds heal right before my eyes and then she slowly transformed into her natural state---a magnificent mermaid.

"Well hello there, Beautiful." I said to Azoria with love and appreciation for her return to life. "Don't ever scare me like that again, I was beside myself with grief the whole time you were gone. I was afraid I'd never see you again."

Azoria opened her eyes slowly, and when she saw my face she said, "Why are you crying, my love? Are you not happy to see me?"

I was so overcome with joy at that point that I couldn't even speak, so I just reached out and gave her a really big hug and a tremendous kiss.

"Wow!" said the princess. "What was that for?"

I couldn't stop smiling, and again, I kissed Azoria with the kind of passion reserved only for soul mates. We were two lovers who had just been reunited after a long time apart. Azoria was happy to learn that I felt the same way about her as she felt about me. The discovery of our hidden love for each other would soon prove to be the essence of something truly spectacular.

✦ 101 ✦

"I cling to my imperfections, as the most important part of my being."
        ---Anatolé France

CHAPTER 11

THE VALLEY OF TROG

Azoria and I rejoined the caravan to Abyssinia, which now included the kingdoms of Melanesia, Kenya, and Morocco. The convoy was entering the most dangerous leg of the journey---the Valley of Trog. It was believed that a terrible sea monster lived inside this trench at the bottom of the sea, and whosoever entered its domain would likely not be seen again. Many have referred to this deadly passageway as Valle de La Muerte (Death Valley). And the giant serpent that haunts it is called the "Troglodyte". According to legend, there has only been rare sightings of the creature because most who've seen it didn't live to tell anyone.

"The ocean current is very strong here," I said to the leaders of each kingdom. "Tell everyone to stay close."

Accepting responsibility for the lives of so many mer-people was a huge undertaking that required me to make decisions as a leader that would ensure the safety of everyone in my care. It was very much like the times I assumed responsibility for the well-being of my younger siblings back home. Seeing the photo of my family on the screen of the smartphone reminded me of a conversation I once had with my thuggish little brother Jamal. At the tender age of only sixteen years old, Jamal had already gained a reputation as being a certified killer and was well on his way to becoming Crescent City's most notorious "hot boy"---a term used to describe young street hustlers down south who kept the block "hot" with police activity because of their nefarious ways.

One evening while I was home visiting my family during a break from college, I had the rare opportunity to sit and talk to Jamal about life, politics, and the miseducation of Black kids in America, albeit the circumstances were anything but normal. The sky was angry, the night was humid, and the devil had gone down to New Orleans:

"You've reached 9-1-1," said the operator. "What is your emergency?" Forgetting that I had called for help, I stood frozen staring at the dark red bloodstain on my new shirt.

"Caller, are you still there?", asked the lady on the phone.

"Yes ma'am, I'm still here." I finally answered.

"Sir, what is your emergency?"

"I'm calling to report a shooting at 5128 Rocheblade Street, apartment 112. Please hurry."

"Police units and EMS are en route to your location."

"Thank you, ma'am." I said before abruptly ending the call and turning my attention back to the crimson stain on my shirt. The blood had come from Jamal, who was sitting on the steps of our building nursing a gunshot wound to his left shoulder. The shooting was a result of an ongoing beef between him and some guys from 'cross the river. I felt it was necessary to call for help, a sentiment that was not endorsed by my thuggish sibling.

"Say bruh! I know you ain't just call them people, huh?!" chided Jamal with a heavy Southern drawl. He was asking me did I call the police.

"Yes," I said. "Now sit your ass right there until the ambulance gets here."

"Say woa-day, I don't need them white folks in my business, ya heard me! Man, I'm hot right nah!" Obviously Jamal was concerned about the outstanding warrants for his arrest, he was worried that the authorities would take him to the infirmary at the jail rather than to the hospital. I knew better than to ask him what he had warrants for. Honestly, I didn't want to know. There was no telling what Jamal had been doing in the streets, and frankly I sometimes questioned whether he knew where to draw the line. I stood there trying my best to conceal the anger I felt toward the senselessness of the situation. It seemed crazy to me that Jamal was even living that way.

"You've just been shot," I snapped at Jamal after quietly brewing for nearly a minute. "What else was I supposed to do?"

Jamal looked at me and then flashed a slick grin knowing that it would reveal the sparkling diamonds embedded in his platinum grill---the hallmark of a young street hustler. By all accounts, Jamal was the epitome of a gangsta.

"Reading all them fancy books done made you soft, 'College Boy'", said Jamal with a devious grin on his face. He knew just how to get under my skin.

"Jamal, I've asked you more than once to not call me that." I said through gritted teeth, "You're really pushing it." For some reason Jamal felt resentment toward me, I believe he was under the impression that I had turned my back on the hood. In his eyes, I was just another sellout, aka, College Boy.

"Listen to me Jamal, I know that my going away to college didn't sit well with you, but you need to get over it. I'm not going to sit here and apologize for wanting a better life."

"Ol' bitch-ass-nigga! Ain't nobody stopping you from having a better life. Yo' pussy-ass just scared to get outche' and hustle for what you want. You scared to be outche' with all us real niggas, that's why you ran yo' scary ass to Baton Rouge to go hide off at Southern. Then you come back round here talk'n proper and shit, tryna sound like them white folks--Boy stop!"

My jaws tightened and I became enraged after hearing what Jamal thought of me. Didn't he know that Southern University was the largest predominantly Black college in the country? The nerve of him to make such an accusation.

"Listen, you little bastard! I'm fully aware of who I am and where I come from. I've never pretended to be someone I'm not. So you better watch your mouth, or my educated ass is going to---"

"What, nigga?!" Jamal growled as he jumped up and pulled a loaded semiautomatic pistol from his waistband. He pointed the weapon right in my face and said, "Nigga, if you wasn't my brother I'd blow yo' motherfuckin' brains out!"

"That's just what I'm talking about, right there." I said in a calm, rational manner hoping that the situation wouldn't get out of hand. "That's why there's so much violence out here in these streets, Jamal, because you guys are quick to pull out a gun thinking it's the only way to resolve your disputes. Why is that? Why do you even need a gun?"

Jamal stared at me for a long while with an expression on his face that I could not decipher, the situation was growing more tense, and I didn't want to provoke him because his 9mm pistol was still pointed at my face.

"For a 'College Boy' you kinda slow. These niggas outche ain't playin'. Everybody and they grandma is totin' choppas with big clips: AK's, AR-15's, Mack-11's. My lil' potnah even got a Drako that spit a hundred rounds. So what you expect me to do, bruh? You think I'mma fuck around and get caught outche without my 'Nina Ross'? We in a motherfuckin' concrete jungle, nigga. And ain't nobody fitnah come round here fuckin' with me unless they wanna wind up with a full clip in they ass. I been 'bout that dumb-shit, ya heard me!"

"I understand your frustration, Jamal, but why do you hate the police so much? They really have a hard job." Jamal cocked back the hammer on his weapon and readjusted his grip while slightly squeezing harder on the trigger. Geesh!, what was I thinking!

"You know what, dawg," said Jamal as he lowered his gun and glared at me. "You is really fucked up. You put too much faith in them white folks. Them crackas ain't outche to 'serve and protect' nobody round here. All them bitches do is harass niggas and abuse they authority on some white power shit. They the motherfuckas outche doin' the most dirt, any huh. Who you think be sellin' the most guns and dope in the hood? It sure the fuck ain't us! Niggas is barely eatin' round this bitch. Yeah, some of these niggas might look like big-tymers but they really just be stunt'n for them hoes. All the while, them jump-out boys and dirty cops outche raidin' niggas' stash-houses, pimpin' hoes, movin' work, settin' niggas up, plant'n false evidence, puttin' hits on niggas, all type of shit! And believe one thing, woa-day, them white boys quick to choke yo ass to death outche while ain't nobody watching. So I'mma tell ya like this, don't be asking me why the fuck I got a gun. Go ask them white folks, ol' bitch-ass-nigga!"

Though I sympathized with my brother's plight, he had definitely crossed the line. I decided that I would make him respect me one way or the other.

"I told you to watch your mouth, Jamal. Now you leave me no choice." I threw a wild punch and hit Jamal in the mouth with a closed fist, knocking him to ground and then wrestling the gun away from him. I tossed the weapon aside and then the two of us went at it. Even with a wounded shoulder, Jamal was a handful. For a moment I thought that he might actually get the best of me, but thankfully, Mama heard the commotion we were making and came running outside to break us up. She picked up Jamal's gun and fired one shot into the air, then tucked the pistol in her bosom and told us that if we didn't stop fighting, she was going to whip both our asses. And she meant every word. Once things cooled off between Jamal and me, Mama went back inside and closed the door behind her, leaving us to work things out on our own.

"Listen, Jamal. You're my little brother and I love you, bruh. But I can't allow you to keep disrespecting that way, you feel me dawg?"

"Nigga, fuck you! As soon as my shoulder get back right I'mma beat yo motherfuckin' ass, bitch! You feel me dawg?"

Jamal and I had had many fights growing up, because neither of us was willing to compromise when it came to having differences of opinions. Well, it was high time that one of us tried a new approach. I was optimistic about getting to the root of what was causing our dysfunctional relationship. I would at least try to reason with him and explain my point of view in hopes that it would make a difference. If not, then the fighting would continue until one of us conceded to the other.

"Jamal, let me ask you something," I said as politely as I could.

"What, nigga?!" he snapped at me. And only by the grace of God was I able to refrain from laying my hands on him again.

"Tell me, how do you plan on not becoming a statistic out here in these streets? The war on drugs isn't over, you know? Instead of complaining, you should get involved with organizations that are about restoring equity to our community and working with local law enforcement to help stamp out crime."

Jamal looked at me as though I were a perfect stranger, someone who had wandered into our neighborhood by chance and had gotten lost. He sat down on the steps of our building and shook his head at how naive I was when it came to the reality of life in the hood. Though I had spent time hanging out with friends from college and visiting their neighborhoods in Baton Rouge, it wasn't like I was "in the streets", so to speak. Places in Baton Rouge like Scotlandville, Zion City, Dixie, Easy Town, Park Town, Gardere Lane, and Southside aka "The Bottom"--- were very dangerous neighborhoods. I was not a stranger to violence, but I tried to avoid conflict as best I could. In other words:

I'm not a killer... but don't push me.

"Dawg, you really don't get it do you?" said Jamal. "The police are the ones outche merc'n niggas in broad daylight all on video and shit and gettin' away with it. Them white folks don't give a fuck about the problems in the hood. All them crackas care about is lockin' a nigga up and throwin' away the key. It's open season on niggas outche, and every time them bitches shoot a nigga down in cold blood they run that same ol' bullshit-ass line 'bout, 'I was just doing my job'.

Well I'll tell you what, potnah, if them bitches ever roll up on me and try that George Floyd shit, I'mma show'em just how much black lives matter and leave they ass smokin', ya heard me. And for what? All behind some racist-ass cops outche tryna flex they nuts on a nigga like me who really 'bout that murda shit. Man, fuck them hoes! It's whatever, ya heard me."

As much as I hated to admit it, Jamal had a point. Our neighborhood had become a virtual war zone where drugs, guns, and violence were as common as crawfish in the bayou. The police, for whatever reason, showed little interest in resolving the problems that plagued our community. In fact, they seemed more interested in proliferating the "War on Drugs" campaign initiated first by Richard Nixon and then ratified by President Bill Clinton who enacted policies written and provided by "ALEC"---a conglomerate of corporations and special interests groups that lobby for laws beneficial to their profit margins. Clinton signed the legislation that had been prepared by ALEC, and in doing so, paved the way for the creation of paramilitary police agencies and the mass incarceration of Blacks nationwide. Jamal's combative attitude toward the police stemmed from his experiences with them. He had never seen a "good cop" before, so in retrospect, his belligerent attitude was in response to the police brutality and negative reinforcement he witnessed firsthand through years of cruelty.

The sometimes blatant marginalization of Blacks by law enforcement in the projects lends credence to why Jamal bears such disdain for the authorities, actually, he has a right to be angry. His life and his freedom are constantly in jeopardy at the hands of the police. In the eyes of the law, anyone who looks like Jamal---young, Black, with dreads and living in the projects---is considered a "suspect" whether or not a crime has even been committed. Therefore, you're subject to get stopped and searched at any given time for any given reason. Just like when cops pull up to a playground in the hood and make the Black kids line up on their knees on the hot pavement with their hands behind their head, it's a common scene that plays out over and over again in ghettos across America.

After being away in college for four years, it seemed that I had become somewhat detached from the reality of life in the hood. It was like I had completely forgot that there was a war going on. Had it not been for the COVID-19 pandemic, I believe people in this country would have never taken the time to stop and pay attention to the social ills that Blacks have been suffering through for many years. When the world stood still, a new curtain opened up and we were forced to watch the great racial divide which so many of us had learned to turn a blind eye to.

Before the pandemic, a kind of "colorblind racism" existed in America. It had indelibly blended itself into the social norms and was well on its way to becoming a permanent fixture in our societal landscape. We all accepted it to a certain degree, but I don't think any of us realized the gravity of what our complacency could have led to had not the pandemic intervened.

Be that as it may, Jamal needed to understand that in order to overcome the vestiges of the "Jim Crow South", he must put down the gun and pick up the pen and express his anger in a more effective manner. I was determined to enlighten him about the prison industrial complex and give him an in-depth look at the true history of Louisiana's modern day slave trade, also known as the criminal justice system.

College had taught me many things I wish I had known while growing up in the Calliope. The kinds of books we were required to read in school did not accurately depict the Black race. Grotesque images of African slaves clad in chains were etched into our minds at an early age. And the white kids in class who assumed the books correctly described the origin of Black people gained a false sense of superiority after reading the false accounts. Those bleak lessons contained plenty of misconceptions about people of color---both past and present. Proclaiming erroneously that

Blacks came into existence as slaves, the books created fertile ground in the minds of some of the white kids, which was exactly where the first seeds of bigotry were sowed and the great racial divide began. I took a moment to remind Jamal that it wasn't that long ago in New Orleans that Blacks were made to believe the color of our skin somehow made us inferior to whites. When in fact the Black man---like the Aztec----was civilized when the dominant branches of Caucasians were still savage. I said to him as eloquently as I could:

"Jamal, we mustn't succumb to the negative stereotypes that have been placed on us by those who seek to oppress the Black race. We have to be Changeseekers---devoted individuals with the ability to shape the future and restore equity to the way in which we are governed---and speak truth to power by never giving up on what we believe in. I've seen you stand up to guys twice your size and make them respect you. And that's the same vigor and strength you must bring to bear on those who would stand in the way of our efforts to stimulate socioeconomic growth and independence within our own communities."

I glanced over at Jamal and saw that he was listening closely to what I was saying. Which was quite surprising because usually he would tune me out whenever I'd start talking about the "Black condition" and other social justice issues we face as African Americans living in the Dirty South.

"You talk'n some good shit right nah, ya heard me," said Jamal. "I saw you on TV at that rally that time talk'n 'bout how them crack---I mean them white folks---made a law designed to keep Black folks in slavery. I didn't really understand how it went, but you sure had them bitches shook up the way you said it."

Jamal was referring to the speech I gave at a rally in front of the State Capitol building in downtown Baton Rouge during Black History Month. It was covered by national and international news outlets, so my message was heard around the world. I recited it again just for my little brother:

As president of the Southern University Student Government Association, I want to welcome you all to a brand new celebration of Black History

Month---it is time to clear the air. There is an organization in the state of Louisiana that is operating an "ethnic cleansing," multimillion dollar enterprise primarily designed to enslave and oppress Black people. A legalized slave trade euphemistically known as the "criminal justice system".

Now that I have your attention, let me tell you a story that involves the lives of thousands of Black people who have been cast back into slavery and remain there even now. I'm speaking about the incarcerated citizens being held in bondage in the Louisiana State Penitentiary at Angola---an 18,000 acre modern day slave plantation that sits comfortably in an Antebellum wasteland that time has forgotten. Many who have been captured and brought there are "living monuments" to Jim Crow, victims of a racist law enacted by white supremacists to silence Black jurors and to "perpetuate the supremacy of the Anglo-Saxon race in Louisiana."

But I say to you today, that these victims of modern day slavery in America are changing the course of human history with the stroke of a pen. Two remarkable prisoners calling themselves "Phantoms" have petitioned the Department of Justice on the grounds of being racially discriminated against by the State's non-unanimous jury law. Which is also known as "10-2" or a "Jim Crow Jury"---Louisiana was one of only two states that sent people to prison for life without the unanimous consent of all 12 jurors. The DA had only to get ten of the twelve jurors to agree in order to win a conviction. The historic complaint filed by the two Phantoms gained overwhelming public support, which prompted the Civil Rights Division of the Department of Justice to open an investigation into their claims. Ultimately, all funding to state agencies associated with the criminal justice system were suspended due to evidence of the ongoing effects of racial discrimination determined by the U. S. Supreme Court's landmark decision in Ramos vs Louisiana, where it was ruled that non-unanimous juries were unconstitutional and were created with racist intent.

Unlike the irresponsible rhetoric spewed by former President Donald Trump that led to the shameful insurrection at the U. S. Capitol, I'm calling on all of you in this country who are listening to my voice to exercise your civic duty peacefully. Let us come together and restore equity---the spirit and habit of fairness---to our institutions of justice now and forever. Let us tend to the unfinished business that was begun by early civil rights leaders who vowed, wholeheartedly, to uphold the principles of fairness and equality that *have made this county what it is today. Let us tend to the unfinished business of removing monuments of hate and bigotry not only from public display but from the annals of our legal system where racist laws enacted by white supremacists threaten to jeopardize our efforts to form a more perfect union. This is our moment, America. Our golden opportunity to heal racial wounds that have been festering for far too long. Only in solidarity can we embrace the future with confidence and protect the sanctity of freedom for all.*

May God bless the oppressed who continue their struggle for freedom, and may God bless those who hear their cries and move to action.

"Man, that's the realest shit I ever heard," said my little brother as he pondered the message I had just given him. "You make it sound like we still living in slave times.""Actually, Jamal, in some ways we still are." I said while Googling the Thirteenth Amendment on my smartphone. "Here, take a look at this."

Jamal took hold of the phone and started reading the Thirteenth Amendment out loud."AMENDMENT XIII. Slavery abolished... Neither slavery nor involuntary servitude, EXCEPT AS A PUNISHMENT FOR CRIME... shall exist within the United States---What the fuck?!"

"Yes, it's true, Jamal. If you're convicted of a crime---justly or not---it means that the state of Louisiana will place you back into slavery, real slavery."

Jamal stared angrily at the words on the screen, for he was beginning to understand how badly the system was rigged against him---and he felt played.

"Man, I been outche beef'n with niggas over streets that don't even belong to us, and all the while them white folks been going with they move trynna put a nigga back in slavery. Them bitches a fool wit' it!" Jamal was fuming over how blind he had been to the bigger picture. And I was about to enlighten him even more.

"Since you mentioned streets, do you know that many of the names that appear on street signs in our city belonged to white supremacists? Streets like Governor Nicholls, Claiborne Avenue, Lee's Circle, Lafayette Street, Dumaine, Gravier, Carondelet, Baronne, Carrollton, Napoleon, and others."

"Man, how you know so much about so many things, big brother?" said Jamal with a tinge of pride in his voice that I wasn't accustomed to hearing. "You really been learning a lot at that college you go to, and I'm glad you giving me the game on some shit I ain't know about. But bruh, I'm trynna figure out how them white folks make money from locking boo-koo niggas up?"

"Jamal, listen to me closely," I said as sat down beside him and put pressure on the gunshot wound to his shoulder. "Here's a brief history lesson you won't hear about in public school. Major James, a retired Major of the Confederate army, is the guy who sold Angola to the State and presided over 25 years of the most cynical, profit-oriented and brutal prison regime in Louisiana history. The origins of modern corrections in this state can be found in Major James' administration of Angola. His guiding principles included the isolation of inmates from public and political view, the emphasis on economy and cheapness in prison operations, agricultural labor, and the perpetuation of the pre-Civil War racist mentality. His scheme was known as convict leasing, and it utilized Black Codes to arrest, prosecute, and convict Blacks in order to provide a steady supply of free laborers to fulfill the demand for work normally done by slaves. So to answer your question, in the same way that Major James benefitted from Louisiana's Jim Crow Jury scheme in the post-Civil War era, the Louisiana Sheriffs' Association today is profiting from a similar form of convict leasing by housing state inmates and using them for bargaining chips.

Louisiana officials struggled to meet the conditions of a federal judge's ruling that the state's prisons were too crowded, so they came up with the money-saving gambit of putting state inmates in local jails. The state then began signing contracts in which corrections officials promised to fill beds in yet-to-be-built jails, and many Louisiana sheriffs used the deals to get financing for a jail building boom. Add that to the fact that building prisons in rural, mostly white districts create jobs that produce economic stimulus in places where normally the residents would have to rely on welfare. These new prisons are then stuffed to the gill with Black 'criminals' who are counted in census reports as 'residents' of the districts in which the prisons are built, qualifying those areas to reap greater tax revenues and federal benefits. Not to mention larger representation in state legislature. No different from rice, cotton, and sugarcane, Black inmates are seen as an indispensable commodity in Louisiana. In fact, John Oliver Killens said it best when he wrote:

'The American Negro is an Anglo-Saxon invention, a role that the Anglo-Saxon gentlemen invented for the Black man to play in the drama known euphemistically as the American Way of Life! It began as an economic expedient... because you wanted somebody to work for nothing. It's still that, but now, it is much more."'

The ambulance finally arrived and took my little brother to the hospital. Our conversation that day had been a defining moment in both our lives. A new sense of respect and admiration had been shown toward me by Jamal, but what I was most happy about was the promise he made to me that he would get more involved in the struggle for social justice and teach others what he had learned. It gave me hope for the future. But at the moment, I had bigger problems...

"My lord, the rulers of Melanesia and Kenya have expressed grave concerns about venturing into the Valley of Trog," said King Claudius. "Many of their citizens have never returned from this valley, and that is why they live in great fear of the giant sea serpent that lurks within these canyon walls. Even after I told them about how you singlehandedly conquered the Kurnool at Anog, still, they are afraid."

I turned toward Claudius and said, "Then go and remind them that the Reckoning has begun, and so has my quest to fulfil the prophecy. If the creature inside these walls attempts to stand in my way then it, too, will taste my wrath."

The King went back and relayed my message to the leaders to ease their anxiety and bolster confidence in our mission to reach Abyssinia. But as fate would have it, there came a disturbance in the canyon. The creature was on the move and had been spotted by one of the guards. Suddenly, the giant head of a magnificent sea serpent emerged from the darkness followed by a long, spindle-like body that was the length of a thousand ships! The Troglodyte seemed to have no end as it rose up from the floor of the valley.

"Everyone stay calm and stay together!" I shouted. "Keep the women and children away from the canyon walls!"

Pandemonium erupted when the citizens of Kenya came under attack by the beast they so greatly feared.

"Help us, my lord! The beast means to kill us all!" I heard the voices of the Kenyans cry out to me. But as I rushed to save them, the wicked sea serpent filled the ocean with pitch-black ink that came spewing from its nostrils. It used the cloudy water to make off with a slew of Kenya's citizens.

"Where is the serpent? Can anyone see the Troglodyte?" I shouted in vain, because no one saw anything in the midst of the confusion down in the murky depths of the ocean. Then suddenly---

"Look out, D'Shawn!" Azoria's voice rang out in the deep, "The beast is coming your way! Look behind you!"

But it was too late....

The Troglodyte was a creature of unimaginable strength, one that reminded me of the blurry photographs I'd seen of the legendary Loch Ness Monster---except this beast was much larger. It swallowed me down its long esophagus where I joined the Kenyans in the bottomless pit serving as the creature's belly. The harrowing trip down its throat took nearly six minutes, and gauging from the speed I was traveling, I estimated the distance to be about a quarter mile. Which gives you some perspective on how big this creature was.

I felt it coming this time, the metamorphosis I mean. It started with a memory of an incident I had witnessed while fishing for bass at University Lake on the campus of LSU in Baton Rouge. I saw a remarkable struggle for survival take place on the lake. A ruckus broke out right beside my boat and when I looked to see what it was, I saw a speedy little catfish trapped in the mouth of a large water moccasin. The venomous snake caught the little fish but didn't take into account the fierce nature of its intended victim. The feisty catfish waited until the snake completely swallowed it, and then that's when the real fighting began. The little catfish suddenly sprang forward its razor sharp fins with surgical precision, slicing open the snake's belly and spilling the serpent's intestines into the lake as it freed itself and swam off without a scratch. The metamorphosis decided that I should become like that little catfish. It provided me with two enormous fins, and when I sprang them forward the Troglodyte screamed out in pain and began convulsing wildly as I freed the Kenyans and myself from the belly of this great beast.

Now wounded, the Troglodyte tried to escape back into the depths of the valley. But since I vowed that it would taste my wrath, I pursued the beast with all my might.

"D'Shawn! Noooo!" screamed Azoria. "The creature is known to heal itself very quickly, you must never follow the Troglodyte into its den." I heard Azoria loud and clear, but I had no intention on heeding the warning she had given me. I had set out to rid her world of evil things and that's exactly what I planned to do. I chased the great sea serpent into the abyss where a bloody battle commenced. It raged on for over an hour until finally death had claimed its prize. I dismembered the beast and then returned to the caravan where everyone was holding a collective breath praying that I would emerge victorious---and I did.

"To all the kingdoms I say to you, the monster that terrorized those who entered this valley will never again show its face. For I have slayed the dragon!" I boasted in a booming voice that shook the entire gorge. "This demon of the deep is no more!" There came thunderous applause from the masses gathered tightly together in the Valley of Trog. The roar of the crowd could be heard throughout the ocean as once more everyone began chanting my name.

Meanwhile, Azoria was staring at me with a huge smile on her face. Because standing before her was her knight in shining armor, a hero whom she had dreamed would one day come and rescue her people from the evil that had befallen them. And I was glad to be of service.

The convoy continued moving through the Valley of Trog and passed by the mysterious Balkan Pyramids before finally reaching the beautiful escarpment known as La Inagua. It would be the final crossing before arriving at Abyssinia. Every mer-person in existence was now part of this historic pilgrimage headed to the grandest mer-kingdom ever built. Most of them had never actually seen Abyssinia but had heard many stories about its magnificent beauty. The stage was now set for the ultimate showdown.

Welcome... to the end of days.

"Show me your faith without deeds, and I will show you my faith by what I do. You believe there is one God. Good! Even the demons believe that---and shudder."

---James 2:18-19

CHAPTER 12

PURGATORY: POINT OF NO RETURN

The beautiful kingdom of Abyssinia came into view as the caravan crossed La Inagua. There were now four hundred twenty-six kingdoms joined together for one last stand against their ancient enemy called Sapian. King Claudius, ruler of Anog, requested a final conference with me before entering into the underwater "Taj Mahal" known as Abyssinia. He brought with him a Great Elder from one of the first mer-kingdoms to ever exist, the kingdom was called Kush.

"Now is not a good time, Claudius. I'm in the middle of----"

"Hush!, D'Shawn," demanded Claudius. "This matter is very important, and you must listen at once. The Great Elder Romulus has an urgent message for you. He insisted that it be delivered in person. Romulus is the oldest and wisest wizard in all the kingdoms."

The elderly wizard was uncharacteristically tall for a mer-person, and his arms and fingers were disproportionately long to the point where they made him look creepy. But all things aside, I wanted to hear what he had to say.

"Forgive me for arriving so late in the hour, my lord, but I am well along in age and the journey here was a difficult one indeed."

I sensed great wisdom in the wizard's voice and saw in his pale blue eyes the burden of knowing what others did not. Romulus had come to share a guarded secret that he alone had carried his entire life. It concerned the prophecy, and ultimately the fate of the world. "Though the prophecy states that a pivotal battle between the forces of good and evil will take place in Abyssinia, it is a bit misleading" said Romulus. "I know this to be true because... Abyssinia no longer exists."

King Claudius and I looked at each other, then turned our attention back to Romulus. Apparently, there was more startling news to come.

"The Great Prophecy has been misinterpreted by many false prophets who simply did not understand the writings," explained Romulus. "But fear not, my lord, the oracle will soon show you the way."

"What oracle? Show me the way to where?" I asked the wizard. "Tell me, Romulus, how am I supposed to understand any of this?"

"Lord D'Shawn, my time here is nearing an end and I do realize there is still much you do not understand. But you mustn't worry. Let faith be your guide and you will find your destiny soon enough." I suddenly realized that the Great Elder's faded skin and slurred speech indicated that he was nearing death. The clock was now ticking, and every second counted. "You will soon bear witness to remarkable things meant only for the eyes of the immortal--do not shun them. For they are the keys to the devil's undoing." There was a brief pause while the dying wizard struggled to catch his breath, then defiantly, he continued to relay his message.

"When you enter the place that was once Abyssinia, you will discover a doorway that will seem like the gateway to heaven, but do not be deceived. Inside this place lies a virtu---"

"Great Romulus, I hate to interrupt you, but why do you keep referring to Abyssinia as if it doesn't exist?" I said out of desperation because I needed to be sure that Romulus was coherent. "Surely you can see that the kingdom is right there!" I said while pointing toward the magnificent kingdom in the distance. But the wise old wizard did not look in the direction I was pointing. Instead, he slowly approached me and explained the truth about what was in the distance.

"My lord, that which you see is not our beloved Abyssinia." The wizard then placed his hand on my shoulder, looked me in the eye and said, "The Kingdom of Abyssinia has already fallen to the beast and his armies. Nothing remains except that which the devil wishes you to see."

"That's crazy!" shouted King Claudius. "How can that be?"

"What you're looking at is an illusion created by the beast to lure our entire species into his ghostly realm where his armies can annihilate us once and for all. Remember, the devil too knows what is written in the prophecy."

"Romulus, why didn't you tell us this sooner?" I asked. "You could have saved us a lot of trouble, you know."

"The prophecy must be fulfilled as it was written," said the wise ol' wizard. "Though the place that was once Abyssinia is now only an illusion, still, you must go there to do battle with the leviathan---as it is written. Had I disclosed this information to you any sooner, it would have given Sapian time to devise another scheme. Have you forgotten that the dragon sees everything? Be warned, my lord! Now that my secret has been revealed, nothing will be as it seems inside the illusion. The beast is already attempting to alter things as we speak. Also, the citizens of what was once Abyssinia are neither alive nor dead---they are somewhere in between. Like empty vessels possessed by the dragon's black magic, they do the devil's bidding. The enchanted realm that you are about to enter is called Purgatory."

The Great Elder suddenly collapsed on the ocean floor, his frail body looking like twigs that had been broken and set in a pile. I rushed over to be at his side as he lay dying, gasping for his last breath. With trembling hands, the Great Elder placed a small scroll in my palm. And as I looked down at the tiny epistle he'd bestowed upon me, the great wizard gave his final prediction:

"Do not surrender, my lord! For in the darkest hour there will come another!" And just like that, he was gone. Romulus died in my arms and the ocean felt colder than it ever did before.

"Sleep now, gentle wizard," I whispered as I folded Romulus's long arms across his chest and bid him farewell. When I looked toward Abyssinia again, it no longer appeared to be real, and the words of the Great Elder were echoing loudly inside my mind:

"The enchanted realm that you are about to enter is called Purgatory... Purgatory... Purgatory."

"What did you make of Romulus's revelation?" I asked King Claudius.

"I never imagined anything as bizarre as what the Great Elder just said about Abyssinia," replied the bewildered king. "It has always been my belief that the keepers of the Great Prophecy were in complete agreement about what was written despite the many translations that came over time."

There was an awkward silence that lasted longer than either of us intended. We were obviously pondering what we had just witnessed but simply could not wrap our head around the situation. The Great Elder's message had left us in uncharted territory and neither of us saw it coming. Finally, Claudius broke the silence with an inquiry:

"D'Shawn, what are you going to do?"

"What do you mean, what am I going to do?' I'm not the one who went around filling my head with all that stuff about 'you're the Chosen One' and 'it's your destiny to lead us to the Promised Land'." I bemoaned. "You know what?---I'm gett'n the hell outta here!"

"D'Shawn, you can't just leave!" shouted Claudius. "What about the Reckoning?"

"Claudius, didn't you just hear what Romulus said? None of this is real! The whole kingdom is a goddamn illusion! Everything was supposed to go according to the prophecy. But, nooooo!, you had to go and bring Romulus up in here looking like the

Crypt Keeper from "Tales from the Crypt" talking about illusions and oracles and black magic! Oh!, and let's not forget about the citizens of what was once Abyssinia, about them being neither alive nor dead---but somewhere in between. What the hell did he mean by that? Was he talking about zombies?" My tantrum only added to the King's bewilderment, leaving him feeling dejected and confused. I watched his spirit turn a dark shade of melancholy right before my eyes.

"Claudius, I'm sorry. This is not your fault." I offered the King my sincerest apology. "We've been through a lot, you and I, and maybe the stress is starting to get to me. Not to mention there's an evil lizard running around threatening to destroy the world."

"Sapian is not actually a lizard," the King quietly interjected. "He is a hellish dem---"

"Claudius, I really don't give a damn what Sapian is," I interjected back. "Obviously, you're missing the point. For all I know, even you might be an illusion!"

"Don't be ridiculous!" chided the King. "Only an asshole like you would even say such a thing."

"Who you calling an asshole?! Man, I will come over there and break my foot off in your---"

"D'Shawn!" yelled Azoria just in the nick of time. "What in the world is going on here? Why are the two of you arguing?" If there was anyone who could restore order to this chaos, it was Azoria.

"You should be ashamed of yourselves!" declared the princess. "You're behaving like a couple of spoiled children. In case you didn't know it, there's a war brewing just beyond La Inagua that will determine the fate of our world. And here you are bickering amongst yourselves before the fighting even begins. Both of you are leaders! Now, act like it!" Azoria's scolding abruptly ended our confrontation and put things back into perspective. Then---for the first time since joining us---she noticed Romulus's stiff, lifeless body laying at my feet.

"Father, what's going on? Why is the Great Elder lying on the floor?" Before Claudius could explain what happened, in came

Zenobia who demanded answers of her own."Claudius, there had better be a good explanation for the racket you two have been making," said Zenobia with a fiery attitude and noticeable ire in her voice. "Well Claudius, I'm waiting."

"Yea Claudius, why don't you tell your wife how you brought the 'Crypt Keeper' guy in here and ruined everything," I said mockingly. "I'm sure she'd love to hear all about it.""Shut up, D'Shawn!" shouted the royal family in unison.

Queen Zenobia shot me an angry look for the disparaging remark I made toward the Great Elder. The strange thing about it was that normally I showed respect to all my elders, it's how I was raised. So being disrespectful to Romulus and the King was completely out of character for me. Yet it happened, and I wasn't sure of the reason. I was starting to suspect that it had something to do with the Quintess, like perhaps it was affecting me in ways I hadn't realized. I now possessed an extremely aggressive nature that felt, well, alien to me.

"Your Royal Highnesses," I said to King Claudius and his wife on bended knee. "I humbly apologize for the way I've been be-having lately. Forgive my lack of decorum, I will certainly try to do better going forward."

The royal couple acknowledged me with a nod of approval, and everything was as right as rain again---at least for the time being. Zenobia turned her attention back on the King, she and Azoria were waiting to hear about what Romulus said before he died.

While Claudius offered them his account of what was said, I informed the citizens of Kush that Romulus had passed away and granted them permission to conduct a burial ceremony to honor the Crypt Keep---I mean, the wizard one last time.

"...and then the Great Elder Romulus said that this place was called Purgatory." King Claudius said at the conclusion of his explanation to his wife and daughter.

"My goodness!" said the Queen. "That is unbelievable!"

"Yeah, tell me about it." Claudius mumbled in response.

"What does D'Shawn plan to do now that everything's changed?" asked Zenobia.

"Well, he's kind of touchy about being asked anything regarding his plans," the King warned. "That's what started our argument earlier." As usual, Zenobia paid her husband no mind. She politely proceeded to take matters into her own hands.

"That's just ridiculous," chided Zenobia. "I'll get to the bottom of this mess right away!"

"But wait, honey!" pleaded Claudius. "I don't think it is a good time to---" He was too late, Zenobia was on the warpath.

She approached me with her hands planted firmly on her hips and said, "In light of what the Great Elder revealed to you, how do you plan to defeat the dragon and deliver us to Atlantica?"

I glanced at Claudius as if to say, "Don't you have any control over your wife?"

He shrugged his shoulders and gave me a look like, "Are you fucking kidding me?"

Zenobia now had her arms folded waiting on me to respond.

"Listen here, 'Boss Lady'!" I said to the fuming queen. "Don't go getting your panties in a bunch, I'm the 'Big Ku una' around here and what I say, go---"

"How dare you speak to me that way?!" complained Zenobia. "I am to be addressed as Queen Zenobia! And from now on you will call me by my proper title or I'll make you wish you were never born!" I glanced at Claudius again and mumbled under my breath, "I'm already wishing I was never born." He chuckled at my joke, but very discretely.

"Okay then, Queen Zenobia." I said to her bourgeoisie ass. "If we're using proper titles and all, shouldn't you be addressing me as Lord D'Shawn?"

The Queen was fuming even more at this point. And to add gas to the fire Claudius inadvertently opened his mouth and said, "Well dear, he has a good point there." Zenobia gave him the same icy glare she had given me moments earlier. I intuitively went over and gave the King a "high-five" knowing full well that such an impromptu display of male bonding would get Zenobia's goat.

"Thanks for getting my back, K. C. (King Claudius)!" I said while making sure Zenobia saw the huge grin plastered upon my face.

"Fo' shiggedy, D'Shizzle," said the King while trying his hand at a little West Coast banter.Meanwhile, Zenobia cut her eyes at us in disgust---and we loved it.

"You two deserve each other," she ranted. "I can't stand the sight of either of you!" Azoria quickly came to her mother's aid.

"Don't worry, Mama---I got this," she said while approaching me with that same look in her eyes as when I got carried away with "filming" the whales.

"D'Shawn, since you claim to be the 'Big Ku una' around here, what are you planning to do about the Reckoning?"

"Didn't you just hear me tell your bossy-ass mama to stop asking me about my plans?" I said while making sure to keep lots of distance between us. "See if you can get this through your thick skull, princess. I don't have to explain myself to you or your mama. Whatever I plan to do is none of your business, O-Kulllllllll!" I hit her the "Cardi B" tongue roll and Azoria just smiled, which made me even more nervous than if she had cussed me out.

"Well Mama, you know what this means don't you?" said Azoria while glancing under eyed at the Queen.

"I most certainly do," replied Zenobia. "It means he hasn't the slightest clue what to do next." The Queen and her daughter shared a long laugh at my expense. I tried not to let it bother me, but they were laying it on pretty damn thick.

"Okay, that's it! That's the last goddamn straw!" I screamed to no avail. Even Claudius was laughing with them at that point.

"Okay goddammit! The very next person that asks me about my plans is gonna get the taste slapped right out of his mouth!"

Just then, a gangly lieutenant came in with a question:

"My lord, what plans have thee for the armies?" I turned and I saw Azoria and her parents standing there trying to hold back their laughter. But one of them snickered out loud and started a chain reaction involving contagious giggling that soon turned into boisterous laughter and spread throughout the crowd. The next thing I knew, we were all rolling around on the floor in stitches laughing our asses off for no particular reason. The poor lieutenant stood there gawking at us as if we had all gone mad. But there was no cause for concern, we were simply having a "family moment"---one of many to come.

✦ 129 ✦

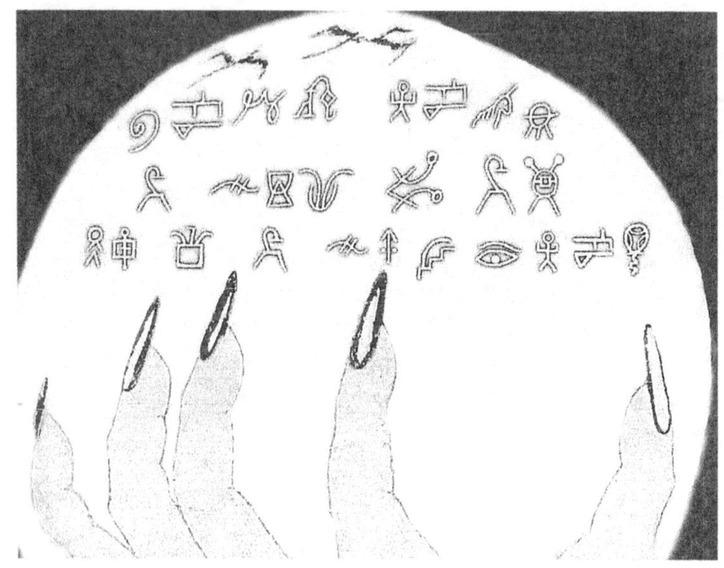

"He made his son pass through the fire, practiced witchcraft and used divination... He did much evil in the sight of the Lord provoking Him to anger."---2 Kings 21:6

CHAPTER 13

THE ORACLE AND THE RAINBOW

The time had finally come for me to face the wicked beast known as Sapian. I could sense his evil presence hovering over the illusion like an ominous black cloud. Not a single living creature went anywhere near the ghostly kingdom, it was as if they too sensed the evilness inside the place that was once Abyssinia.

With Claudius by my side, I looked out at the millions of mer-warriors under my command---their eyes glowing fiery red with fury, their weapons glistening beneath the ocean blue---and I saw the enormous pride emanating from them. I was immediately reminded of what was at stake, either we would defeat the dragon and fulfill the prophecy, or we would all die together right here on this battlefield. And with that in mind, I gave the order to attack!

At once, millions upon millions of mer-warriors descended on the ghost of Abyssinia like a plague of hungry locusts ready to engage whatever horrors lie in wait behind its dreamy façade. Suddenly, the ocean moaned as lightning flashed beneath the water and thunder clapped loudly in our ears. A great darkness befell the kingdom and devoured all light, leaving me no choice but to halt the attack.

"Stand down!" I commanded the armies of mer-warriors. "Hold your positions and wait for my signal!"

"Look, my lord!" shouted one of the warriors. "Something is coming from the direction of the kingdom!"

"Ready your weapons!" I said while focusing on the object coming our way. We braced ourselves for an attack, but when the object got closer we couldn't believe our eyes.

Here we were at the precipice of war, and out of nowhere comes this little white dolphin frantically swimming towards us as if something was chasing it---something unseen in the darkness. The mystical creature was in distress, and for good reason. The monstrous beast that was chasing it soon emerged from the abyss like a furious Titan----it was a giant squid!

"Hold your positions!" I commanded once again. "It could be a trick of some kind!"

The squid was the size of a mountain and yet was amazingly fast, it appeared that the dolphin would not escape the reach of its deadly tentacles.

But why would a creature that large go after such a small meal? I asked myself. Then I remembered the words spoken by the Great Elder Romulus:

"...fear not, my lord, the oracle will soon show you the way." I immediately gave new orders!

"Let no harm come to the dolphin! It is the oracle!" On my command, legions of mer-warriors swarmed the giant squid like a horde of killer bees. Though the beast was caught off guard, it still managed to grab dozens of warriors with its long tentacles and strangled them to death. That's when the ferocity of the mer-warriors went on full display, and they began tearing the squid limb from limb and ripping its body to shreds. In a matter of seconds, there was nothing left but bits and pieces of the formidable beast raining down on the ocean floor. The little white dolphin, meanwhile, after realizing the squid was dead, swam up to me and snuggled its beak next to my chest as if to thank me for saving its life. It started chirping and making all sorts of clicking noises as it swam about with excitement glad to be alive.

"I hope I was right about you," I said to the peculiar looking animal. "I also hope that you have something useful to show me." The white dolphin continued to swim in circles chirping and whistling and nudging me playfully, but then it stopped right in front of me and said, "I've come to show you a great secret---Yep! Yep!"

What the fuck?!

"This is not happening!" I said in disbelief of the talking dolphin. "I'm not about to stand here and converse with a frickin' fish!"

The little dolphin tilted its head slightly and said, "But you would converse with a mermaid, yep?!"

Damn! The oracle made a good point. I had to remind myself that in Azoria's world anything was possible---even a talking fish.

"Okay, you've made your point," I conceded to the oracle. "All I know is that when this shit is over, I'm going to need some serious therapy. Now show me this big secret of yours." The oracle started swimming in circles again, but this time when the dolphin stopped, it posed a question to me in the form of a riddle:

"There's something you must seek--Yep! Yep!---which can be seen over peaks and even in the ocean spray. Click! Click! Click!. For forty days and forty nights the pitter-patter, pitter-patter brought our worlds together as one. The thing you must seek is a promise to keep---a divine reminder that our worlds shall never again meet Click! Click! Click!. It is spoken about in fables and tales about gold, but for you, dear D'Shawn, it shall be the gateway to heaven if you can name it before this riddle grows cold. So tell me great savior, if you are truly the shepherd sent to protect God's sheep, what is the name of the thing that you must so earnestly seek?"

I was completely taken aback! Not because I didn't know the answer to the riddle but because I was shocked that the oracle knew what was written in the book of Genesis. I mean, how was it that a dolphin knew about the covenant made between God and Noah which was described in the ninth chapter of Genesis? Something wasn't right, I sensed a strangeness in the way that this whole scenario was playing out. But I figured it would be best that I answered the riddle before some other weird shit popped off. So I looked at the oracle and offered it my response to the riddle:

"When you said that rains (pitter patter, pitter-patter) brought our worlds together as one, you were obviously referring to the Great Flood where God made it rain for forty days and forty nights, turning the world into one giant ocean. You also mentioned the promise that God made to Noah that He would never again send such a flood to destroy the earth. And as a 'divine reminder' of this promise, God placed a beautiful arc in the heavens above the sea. A bright and colorful miracle that can be seen over mountain peaks and even in the ocean spray."

"Quickly D'Shawn! Tell me the name of the thing you must seek! Speak it now, or you will never know the secrets I keep--- Yep! Yep!"

"The thing I must seek is a rainbow."

At that very moment a brilliant beam of pure sunlight pierced the ocean depths and entered the oracle, turning the little white dolphin into a living prism. The oracle's translucent body began casting off a beautiful array of vibrant colors that came together and formed a magnificent rainbow beneath the sea. Now looking like "sparkling crystal", the mystic creature projected the full spectrum of colors contained in a rainbow directly into the heart of Abyssinia.

"D'Shawn, you have proven that you are truly 'the Chosen One' sent to fulfill the Great Prophecy," said the oracle. "Now you must go into the place that was once Abyssinia, but do not venture outside of the rainbow. For if you do, then you will become like those whose souls have been trapped in Purgatory and you will remain there until the Judgement----Yep! Yep! Follow the rainbow, it is your key to the Abyss, and it will guarantee safe passage through the gates of Purgatory. But beware! For you will soon have to enter the Netherworld----Yep! Yep!---where the great dragon sits quietly waiting in the shadows for you to arrive... Sapian knows you're coming."

The glistening oracle then approached me and said, "There is one other riddle you must solve which involves a different kind of key Click! Click! Click!. The future you can see if you peep inside of me---Yep! Yep!"

"What key are you talking about?" I asked the oracle, "I don't understand what you mean. How am I supposed to---"

BRRrrrmmmm!

The oracle's mouth slowly opened up, allowing me to see a vision of the future through a magical glass lens leading down into its body. Studying the vision with intense concern, I saw images of Azoria and me walking hand-in-hand together, but the strange thing was... we were in New Orleans.

The New Orleans Saints had just won their latest Super Bowl and the French Quarter was filled with screaming fans hollering, "Who DAT?!", and dancing in the streets. It was like Mardi Gras all over again!

In the vision, me and Azoria were walking up Bourbon Street toward the Royal Sonesta Hotel when we noticed a small bookstore sitting in the shadow of the building next to it. There were several dimly lit lanterns dangling from the rust-covered awning that protruded downward at an odd angle in front of the building. Even without there being the slightest hint of a breeze blowing, the rickety old lanterns were swinging to and fro like there was a storm brewing nearby. I also noticed that there was a large glass window in front of the store through which hundreds of books could be seen from the sidewalk outside. Many of the books sitting on the shelves near the window looked very old. And based on the store's rustic décor, I assumed that part of its inventory dealt with antiques, but I couldn't be sure because there was no sign posted on the outside of the building telling you what kind of shop it was.

We tried to go inside but the door wouldn't open. That's when we noticed the table with the crystal ball on it sitting beside the entrance. There was also a note laying on the table that read, "Touch the crystal ball with your left hand and then close your eyes." I watched Azoria reach out her hand in the vision, and like magic, the door to the bookstore opened by itself and we went inside and started looking around. There were thousands and thousands of books on the shelves throughout the store, which now appeared to be much larger on the inside than how it looked from the sidewalk. Azoria began rummaging through a litany of encyclopedias that were lined up along the far wall of the shop and standing next to her was an empty suit of armor belonging to a knight. A few minutes later I saw myself rushing over to where she was standing, and when I got there she was holding what appeared to be an encyclopedia containing some type of crude writing. The book's title was deeply carved into the fleshy material on the cover and was written in a Gothic style calligraphy that was as ancient as the rest of the relics inside the strange little shop.

I watched Azoria run her fingers across the letters in the title right before she dropped the book and suddenly backed away from the wall. When the large book landed on the floor, it sent clouds of dust and cobwebs flying everywhere. Once the dust settled, the book's title was clearly revealed: Ex Libris Mirabilia. It was a Latin term meaning "from the books of miracles".

Suddenly an old woman appeared from behind the counter wearing a tattered black dress with long, moth-eaten sleeves on it that stretched all the way down to the tips of her black fingernails. Something was very peculiar about the old hag, but I couldn't quite put my finger on it. She moved closer toward Azoria and I noticed that her hair was in dreadlocks, I could see them sticking out from beneath the pointy hat she was wearing and there was also a huge white broach shaped like a human skull pinned to the front of her black afghan. The witch's face was partially covered by a sequenced veil that draped down from the brim of her hat, leaving her eerie looking eyes barely visible in the shadowy realm disguised as a bookstore. And though I could see her mouth moving in the vision, it wasn't enough to make out what she was saying. But judging from the expression on Azoria's face, it was plain to see that whatever the witch said must have frightened Azoria a great deal---she looked completely terrified.

The old hag then reached out her long, bony hand and beckoned for Azoria to hand her the book that had fallen on the floor. I could see Azoria's hands trembling uncontrollably as she gave the witch what she asked for. The creepy old lady in the bookstore steadily moved closer toward Azoria, who seemed to be paralyzed with fear and could not run away from the witch. There were tears streaming down Azoria's face like tiny waterfalls, and for some reason I stood there unable to help her. It appeared that I too had become paralyzed. Frozen. Bewitched.

Once the witch took possession of the book, she opened it and removed a marker that had been placed inside. She then pointed to a glowing chart that was filled with glyphs and alphabets and was labeled The Key of Adwah.

The hieroglyphic cipher was encapsulated inside decorative ribbons laced with musical notes, and at the top corners was a pair of angelic cherubim adorned with wings and gleaming halos positioned directly above their head. The cherubim symbolized unconditional love and everlasting faith, a manifestation of God's gift to humanity.

After revealing the chart to Azoria, the witch threw back her head and let out a bloodcurdling scream as her body levitated off the floor into midair. She then began swirling around and chanting loudly in a strange language. The bookstore immediately went dark, but still I could see myself moving through the darkness knocking over several book displays as I tried to reach Azoria. That's when the witch cornered me and began whispering something in my ear. Soon afterwards, symbols from the key started appearing above her head. I couldn't make them out at first because my focus was on getting to Azoria, and as soon as I was able to break free from the witch I rushed over to where Azoria was standing and we immediately headed toward the exit----but unfortunately, the door was jammed.

We started pounding our fists against the large glass window at the front of the store hoping that someone out on the sidewalk would see us in need of help and call the police. But the people who were passing by right outside the window never once looked in the direction of the store. At that point in the vision, I peered deeper into the mouth of the oracle because something had entered the bookstore and quietly hid itself in the shadows behind us. Then, out of nowhere steps a humongous dragon that had streams of liquid fire pouring from its nostrils. The dragon inhaled a deep breath and then breathed fire like you wouldn't believe. The witch was instantly set on fire while still swirling in the air, and the glowing symbols, meanwhile, were now hovering over the head of the dragon.

"Study the markings well Click! Click! Click!," said the oracle as it startled me by speaking while I was completely engrossed in watching the vision. "You must first solve the riddle of a man if you are to defeat the red dragon at his own game----Yep! Yep!"

Taking heed to what the oracle said, I immediately began focusing on the symbols above the dragon's head.

Studying them.

Deciphering them.

Memorizing them in sequence.

In the vision, meanwhile, the dragon was focusing on us---Azoria and me. Again the monster took in a deep breath but before it began its rain of fire, the oracle closed the portal and the vision ended the same way it began...

BRRrrrmmmm!

"I say to you again, great D'Shawn, follow the rainbow Click! Click! Click!. It is the key to the Abyss---the dragon's lair---and you mustn't venture outside the light. Remember, it was destiny that led you here but only faith will protect you in the presence of the devil----Yep! Yep!"

The oracle then swam off into the distance leaving me to contemplate the things I had been shown. Once I had drawn my conclusion, I turned to King Claudius and said, "Your Highness, I am going in alone, and I want you to take command of the armies in my absence. If I don't return by dawn then order the attack and destroy everything in sight!"

"Yes, my lord. I will do as you wish," said Claudius speaking as though he was sending his own son off to war. His voice trembled with sadness, and I could sense the grave concern he held for me in his heart.

"D'Shawn, when my daughter first brought you before me, I was foolish in my haste to judge you, and for that, I am deeply sorry. You have proven to be extremely wise and courageous, and I am honored to serve under your command."

I had not heard the King speak in such a manner before, his sincere words touched my heart in a way that felt unfamiliar to me. I never had the opportunity to bond with my father. I was very young when he was wrongfully convicted and sent to prison for life. And though he tried his best to stay in touch with the family, the shame he felt for not being able to provide for us from behind bars led to our correspondences becoming less and less as the years rolled by. It was heartbreaking to say the least, and here was this mighty king offering me the opportunity to experience a father's love... how amazing was that?

"Claudius, don't you go getting all mushy on me right now," I joked with the King to lighten the mood. "We still have plenty of work to do, starting with getting rid of this stupid lizard and then finding Atlantica."

"But D'Shawn, I've told that Sapian is not a liz---"

"Good grief, Claudius! I know he's not a lizard!" I said as I interrupted the King. "For crying out loud, do you have any sense of humor at all?"

Claudius managed to produce a placid smile on his weary face, but it didn't erase the worry in his eyes. He knew, as did I, that the treacherous journey upon which I was about to embark could very well turn out to be my last.

✦ 143 ✦

"We all drink from wells we didn't dig, and warm ourselves by fires we didn't build."
---Mark Shields

CHAPTER 14

FEAR NO EVIL

I followed the rainbow through the gates of Purgatory and then made my way toward the heart of Abyssinia where the citizens of the once glorious kingdom were now under the spell of the beast. They appeared to be in great fear of the light that radiated from the luminous arc beaming down from the heavens above. These Abyssinian monsters were terrifying beyond belief, and I could see them staring at me with eyes that were as lifeless as those of the Great White shark. But even though I walked through the valley of the shadow of death inside the ghostly kingdom, I would fear no evil---for I knew that the Lord was with me every step of the way. In fact, I saw this as an opportunity to have a little fun with the locals.

"Hey lah bas! Come nah!" I said with a heavy Southern drawl sounding like Jamal. "Can I come over there and holla at ch'all for a minute?" The lost souls of Abyssinia curiously stared at me as I strutted around with an exaggerated swagger pretending to be a Southern pimp.

"Say lil' mama, why don't ch'all come back to New Orleans with me so we can go to the Mardi Gras, ya heard me," I said to an

Abyssinian female standing with a group of her friends. "Come nah cheah, we gon' act bad in dat city, yeah. And ain't nobody gon' stop our shine. I bet ch'all ain't never danced at a second line, huh? Let me show ya how we do it in the Big Easy, baby!" I started buck jumping to an imaginary second line drum cadence and the Abyssinian females looked on in complete amazement. They didn't know what to make of the strange deity who spoke an "ebonic" dialect that came from the streets of New Orleans. The next thing I knew, the entire group of Abyssinian broads caught on to that New Orleans rhythm and man them girls went buck wild! They started twerking and "p-poppin" like they was out the Melphomine projects. This one lil' broad did a handstand and made her butt cheeks clap underwater in slow motion. I said to myself, "You go girl!."

I joined the second line and threw my hands up high so they could see the diamond encrusted bracelet I had made with the jewels from the beach. Man, you should've seen them diamonds twinkling and glistening in the bright light coming from the rainbow, I was blinding them hoes! Then I started singing one of my favorite Cash Money classics: "...every time I come around yo' city---Bling! Bling! Pinky ring worth about fifty---Bling! Bling! Every time I buy a new ride---Bling! Bling! Lorenzo's on Yokohama tires---Bling! Bling!"

Moments later when I reached the heart of Abyssinia, the safe haven that had protected me from the creepy zombies suddenly disappeared.

"Hey! Who turned off my rainbow?!" I shouted. "C'mon! Stop playing!"

The creepy monsters then began to emerge from the shadows and started coming toward me. "Hey guys, you know I was just kidding about the whole 'pimp' thing, right?"

They were not amused at all by my teasing, in fact, the creatures quickened their approach and just when they were about to pounce on me from every direction---Ka-Boom! A massive explosion rocked the area and sent shockwaves through the ocean depths scattering the Abyssinian zombies like roaches when the lights go on. I knew that it could only mean one thing... the devil had finally arrived.

First I heard the serpent's hiss, then the beast made a bellowing sound like an alligator, a low guttural growl that signified there was a monster nearby. Then I heard people screaming and moaning and there were multiple voices speaking in different languages all at the same time. The red dragon was obviously showing off his many talents.

"Welcome, D'Shawn. I've been expecting you," said the ancient dragon with bated breath. "There is much we need to discuss, you and I." Sapian's voice sounded like a raging storm, and it seemed to come from everywhere. I'm not gonna lie, I was a little shaken at first, but it didn't take long for me to remember why I had come to confront this demon from the Underworld.

"Hello, lizard." I said while brandishing a toothy smile, "It's good to finally make your acquaintance. How 'bout we grab a couple of beers and talk sports? I don't take it that you're a Saints fan, right?"

The ancient leviathan wasn't sure what was going on, he couldn't fathom being spoken to in such a lackadaisical manner.

"Do you have any idea to whom you are speaking?!" Sapian chided, "Do you know who I am, D'Shawn? I don't believe you do."

"Au contraire, mon Cheré!" I said with an excellent French accent. "I most certainly do know who you are. You're the 'Gatherer of Souls', the 'Sultan of Sin', and the 'Demon of the Dark'. You're 'Boltazar the Wicked' and 'Zulamon the Deceiver'. You're 'El Diablo' and 'Raz Skatzchezin of the Dead Sea'. You're 'Ragamuffin' and the creature known as 'Krampus'. You're the 'Kraken' and the sea monster 'Gretchen of the Deep'. And you're the red dragon humbly known as 'Sapian' by the mer-people. So yes, I know exactly to whom I am speaking." I finished with a smirk and a chuckle. Now it was time to really piss off the dragon. "Oh,

I almost forgot to tell you that your reign of terror is officially over. And from now on the only thing you'll be called is a lizard ést mour." Both my candor and the unusual phrase I had used to describe him intrigued the dragon to no end. Sapian was curious to the point where he was forced to ask me what it meant.

"D'Shawn, tell me again the name you mentioned. I want to know what it means."

I looked around as if checking to see if anyone was listening, then I whispered to the dragon saying, "Are you sure you want to know?"

"Yes, D'Shawn. I'm curious about the name. I'm asking that you tell me what it means."

As I prepared to translate the phrase for the dragon, a sly grin crept into the corners of my mouth, and I relished the moment.

"Well, great and powerful Sapian, ruler of the Underworld, demon extraordinaire, murderer of women and children, deceiver of man, emperor of evil, conqueror of---"

"Okay! Enough with the accolades! Get on with it!" demanded Sapian after realizing that I was making fun of him.

"The phrase that you are so curious about is more of a promise than a name," I said with a devilish grin. "Because once I tell you what it means, I promise you won't like it." The dragon, though still remaining unseen, gave me the impression that he was feeling a bit apprehensive about finding out what I had called him---but it was too late to turn back now.

"The term lizard ést mour simply means 'dead lizard', and that's exactly what you're going to be once you show your ugly face, you despicable bastard!" The dragon became enraged and then went absolutely berserk.

"Why you insignificant little fool! How dare you speak to me with such insolence! I'll snatch your soul right out of that pathetic carcass of yours and shit down your throat! Don't play with me---I am not to be trifled with!"

I stood with my arms folded and calmly replied, "Who do you think you are bitch, Donald Trump?"

Sapian was so mad that he almost slipped and revealed a secret that he's been keeping from me. He managed to catch himself in the nick of time... but the temptation was still there.

"D'Shawn, if you keep it up, I'm going to tell you something that will open your eyes to a glorious truth that will destroy your belief in many things."

"What do you know about 'truth'? You're the biggest liar there ever was. But don't worry, bitch, you'll soon be just another lizard ést mour and I'll be the one taking a dump down your throat."

"Based on the auspicious nature of our conversation, I can't understand why you insist on calling me that?" said the dragon sarcastically. "I thought you'd be more clairvoyant than to think of me that way, but I guess I was wrong. You're about as uncouth as a jackal."

"First of all, fuck you! And second of all, here's your 'clairvoyance' right here, buddy!" I reached for my crouch forgetting that in my current form of a merman, my genitalia was not where it would normally be.

Damn!

"What are you doing?" asked the dragon when seeing me make the odd gesture. "You look ridiculous."

"Yo' ugly mama look ridiculous!" I could feel my little brother Jamal coming out in me. "Why don't you stop being such a bitch and show me where you are so we can get it on?!"

"Well D'Shawn, I'm glad that you'd like to join me in the Netherworld. Quite frankly, I think it's a great idea. I wish you could bring your little girlfriend along too---her and her mama--- we could have ourselves an orgy that's out of this world!"

Sapian was trying to get me back for what I said earlier, and the bitch was doing a very good job of it too. Man, I was mad as hell when hearing the misogynistic comments being spewed from the devil's mouth.

"C'mon D'Shawn, give me my due," said the dragon. "I wonder if Azoria's cat tastes like sushi... you think?"

"I'm gonna rip your filthy tongue right outta that filthy mouth of yours!" I yelled at the dragon. "You're a coward-ass bitch and I'm gonna whip yo' ass as soon as I get my hands on you!"

"Sticks and stones may break my bones," Sapian said with a laugh. "But I'd still like to taste some of that sushi!"

Y'all, I'mma kill this bitch!

✦ 150 ✦

✦

" ...the archangel Michael, when he was disputing with the devil... did not dare bring a slanderous accusation against him, but said, 'The Lord rebuke you!'"
    ---Jude 9

CHAPTER 15

DRAGON'S LAIR

I immediately transformed into a formidable beast with bulging muscles and arms the size of battleships. Even though I had grown taller than Mt. Everest, the metamorphosis continued increasing my size in anticipation of the enemy I would soon face. It was preparing me for the ultimate battle, a duel to the death between me and the devil.

Moments later, Sapian opened a giant portal that led directly into the Netherworld, and as I peered through the opening I saw countless souls being tortured and tormented in Hell. I had to remind myself that this, too, was part of the illusion, part of the devil's diabolical plan to distract me from the real reason he destroyed Abyssinia and brought me here.

"What's the matter, D'Shawn?" the dragon teased. "Are you afraid to step into my world?"

"I'm not afraid of anything, lizard!" I shouted back at the dragon while scanning the portal's entrance looking for booby traps.

Sapian was definitely trying to play with my mind---that low down son-of-a-bitch!---but I knew I had to stay sharp, or I would lose not just my sanity but my life, as well. What's funny though, is that I imagined that the Netherworld would be a fiery hell where all you heard were the screams and moans of tortured souls being poked with pitchforks held by hideous demons. But to the contrary, it turned out to be a desolate wasteland of darkness and silence, a dead universe where there was no light, no life, and absolutely no love. I began contemplating my next move when, out of nowhere a cloven hoof struck me in the face and rendered me unconscious. When I came to, Sapian was towering over me wearing an evil grin. The dragon was twice the size I had grown.

"You arrogant little fool!" roared Sapian. "Did you really think you could come into my world and destroy me?!"

The leviathan grabbed me by the throat, picked me up, and began to examine me as if I were some kind of insect.

"Oh, you poor child," said the red dragon with a sneer. "Your suffering will be legendary... even in Hell!"

Sapian was indeed a terrifying sight to behold. His gigantic head was shaped like that of a ram with curled horns sprouting from each side and ending with a sharp point. The dragon's eyes were freakish and reptilian like those of a pit viper, and out of his back grew the giant wings of a Vampire bat. Sapian had the upper body of a man, but he stood on the hind legs of a bull and had skin that was as scarlet-red as boiled crawfish. I couldn't stare at him for long without getting sick to my stomach thinking about the countless lives he had destroyed with his wickedness.

"You don't scare me, Sapian!" I managed to say despite having the dragon's claws wrapped around my throat. "Now put me down so that I can fulfill the prophecy."

"Foolish mortal! You have been deceived!" said Sapian while basking in the glory of his diabolical charade. "There is no prophecy, you idiot. There is only that which was given to the first Elders. I planted false visions in their mind and instructed them to record what they were shown. Being the good 'shepherds' that they were, they each went forth and spread the 'gospel' to all the little sheep and made them into believers. Does that sound familiar, D'Shawn?" said the devil as a loud, sinister laugh escaped his throat and filled my heart with rage.

"You're a liar!" I yelled at the dragon, "The prophecy is real! And I'm the savior who's been sent to destroy you!"

"Fool! You've lost your mind!" said the devil. "And for that I'm going to reward you by telling you a secret that no mortal has ever known. But first, my little beasty, there's something I want to show you."

Sapian released the grip he'd held on my throat and placed me back on solid ground, my initial thought was to kill him right away, but then I remembered the words of the Great Elder Romulus when he said to me:

"You will soon bear witness to remarkable things meant only for the eyes of the immortal---do not shun them. For they are the keys to the devil's undoing."

Trusting the wizard's great wisdom, I refrained from killing the dragon and instead, followed the beguiling beast deep into the Netherworld. We eventually arrived at a luxurious cathedral that was filled with religious artifacts of every kind. This magnificent building had many rooms, and inside them were exquisite oil paintings in beautifully designed gold frames hanging on the walls. The rooms had jade statues of famous saints on display, mounted on pedestals made of pure marble sitting in front of detailed carvings depicting events described in the book of Revelation. I knew a couple of the paintings by name, like the one called "The Last Supper" painted by Leonardo da Vinci, and the painting by Michelangelo that was named "Creation" which is displayed on the ceiling of the Sistine Chapel in Rome.

"Why are you showing me this?" I asked, but the devil ignored the question because he was busy plotting on how best to relay the secret that he was dying to reveal.

I knew the devil was setting the stage for his dramatic bombshell to get dropped at the precise moment---unfortunately, there was nothing I could do but wait for it.

"Come closer great savior of the mer-people," said the dragon. "Tell me, D'Shawn, what do you make of these?"

The ancient leviathan pointed to a row of books and scrolls that were carefully organized in chronological order beginning with the Hebrew Bible, which dated back to around 500 B.C. and ending with the King James Bible. The biblical translations continued in historical succession following the Hebrew Bible in this order: Latin Vulgate Translation (383 A.D.), Alcuin Bible (800 A.D.), Paris Bible (1200 A.D.), Wycliffe Bible (1382), Gutenberg Bible (1455), Erasmus Translation (1516), Luther Bible (1522), Tyndale Translation (1526), Coverdale Bible (1535), Matthew Bible (1537), Great Bible (1539), Geneva Bible (1560), Bishops' Bible (1568), Douay-Rheims Bible (1582), King James Bible (1611).

"They appear to be various translations of the Holy Scriptures," I said in response to Sapian's question.

"My, my, my... you're not as dense as I thought. I'm impressed," said the dragon while thumbing through the pages of the King James Version of the Bible. The movement of the devil's hand drew my attention in a way that I didn't expect, causing me to lose track of where I was and only focus on what was in front of me. Watching the hypnotic motions of the dragon's hand was like listening to a subtle lullaby and I soon fell under Sapian's spell as he conjured up a different version of how the Gospel of Christ was created. The dragon showed me a vision, and in the vision this is what I saw...

The archangel Michael---while standing amid a smokey haze of ash and vapors---was preparing to slay an unruly angel whose face was hidden by the mist. Then out of heaven came a gleaming light that caused the fighting to stop. A voice in the light was speaking to the angels using a language I hadn't heard before. In the very next instance, the angel who had been fighting with Michael was taken away by a celestial creature traveling faster than the speed of light. It was able to move back and forth between the spirit realm and the realm of the living, and it came and saved the fallen angel from Michael's sword. At first I thought it was Azrael, the Angel of Death. Or that maybe it was Azazel, the evil spirit in the wilderness to whom a scapegoat was sent on the Day of Atonement---but it turned out to be neither of them. The ambiguous creature carried the fallen angel to Earth's realm and together they began plotting against mankind by creating mighty empires and empowering false prophets with the authority to rule them. The evil hearted rulers intentionally began to wage war against their enemies in the name of God. Many propaganda campaigns were launched to further divide the people but none as successful as that involving the infamous "Protocols of the Learned Elders of Zion", a widely distributed false doctrine vilifying Jews and endorsed by Adolf Hitler himself. It was an effective means of spreading heresy and lies that ultimately led to the deaths of many Innocent people. Similarly, throughout the course of history, false prophets have used the Holy Scriptures for their own selfish interests such as enslaving and controlling the minds of "true believers" who never question the Word of God.

But as more and more translations of the Bible were written, the greater the conflicts of religion became. For the most part, people were afraid to speak out against some of the ambiguous interpretations of the Bible in fear of being accused of blasphemy and put to death without a trial.

All throughout the vision the ambiguous spirit travelled back and forth between realms as though it was searching for something. Finally, after many cycles, the mysterious phantom reappeared holding a fiery scepter that had a huge dagger at one end and at the other was a ram's head made of pure crystal. The scepter was used to possess the minds of influential people, particularly those who were the rulers of kingdoms, empires, and powerful nations.

In the vision, the entity's most triumphant moment came when it possessed the mind of a conniving Scottish ruler named King James VI (who was also known as King James I). It just so happened that King James was the cousin of the most powerful woman in the world at the time, the Queen of England, Queen Elizabeth I. Immediately following Queen Elizabeth's death in 1603, King James inherited the throne of England and was catapulted into the highest seat of power in the land.

During the course of the 16th century, England went back and forth, going from one reign to the next between Protestant and anti-Protestant régimes. Because of this, England wound up with two competing versions of the Holy Scriptures. One was the Geneva Bible that had been published in 1560 by a small group of Scots and English Calvinists in Geneva. King James loved the book for its wisdom but disliked its anti-royal sentiment. It was for that same reason the Elizabethan church took it upon itself to produce another version of the Gospel called the Bishop's Bible, which had been quickly translated by 12 of the Queen's bishops in 1568. People had little use for the Bishop's Bible because of its aristocratic tone---there was actually a picture of Queen Elizabeth herself on the title page of the book. Most people regarded the Bishop's Bible as an ecclesiastical showpiece and nothing more.

Faced with this dilemma, King James decided to publish his own version of the Bible. He summoned together 54 scholars from around the world. Men like Lancelot Andrews, dean of Westminster, an expert in the ancient languages. He also recruited John Layfield, a soldier who fought the Spanish in Puerto Rico. And there was also a gentleman by the name of Hadrian a Saravia, who was half-Flemish, half-Spanish. George Abbot, author of a bestselling guide to the world was part of the group as well. King James's entourage also included several Arab scholars and expert mathematicians like William Bedwell and Henry Savile. But the most controversial member of the group was a man named Richard "Dutch" Thompson---a brilliant specialist in Latin but had a reputation of being a drunkard.

By the year 1611, the King James Version of the Bible was published. King James had successfully created a masterful compilation of all the earlier translations of the Holy Bible. The words were chosen in such a way that even those who weren't followers of Christ Jesus could not turn away from the book's universal wisdom. In fact, even Rastafarians chant psalms from the King James Bible every morning on Bobo Hill outside Kingston, Jamaica, facing east into the rising sun.

As I came out of the spell, the vision quickly faded away and I saw Sapian standing next to me with his sharp claws planted firmly atop the King James Bible, the last book in the series of bibles on display inside the grand cathedral.

"So you see, D'Shawn, everything that you were told about the prophecy, and even your God, was a lie. A magnificent gambit purposely created for the sole purpose of enslaving not only the minds of men but your souls as well," boasted the red dragon as he turned and greeted me with an evil grin. Sapian was ready to reveal his secret, the one he has kept quiet about since the beginning of time.

"D'Shawn, the entity you saw in the vision who rescued the fallen angel from Michael's sword is standing right before you...," Sapian said with a twinkle in his eye, "It was me! I am him! The Master of Deceit! The Lord of the Flies! I am---ABSOLU-TION!"

While basking in his own glory, Sapian continued praising his underhanded deeds.

"It was I who possessed the mind of that conniving bastard whose name appears on the cover of the very book that I'm holding right here. I alone am responsible for the annihilation of countless civilizations through the use of my ambiguously written dogmas which have spawned deadly conflicts such as the Holy War and other prolific religious battles throughout history. And now I have used you to bring the mer-people to Abyssinia so that I can destroy their wretched race once and for all!"

The red dragon suddenly ripped the King James Bible in half setting ablaze both the Old Testament and New Testament with his fiery breath. The devil reveled in his apparent victory over mankind and the mer-people whom he so vehemently despised.

Standing next to the giant reflecting pool at the center of the cathedral, the dragon performed his grand finale.

"Come now great savior of the mer-people, cast your eyes upon the water and behold the power of a real god!" I peered into the reflecting pool and I saw the Kingdom of Abyssinia and all the mer-warriors who had been under my command. King Claudius was preparing them for an all-out assault just like I instructed him to. But neither he nor the warriors had any idea what was waiting for them inside the illusion that was once Abyssinia. The dragon had arranged an ambush that was set to start the moment they entered the ghostly kingdom. A virtual death-trap with no way out.

Damn.

"Theolonius D'Shawn Atlanticus," the dragon roared. "Now you will bear witness to the end of all things!"

As millions of mer-warriors entered the ghostly kingdom they came face-to-face with hordes of hideous monsters, many of whom were the same creatures that I had dispatched during the attack on Anog. Sapian had resurrected an army of zombies and staged an ambush of biblical proportions. Wave after wave of Wutu, Kaxapix, Nehru, and Kurnool descended upon the disoriented mer-warriors like the torrential rains of the Serengeti. I watched as the slaughter unfolded in living color on the glassy surface of the reflecting pool.

"You coward!" I yelled at the dragon. "Why did you use black magic to bring back the hordes? How can the mer-people defend themselves against a suicide squad of misfits that you've conjured up from the grave with your sorcery and witchcraft bullshit?!"

"You shouldn't worry about them, D'Shawn," said the dragon. "What you should really be worried about is what's going to happen once this is done."

"What's that supposed to mean?" I asked.

"It means that once I've annihilated all living things, it'll be just you and me for eternity... imagine the fun we will have. Ha-ha-ha-ha!"

Meanwhile, back at La Inagua, Azoria was conferring with her mother about the situation at hand.

"Mama, I will go and find D'Shawn before it is too late," said the princess with obvious desperation in her voice.

"No, my child, it's much too dangerous! We have to remain here in La Inagua until we receive word from your father that the coast is clear. He has commanded us not to go near the illusion and we will obey him."

"But Mama, our armies are being wiped out! Where could he have gone?"

By noon the next day, the armies of mer-warriors nearly had been vanquished from existence. It appeared that in the darkest hour evil would prevail. Azoria lay sobbing on the ocean floor while her mother Zenobia tried her best to comfort her.

"Now, now my darling, you mustn't cry. We will find refuge elsewhere and live to fight another day. Come now, we must flee this place, for our enemies will soon be upon us if we stay." Queen Zenobia was trying to protect her daughter from the ferocious monsters that were headed their way. But it was too late... S-S-SWUUTHH! S-S-SWUUTHH! S-S-SWUUTHH!

Three razor sharp harpoons hurled by members of the Kurnool struck the Queen and sent her body crashing to the ocean floor.

"Mama, Noooo!" screamed Azoria. "Please get up! Don't you dare leave me here alone!" Queen Zenobia, even after being mortally wounded, maintained her poise and remained the majestic, loving parent that Azoria had always known.

"My dear sweet Azoria," said Zenobia to the weeping princess. "This is truly our darkest hour, so you must be brave now more than ever. My spirit will always guide you, my love. Keep the faith and never forsake what your heart tells you, because true wisdom comes from within---there will be things you won't be able to see with your eyes but trust your heart and it will give you sight where none exists. Farewell, my love." And just like that, she was gone.

Azoria held her mother in her arms one last time before letting loose a primordial scream like the mothers who cried out in the Calliope. Then, as if her soul had been set ablaze, the mermaid princess felt a burning anger raging within her.

"My world will not end this way!" Azoria roared. "Do you hear me dragon?! Vengeance shall be mine!"

"Your little princess has a fiery temper," said the red dragon while peering into the reflecting pool. "I see now why you are so blinded by her spirited charm."

"Leave Azoria out of this, Sapian! This is between you and me!"

"Foolish boy!" The dragon roared. "There is no 'you and me'! You're nothing to me, nothing at all!"

I lowered my head as if the dragon's words had caused me great distress. Sapian noticed it right away and saw it as a sign of weakness, so he decided to further ridicule me with his wicked banter.

"Now who would've thought that a mermaid princess would share her precious Quintess with the likes of you? A fool from the 'gutta' who now believes that he's a savior from an ancient prophecy sent to rescue the mer-people from tyranny. You're fucking ridiculous, that's what you are."

"Kiss my ass, lizard!"

"Oh! I'm much more than that, D'Shawn," said the wicked leviathan. "If you wasn't so damn naive you'd know that I am called by many names in many worlds. Perhaps you'll feel more at home if I were to tell you my name in your world."

"The only name that I have for you is Lizard 'est Mour!" I forced the words from my mouth making sure to clothe them in the vilest tone I could muster.

"Come closer!" The dragon demanded. "I have something to tell you."

Sapian leaned in close to me and said, "In your world... I am called Lucifer!"

"LIAR!" I shouted at the dragon startling him. "Now you have sealed your doom, stupid lizard."

I started chanting the same words that had been spoken by the witch in the bookstore. I had memorized the symbols that appeared above the dragon's head while the witch cast her spell, and now I was using them to open the portal to the Netherworld. Unbeknownst to the dragon, I was secretly given a replica of the Key of Adwah by the Great Elder Romulus. The wise old king handed it to me as he lay dying in my arms, and he said to me:

"This key opens many doors, and you must guard it with your very life. It belonged to a sea goddess named Willeaux (Willow) but was stolen by dark elves and used for nefarious purposes. Willeaux named the Key of Adwah after her daughter, Adwahlena. In their native language the word adwah

means to 'emit love', but when read or written backward, the definition then says to 'evol(ve) time', which is precisely why the dark elves stole the key. They aligned the encryptions in reverse and were able to manipulate time by travelling through portals to reach alternate realms throughout the universe where they gathered weapons, technology, medicines, gold, and other riches before disappearing back into the vortexes that had been opened with magic spells conjured by the symbols in the Key of Adwah. You must find the oracle; only then will you see what the future truly holds."

The reason I made fun of the Great Elder Romulus was so that the dragon wouldn't grow suspicious and discover my plan. I had memorized the symbols in the vision showed to me by the oracle, and then used the Key of Adwah to decipher the spell invoked by the witch when she opened the portal in the bookstore. She had arranged the symbols in the following order:

"Adwah! Adwah! Adwah!" I shouted after reciting the spell. The words burst from my throat and revealed an enigmatic power capable of opening doors to other worlds. And just like the Great Elder Romulus had predicted, there came another.

"Someone has entered my realm!" Sapian cried, "But how?! No one has the power to do such a thing! It's impossible!"

Entering the Netherworld and standing taller than Sapian himself, was Princess Azoria. She brought with her all the armies of mer-warriors that were under my command and not a single soul had been lost. Also with Azoria was her father, the King. And standing next to him looking as stunning as ever was his beautiful wife, Queen Zenobia.

"What is this?! Something's not right!" Sapian said while looking befuddled and distraught. "I saw all of you in the reflecting pool, and I watched you die!"

"What you saw, stupid lizard, was an illusion," said Azoria. "One that was created by a very powerful god who is more cunning than you could ever imagine... and he's standing right behind you." Sapian looked over his shoulder at me and noticed that I was once again smiling like an amphibious Cheshire cat.

"No! No! No! This is all wrong!" The dragon bemoaned while trying to make sense of what had just happened. He soon realized that it was because of the "second resurrection" where I shared my Quintess with Azoria that she too became godlike. It had been foretold by the Great Elder Romulus when he said, "Do not surrender! For in the darkest hour there will come another!" The wise old wizard was referring to Azoria, but the dragon missed it.

My plan was made long before reaching Abyssinia. I knew that Sapian was watching---and listening to---everything that was going on, so as part of the plan, I voluntarily entered the Netherworld to be a decoy while Azoria and the mer-warriors secretly wiped out Sapian's army of zombies waiting inside the haunted kingdom.

"My lord, it is time to finish it!" shouted Azoria with her fist raised high above her head in a display of solidarity and pride. "Fulfill your destiny! Let it be done!"

Crever pour lizard! (Death to the lizard!)

✦ 164 ✦

"In that day the Lord will punish Leviathan... the twisted serpent; And He will kill the dragon who lives in the sea."
        ---Isaiah 27:1

CHAPTER 16

FEAST OF GENESIS

Azoria and I, along with millions of mer-warriors, converged and attacked the red dragon like sharks in a feeding frenzy. Sapian tried to retaliate by spewing plumes of purple haze from his nostrils hoping it would allow him to slip away undetected. But when that didn't work, the dragon divided himself into hordes of biblical monsters and I began to recall some eerie similarities between the events that led me here and what is written in the ninth chapter of Revelation:

...a star had fallen from the sky to the earth (a reference that Azoria had made toward me), the star was given a key (the Key of Adwah) to the tunnel leading to the Abyss (Abyssinia). When the star opened the Abyss smoke rose up like smoke from a huge furnace (Sapian's hellfire). Out of the smoke came locusts... they were given power like the power of scorpions... the locusts looked like horses ready for battle... their faces looked like human faces. Their hair was like woman's hair. Their teeth were like lion's teeth (the mer-warriors).

It was obvious the dragon knew what was written in the prophecy and the Bible because what the beast did next came straight from the thirteenth chapter of Revelation:

I saw a beast coming out of the sea. He had ten horns and seven heads... the beast I saw looked like a leopard. But he had feet like a bear and a mouth like a lion. The dragon gave the beast his power.

There could be no mistaking that a war was about to begin. Monsters galore sprung from Sapian's body and began an all-out attack. The moment the first bodies collided, and weapons were swung, an explosion of blood spilled into the ocean and ignited rage on both sides of the war. Not only were the mer-warriors using swords on their enemies, they were also attacking them using their fangs and razor sharp claws slashing the enemies' throats and ripping off their heads.

Sapian's army used brutal tactics as well. Wounded mer-warriors would become food for the demon horde, eaten alive by nameless creatures with an appetite for flesh. As if that weren't enough, the dragon attempted to cast a spell using black magic---a kind of witchcraft that was forbidden in many realms---to beef up the hordes and immobilize the mer-warriors. But in his weakened condition of being divided into so many monsters, the spell backfired. Instead of destroying the mer-warriors the spell made them invisible, and that's when the real bloodbath began.

The invisible armies of mer-warriors started savagely making their way toward victory against the devil and his minions. In desperation, the dragon summoned the remaining monsters back into his body hoping to restore his strength, and that's precisely when Azoria and I launched our assault. We latched onto the dragon like two ferocious lions, leaving Sapian with no place to run. Everything was going exactly how I planned it, and now, Sapian was right where I wanted him.

"Not too bad for a guy from the 'gutta', huh lizard?" I teased the befuddled Sapian. "Haven't you ever heard that you can't judge a book by the cover?"

Azoria and I pinned the dragon down so that the wizards could come in and work their magic. They all came together---one from each of the 426 kingdoms---and joined hands while forming a gigantic circle around the dragon. Sapian's reptilian eyes watched the wizards closely, he had no idea what was in store for him. But one thing was certain---the dragon was afraid.

Dressed in colorful African dashikis representing their respective kingdoms, the wizards prepared to perform a ritual that had never been tried before. Never in history had so many of them gathered for a common cause. The miraculous feat they were about to attempt would call for them defy the laws of magic and of nature, and even cost many of the wizards their lives. But it was a sacrifice they were willing to make for the sake of their people.

With hands joined and their magic united, the mystic augurs brought forth a phenomenal force more powerful than a trillion supernovas combined. The Great Elders referred to it as God-swind, the strongest magic force in the universe. No human was ever supposed to witness its power---I would be the first.

"Sapian, you are now bound by powers beyond your knowledge, and you will suffer greatly because of what you've done." I said in a loud and thunderous voice that shook the Netherworld like never before. "Because of the insufferable cruelty you've deliberately inflicted upon countless generations of living beings, I have arranged for you a special surprise."

On my command the wizards began chanting and swaying until all at once they were driven into a deep trance. The dragon stared as the augurs' metaphysical essence transcended their bodies like ghosts in the darkness. The spirit-beings that emerged from the entranced wizards bounded the dragon in heavy chains and locked them with a magic seal that could not be broken for a thousand years. Then they took hold of the dragon and prepared to cast him into Godswind, which led straight down into the fiery Abyss. But before his banishment could be executed, Sapian turned to me and cried out, "There can be no good without evil, nor love without hate. I am only the conduit through which chaos is assimilated. Without me, and without it, your existence has no meaning. So why then am I being punished for causing mayhem and suffering, the very thing that your God sent me here to do?"

The red dragon then looked up toward heaven and spoke in a language that sounded like an ancient form of Italian saying, "Ordina questo amore o tu che m'ami! (O thou who lovest me, set this love in order!)" The spirit-beings cast the red dragon into Godswind banishing him for a thousand years and ending the war in victory.

"You did it, D'Shawn! You defeated the red dragon!" shouted Azoria as she and the mer-warriors gathered around and started chanting my name. There was a tremendous light that shined throughout the ocean and the world. Every living creature could see and feel its warmth and somehow knew that the world had changed for the better. The prophecy was now fulfilled.

As if by magic, the illusion that was once Abyssinia slowly began to fade, and in its place appeared a new kingdom---the Kingdom of Atlantica.

"Oh my god! Look how beautiful it is!" said Azoria as she witnessed the birth of an absolute paradise beneath the sea.

The immaculate kingdom reminded me of Disneyland, except it was a million times more splendid and was filled with real magic. Atlantica stretched in every direction for as far as the eye could see, and there were no words to describe the amazing things inside.

"Azoria, are you seeing what I'm seeing?" I asked the princess. "Can something actually be this beautiful?" Though the kingdom was underwater, there was a clear blue sky above it filled with colorful ribbons carrying pure sunshine to every corner of Atlantica. The pulsating beams of light changed from blue to yellow to green to orange to red to fuchsia and then back to blue before starting all over again.

"My love," said Azoria. "You have delivered us to the Promised Land just as the prophecy said you would. And now all may bask in the glory of heaven on earth."

The armies of mer-warriors began returning back through the portal and seeing for themselves what had become of the illusion. Yes, the prophecy was fulfilled. And a magnificent celebration began that lasted six days and seven nights. On the seventh night King Claudius hosted a royal banquet in honor of the heroic actions taken to save all life on earth. Before sitting down to feast on the delicious food in front of us, the King asked me to say a few words to those who had gathered for this stupendous occasion:

"To the citizens of this brave new world I say to you, there will be no ruler over Atlantica. Everyone is welcome. Atlantica belongs to all, and to all shall it serve without prejudice or scorn. Never again shall the threat of annihilation, tyranny, or oppression befall any citizen of this great kingdom. And never again shall any of you be forced to live in fear of the red dragon's treachery and deceit. Azoria and I shall serve as guardians of Atlantica, assuring that everyone remains safe within these hallowed walls. So let us now make a toast to this glorious day and give thanks to God Almighty." I said to the millions of mer-people who were now gathered around me. "I want you all to know there is only one true God and His name is Jesus Christ, our Lord. We shall worship Him with all our heart, and with all our mind, and our soul forever and ever! Amen."

"A toast then!" shouted Azoria as she raised a golden chalice laced with red rubies, sparkling diamonds, and bearing a 'Genesis' crest that symbolized a new beginning. "A toast to our Lord and Savior Jesus Christ!"

There was joy throughout the kingdom and everyone could sense that something exciting was on the horizon. Atlantica not only gave them hope for the future, it brought them closure for the suffering they had endured to get here. The banquet that night was very special because it commemorated a new beginning for us all. We named it, in fact, The Feast of Genesis.

"And I saw an angel coming down out of heaven, having the key to the Abyss and holding a great chain. He seized the dragon, that ancient serpent, who is the devil, ...and locked and sealed it over him, to keep him from deceiving the nations anymore until the thousand years were ended. After that he must be set free for a short time."

---Revelation 20:1-3

CHAPTER 17

KINGDOM COME

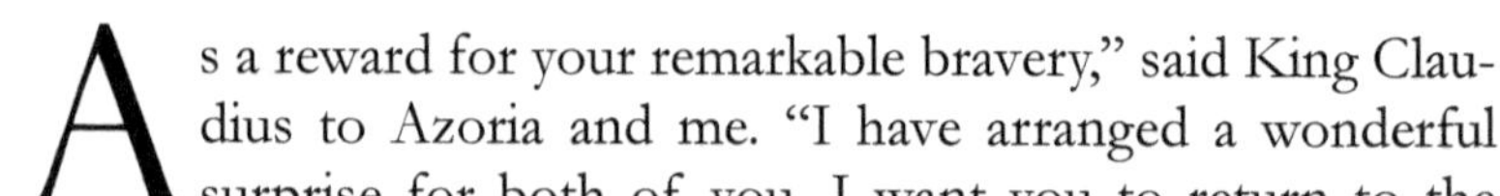

A s a reward for your remarkable bravery," said King Claudius to Azoria and me. "I have arranged a wonderful surprise for both of you. I want you to return to the Galactic Island and---" '

'Excuse me, Your Highness," I interrupted. "There's something I need to tell you about the island."

"You mean about your wrath upon the Lycan?" said King Claudius while his eyes glared at me from beneath his furrowed brow. "I'm quite aware of the desolation you caused while avenging my daughter's unfortunate brush with death. But we'll discuss that at a later time, right now I want you to do as I've asked and return to the Galactic Island at once." Without any further adieu, Azoria and I set out toward the island at her father's request. Neither of us knew what to expect nor had a clue as to why the King was so adamant about us going there. But little did we know, King Claudius had instructed the remaining wizards who survived Godswind to travel ahead of us and restore the island to its original splendor. The wizards used the last of their magic to transform what was once a bloody battlefield into a tropical paradise unlike any on earth. It had plush green forests full of all kinds of exotic birds: peacocks, macaws, crested cockatoos, large-billed toucans, and tall flamingos with rosy-white plumage, scarlet wing covets and shiny black quills. Twenty-five stunning waterfalls now lined the interior of the island, they met at the base of a magnificent mountain where the shimmering falls spilled into a crystal-clear lake the size of Yellowstone. Sitting atop the lake's glassy surface, majestic swans gathered together in small groups like families on a picnic after Sunday morning service at church. They cuddled one another while playing in the cool summer breeze blowing briskly across the lake. The thoughtful wizards even replaced the thundering volcanoes with a spectacular view of the ocean that could be seen through a series of enclaves carefully carved in the hills west of the bay. On the island's northern coast the wizards placed high mountains that seemed to grow even taller with each passing cloud that scrapped its peak. Some were so tall that snow caps formed on top of them. And whenever the sunlight shined on the glistening ice caps, it caused the mountaintops to sparkle brightly against the dark blue morning sky---a sight that was absolutely breathtaking.

"D'Shawn, how is this possible?" said Azoria while staring at paradise in front of us. "Wow! This is truly amazing!"

"Your father really out did himself with this one." I said to Azoria, "Some daughters get a car or maybe even a pony, but your dad gave you a whole damn island!"

"Yes, I know!" said Azoria. "So what are we waiting for? Last one to the beach is a rotten egg." We went racing toward the island like a couple of newlyweds on vacation, splashing water in each other's face and wrestling until we were both out of breath. When we finally reached the island Azoria initiated a coquettish game of hide-and-seek, she told me to count backwards from a hundred and then she darted into the forest to hide.

"...5, 4, 3, 2, 1! Ready or not, here I come!" I shouted out loud so that Azoria would know the hunt was on. I first searched for Azoria in all the obvious places: behind the bushes along the beach, in the tall grass leading into the woods, inside the caves nearby. But I couldn't find her anywhere. "Come out, Azoria!" I shouted, "You win! I give up!"

Several minutes went by and still no sign of her. I could feel panic starting to build up inside of me as thoughts of Azoria being in trouble flooded my mind. I immediately started combing the island from top to bottom, searching anywhere and everywhere, leaving no stone unturned. And as I approached the clearing where she and I first met, there she stood once more with her body dripping wet and wearing nothing but a smile. It was like déjà vu, she looked absolutely gorgeous with her hair twisted into micro-braids and decorated with little white seashells. A bright yellow jasmine had been carefully placed behind her right ear, and just below her neck hung a beautiful lei made of red, white, and pink rose petals.

"You look very sexy standing there, Azoria." I said while observing her immaculate booty---I mean, beauty. "You had me worried there for a minute. I was beginning to think that you were in trouble and needed my help, I'm glad to see that you're okay."

Azoria smiled at me and then licked her lips like one of those temptress broads in the movies. I can't lie, she was really turning me on in a major way, and she knew it too.

"C'mon princess, don't do me like that. Don't get me all worked up for nothing, ya heard me." Azoria beckoned me to join her, and I wasted no time making my way over to where she was standing. Once there, I stared into her eyes, and for the first time she stared back into mine. Azoria then noticed that the color of my eyes was a unique blend of chestnut brown mixed with hazel, she only saw it when the sunlight came shining down through the trees and washed over my caramel-colored face. The hazel in my brown eyes captivated her to the point where she could hardly breathe. The more she stared at me the more enchanted she became, and the more passionate. I was surprised when Azoria asked me to undress and then pressed her naked body next to mine.

"You sure you're ready for this?" I said while gently caressing her big round butt and nibbling on her earlobes. I had already discovered her erogenous zones and was making her tingle with excitement like never before. She started slowly rubbing her fingers through the wave patterns in my hair thinking to herself that she's never been with a guy like me---except in her wildest dreams.

The young sea goddess was anxious to explore her sexuality and experience love from a human perspective. After all, she was out of her father's house---the ocean---and was on her own for the first time in her life. All she wanted now was to share her newfound freedom with the man she loved. "D'Shawn, now that we're alone, there's something I want to ask you?" said the gorgeous princess. "Do you remember what you told me would happen the next time I got caught without my tail?"

"Yes, as a matter of fact I do." I replied.

"Well, did you mean it?"

Azoria was referring to the comment I made after she chopped on me for not understanding how telepathy worked. I told her the next time I caught her without her tail, meaning in human form, I'd show her who was more gullible when it came to sex. Then I telepathically projected pornographic images into her mind that were so explicit she started cussing and screaming and couldn't stop blushing.

"Of course I meant it, at the time. But why are you bringing it up now?" The look that Azoria gave me when I asked her that question confirmed what I had suspected all along. I had always sensed that there was something very powerful between us that felt primordial in nature. A strong animal magnetism that could not be explained but was definitely real. Somehow I knew that we were destined to be together from the moment I saw her, and there was nothing that either of us could do but follow our hearts and let the magic unfurl.

"Come closer, my love," said Azoria. "I have a surprise for you, but first you must close your eyes." I did as she requested, and the next thing I knew I was lying on my back blindfolded with a piece of garment that had been torn from Azoria's outfit. The blindfold was secure but not too tight, and I assured her that I couldn't see a thing with it on. She told me to relax, and then she gently placed my head on a soft bed of roses and began running her fingers through the hair on my chest. I began to notice the sweet scent of jasmine coming from the exotic flower in Azoria's hair, but I also detected another scent which added mystery to the plot as I tried to figure out what was happening on the other side of my blindfold.

"Hey Azoria, what's up with the coconuts?" I said with a smile, letting her know that I was at least aware of that.

"Hush, fool. I'm about to make all your dreams come true. So don't ruin it by talking."

Nuff said.

I decided to shut up and enjoy the magical evening with no questions asked. I laid back while Azoria slowly ran her hands down my chest toward my genitals and began pouring warm coconut oil on my testicles and my penis. Before long, my entire body, and hers, was covered in scented coconut oil just like in the fantasy I had when I first laid eyes on her in the forest. That night I learned that coconut oil is an amazing aphrodisiac. Apparently Azoria knew more than I had given her credit for. After the exhilarating coconut bath, Azoria climbed on top of me and started grinding her soft, moist vagina against my throbbing hard penis as if to gauge how well endowed I was.

"Impressive," I heard her say. "I'm really going to enjoy this." I could see right away that I was in for a helluva night. This broad was the epitome of a love goddess, she had the attributes to seduce any man she wanted: gorgeous skin, a sultry voice, pretty white teeth, voluptuous breasts, luscious lips, thick thighs with a small waist, and the kind of ass that could turn a grown man into a crybaby.

While Azoria and me lay naked in the forest next to a beautiful lake surrounded by cascading waterfalls and majestic mountains, exotic birds serenaded us with their love songs, creating a romantic atmosphere unlike any other place on earth. It reminded me of that scene in "Jason's Lyric" where the two main characters---Jason and Lyric---made love while lying next to a sleepy bayou in a field of beautiful flowers. The mood was set, the night was young, and we was just getting started. I gently placed my hands on the smooth indentations of Azoria's tiny waist and guided her body slightly to the left so that my fully erect penis could slide deep inside her sugary walls and ignite her soul.

"Oh, my god!" screamed Azoria as my anaconda hit its mark. "D'Shawn, that feels so amazing! Don't stop!"I instinctively moved my hands toward her plump, sexy brown ass and started squeezing it, positioning her body once again in the right spot so that with each stroke she could feel the friction of my enormous cock rubbing against her clit driving her wild. I was hitting it so good that she didn't even notice that my blindfold had come off.

"Oh! Oh! Oh! Oh!" was all I heard. And then suddenly she shouted, "Oh, my god! I'm cummiiiiiiiing!"

I lifted Azoria's head so that her golden braids lay across my face, and that's when she looked into my eyes and completely surrendered herself to me---mind, body, and soul.She unfolded like a flower in bloom and gave herself completely to the one man who knew her body better than she. It was as though we had been joined as one, but not by a Quintess---this was something very different. We made love all through the night until the sun came up the next morning, and when we were finally done, Azoria lay atop me with her body covered in glistening beads of sweat, still quivering from having multiple orgasms and trying to catch her breath. We kissed, we talked, we laughed. I will never forget that special night or the sweet taste of Azoria's tongue inside my mouth---pure ambrosia.

As we lay side-by-side on the beach reminiscing about the night before, Azoria and I realized that our little love-making marathon officially consummated our union, leaving the ocean's gentle lullaby to sweep us into a blissful, magical, incredible sleep.

✦ 178 ✦

"All that Adam had, all that Caesar could, you have and can do... Build, therefore, your own world"
    ---Ralph Waldo Emerson

CHAPTER 18

PIRATES' REPRIEVE

Azoria and I awoke the next day feeling relaxed and in love, we cuddled one another while bathing in the soothing warmth of the morning sun, and later went skinny dipping out in the ocean and hunting for clams. "I'm having the best time ever, my love," said the glowing princess. "I've never been so happy in my entire life." I stood behind her gently kissing the nape of her neck while coddling her supple breasts with my hands.

Azoria struggled to contol herself, she felt a rush of burning desire coursing through her body and making her so, so wet. "D'Shawn, you're getting me all worked again, and I don't have the energy for another rodeo like the one we had last night. I don't know what got into you, but you really wore me out down there."

In light of the challenge we had going, I was determined to make a lasting impression on Azoria so there'd be no question as to who was more gullible when it came to the sex game. And now she had basically admitted that I was the truth in bed---Mission Accomplished. I immediately started talking shit.

"I beat the stuffin' out that muffin' last night, I'm the last of a dying breed---you ain't know?!"

"Boy, please!" Azoria snapped back with a heavy New Orleans drawl saying, "I gave yo' ass a lil' taste of this hot Creole pooh-nanny and you went straight to sleep like itty-bitty baby. You don't remember that?"

"No, I don't remember that at all." I shamefully admitted.

"That's because you was fast asleep, pimp." Azoria's slick tone and bossy swag left no doubt that she had won the challenge. And that's when she hit me with a hot track of her own. "I'm like Rick Ross, ya heard me. I got that A-1 portico!" said Azoria, still bragging about winning the challenge. Then with plenty of vibrato in her voice she hit me with Rick Ross's one word catch phrase... HUMPH!

Azoria's one jazzy broad.

I may have lost the contest but that didn't stop me from gettin' my groove on last night during foreplay. My rendition of Marvin Gaye's "Sexual Healing" really turned Azoria on and she kept complimenting me on my singing.

"That's quite a voice you have, D'Shawn. Where did you learn to sing like that?" she asked me.

"Baby, music is the soul of New Orleans. I was listening to jazz while still in my mama's womb waiting to jump out and start dancing in a second line."

"D'Shawn, I really love the way you talk about New Orleans, it must be a wonderful kingdom." said Azoria. "I hope to visit it some day, it sounds like a very romantic place."

I laughed at the thought of New Orleans being a real kingdom, I couldn't even picture the Calliope in that context.

"Hey, are you planning to meet with my father today?" asked Azoria.

"No, I wasn't planning to. But I guess it wouldn't be a bad idea to see how things are going in Atlantica."

"He really likes you, you know."

"Yeah well, I like him too. I think he's pretty cool, for a king and all."

"Oh, you're just saying that because you're screwing his daughter."

"Hey! That's not true, Azoria. I would have screwed you even if I didn't like your father. Wait! That didn't come out right, I meant to say that I---"

"Just shut up, D'Shawn," said Azoria with an attitude. "Hurry up and get dressed so we can have breakfast with my parents in Atlantica. You're such an asshole." I'm a guy, and like most guys, I used to wonder why people would always say that women are from Venus and men are from Mars, but now I'm starting get it. I made one little remark and boom!, Azoria started trippin' and shit. But luckily, like Sade said, I'm a smooth operator.

"Okay Azoria, I'll get dressed so we can join your folks for breakfast, no problem sweetheart. I'll even whip up one of my famous omelets for the occasion." Man, I was so smooth that she didn't even have a chance to come up with a sarcastic rebuttal.

Damn! Spoke too soon.

"Let's not forget what happened the last time you made an omelet, mushroom boy," said Azoria with a huge smirk on her face. "I don't think my parents would fancy running up and down the beach naked while singing Christmas carols, do you?"

Smart-ass.

"What'd you say?!"

"Oh!, nothing." I replied.

"You're this close from getting that ass whipped, ya heard me." Azoria said while demonstrating the distance by holding up two fingers less than an inch apart, and still talking like she was from New Orleans.

"Yeah right, whatever." I said to myself. "Just hurry up." While she was getting dressed, a peculiar thought came to mind, one that raised a serious question.

"Hey Azoria, if the Lycan' was the only creature on the island, then where did all the eggs come from that I used when making my omelets?"

"They came from the Ooplahs," she said in a nonchalant sort of way.

"What the hell are Ooplahs?" I asked.

"Ooplahs are mystic creatures that resemble giant sea turtles but have six heads and a long tail like an eel's. They sometimes nest on the island during mating season, especially when the seas are rough and the tides are too strong for most predators to follow them. They are excellent swimmers and can spend weeks underwater without coming up for air even once. The Lycan', however, had them at a disadvantage. It would watch the Ooplahs lay their eggs in the nests and then patiently wait for the hatchlings to be born so that it could eat them."

"Eat the hatchlings?!" I said in disbelief.

"Not just the hatchlings," Azoria explained. "It would eat their mothers as well. You see, once the eggs were ready to hatch, the mother turtles would always return to the island with food for their young and that's when the Lycan' would appear out of nowhere and devour them all. Pretty gruesome, huh?"

I solemnly stared at the ocean thinking what a horrible beast the Lycan' was. How could something created by magic be so cruel? It wasn't like the creature needed to eat the Ooplahs in order to survive, its sole reason for being on the island was to do its master's bidding, and I'm sure Sapian had no interest in killing baby sea turtles. So it's reasonable to believe that the Lycan' ate the Ooplahs purely for the hell of it, and nothing more.

"You know what? I'm glad I killed the bastard." I said to Azoria who then turned to me and replied, "Yeah, and so are the Ooplahs."

"Wait a minute! Speaking of the Ooplahs," I said as the thought suddenly occurred to me that none of it explained where the gigantic egg had come from that I used to make my omelet. "What about the 50 pound egg with the glossy pink shell I found? You know, the 'Volkswagen' egg?" I asked Azoria who stood there looking at me as if she had no idea what I was talking about.

"I've never known the Ooplahs to lay an egg such as that," said Azoria. "Are you sure you're not exaggerating?"

"Hell naw! That egg was big as a motherfuc---" And that's when it hit me. "Oh shit! I think I know what happened!" Come to think of it, I was still suffering the effects of those damn mushrooms when telling the story about the omelet. That explains how the details got so grossly distorted. There never was a giant egg. I imagined the whole thing.

Well, I'll be damned!

Azoria and I returned to Atlantica where we sat down to a nice breakfast served by Queen Zenobia. She had prepared a marvelous seaweed soufflé and buttered muffins along with one of Azoria's favorite appetizers: shrimp-flavored crepe suzettes.

"Now Mama, you know how much I love these little pancakes of yours. Once I start eating them I can't stop. What are you trying to do, make me fat?" Azoria joked.

"Well, you can see how much your father enjoys my cooking, he's getting more and more um... robust around the middle." said Zenobia while patting the King on his big round belly. Azoria and I chuckled at the sight.Meanwhile, high above Atlantica on the open seas there were explosions going off one after another resounding loudly in the deep.

"What's that noise?" I asked, but no one at table answered me. They all just sat there pretending like they didn't hear the explosions. "I know y'all heard that. So what gives?" Again I questioned the the noise overhead and again everyone played dumb.

"What noise are you talking about, D'Shawn?" said Azoria. "I didn't hear anything. What about you, Mama? Did you hear something?"

"No, not a thing." Lied Zenobia, "I have no idea what he's talking about. What noise?"

BOOM! BOOM! BOOM! BOOM! BOOM!

"That noise."

I quickly swam toward the surface like a speeding torpedo and soon emerged in the swell of a huge wave. Once the sea levelled out and gave way to a spectacular horizon, my eyes caught a glimpse of an unusual sight: a wooden ship carrying a howling crew of rowdy, swashbuckling pirates! *What the hell?!*

The sturdy little vessel was returning cannon fire at an armada of heavily armed British war ships that appeared to be chasing it. The pirate ship's blazing cannons were blowing holes the size of swimming pools in the hulls of the British ships and leaving long trails of smoldering debris on the surface of the water with no regard for the oceanic creatures below. Azoria's head soon broke the surface as she arrived on the scene and pulled up next to me. She was not at all surprised by what she saw. "They're all a bunch of barbarians!" she complained. "Every last one of them! We don't get a moment's peace whenever they come around."

I made no immediate comments because I was still reeling from the events that were unfolding before my eyes. But as soon as I was able to get a grip on myself, best believe I grilled the little mermaid by asking a slew of questions regarding the pirates

"Okay Azoria, explain to me how a ship full of pirates is sitting less than fifty feet from us with big frickin' cannons sticking out of it?" She purposely avoided making eye contact, which to me, meant she was trying to come up with something just to shut me up. But I already had my next question cocked and ready to go.

"Also, if I'm the only human in your world, then who are all those people on the ships?" I said, before suddenly remembering the sunken wreck that Azoria and me came across on our way to Anog. Then it dawned on me that the ships in front of us were old as hell.

"What's wrong, D'Shawn? Are you okay?" said Azoria as she could see the wheels inside my head turning.

"No, I'm not okay. Something is very fishy about this whole scenario and I plan to get to the bottom of it real soon."I had the look of someone who wasn't sure whether he was dreaming or awake. I was going to solve this mystery if it was the last thing I did.

"You said I came here from another world." I reminded Azoria. "Well, those ships don't look all that 'alien' to me."

"I didn't say that you were from another planet, D'Shawn, I only said that you were not of this world, my world."I looked at Azoria as if she was speaking a foreign language

"What does that mean?" I asked.

"It means exactly what I said." Azoria replied, "You're not from a different planet, silly. You're from different time."It suddenly dawned on me that the nearby ships were from the 18th century.

"Holy shit!" I shouted. "I've travelled back in time!" None of it made sense. In fact, I began to question everything at that point. "Wait a minute!" I said to Azoria. "Even if I have somehow managed to travel back in time, it doesn't explain why you're here. There weren't any mermaids back in the 18th century. Nor at any other time for that matter."

"How do you know that?" said Azoria

"I know because mermaids aren't real!" I said back to her.

"Well then, asshole, how do you explain the fact that you're having an argument with a mermaid at this very moment?!" Azoria said as she balled up her fists and got right in my face. "Another thing, if mermaids have never existed then how do you even know what a mermaid is?"

"Everyone knows what a mermaid is because we read about them in books."

"What kind of books?" Azoria asked.

"The kind filled with fairy tales and fantasies," I said with a softer tone now realizing I was a bit out of line with the comments I made.

"Well, did you read about any pirates in those books?"

"Yes, of course I have, Azoria. But pirates are real."

"So are mermaids," said the princess with a smile. "And if you don't believe me, maybe this'll help." The gorgeous sea nymph---and love of my life---kissed me so passionately that I forgot what we were even arguing about. When I opened my eyes I could see that the scene around me was spinning out of control: cannons blasting, pirates yelling, clouds of smoke swirling overhead.

"D'Shawn, my love," said Azoria with grave concern in her voice. "Listen to me closely, Sapian not only terrorized the citizens of my world, he also brought death and famine to the people of your world, particularly in regions considered to be holy land. The red dragon has always pitted tribe against tribe using divisive means to create civil unrest amongst the people. Sapian would use their differences of religion, race, color, creed, ethnic, and in some cases sexual identity to sow seeds of discord and then reap hatred that never ends. Tell me, D'Shawn, in the stories you've read about mermaids and pirates was there any mention of a giant serpent that plagued the seven seas?"

"Yes, such a monster was often mentioned, but like I said, the stories were just fairy tales."

"Well my love, even fairy tales have to begin somewhere."

The British armada ended their pursuit of the pirates and slowly disappeared into the horizon, leaving the badly damaged pirate ship and its crew of hooligans drifting toward the Galactic Island. The ship's heavy anchor plunged into the ocean near Bling Bling Lagoon scaring the fishes below and causing huge ripples to go rolling toward the beach. Moments later, Azoria and I watched as several small boats departed the main ship and headed for the shore. I thought to myself: "What if the jewels I found belong to the pirates?" Hmm, the plot thickens.

"Those murderous bastards are heading toward the island!" Azoria screamed, "We must stop them at once!"

"But they have as much right to go to the island as we do." I said out of guilt for having took the pirates' treasure. "They're probably just looking for something that belongs to them."Azoria didn't understand why I was suddenly taking up for the pirates, nor did she care.

"The Galactic Island is our home, D'Shawn. And those pirates are trespassing!" She took off with a vengeance. Azoria was convinced that the island was ours and the pirates had no business being there. The enraged mermaid torpedoed beneath the surface of the water like a killer whale on the hunt, and with one mighty blow from her magnificent tail she capsized the lead vessel and sent a dozen pirates sailing through the air screaming for their lives.

"Ahoy!" shouted a pirate from another boat. "Mermaid off the starboard bow!"

"Arrgh!" growled the leader of the pirates. "What are ye waitin' for? Kill the wretched sea witch at once!" On his command, a flurry of sharp harpoons rained down into the ocean near Azoria but it didn't phase her one bit. Mermaids are elusive creatures by nature, so she was able to easily dodge the harpoons while darting in and out of the water with the finesse of a sea lion. But the fun and games abruptly ended when the furious mermaid resurfaced just a few yards from the dinghy carrying the captain---and she was a sight to behold: her body glistening in the moonlight, her golden braids flowing in the ocean breeze, her fiery eyes glowing bright red with fury, her sharp fangs visible from a distance ready to rip flesh from bone. Azoria gave the pirates a deadly warning.

"Leave here at once! And never return!" she roared. "For if you don't, you will never leave at all!"

The captain---a short, chubby fellow who looked like a black Danny De Vito---pulled out a derringer from his oversized cummerbund and fired a single shot at Azoria's head. The fiery bullet missed her face by inches and when it entered the ocean it sounded like a red-hot poker being doused in cold water.

After missing with his derringer, the grimy looking captain hurled a ridiculously large harpoon at Azoria's chest. But before the weapon could hit its mark I reached up from beneath the surface of the water and grabbed the harpoon in mid flight, snapping it like a giant toothpick. The loud noise sounded like a utility pole being broken in half. The pirates had crossed the line and it was time for me to join Azoria and defend the sanctuary given to us by her father, King Claudius. Speaking of the King, this time when the metamorphosis took hold, it transformed me into a gigantic merman who bore a likeness to King Claudius himself, and was even holding a trident the size of a billboard. In the form of this giant ruler, I began rising up out of the sea like a mighty Titan, growing taller and taller until every single pirate had to look straight up in the sky to see my face.

"My name is D'Shawn, guardian of the island you see before you." I said to the pirates in a thunderous voice. "You're not welcome here and you must leave at once!" To everyone's surprise, especially his crew, the chubby captain jumped in a dinghy and boldly approached me with a request. "Ahoy there, matey!," said the smelly captain with a gap-toothed smile that showed his yellow teeth and black gums. "I be known as Azuru-Chi (uh-ZOO-roo-kye), the captain of ye yonder vessel the Black Scorpion. I'm sure you can see, good sir, that me ship's been damaged by them varmints who attacked me and me crew."

"I'm sure they had good reason." I said with obvious contempt in my voice.

"Well matey, the reason is neither here nor there. I only ask that me and me crew here be permitted to gather a few materials from ye fair island so as to repair me vessel. Afterwards, we'll gladly shove off and never again set hide nor hair on her precious shores. You have my word."

Pirate or not, I didn't trust Azuru-Chi, but due to the circumstances I decided to grant him and his crew a reprieve that would allow them a brief suspension of my demand for their immediate departure and give them time to fix their ship.

"Very well then, you and your men have until dawn tomorrow to gather what you need. Not a moment longer."

"Thank you, kind sir," said Azuru-Chi while mockingly bowing to me as if he were a loyal subject in the company of a king. "Ye be's a most gracious host, Great D'Shawn! Arrgh!"

Cheers rose up from his crew as they realized their lives would be spared, at least till dawn. But the captain was less than thrilled about the bargain that had been made. I could sense the deceit in him, and the way he cut his eyes at me was a sure sign that he was up to something. So I reminded him once again of our arrangement:

"Azuru-Chi, do not attempt to exceed the deadline you've been given to leave the island. Consider this your final warning." And with that, Azoria and I disappeared into the ocean like spirits in the wind.

While most of the pirate crew was out gathering supplies for the repairs, the captain and a few of his most trusted henchmen went on a treasure hunt that lasted throughout the night. Azuru-Chi was hoping to find the cache of jewels he buried the last time he was on the island. Little did he know, the jewels had already been discovered by yours truly.

"Arrgh! Where's me treasure?!' screamed Azuru-Chi. "It was right here and now it's gone!"The captain was right, his precious 'booty' had been thoroughly plundered and it was a well-known fact that pirates would rather die than have their treasure taken without a fight.

"That sea devil stole me treasure!" complained the captain. "And now he thinks him and his sea witch mate can run me off like a scalded dog! Arrgh! I'll cut off his head and feed it to the sharks! This means war!"

"Your rulers are rebels and companions of thieves; everyone loves a bribe and chases after rewards. They do not defend the orphan, nor does the widow's plea come before them. Therefore the Lord God of hosts, the Mighty One of Israel, declares, 'Ah, I will be relieved of My adversaries and avenge Myself on My foes.'"

---Isaiah 1: 23-24

CHAPTER 19

IN SEARCH OF CHLOEY

Azuru-Chi cussed up a storm as he rallied his fellow pirates and began preparing for war against those he blamed for his missing treasure. They drank rum and sung songs of war that only pirates knew, and Azuru-Chi led them in chanting the pirate's secret oath---an oath by which all pirates lived, fought, and died. The enraged captain was hellbent on repossessing his lost treasure trove. He and his henchmen returned to the ship and found that the repairs had been completed in record time. They set sail just before dawn, right on schedule. But that of course was not the end of it, not hardly.

Azoria and I watched from a distance as the Black Scorpion, tattered and bruised, crept slowly toward the horizon and the open sea. "Well that's the last we'll see of that bunch." I said with an optimistic tone.

"I seriously doubt that, my love," said Azoria. "Pirates are quite deceitful and will say and do anything to get what they want."

"But all they wanted was to get materials to repair their ship," I said as if defending my decision to allow them one night on the island. "And now that they've gone we won't have anymore trouble, right?" Azoria looked over at me and very nonchalantly said, "What have you heard about pirates, that they're honest, goodhearted people or just the opposite?" I knew exactly where Azoria was going with her line of questioning; she believed that my decision to give the pirates a reprieve was wrong. Still, I continued defending my position on the matter.

"For your information, Azoria, I've read books that not only spoke about bad pirates but good pirates as well. There was one particular pirate I read about who actually became a prestigious hero, his name was Jean Lafitte." I proudly boasted, "He was one of the most famous pirates to sail near New Orleans in the waters of Barataria Bay. Jean Lafitte warned the generals in New Orleans that the British were planning an attack, and even offered to fight for America."

Azoria folded her arms and stared at me as though she wasn't buying a word I said. She knew all too well about the dealings of pirates.

"You may be right, my love, but this Azuru-Chi character is certainly no Jean Lafitte. You can rest assured there's going to be trouble ahead, and plenty of it."While me and the princess returned to Atlantica and began preparing a doctrine with guidelines that would ensure harmony and peace throughout the kingdom, the despicable Azuru-Chi was busy organizing a plot for revenge. He sent out word to other ships' captains telling them to meet him at Cam Island, a secret stretch of land in the middle of nowhere and known only to the most dangerous, black-hearted pirates there was.

"Arrgh! I want him skinned alive!" Azuru-Chi shouted. "No one steals me treasure without a fight!"

"Skinned alive! Skinned alive! Squaaawwk!" screamed the big green parrot sitting on Azuru-Chi's shoulder named Ditto.

"Hush ya beak ye mangy pigeon before I pluck ya feathery hide and boil ya in hot squid oil!" chided the ornery pirate. And that's when Ditto started fumbling over the lyrics to "Old Town Road" by Lil Nas X:

"I got the horses in the back, horse stock is attached, hat's matte is black got the boot shields black to match. Ridin' on a horse, you can whip your Porsche, I been in the valley you ain't been up off that porch now---Can't nobody tell me noth-iiing, you can't tell me noth-iiing! Can't nobody tell me noth-iiing, you can't tell me noth-iiing! Squaaawwk!"

"Ditto! If you don't stop ye mindless gibbering, then it's off with ya head! Arrgh!"

Ditto was an unusual bird, to say the least. Azuru-Chi won him---or rather got stuck with him---after killing his previous owner for cheating in a game of "cutthroat". Rumor has it that Ditto was discovered long ago by a band of travelling Gypsies. They claimed to have found him inside a strange capsule full of artifacts from a time yet to come. The capsule was said to contain mystic items such as wristwatches and smartphones, and a pair of virtual reality goggles that came with a set of flying drones. There was also an extensive movie and music collection inside, which was where Ditto got his strange vocabulary from. The parrot was mimicking lyrics and lines from songs and movies of the twentieth and twenty-first centuries... "It's Friday. You ain't got no job. You ain't got shit to do! I'mma get you high today! Squaaawwk!"

Azuru-Chi and his crew sailed for the Isle of Cam, which most pirates referred to as Cam Island. It was home to a ferocious colony of fire-breathing dragons known as the Cammill. Legend has it that whosoever captures the leader of the colony will be granted a single wish. The legend has led many pirates to their deaths and many more will follow because the Cammill are the deadliest creatures in the world, especially after dark. The island's name, in fact, is an abbreviation for the word "camisado" which means "an attack by night". And the dragons have surely earned their moniker---death from above. Azuru-Chi planned to lure Azoria and me to Cam Island and pit us against the deadly

Cammill. Then, in the midst of battle, he would sneak back to the Galactic Island and reclaim his lost treasure. The conniving pirate put out a trolling net in order to capture a school of dolphins that were playfully following his ship. Once the dolphins were in the net, the evil captain left them trapped alongside the vessel so that their sporadic struggling would attract the attention of any nearby mer-people. A second net was made ready for the first brave soul who attempted to rescue the dolphins.

Less than a mile away, the little mermaid named Chloey was playing with her younger sister Jacie when she heard a noise from up above.

"Look Jacie!" shouted Chloey. "The poor dolphins are trapped, we have to help them."

"Chloey wait!" Jacie pleaded. "We should go get D'Shawn and Azoria, they'll know what to do."

"There isn't enough time. The pirates will be gone by then," said Chloey. "I'm going to follow the ship, just tell D'Shawn and Azoria to hurry." Jacie raced off to find help while Chloey stayed behind to comfort the frightened dolphins in the net.

"Everything's going to be alright little ones. Help is coming." whispered the little mermaid. "Shhh! The pirates will find me if you keep splash---"

Without warning, the second net hit the water and quickly closed around Chloey, trapping her inside a knotted and tangled prison. As the pirates started hauling in their catch, Chloey fought with all her tiny might to get free but couldn't, the net was just too strong. The more she struggled the more entangled she became, and now the struggle was over. "We got it Cap'n!" one of the pirates yelled. "It's a little one!"

"Arrgh! Let's get this show on the road!" Azuru-Chi yelled to his men. "It's time to catch a rat!" The pirates dragged Chloey aboard the ship and when they cut the net open, she tumbled out onto the deck with a loud thump. The men were laughing and dancing around in a circle taunting the little mermaid, some of them even spit foul smelling rum in her face and hair. Chloey cried out for her mother as the rum burned her eyes, she was all alone and in a world of trouble... it was a dark day in paradise and Chloey was getting her first taste of life above the ocean.Word of Chloey's abduction was quickly spreading throughout Atlantica, and when Azoria got the news she immediately informed me of the tragic events.

"D'Shawn, come quickly! Chloey's been taken!" said Azoria.

"Taken where? By who?" I asked.

"The pirates took her aboard their ship and we can't find them anywhere! It was the same bastards who were here just days ago. It was Azuru-Chi!"A burning anger began brewing inside of me along with an overwhelming sense of regret. I felt completely responsible for Chloey's abduction; in hindsight, I should've eliminated the pirates when I had the chance. Nevertheless, I would let nothing stop me from finding the pirates who did this and killing every last one of them. Legions upon legions of mer-warriors went in search of Chloey, leaping high into the air and calling her name before gravity forced them back into the rolling sea.

What an awesome sight to behold, this spectacle was unprecedented because these reclusive creatures rarely ventured to the surface, and now here they were in plain sight by the millions.

"Azuru-Chi, you and those who are with you will feel my wrath!" I roared loudly across the ocean so that all could hear my voice, especially the pirates whom I intended to slaughter. "None of you will escape Death, for she is my concubine---a treacherous harlot whose only pleasure is being in the company of those whom I despise. She is coming for you... and so am I."

And so began the metamorphosis.

Azoria stood silent, she hadn't heard me speak that way before and it terrified her to no end. There was a dark, ominous tone in my voice that frightened her, and for the first time ever---Azoria was really afraid of what I might do. And she had good reason to.

"Land ho! Cam Island straight ahead Cap'n!" shouted one of the pirates who was positioned high above the ship's deck in the crow's nest.

"Arrgh! Water the little shrimp. We don't want it stinking up the place, now do we men?" Azuru-Chi made fun of Chloey who sat inside a tiny net that was dangling from a rope tied to the captain's wheel.

"No sir Cap'n! We don't want that," joked one of the pirates as the rest were laughing and spinning the net around trying to make Chloey dizzy and sick. Someone from the mob of cutthroats doused the little mermaid in the face with a bucket of filthy, stale seawater causing her to once again cry out for her mother. "Mommy! Mommy! Where are you? I can't see!"

"Shut ye little pie hole ya stinkin' sea witch! Arrgh! I'll take this here harpoon and gut ya down the middle, ye'll make a nice tuna fish sandwich. Arrgh!" Azuru-Chi taunted.

"I want my mommy!" cried Chloey.

"And I want me treasure! Now one more word and it's off with ya head! Arrgh!"

Chloey bit down on her lip and tried her best to stop crying because she wanted to be brave for her people. That's when Azuru-Chi stared into her eyes and noticed they had suddenly turned bright red---she was no longer afraid of him. The salty old sea captain knew all too well what it meant when a mermaid's eyes began to glow that way, and he quickly backed away from the net.

My anger at Chloey's abduction ignited the metamorphosis and brought forth a prehistoric juggernaut known as the Megalodon, a gigantic sea monster that's the ancestor to the Great White Shark. Unlike modern day Great Whites (Carcharodon carcharias), Megalodon was the size of a luxury yacht! Yes, the metamorphosis transformed me into the most fearsome creature the ocean's ever known. I was now equipped with nature's most sophisticated sonar navigation system and was able to quickly pinpoint the Black Scorpion---Azuru-Chi's ship---though it was hundreds of miles away. A series of small tsunamis was left in my wake as I torpedoed toward the unsuspecting horde of soon to be dead pirates. A dozen more ships had joined the Black Scorpion and dropped anchor off the coast of Cam Island. The pirates were conspiring against me, but it was too late for them to put their plan in effect. On the horizon appeared a dorsal fin that was as tall as a building---Megalodon had arrived!

"Ahoy below!" shouted the lookout from the crow's nest. "A beastly creature approaches from the west! The beast is coming! The beast is coming!"Azuru-Chi ran toward the ship's wheel carrying a spyglass that hung from a silver chain he wore around his neck. He took and pointed it in the direction of the creature, and when the image came into focus Azuru-Chi dropped the spyglass and ran for the nearest dinghy.

"Arrgh! It's every man for himself!" shouted the captain as he boarded the dinghy alone. "The beast means to kill us all!"The rest of the pirates followed suit and quickly started to abandon ship after hearing Azuru-Chi screaming at the top of his lungs saying, "Swim for ya lives! Swim for ya lives!" But for many of them it was already too late.

In my new form as the great beast Megalodon, I went crashing into the first ship with tremendous force smashing its wooden frame into a million pieces. Megalodon's giant serrated teeth chomped down on the pirates who landed in the water cutting them to shreds and turning the crystal blue ocean into a sea of red. The few who managed to escape the monstrous jaws of Megalodon swam toward the beach and took refuge on Cam Island. They watched helplessly as the gigantic shark devoured their shipmates one by one. The screams coming from the ocean told a horrific story that left the surviving pirates shaking in their boots. Megalodon was on a rampage destroying every ship in sight, but when the beast came upon the Black Scorpion, it was my turn to seek revenge.I quickly returned to human form and climbed aboard Azuru-Chi's ship in search of Chloey.

"Chloey! Where are you, sweetheart?" I called out to her.

"I'm over here!" a little voice cried out from behind a stack of crates. "I knew you would come for me, D'Shawn! I just knew it!"After freeing Chloey from the net I held her tightly in my arms and praised the Lord above for allowing me to get to her in time

"Chloey, sweetheart, I am so sorry for what happened …" I said on bended knee. "I should've dealt with those horrible men when I had the chance."

"It's alright, D'Shawn. I wasn't afraid of them." Chloey said with a warm smile that melted my heart; it was a sure sign that I had been forgiven. "D'Shawn, I was worried that you and Azoria would be angry with me for not leaving with Jacie to get help. But I was only trying to save the dolphins that had gotten trapped by those nasty pirates."

"I know sweetheart, and you did the right thing. The dolphins are safe because of you. But now I want you to return to Atlantica as quickly as you can, okay. And no matter what you hear… do not look back."

"Okay," said little Chloey in the cutest voice. "But what about the pirates? They hurt me, you know."

The world around me turned blood-red as my temper flared and rage swelled in the cockles of my heart. I listened as Chloey told me about her ordeal aboard the ship at the hands of Azuru-Chi and his crew.

"The pirates pulled me from the water and slammed me down hard on the deck of the ship, then started spitting yucky stuff in my face and all over my hair." While the little mermaid continued telling me her story, my eyes searched the shores of Cam Island looking for those who were responsible for torturing her.

"…and when I started to cry because my eyes burned, the fat captain said he was going to cut off my head." The transformation began without my permission and I had only seconds to warn Chloey before the next monster was brought to life.

"Chloey! Get off the ship right now! Hurry sweetie! And remember, don't look back!"

The little mermaid made a high-pitched squeal before leaping from the bow of the ship and swimming for Atlantica. Once I saw that she had reached a safe distance, I surrendered myself to the metamorphosis and began ripping away at my flesh until the Wolf in the Darkness came forth. A thick red fog slowly began to surround the ship and I could hear myself screaming like a banshee. It was a horrifying scream that literally pierced the souls of the pirates on the island who heard it. They stared in the ship's direction trying to figure out what kind of animal could make such a bloodcurdling sound. Then suddenly, out of the crimson fog came the answer...

Two giant hooves emerged from the fog and entered the ocean with a splash. Then a pair of humongous wings appeared over the sails, they were like the wings of a Vampire bat stretching out far beyond the length of the ship while casting an ominous shadow over the beach where the pirates stood petrified at what they were witnessing. Rising above the wings came a gigantic head with curled horns on it like a ram; then the pirates spotted those reptilian eyes and instantly began screaming out the name Sapian. Yes, I had taken the form of the diabolical red dragon himself. Streams of liquid fire started raining down from my nostrils while a giant forked tongue formed inside my mouth. I couldn't believe how much rage there was inside the belly of the beast. The pirates on the beach started running in every direction but their fate was already sealed. By the handful, I snatched them up with my claws and tossed them in my mouth like popcorn shrimp as I chomped, chomped, chomped their asses to death. Suddenly, out of nowhere, came a blast of searing heat that hit the back of my head like a flamethrower.

"What the hell?!" I yelled while rubbing the bald patch where my hair used to be. I turned and I saw a ferocious little dragon hovering in the air preparing to breathe fire at me once again. But before the little bastard could muster another burst, I reached back and swatted his ass as hard as I could. "Take that! You little bitch!" I said as the Cammill dragon went soaring through the air and crashed into the ocean with a huge splash.

"Sapian! How'd you escape the Underworld? And what have you done with D'Shawn?!"

I knew that voice. "Turn and face me you coward!" I slowly turned around and there was Azoria standing nine stories tall with her claws bared and her long, curved fangs dripping with venom.

"Azoria wait! It's me!" I said while raising my hands to show her I was not a threat. "It's me, D'Shawn. Calm down and listen to me. You and I banished the real Sapian for a thousand years. Remember?"

"Then why are you masquerading as him? Are you trying to get yourself killed?" chided Azoria.

"Of course not! But I became so enraged at what the pirates did to Chloey, that the only thing the metamorphosis could relate to with that much rage was Sapian. And look what happened to my head, some little fire-breathing mosquito burned my scalp and fried a bald spot in my hair."

"D'Shawn, do you not realize what island we're on?" said the princess.

"Who cares? In a few minutes this whole place is going to be covered in blood, once I catch the rest of those bastards who tortured Chloey."

"You may want to reconsider that once you hear what I have to say." Azoria knew the legend of Cam Island from listening to stories told by the Great Elders. She has always had a special interest in knowing such things. "Camisado was the island's original name, and the dragons you see flying overhead are the Cammill." Azoria explained. "Are you listening to me, D'Shawn?"

"Yeah, I'm listening, but why should I care about a bunch of flying mosquitoes that go around setting heads on fire?"

"It's believed that whosoever captures the leader of those so-called mosquitoes will be granted a single wish in exchange for its freedom."

"That's a bunch of bull. No one can make a wish and have it magically come true. That only happens in fairy tales."

"Yeah, I guess you're right. Believing that a wish can be granted is like believing in sea monsters and werewolves and dragons and oracles and wizards and mermaids and---"

"Alright, alright I get it! You've made your point, Azoria!" I conceded. "But you know what? I really hate it when you make it so obvious that I'm wrong."

"That's too bad, because I really enjoy it---and you are wrong all the time." She said with a beaming smile on her face. "Now listen, D'Shawn, I want you to promise me something."

"Sure, anything."

"Promise me that Azuru-Chi won't live beyond this day."

"Oh! You have my word! That chubby son-of-a-bitch is as good as dead."

"Good. Because I ran into to Chloey on her way back to Atlantica and she told me what that pig Azuru-Chi said to her. I'll track down the other pirates while you dispatch that despicable rat of a captain. But most importantly, I want you to find the leader of the Cammill and make your wish."

"Yeah, about the leader..." I said with downward cast eyes. "I've been meaning to tell you that---"

"Tell me what, D'Shawn? What are you talking about?"

"I believe I may have already killed the leader of the dragons." I said to Azoria who simply stared at me with a curious expression.

"What in the world are you talking about, my love?"

"Well, just before you showed up, I swatted the dragon that torched my scalp right out of the air and I'm pretty sure it's dead. So what if that was the leader?"

"D'Shawn, the leader of the colony is the queen dragon and she doesn't have wings. But you have to be extremely cautious in her pursuit because the rest of the colony will defend her to the death." I appreciated her concern and her wisdom. Azoria was like my guardian angel, always there protecting me from dangerous things.

"Well, I guess it's time to catch a dragon by the tail, and a pirate by the throat." I said half jokingly. "You be careful Azoria, and don't do anything crazy like... well, like I would do." She flashed a devilish grin and then went on the hunt for the remaining members of Azuru-Chi's crew. It didn't take long for her to catch up to the first band of pirates trying to escape through the dense woods that covered the island. She brutally killed them one by one, smearing their bloody guts on the barks of trees so that the other pirates would know that she meant business. Azoria had become a formidable beast and she would leave no stone unturned until every last pirate was dead and accounted for. She was turning Cam Island into a blood soaked battleground that re-sembled the one left after I sought my revenge against the Lycan. In fact, Azoria was worst than me!

Now if that ain't a hot-girl, whaddaya call that?

✦ 205 ✦

"It follows that any being, if it vary however slightly in any manner profitable to itself, under the complex and sometimes varying conditions of life, will have a better chance of surviving, and thus be naturally selected."

---Charles Darwin

"...God created man in his own image... male and female he created them."

---Genesis 1:27

CHAPTER 20

WISH UPON A STAR

Deep inside a secluded cavern Azuru-Chi showed his true cowardice by hiding himself away from his own men. His plan was to wait there a couple of days and then flee the island and gather a new crew of faithful pirates. The cave was perfectly hidden behind a cascading waterfall, it was only by sheer coincidence that Azuru-Chi was able to spot the entrance at all. A fallen tree had temporarily blocked the river's flow above the cliff, creating a stoppage and allowing for Azuru-Chi to spot the opening from down in the forest. He quickly scrambled up the cliff and crawled inside the cave just in time before the tree snapped under the pressure of the current and the rushing water came tumbling down the falls again. The cascading water shielded the entrance once more, making for a smooth getaway. Or so it seemed.

The further Azuru-Chi ventured into the cave the roomier it became. He had entered on his hands and knees but eventually was able to stand up straight and had plenty of room to spare. "Ahoy there!" yelled Azuru-Chi when he noticed a flickering light further down the corridor glowing brightly against the wall. "Who be's there? Arrgh! What bewitchery be's this?" After no one answered him, Azuru-Chi followed the light until he came upon some strange writing on the walls. It was a message written in dragon's blood and this is what it said:

WALK XVI PACES * TURN LEFT * PLACE BOTH HANDS IN SPACES AND FIND DEATH *

"Walk 16 paces, then turn to me left. Place me hands in spaces and find death." Azuru-Chi said while reading the message for the third time. He was determined to solve the riddle so he kept reading it over and over until finally it came to him. "Arrgh! Death be's the Cammill! This here's me map to the queen dragon!"

Ecstatic about possibly locating the leader of the colony and being granted a wish, the greedy pirate quickly stepped off sixteen paces then turned to his left. But all he found was a dead end. "Arrgh! I'm supposed to place me hands in spaces but there be's no spaces!" Suddenly out of nowhere Ditto shows up and plants himself firmly atop Azuru-Chi's shoulder. "Ditto! What be's ya, some kind of homing pigeon? How'd ya get in here? Nevermind, just get ya mangy claws off me!" Though Azuru-Chi feigned like he was angry, that ol' crusty pirate was actually glad to see his talkative parrot show up. Well, at least until he realized that Ditto had been in the cave too long and had gone completely mad. The crazed parrot snatched off the diamond earring that Azuru-Chi wore in his right earlobe, swallowed it, then started dancing around on the captain's shoulder while singing a medley that included Lorde's song "Royals" and Nu Breed's rebel anthem "Land of the Lost": *"...We're driving Cadillacs in our dreams! But everybody's like Maybachs, Crys-Tal, diamonds on your timepiece, jet planes, is-lands, tigers on a gold leash! We don't c-a-a-a-re, we aren't caught up in your love affair. And we'll never be roy-y-y-a-als... Squaaawwk!" On them back ro-o-ads where them alligators crawl, and the swampland we ain't worried 'bout no law. You can find m-e-e in the woods with my dogs, under pine tre-e-s in the land of the lost. I've been drinking on this whiskey got my head up in the clouds, and if this world keep fuck-ing with me I ain't never coming down... Squaaawwk!"*

"That be's it! That be's the last I'll hear of ye senseless gibberish!" Azuru-Chi was fuming as he reached over and grabbed Ditto by the neck and tried to choke the life out of him. But the feisty parrot started pecking away at Azuru-Chi's hand with its sharp beak forcing the crusty pirate to let go. Then the angry bird began fluttering its wings hitting Azuru-Chi with a barrage of licks that left him dazed and scarred with feathers lodged in his greasy skin. And before Ditto fled the cave, he sang one final message to Azuru-Chi: "You've been hit by! You've been struck by! A smo-o-o-th criminal! Squaaawwk!"

Back at the wall, the grumpy captain contemplated his next move. He stood silent mulling over the directions written on the wall. "Arrgh! Yonder map say me spaces should be right here. Stupid map!" He didn't see any spaces in front of him but when he threw up his hands in frustration, Azuru-Chi suddenly felt something scrape across his chubby knuckles. "Bligh me!" he shouted. "What be's this?" Looking up, he was startled by what he saw. "How'd they get there?"

Two long ropes with nooses at one end were dangling just above the pirate's head, giving him the "spaces" he was looking for. "That be's a right fine map after all, it led me straight to me spaces." Azuru-Chi foolishly followed the message and put his hands inside the nooses. Then with only a slight tug on the rope, ZOoooOM! He took off like a rocket screaming, "Weeeee!" as he flew through the air at incredible speeds. The puggy pirate zoomed through the cavern inside a smooth, cylinder-like passageway that had been meticulously carved out by the Cammill. Two large boulders were tied to the other end of the ropes as counterweights; they went tumbling down the inside wall of a volcano, leaving a trail of ash and cinder lingering in the darkness.

The giant rocks eventually slammed into the bottom of the volcano leaving Azuru-Chi dangling with his feet several inches off the ground, the more he struggled to get free the more the nooses tightened around his chubby wrists. He looked and he saw a group of odd shaped boulders sitting on a bed of straw over in the corner where there was more writing on the wall. The message above the boulders was also written in dragon's blood:

*YOU HAVE COME SEEKING DEATH AND DEATH YOU WILL FIND * OUR YOUNG ARE READY TO FEED AND ON YOUR ROTTING CARCASS THEY WILL DINE

The bed of straw turned out to be a giant nest and the odd looking boulders were actually eggs the size of igloos. "Shiver me timbers!" cried the captain. "Those be dragon eggs!" It was true, he had stumbled upon a nest full of dragon eggs that had been laid by the queen dragon herself. The writing on the walls was part of an elaborate trap set by the dragons to lure in greedy pirates who came searching for a wish. Azuru-Chi hadn't noticed it before but there were skeletons all around the cave belonging to pirates who had fallen into the trap and had served as food for earlier broods of baby dragons. And unfortunately for him, the next brood was ready to hatch.

Azuru-Chi's attention was suddenly drawn to the largest egg in the nest, it wobbled and then made a loud cracking noise like a splitting windshield. "The little beasties are breaking out of their shells! Arrgh! I be's in deep shit!" Knowing that the baby Cammill would soon be loose in the cave, Azuru-Chi tried desperately to free himself from the ropes one last time. But when he yanked his arms downward, the ropes cut deep into his skin turning his knobby fingers dark purple and making him squeal like the pig he was.As the cracking noise grew louder, so did Azuru-Chi's bellowing. He was yelling at the top of his lungs hoping that one of his shipmates would hear his pleas for help and come to his rescue. But he had abandoned them on purpose and hid in the cave alone, waiting for his chance to gather a new crew of bloodthirsty pirates that would sail with him. Now facing his impending doom, the ornery pirate looked toward the nest and began cussing out the young dragons even before they were fully hatched:

"Arrgh! I'd rather be's tarred and feathered than be's eaten by you scummy fuckin' beasts! I hope ye fuckers choke on me greasy balls! Ya filthy flying scum! Arrgh!"

The largest egg in the nest broke open and out popped a ferocious mini version of the adult dragons flying around outside. The baby dragon was about the size of a rhinoceros and was covered in a slimy liquid that instantly filled the air with a putrid odor. The beast stared directly at the pirate and then let out a harrowing, screeching sound from deep inside its throat; the eerie high-pitched cry stirred the rest of the brood and caused the remaining eggs to begin breaking open.

"Shiver me timbers!" cried Azuru-Chi. "I be's pickings for the birds! Arrgh!" That's about the time I arrived on the scene. I had transformed into a giant Vampire bat with specialized hearing and sonar capabilities to track Azuru-Chi through the dark caverns after picking up his nasty scent near the waterfall. Once I found him dangling from the ropes inside the dragon's den, I became a vile creature and perched myself in the corner like a wolf in the darkness with glowing red eyes.

"Consider yourself lucky, you disgusting bastard." I hissed at the pirate from the shadows. "If not for the hatchlings needing you as a meal, I would rip your fucking head off and eat your worthless ass myself."

"What devil be's you?!" cried the terrified captain.

"I am the same devil that allowed you and your men to gather material from the Galactic Island. And you repaid me by abducting a child and using her as bait to lure me here to Cam Island!" As images of the pirates torturing Chloey flooded my thoughts, the metamorphosis was triggered yet again. "Well, here I am! Motherfucker!"

I emerged from the shadows as a savage beast and immediately began ripping the pirate apart. I could hear him screaming as huge chucks of his blubbery flesh splattered against the wall and the salty taste of his blood filled my mouth. I was a blur of pure rage, and the beast I had become showed no mercy to the pirate, it grabbed hold of Azuru-Chi by the throat and tore out his Adam's Apple leaving a gaping hole in the pirate's neck with streams of blood squirting all over the walls and ceiling of the cave. A look of sheer terror was in Azuru-Chi's eyes as he and the beast I had become stood face-to-face. The dying pirate stared hopelessly into my pitch black eyes, shaking and quivering and bleeding profusely from his wounds---even death could not save him from my wrath.

After ripping out his tongue and eating it right in front of him, I slashed his stomach wide open and watched his bowels spill onto the floor in a steaming pile of half digested fish heads and raw eels. Apparently, he was a rotten bastard to the core. The only part of him I didn't eat was his left arm which was tattooed with a much earlier version of one of Ice Cube's most famous lines, "Life ain't nothing but bitches and money!". But Azuru-Chi's tattoo said, "Life Be's Nothing But Wenches and Gold!".

His arm was left dangling inside the cave after I snatched the rest of his body down from the ropes and disappeared into the dark caverns like a wild beast. That bastard definitely got what was coming to him, so good riddance. Now it was time for me to find the queen dragon and make my wish.

After gorging myself on Azuru-Chi's blubbery hide, I retired to a quiet, shady area beneath some trees and fell fast asleep. I awoke a few minutes later and found that I had resumed my human form. I was so happy that I went running naked toward the ocean to go for a swim---but there was just one problem. Cam Island was teeming with fire-breathing reptiles, making it an extremely unsuitable environment for skinny dipping.

Just before I could reach the water's edge, a searing blast of heat toasted my naked buns and roasted my dangling balls like chestnuts on an open fire. "Whoa! What the hell?!" I yelled as I turned to find a gangly six-winged Cammill dragon rapidly coming toward me. "That shit really burns, you know!" I shouted at the dragon while fanning my balls. "How'd you like it if I was to set your balls ablaze?!" I suddenly felt that familiar sensation in the pit of my stomach and immediately knew that a formidable monster would soon be unleashed because of the trigger happy metamorphosis... And I was right. "Here we go again..." I said to myself as the next creature emerged from within me with ten horns and the ability to breathe fire. It began torching everything in sight including the dragon's balls--and let me tell you---the dragon wasn't too happy about it.

Meanwhile, Azoria was in a fierce battle of her own. She had turned into a creature that stood taller than the tallest tree on the island, but her enormous size didn't stop the Cammill dragons from attacking her. The flying menace came from every direction screeching loudly and slashing at her throat with their sharp tails as they flew by. The dragons looked like a giant swarm of killer bees carrying flamethrowers---real deadly sons-of-bitches. After dispatching with the dragon that liked to roast nuts, I rejoined Azoria and began slaughtering her attackers by the dozen.

"Need a hand with these mosquitoes, ma'am?" I joked with the princess.

"Why yes, I most certainly could use a hand here," said Azoria with a sly grin. I knew she could have handled the Cammill on her own, but I wanted her to see how chivalrous and manly I was.

Thousands and thousands of mer-people started gathering off the coast of the island to watch us extinguish the Cammill's fiery siege. Azoria and me were a great team, a force to be reckoned with, and it made her people proud to see us standing together fighting side-by-side. Finally after nearly three hours of constant fighting, I killed the last flying dragon by crushing its head and splattering its brains all over the place. With no more Cammill dragons to protect her, the queen's ass was mine.

Azoria told me to go ahead of her and she would catch up later. The princess then returned to the beach and rejoined her people who were waiting out in the bay. I, meanwhile, continued my quest. I began searching the forests for the queen dragon's lair but I came up empty. So that led me to look in other places on the island that I really didn't want to go to. Dark, scary places with nasty little parasites crawling on the ground and flesh-eating fungi growing on the walls illuminating the dark caves with an eerie aura that reminded me of Halloween and haunted houses. Something odd caught my attention while exiting one of the caves. There was a strange colored flame shooting out the top of a volcano which was not active at all. And I thought to myself, "How can a dormant volcano spew flames without erupting?" Then it hit me---

Dragon's fire!

The strange flames were coming from the nostrils of the humongous dragon hiding inside the volcano, the Queen. She was already preparing to hatch another brood of baby dragons after the last one had been destroyed during my wrath upon the pirate Azuru-Chi.

I climbed to the top of the volcano and then slowly made my way down the inside wall hoping to surprise the beast. But she was already on to me, I just didn't know it.

"Why have you come here?" said the queen of the once mighty Cammill with her eyes still closed as though she was asleep. "You have desolated my colony and murdered my young. Have you any idea what I'm going to do to you?"

"Nope. Not a clue." I said, being the smart-ass that I am.

"Your annoying, self-assertive humor won't go over well with me, Cartrell."

"Who the hell is Cartrell?" I asked the queen dragon.

"Wouldn't you like to know," she answered with a devilish grin. "After all, it's the reason you're here."

"I came here to get a wish. Not to find out about some dude named Cartrell."

The queen dragon finally opened her reptilian eyes and stared at me with the look of a cobra preparing to strike. She then made a great yawn and I stared at the rows of dagger-like teeth stretching around her gaping jaws that spanned the length of two football fields across. The great beast impressed me with her tremendous roar that sent goosebumps racing down my arms and left the walls of the volcano trembling violently. She then spewed fire from her nostrils that was so hot it melted the stalactite hanging from the roof of the cavern and caused it to come raining down mixing with the burning rocks and creating a river of molten lava between us.

"You cunning bitch!" I said as the clever queen dragon made her escape through a hidden passage at the rear of her den. "I'll get you, my pretty! ...And your little dog too."

The queen dragon's escape tunnel led directly to the deepest depths of the ocean where she was well equipped to survive the enormous pressure found far beneath the surface.I stood alone inside the smoldering dragon's den thinking of how my hope of being granted a wish was now lost.

"Damn! This was all for nothing. The queen dragon has gotten away and there's no way I'll be able to find her again." I said while feeling dejected and exhausted from the fight with the Cammill earlier.

"Well, I wouldn't exactly say that," Azoria commented as she walked up behind me and put her arms around my waist. "Now that she's entered the ocean, she's in my world. And finding her won't be as difficult as you may think. Come, my love. Walk with me back to the beach and I will show you something that's quite magical indeed." Azoria took me by the hand and led me back to the ocean's edge where I looked and I saw mer-people gathered together out in bay for as far as the eye could see. Reaching behind her neck, Azoria unfastened the chain that held the exquisite heart-shaped blue diamond she so eloquently wore. It resembled the one worn by "Rose" in the epic film "Titanic"; the one referred to as the Heart of the Ocean.The magnificent gem started glowing brilliantly and there were voices---beautiful voices---singing glorious music that sounded like gospel, but with a distinctively urban vibe to it.

"Azoria! Do you hear that?" I said with excitement. "It sounds like an enormous hip-hop choir!"

"Yes my love, I hear it," said the princess with a gentle smile. "And so do they."

Azoria pointed out over the ocean and I saw a couple of familiar looking creatures making their way through crowds of the mer-people and heading toward us. I had encountered the creatures on many unfortunate occasions, but this time they were joined by thousands of others that looked just like them. "Holy shit! It's a Gemini invasion!" I said while watching more and more of them appear on the horizon. "How is this possible?"

Come to find out, the twin dragons I encountered earlier were part of a legion of guardians that all looked exactly alike. Azoria began explaining that Gemini were superb hunters that could be summoned with the mystic jewel she was holding in her hands

The blue diamond was given to her as a gift from her father, and he told her that if she truly needed them, they would come. Azoria summoned two of them to the Galactic Island and gave them instructions to protect me.

They made sure I remained safe from the certain death that I would have suffered had I ventured into the water unprotected.

All this time I thought the dragons were just a couple of obnoxious assholes. Well I'll be damn!

Azoria instructed the Gemini legion to hunt down the queen dragon and bring her back to Cam Island through the same tunnel she had used during her escape. The supreme hunters immediately began combing the ocean from top to bottom leaving no crevice unchecked. They communicated with one another using telepathy in the shallows and 3-D sonar when scouring the ocean depths and trenches.

Less than two hours into the hunt, a group of them found the queen dragon hiding inside a natural fissure with only the tip of her nostrils sticking out. They aggressively grabbed hold of her and a great tug-of-war began. She had buried herself deep inside the hole and was fiercely fighting the Gemini dragons like a vicious moray eel. There was biting and clawing and pushing and pulling until eventually the queen dragon was snatched out of the hole and corralled by the hunters whose numbers grew expeditiously after the call went out that the queen had been found. Soon hundreds of Gemini dragons showed up to assist their brothers-in-arms with containing and subduing the fierce Queen of the Cammill. She was hissing loudly and striking out at them like a King Cobra cornered by an army of mongooses. But the mighty Gemini legion was extremely ferocious themselves, and was able to impose their will on the queen and make her bow down in defeat.

Once the battle was over, the army of Gemini parted in half leaving open a single path for the queen dragon to follow. The path led directly back to Cam Island, and though it was the last place the queen dragon wanted to be, she knew it was better than facing the ocean's most deadly apex predators---Gemini.

The moment she returned back through the tunnel and entered the volcano, I pounced on her ass like a hungry lion and secured her with a hundred chains tied to anchors. I wasn't taking any chances of losing her again, this time preparations had been made to ensure that she could not escape. Gemini guarded all the subterranean exits while Azoria kept a close eye on the queen dragon from above as she positioned herself at the volcano's crest. Meanwhile, I stared into the dragon's eyes and laid down my demands

"Be still!" I commanded the beast. "You will not trick me again!"The queen dragon was bucking and biting at the chains and anchors that were wrapped around her neck. I had gathered them from the fleets of sunken pirate ships lodged in the soft ocean mud beneath Cam Island.

"You are the last of your kind," I said to the dragon. "So if you want to stay alive in order to recolonize the island, then you must first grant my wish."

The humongous dragon slowly settled down and began listening to the compromise I was offering her. She soon realized that recolonization was her best option, and so she turned toward me and nodded her head in agreement with my offer. I then approached her and cautiously began removing the heavy chains which had gotten so badly tangled around her throat that she couldn't breathe

"Easy now," I said as I lifted the final anchor setting her completely free. "I want you to make a passage through the wall of the volcano using your gift of fire, and then follow me down to the beach."

"As you wish, Cartrell." The dragon said while giving me a devilish look that left me feeling very uneasy about our arrangement.

"Listen bitch! That wasn't a wish, it was a command. And stop calling me Cartrell."

"As you command," the queen dragon snickered. "After all, this is your world, Great D'Shawn."

"I don't know what kind of game you're playing, but you better chill out!"

"Or what?" said the beast while secretly taking in a deep breath.

"Or I'm going to skin your motherfuc---"
WWWHHOOOOSSSSHHHH!
A tremendous ball of fire flew out of the dragon's mouth and blasted a hole in the wall of the volcano big enough to sail an ocean liner through. The dragon was showing off the awesome power she possessed. The fireball missed my head by inches, and had it hit me, I would have been nothing but a pile of ash.

"You crazy bitch! Try that shit again and I'mma sic the entire Gemini legion on your fire-breathing ass!"

The queen dragon shook off the volcanic ash that had accumulated atop her scales and then slowly made her way through the gigantic doorway made by the fireball. She followed me back to the beach where Azoria and the others were waiting anxiously for my return. As soon as I came out of the forest I heard cheering and screaming and saw mermaids leaping out of the water happy to see me again. But then shock and panic quickly struck when the crowds of mer-people saw a pair of giant horns appeared above the palm trees casting an ominous shadow over the entire bay.

"It's okay guys!" I shouted from the beach. "She's with me, we've made an arrangement."

"D'Shawn, have you lost your mind?" said Azoria as she was preparing to transform and attack the queen dragon. "She can't be trusted, she's planning to kill you for destroying the colony. I sense it in her thoughts."

"It's been settled, Azoria. I've convinced her that recolonizing the island is more important than taking revenge on me for what happened here. Isn't that right, dragon?"I could see in hers eyes that she was tempted to incinerate me and kill as many mer-people as she could. But in the back of her mind she kept thinking about the colony. It was her duty to ensure the continuation of her kind, and what better way for her to seek revenge than to raise her own army of killer dragons and send them to hunt me down. I turned to Azoria and asked her to have the Gemini legion guard the queen dragon while she and I went for a walk along the beach.

"D'Shawn, have you decided what you're going to wish for?" asked Azoria as we walked hand-in-hand looking at the beautiful sunset over the ocean.

"Yes, there's been only one thing I've wanted since the beginning." I replied.

"And what's that, my love?" said the princess in a way that almost made me change my mind. But I reached into my pocket and pulled out the photo of my family back home in New Orleans and said, "This is a picture of my mom, her name is Brenda. And those are my brothers and sisters: Brandon, Samantha, Brittney, Jamal, Sebastian, Unique', Devontae', Elexus, and Darrius. I remember them now, and I miss them dearly."

"What about me, my love?" said Azoria with tears threatening to spill from her eyes. "Have you no feelings for me anymore?"

"Of course I do, Azoria. But I have to return home, my family really needs me. Besides, I want to live in my own city, my own world, my own time. Surely you can understand that, can't you?"The princess lowered her head because at that moment she realized that I would be leaving soon. Though her heart was broken by the fact that she was losing me, Azoria put on a happy face and said her goodbyes.

"Yes, my love. Your time here has ended, your family needs you there with them and I'm sure they're awaiting your safe return. I want you to promise me one thing," said Azoria as the tears finally began falling from my eyes. "Promise me that you'll never forget the love we share."I suddenly found myself struggling to hold my composure, and when I tried to speak nothing came out because I was too choked up. Azoria was the love of my life, and I would have moved heaven and earth to protect her. But my mind was made up and it was time to say goodbye.

"Azoria, please don't cry," I said while wiping the tears from her beautiful eyes. "Everything's going to be alright, I promise. And one day I will come back and find you because our love is timeless and has no boundaries, whatsoever."

"I'll be waiting, my love," said Azoria as she gave me a big hug and a long, passionate kiss that almost made me change my mind again. "You're my knight in shining armor, you know that right?" I smiled so big that every tooth in my mouth was showing.

"Something just struck me as being quite ironic." said the princess.

"What's that, Azoria?"

"Well, remember how you came into my world like a shooting star, the same kind that people place wishes upon?"

"Yeah, so?" I said, still not sure where she was going with this.

"Don't you think it's ironic that in a few minutes the dragon will place a wish upon a star?"

"Wow! I never thought of it that way. That is pretty ironic. I like how you came up with such a cool analogy. You're one smart mermaid, Azoria."

"Mermaids only exist in fairy tales, remember?" the princess joked.

"Well, even fairy tales have to begin somewhere." I said, and then we laughed out loud at the remark.

"I'm really going to miss you, my love," Azoria was once again fighting back tears. "You have made a lasting impression on everyone here and we will not forget you or the brave things you've done to save us."

"Azoria please don't make this any harder for me than it already is. I'mma 'bout to cry over here." The princess gave me a warm hug and said, "I don't know how I'm going to go on without you, but I know it's time to let you go." Then she poked fun of her royal status using a Shakespearean like swagger saying, "Maketh thou request to the dragon and allow thy faith to guide thee to the place thou calleth home."I held the princess tightly in my arms trying to take in every detail of her essence, I wanted to remember her in every way possible: the scent of her hair, the feel of her warm body next to me, the loving tone of her voice, the magic in her eyes. We shared one last kiss before returning to the bay where the queen dragon was waiting to grant my wish.

"Dragon!" I shouted as I walked up and stood before the great beast. "I am not of this world. My wish is to return to my own world in my own time. No more tricks! I now command you to grant my wish! Do it now!"

The queen dragon slowly took in a deep breath inhaling for almost a full minute. Then as everyone was starting to get uneasy, a stream of dark blue smoke began seeping from the dragon's nostrils and her huge belly started glowing with a cerulean blue aura that lit up the night like a giant glow stick. The whole area surrounding the bay was bathed in the warm blue light that was coming from the belly of the beast, it was even being reflected off the water as waves came crashing onto the crystalline sands bordering the mystical Island of Cam. "D'Shawn, please be careful," shouted Azoria from a distance. "Now that her lungs are full she can breathe out fire at any moment!"I stood my ground and bravely stared into the dragon's eyes willing to risk it all for a chance to go home.

"Do not be foolish dragon, remember the colony." I warned the beast. "If I die here tonight, so will you."The queen dragon angrily glared at me before exhaling a thick blue haze of smoke and ash, making Cam Island practically invisible to the mer-people wading in the shallow waters out in the bay. Azoria and the citizens of Atlantica began to shout: "Where's the dragon?! Can anyone see the queen dragon?!" But when the smoke cleared the dragon was gone!

...And so was I.

✦ 223 ✦

"After this I looked, and there before me was a door standing open in heaven... before me was a throne... and the one who sat there had the appearance of jasper and carnelian. A rainbow, resembling an emerald, encircled the throne."

---Revelation 4:1-3

CHAPTER 21

FINAL FANTASY

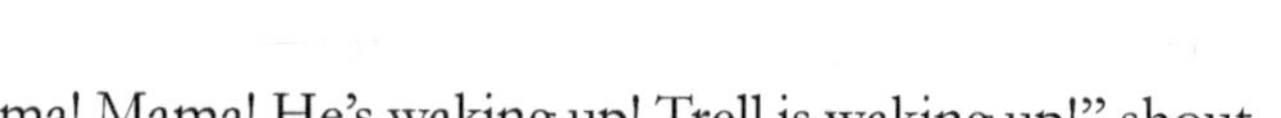

"Mama! Mama! He's waking up! Trell is waking up!" shouted Brittney while standing next to my bed.

"Trell, baby it's Mama. Can you hear me?" I opened my eyes and I saw all the people from the photo standing in the room jumping for joy and hugging one another in celebration of something. "I wonder what's all the excitement about." I thought to myself. Then everything started coming back to me.

"Mama, is it really you?" I said to the middle-aged woman from the photo who now stood beside me smiling and wiping tears from her eyes.

"Yes baby, its really me. It's really Mama," she was so overcome with joy that she started crying and thanking the Lord over and over again. "Thank you Jesus! Thank you Lord! I just want to thank you Father for answering my prayers." My little sister Samantha came over and hugged me tightly, she was wearing a beaming smile.

"Trell, you scared us, we thought you might not wake up again." Sam had a look of grave concern on her face, and it was only then that I realized that I was in a hospital bed with all kinds of tubes and monitors attached to me.

"Mama, what happened to me? Why am I in the hospital?" My mother sensed panic in my voice, and she didn't want me getting riled up to the point where I could possibly go into shock. So she held my hand and in a calm, gentle voice she said, "Baby, you was involved in a terrible incident out in the Gulf. The oil rig you was working on caught fire and exploded---many people lost their lives." My mother grimaced at the thought of how many families were torn apart by the tragedy, she squeezed my hand and again gave thanks to God before continuing to fill me in on what happened.

"Trell, you was the only one who survived the tragedy, even the people who jumped into the water later died from their injuries. Some of them suffered horrific burns and others---Lord have mercy! The news people kept showing all those sharks swimming around the bodies. Baby, there was so many sharks in the water that the rescue crews couldn't get in to save anyone. Thank God you ended up miles away and was found drifting in the Atchafalaya Basin by a couple of fishermen from Pierre Part who were out there hunting alligators. They took you to the hospital near Victor II Boulevard in Morgan City, and from there you was brought by helicopter back here to New Orleans."

"Mama, how long have I been in the hospital?"

"Trell baby, the doctor said I shouldn't say anything about tha---"

"Please Mama! I need to know!"

First she hesitated, then my mother whispered saying, "Well baby, the tragedy took place a little more than three years ago... three years ago... three years ago."

I thought I misunderstood her because there was no way I could have been in the hospital that long. I laughed and said, "Mama, it sounded like you said the incident happened over three years ago."

My mother wasn't laughing. In fact she was staring at me as if waiting for reality to set in. It wasn't until she told me to stay calm that I realized I had heard her correctly.

"No Mama, that can't be right. Why would you say that? Wait, wait, wait... let me think." My heart immediately began pounding against my chest and the machines that were monitoring my vital signs started going crazy.

"Trell baby, you have to calm down. That's why the doctor advised me not to mention how long you've been here." Just then, a team of medical workers came running into the room shouting, "Mr. LeCour! Relax and breathe! Everything's going to be alright." While the male staffers tried to restrain me physically, the female workers used their gentle voices to try and keep me calm. Still, I put up quite a fight.

"Mr. LeCour, you're going to be fine," said one of the cute young nurses after turning off the monitors so that the beeping and chirping would stop.

"You don't want to yank out your I.V., Mr. LeCour," she then said with a smile. "Because if you do, I'll have to stick you again and you're not going to like it very much. Are we clear?"

"Yes ma'am, we're clear." I conceded after realizing what a scene I was making. She gave me a mild sedative to help me relax and then she did a quick evaluation of my condition.

"You're an absolute mystery, Mr. LeCour," the nurse commented while reading my medical chart. "Do you know how fortunate you are to be alive?"I stared in dismay not having the slightest idea what she was talking about. Still, I managed to put on a smile for her.

"The doctor will be in shortly to speak with you and your family. Hopefully the meds I gave you will not have totally kicked in by then, I gave them to you because we really need you to stay calm. If you have any questions, address them to the doctor," said the nurse as she and the other staffers left the room so that I could visit with my family in private.It was great to be able to hug and talk with my sisters and brothers who started cutting up and laughing so loudly that the nurse had to come back in and escort them to the waiting room at the end of the hall. The good thing was that it gave me an opportunity to speak to my mother alone, so I could tell her how sorry I was for everything.

"Mama, I'm really sorry." I said with all sincerity.

"Sorry for what, baby?" she replied.

"I know how badly we needed the money I was going to make working offshore to catch up on paying the bills. And now with the additional expense of me being hospitalized all this time, I don't see how we're going to manage."

My mother's face lit up with a glorious smile and I sat there wondering why was she so happy all of a sudden? "Lord have mercy!" she shouted. "Baby, with all the excitement of you waking up from your coma I completely forgot to tell you the news!"

"What news, Mama?"

"Baby, you're rich! You're filthy rich! Do you hear me?!'"

"Mama, what are you talking about? How can I be rich and I just spent the past three years in a coma?"

"Trell, the oil company you used to work for was at fault. Several people on the company's executive board were arrested and went to prison after it was discovered that they instructed the Chief of Operations on the rig to shut off an expensive safety unit in order to save money. The unit was supposed to prevent explosions like the one that killed all those people. The company tried to cover up everything by releasing a false narrative to the media saying it was a terrorist attack. But a few months later, I got a call in the middle of the night from Mr. Hampton. He told me that he found out what really happened and said that he was going to go public with his findings. And that's exactly what he did. Mr. Hampton promised me that our family would never have to worry about money ever again. He'd gotten his hands on indisputable video evidence that proved the tragic explosion was the company's fault." Even as I sat listening to the excitement in my mother's voice, still, I couldn't fathom the idea of something like this happening to us. Our life in the projects had been full of disappointments, so why would this time be any different, I reasoned. But the more she talked the more convinced I became that maybe, just maybe, our luck had changed.

"The oil company fought the allegations at first, but when Mr. Hampton went public with his video the company's lawyers advised them to settle out of court. Trell, they agreed to pay the sole survivor--- which is you---the largest cash settlement in history. Baby, you're now the richest man in the world!"

The door to my room suddenly burst opened and in came the most beautiful doctor I'd ever seen. She and Azoria could have passed for identical twins.

"Well hello, Mr. LeCour. You're looking quite well I see." I couldn't believe my eyes, I started smiling like a fat kid in a candy store.

"My name is Dr. Collins, I'm your physician," said the lovely doctor. "It's good to see that you are awake and alert."Her name tag read Tanesha A. Collins, but when I saw that gorgeous smile of hers I knew it was Azoria.

"If you're feeling up to it, Mr. LeCour, I may consider giving you an early release from this 'prison'," she joked. "You've been a model patient, I almost hate to see you go. Hey, do you know your mother's been here at your side day and night since you arrived? She's quite a trooper, you're blessed to have her."

"Yes, I know." I said while blowing my mom a kiss. "She's my guardian angel." I was indeed grateful that my mom kept vigil over me as I endured the hardship of being away from home for so long. "It would certainly seem that way. Your miraculous recovery has shocked us all. Even the fact that you were found more than 400 miles from the site of the disaster is incredibly amazing. What did you do, turn into a fish and just swam away?"

"If she only knew." I thought to myself.

"Dr. Collins, you mind if I ask you a personal question?" I said.

"No, not at all. What would you like to know?" she answered with a smile.

"Well, I was just wondering what does the letter 'A' stand for in your name?"

"Wow! I've never been asked that question by one of my patients before. It's the initial for my middle name, which was actually my great-great-grandmother's name who lived on an island in the South Pacific. The 'A' stands for---"

"Azoria!" I shouted out before she could say the name.

"Oh my god! How on earth did you know that?!" she asked. But before I could explain how I knew her middle name, the meds kicked in big time and I felt my eyelids starting to get heavy. The next thing you know, I was snoring like a bear during winter.A great peace had come over me knowing that my soul mate Azoria was there. She had cared for me in this world the same way she took care of me in the other.

"Mrs. LeCour, your son is resting now, but he will be ready to return home with you very soon. I just need to run a few more tests to make sure he's okay," she explained to my mother.

"Bless you darling, you have been so kind to me these past three years, I feel like we're family."

"I feel the same, Mrs. LeCour. It has been my pleasure."

"Please child, call me Ms. Brenda," said my mother as she gave the doctor a hug.

"Okay Ms. Brenda. But only if you call me Tanesha."

"That's a pretty name, but I overheard you telling my son about your great-great-grandmother, I think the name Azoria fits you best." Mama was being very sincere.

"You know what Ms. Brenda? I agree," said Azoria.

"Good, I'm glad that's settled," said my mother in a bossy kind of way. Azoria laughed at how my mom just seemed to take control of the matter.

"Listen, I plan on having a crawfish boil to celebrate my baby's return home, and I insist that you join us."

"Ms. Brenda, I wouldn't miss it for the world." Azoria and my mom hugged each other and then exchanged phone numbers. "You can reach me at this number anytime day or night, Ms. Brenda. I'll be there---I promise."

"Okay nah, I'mma call you soon as my baby gets settled in."

"That'll be great, Ms. Brenda. I'll see you then."

The same week I made it back home from the hospital, my dear, sweet mama arranged a crawfish boil for me at the Lakefront. She invited all the people from the neighborhood to come out and celebrate our family's good fortune---but not everyone was happy for us. Terrence Barkley, better known as "T-Red", showed up with his crew of wannabe gangstas and tried to crash the party.

"Look at that bitch-ass nigga over there, he 'bout to get all that motherfucking money from them white folks and have all our hoes sweat 'n him, ya heard me." T-Red said to his squad. "C'mon, let's set it off in this motherfucker and show that nigga he ain't shit."

The moment I saw him I knew there was going to be trouble, and I damn sure wasn't about to let that clown ruin the special celebration that Mama had worked so hard to put together for me at the Lakefront. So I told that nigga: "Listen woa-day, if y'all got a problem we can take it 'round the corner, ya heard me. It's too many women and children out-chere to start some bullshit."

Me and my brother Jamal had already figured them clowns was gon' come out and try to start some shit at the party. So as soon as I led them niggas 'round the corner, Jamal spun the bend wearing a red bandana over his face and carrying an M-203 with a grenade launcher.

"All you bitch-ass niggas lay it down!" he commanded with his finger on the trigger ready to pull it. Then out of nowhere, several more guys came running toward the action wearing red bandanas over their faces just like Jamal, except they had Glocs, Magnums, choppers, sawed-offs, drakos, 44's, 38's, and I even saw one of them toting a Calico that had a hundred round drum attached to it. I said to myself, "Man, these niggas ready for war!"

T-Red and his crew tried to run but Jamal's clique had already blocked all the exits, and that's when Jamal took out a nickel plated pistol, stuck in T-Red's mouth and made him suck on the barrel like it was a long, shiny dick right in front of all his boys. Them niggas was scared to death, and for good reason. Because my little brother's reputation in the streets was well-known and so was his gang. I stood there looking out of sorts with my hands in my pocket, nervously fidgeting for the brass knuckles I had intended to use if things got physical. Jamal turned and looked at me, and then he said, "Fool, take yo' scary ass back to the party, I got this. Oh!, and tell Mama to save me some crawfish, ya heard me." T-Red and his gang went for a long ride in the back of Jamal's trunk and I never saw them niggas again. As for what happened to 'em, well, Jamal never told me... and I knew better than to ask.

Back at the Lakefront, Azoria showed up to the crawfish boil looking like a movie star. She stepped out of her Maybach coup wearing a Burberry swimsuit with matching sandals and sporting a stylish Louis Vuitton handbag and a pair of $2,000.00 Dolce and Gabbana sunglasses. She was the epitome of a modern Black woman: charming, intelligent, well-spoken, fiercely independent and extremely good at what she does. Her boss swag was obvious from the moment I saw her at the hospital, she looked very confident and there was no question as to who was in charge. Naturally, I tried convincing her to go out with me, but every time I'd ask her on a date she'd politely say, "My career doesn't allow me the time it would take to nurture a romantic entanglement." In other words... I'm in the infamous "friend zone". Azoria had saved my life and I was truly grateful for the care she provided me during my prolonged stay at the hospital. She even came to see me on her off days and spent many long hours comforting my mother and accompanying her to the chapel to pray for me. "Trell, come over here," said Azoria smiling and beckoning for me to join her. "You should give Ms. Brenda a big hug and thank her for putting together such a wonderful party to celebrate your homecoming."

It was indeed a great homecoming, and everyone at the party was enjoying themselves.

"Mama, this is very nice." I said while giving her a big hug as Azoria suggested. "I've missed hanging out with the fam' and having this kind of fun. Thanks mom, for doing such a great job of welcoming me home, I love you dear lady." She squeezed me tightly as tears of joy ran down her face and dampened the blouse she was wearing.

"Baby, I'm so happy that you're home I don't know what to do. I feel like shouting to the world, 'Thank you Jesus! Thank you Lord!'"

"I'm happy too, Mama. But I wish you stop calling me 'baby'---I'mma grown man." I jokingly said while holding back my laughter.

"Trell, now don't you start showing off in front of Azoria," my mother warned. "Because I'll tell her about all those times you peed in the be---"

"C'mon, Mama! I was just playing!" I pleaded. "You know I'mma always be your baby." Azoria was laughing at seeing how Mama always seemed to get the upper hand on me. In fact, both of them found it quite hilarious.

After the settlement, life changed in a major way for our family. There were news crews camping out on the streets leading to our apartment in the Calliope waiting to approach me with questions about how I planned to spend the money. Initially, it was assumed that I, too, had been killed in the explosion. But then I was later found alive by a couple of fishermen. The story of my miraculous rescue made world news, but during their interviews, the Cajun fishermen never once mentioned that when they found me... I was draped in a fortune of jewels.

✦ 233 ✦

"...He sets the needy securely on high away from affliction. And makes his families like a flock. The upright see it and are glad; But all unrighteousness shuts its mouth."
---Psalm 107:41

CHAPTER 22

CHANGE OF VENUE

Shortly after receiving the money from the settlement, I bought Mama a new house and moved her and the rest of the family out of the projects for good. She now owned a multimillion dollar estate located in Bocage Village, a subdivision nestled in the heart of Baton Rouge. The residents of this pristine village community was said to have reached the pinnacle of fine living. From the manicured lawns to the cobblestone streets and marble driveways, Bocage Village was a virtual paradise on earth.

On any day of the week fine dining could be experienced at your choice of several exquisite restaurants near the village. All along Jefferson Highway and College Drive there were eateries serving the best food that anyone could wish for. Their chefs were trained to satisfy any culinary desire one might have, but my mother---had she wanted to---could have put them all to shame. Before I moved the family to Baton Rouge, Mama was a master chef who supervised some of the biggest culinary events in the Crescent City. Her favorite place to cook was at a quaint little restaurant called Dooky Chase's. People came there from all over the world to taste her legendary cooking; they would stand in line for hours just to get a seat inside. And once they were seated, then came the challenge of deciding on which delicious meal to choose. Mama's world famous dishes included her versions of Shrimp Clemenceau, Crawfish Étouffée, Oyster's Rockefeller, Creole Jambalaya, and her rich, creamy Cajun Fettuccini which she called the "Coup de Grace".Those who were dining in the restaurant often pleaded with the servers to ask my mother to come to their table so that they could compliment the chef---and to of course ask her for a recipe or two. They would then insist on taking a picture with my mom, whom they considered "New Orleans's Greatest Chef". Mama was delighted to know that so many people enjoyed her cooking. Fortunately for the eateries near Bocage Village she discovered new passions that came with her new life, and they didn't involve opening her own franchise of Creole restaurants. She was happy just spending time with her kids and seeing us living well and enjoying life.

Not far from the gates of Bocage was an array of antique gift shops and art galleries along with a host of exotic floral boutiques. My mother was spending more time in the shops than in the village. She became so acquainted with the store owners that they started calling her "Bren, the Oprah Winfrey of Bocage Village", a nickname she came to adore.Because of the settlement, our family became richer than most could imagine. And I spared no expense when it came to shopping for my mom. I instructed the contractors whom I hired to build her dream house to install a solid marble Jacuzzi with 24 karat gold facets and set it in the center of her spacious master bedroom. Then I called in a team of highly recommended interior decorators to add waterfalls around the Jacuzzi to help create a tropical rainforest décor with soothing nature sounds, the ambience that resulted was out of this world.

Knowing how frugal my mother was when it came to spending money on herself, I would always hide the price of expensive gifts that I bought for her. Items that were of excessive value would be delivered to her by carrier, and every package would bear the same label: "A gift from an anonymous stranger". Though she knew it was me, Mama never asked about the cost of any of the presents I bought her. She just accepted them with a smile and pretended the "anonymous stranger" was real. To give you an idea of how rich we were, let me tell you about two particular gifts I bought for my mom on her birthday. The first was a Cartier---the Tank Francaise Riviere, to be exact---a 450-diamond, $250,000 version of the most sort after watch line in the company's history. This amazing timepiece was so exquisite its wearer was believed to possess a magic essence... some called it the power of enchantment.

The second gift my mother received that day was Concord's tribute to its Saratoga line, the one of a kind "Exor". This bejeweled timepiece once belonged to the Sultan of Brunei. I acquired it through a rather shady liaison, a Columbian gentleman who went by the name Englique Fernando Escobar: Black hair, dark tan, perfect diction, pearly-white teeth, impeccable taste in women, Englique had it all. Despite his good looks and charming personality, Englique's reputation as a drug lord and arms dealer was a formidable one. He was known for dismembering his enemies and mailing their body parts to their widows and children in neatly wrapped gift boxes tagged with glyphs of unicorns. I became acquainted with him through a mutual friend named Hugo who lives in Columbia but was in the States on unrelated business. Hugo gave me fair warning about Englique before any introductions were made, I was prepared to take the risk because Englique was the only person who could lead me to the gift I wanted for my mom. After our introduction via Skype, he instructed me to fly to Indonesia and he would have someone there to meet me at the airport in Jakarta. Once I landed, a beautiful woman named Myra approached me with a briefcase and asked me a few questions which I knew the answers to only because Englique had given them to me. Then, after insisting that I hold the briefcase, she gave me one final instruction: "Describe the oracle."

What the fuck?!

The handle on the briefcase Myra had asked me to hold was equipped with a high-tech sensor that measures the physiological responses to questions posed to the holder of the briefcase. In other words, the briefcase had been fitted with a polygraph and Myra was giving me a lie detcctor test.

"I'm not sure I understood your question, Myra," I said while trying to figure out how in the world Englique knew about the oracle. I hadn't told anyone about that, not even my mother.

"It wasn't a question, it was a demand," said Myra. "You can either describe the oracle or get back on the plane---the choice is yours."My heart started racing because I knew getting back on the plane wasn't going to be as easy as she made it seem. Englique probably had explosives already aboard ready to be remotely detonated once the plane took off again. So regardless of how strange it might sound to her, I began telling Myra about the oracle in chilling detail: "Well, this may sound kind of weird but the oracle I encountered while in the ocean was being chased by a giant squid and was headed for certain death. It appeared to me in the form of a little white dolphin that I rescued based on what was told to me by the Great Elder Romulus. He said that I would meet the oracle and it would show me what I needed to know in order to defeat Sapian, the red dragon.

"The oracle asked me to solve a riddle, and when I said the answer was a rainbow, the angelic creature transformed itself into a prism made of pure crystal and produced a giant rainbow beneath the ocean. The oracle then opened up its mouth and told me to look inside, so I did. And that's when I saw visions of the future and---"

I immediately stopped talking about the oracle because out the corner of my eye I saw that Myra was struggling to hold back her laughter at what I was saying. I hadn't noticed it before, but she was wearing an earpiece in her left ear and someone on the other end was laughing at my little story.

"Hey, what's so damn funny? And who's that you're talking to?" I said to Myra, who was flat out laughing her head off by now.

"Mr. Escobar says you're a lunatic, and that anyone who's as crazy as you are can't be working for the F.B.I."

"Yeah, well you tell Mr. Escobar I said he can kiss my ass!" I said to myself as I stood there trying to put the pieces of the puzzle together in my head. Little did I know, one of Englique's inside guys at the C.I.A. tapped my mother's phone and overheard her telling one of the church ladies she's friends with, that I sometimes talk in my sleep. She said that she heard me mumbling something about a mermaid, a dragon, and a fish named Oracle. So Englique thought it would be funny to test me by seeing if I would be willing to make a fool of myself rather than deny the story altogether---but in the end, the joke was on him. Several days later one of his cronies checked the results of the lie detector and discovered that I had passed.

My beautiful guide Myra accompanied me on a short cruise from Jakarta to Singapore aboard a privately owned yacht belonging to "Mr. Funnyman" himself, Englique. Arrangements had been made for me to be taken to a secret auction where some of the world's most exclusive treasures were to be sold to the highest bidder. I had my heart (and my wallet) set on getting the one of a kind Exor.

Once we entered the port at Singapore, I was blindfolded and then taken by limo on a long ride. Myra, who remained on the yacht, had instructed me not to remove the blindfold until the car came to a stop and the driver opened my door---I followed her instructions to the letter, so it wasn't until the driver let me out of the car did I take off the blindfold. There before my eyes was an endless field of pink orchids in bloom. They were swaying and dancing in the breeze for as far as the eye could see.

"Where am I?" I asked the petite limo driver standing beside me grinning in his oversized tuxedo and shiny black chauffeur's cap. He didn't speak English apparently, but no matter, because a few moments later a small drone appeared in the sky and began hovering right above my head. Affixed to the side of it was a holographic panel with the flashing message: "Follow Me!" I was of course apprehensive at first, but then I reminded myself that the reason I had traveled all that way was to get my mother the gift of a lifetime. So I left the Chinese limo driver behind and followed the drone into the field of orchids where I soon came upon an area that looked like the ones in those UFO documentaries where they talk about crop circles. The orchids had been laid down in a circular pattern and there were no signs of foot traffic anywhere. The moment I stepped inside the circle I felt dizzy and lightheaded, then I started hearing a humming noise and saw a doorway slowly opening up in the ground. Beyond it was a spiral staircase leading down into a hidden bunker where I saw several people sitting at a table. "Damn! I must be trippin'!" I said to myself.

I cautiously descended the staircase and began eyeing those who had come to the auction hoping to add the Exor to their collection of exquisite timepieces. My game was tight and my money was right, it was time to play with the big boys, the super rich Arabian prince types who came dressed in silk from head to feet... oh yeah, it was on!

With its 118 rare, D-flawless diamonds set in pure platinum, perpetual calendar, and repeater functions, the Exor was the "crem de la crem" of haute joaillerie (high fashion jewelry). I'll admit the competition was fierce, but up against a room full of people with particular tastes in antiquities I held it down for the hood and proved that my wealth was too great for the foreign opposition.

"Sold!" Shouted the Chinese auctioneer, "to the American gentleman who wears the smile of a Cheshire Cat!"

My winning bid for the Exor timepiece was in the amount of $450 million. Mama nearly had a heart attack when it was delivered to the house by armored truck and wrapped in pure silk. She opened up her present and tears started coming down her face.

"Mama, what's wrong?!" I said as I reached for the box in her hand. "Why are you crying?"

Sitting inside the box was the Exor in all its splendor: its diamonds glistening like Spring water, its face perfectly aligned, its band exquisite. The bejeweled timepiece came with its own Certificate of Authenticity which briefly explained the watch's history and listed its extravagant cost. Mama was crying because she knew that I had gone to great lengths to make her birthday wish come true. She had always dreamed of having a one of a kind accessory that she could call her own, and now she had the best one in the whole world. I had never seen her as happy as she was when showing off her new watch to the rest of the family saying, "Look what my 'anonymous stranger' gave me for my birthday." My baby sister Elexus chimed in and said, "Mama, you better marry that man!" And we all laughed until we were completely out of breath. My mother deserved the best that life had to offer, and I planned to do whatever it took to make sure she was taken care of---she was the glue that held our family together and kept us strong, and I remembered the countless sacrifices she made so that I could pursue my dreams. Now it was time for me to make her dreams come true.

I love you Mama.

My mother soon met a nice guy named William, but she called him "Willie" for short. He owned the construction company that I hired to build her new house in Bocage Village. They became well acquainted after Mama took over his crew and appointed herself "Boss in Charge of Everything". She would often complain about this or that and then William would have to come to the house and fix the problem---even though there weren't any problems that needed fixing. They started spending more and more time together and eventually William became a permanent fixture around the house. I didn't mind as long as Mama was happy, but Jamal gave William a hard time and even threatened to kill him if he ever put his hands on our mom. But William wasn't like that, he was genuinely a nice guy and I knew that because I ran a thorough background check on him the moment he asked Mama out on their first date. His company, Pitts Construction LLC, had offices throughout the Gulf Coast region from Texas to Florida. Though he had made a fortune in the construction business, the bulk of his wealth came from a lucrative investment he made in a fledgling computer software company that quickly grew into a powerhouse and is currently listed on the New York Stock Exchange. Several years ago William was invited to a business seminar in Silicon Valley where he listened to a presentation given by a brilliant young MIT graduate named Tao Ming.

Ming headed the software development team at a company called Nanotech Industries, but privately he was working on a prototype of his own that could revolutionize the way we all communicate. William was so impressed with Ming's presentation on telecommunication networks that he arranged a meeting so they could discuss launching a joint business venture. The two men soon entered into a partnership and started a new tech company called Synyl (Sentinel). William was the company's sole investor. Less than a year later, Synyl released the first fully interactive cybernetic language translation software that enabled users to speak any language in the world. Ming's knowledge of nanotechnology and William's bankroll enticed a team of neurologists to join the company. They immediately broke new ground by combining neuroconnectors and nanotechnology in ways no one had thought of. Ming and his team built a powerful microprocessor that was small enough to fit on the tip of a ballpoint pen.

The way it worked was nothing short of genius. A microchip was implanted behind the left or right ear, then the neuroconnectors inside the chip would then be released and would only attach themselves to nerves in the brain running between Broca's area (a region of the left frontal lobe involved in speech) and Wernicke's area (a region of the left temporal lobe involved in processing written and spoken language). The microprocessor, which was being powered by bioelectricity in the brain, enabled the host to not only understand and fluently speak all languages, but write them as well. Ming's revolutionary software, Vox Populi, which means "voice of the people", successfully removed the world's language barriers and made it possible for everyone to speak in the same tongue. Synyl's slogan "One world. One voice." skyrocketed the company to new heights. The latest Robb Report listed its stocks at over 350 billion dollars.

Welcome to the family, Pop.

Brandon and Jamal, two of my younger brothers, were engaged in a heated game of one-on-one basketball in Mama's backyard when they suddenly heard her screaming at them from an upstairs window.

"Put down that ball and come speak to your aunt and uncle!" she yelled, but the boys ignored her and kept right on playing. Which made her call to them a second time but with a bit more attitude: "Bring y'all black asses in this house right now! Don't make me come down there and act a fool in front of our company! Clemus and Joy don' drove all the way from California to see how we doing, so stop bouncing that ball and get y'all asses in this house!"

The basketball court in Mama's backyard was housed inside a green "see-through" mesh enclosure the size of an Olympic swimming pool. Everyone in the family called it the "greenhouse". The boys often played ball at night and the mesh covering protected them from being eaten alive by mosquitoes.

"Mama, hold up a minute! The game is almost over." Brandon shouted, "I'm about to make the last shot!"

"Stop talkin' and shoot the fuckin' ball, chump!" Jamal yelled at Brandon for holding up the game. "I dare you to bring that weak shit in here!"Accepting Jamal's challenge, Brandon tightened his shoelaces, adjusted his shorts, and went charging in the lane hoping to score the winning basket---bad idea.

"GET THAT WEAK SHIT OUTTA HERE!" yelled Jamal after aggressively slamming both the basketball and Brandon to the ground. "You shoulda took the 'J', my nigga."

"That was a flagrant foul!" cried Brandon while dusting off his knees and elbows after the nasty spill he took. "It's still my ball."

"Game's over, dawg." Jamal said as he walked off the court wearing a devilish grin. "I know you heard Mama hollering out the window like she crazy. I ain't fitnah play with that woman and have her coming down here trippin' and shit, ya heard me."

"But that's not fair! You cheated! The game can't end on a foul and I only need one more point!"Jamal ignored his brother's pleas for an opportunity to win the game, leaving him only one option... "I'MMA TELL MAMA!" And there it was---Brandon's equalizer.Jamal knew from experience that going to trial in Mama's courtroom was a one-sided affair with no rebuttals.

"Why you always puttin' Mama in our business?! You know how she be trippin'!" Jamal chided.

"Well, you shoulda thought about that before you cheated me," said Brandon while walking toward the house on his way to rat Jamal out.

"Bitch-ass nigga! Go tell Mama this too!"Jamal swung a vicious right cross and hit Brandon in the face so hard that he blackened his eye and bloodied his nose with a single punch. Brandon screamed and then took off running like a frantic antelope being chased by a hungry cheetah. The poor kid was running for dear life. He raced across the patio and darted through the den before tumbling headfirst into the living room after tripping over Mama's brand new Persian rug.

"Heeelp!" Brandon yelled at the top of his lungs. "Jamal is trying to kill me!"

The only way Brandon was able to keep Jamal at bay was by running around the expensive sectional at the center of the living room and switching directions whenever Jamal would come after him.

"Hey guys, what's going on here?" said William, who had been standing by the bar quietly sipping on a tall glass of Mama's homemade lemonade. "Are you guys okay?"

"Jamal punched me in the face and he won't leave me alone!" Brandon squealed. "Where's Mama?!"

"I believe she's upstairs with your relatives from out of town," said William with a nervous tone. You could actually hear the ice cubes in his drink clinking against the glass because his hands were shaking so bad. William had heard stories about Jamal from the guys on his construction crew who lived in New Orleans. They told him how the police suspected him of being involved in at least a dozen homicides and how the witnesses were afraid to testify against him. To William, Jamal was the real life version of "O-Dog" from "Menace II Society"... young, Black, and just don't give a fuck!---America's nightmare.

"Listen s-s-son," said William, stuttering for the first time ever. "Let's be reasonable here."As William tried to reason with Jamal, Brandon made a dash for the stairs---another bad idea.

"Come here you lil' bitch!" Jamal growled as he grabbed Brandon by the shirt and snatched him off the staircase."(Pip! Pap! Bing-Bada-Boom!)

Jamal landed a flurry of punches that sent Brandon sliding across the freshly waxed woodgrain floor like a hockey puck. Brandon knew at that point there was only one person in the whole world who could save him... "MAAH-MAAAAH!!!"

"Who is that making all that noise?!" Mama yelled from the top of the stairs. "What the hell is going on down there?!"

No one dared to say anything, not even William. Then, like an idiot, I walked into the room after entering the house through the garage and opened my big mouth saying, "Why is Mama yelling like that?"

"Be quiet, nigga!" whispered Jamal in a threatening manner. "Mama trippin' cause I brought that smoke to this clown and he started hollering like a damn fool."I took one look at Brandon's face and then turned to Jamal and said, "Any last words? Because Mama's going to kill you!"

She must've heard me, because the next sound coming from upstairs was her loud voice calling my name.

"Cartrell Victor Damone LeCour! Boy, you better answer me!" Whenever Mama called one of us by our whole name it meant big trouble. Her corporal punishment was swift and exact, and often involved the use of a particular piece of footwear.

"Oooh-wee! Trell you fitnah catch a whuppin'!" said my little sister Unique' while passing Mama in the hallway. "It's 'bout to be some drama up in here, huh Mama? Go 'head nah cheah, handle yo' bizzness!"

"Girl, take yo' lil' messy self back in there and finish your homework." Unique' dashed into her room but before closing the door behind her she yelled, "YOU BETTA RUN FOREST! RUUUUUUN!"

"Trell, if you don't bring your long, choupique looking head up these stairs I'mma come down there and wear yo' tail out with this shoe!" chided Mama while waving her shoe in the air like Conan the Barbarian wielding a sword. I glanced at William as if to say, "I know she's not talking about whipping me---I'm way too grown for that."But William wasn't paying attention, he was still pretty shaken up after seeing how kids from the projects handled disputes. To William, it was a culture shock.

"Trell," he pleaded. "Perhaps you should do as your mother asked and head upstairs." But I flat out refused, citing the fact that I wasn't the one who gave Brandon the black eye. Therefore, I felt that I was justified in standing my ground.

"I can't believe she still thinks she can intimidate me with that ol' shoe of hers." I said to William, "Doesn't she realize I'm a grown-ass man?"William kept quiet because he didn't want the burden of having to choose sides in the matter. But the fact that I was talking under my breath about disobeying my mother made him skeptical.

"You know what, I'm tired of this shit." I said loudly enough to where only the people downstairs could hear me, "I wish she would come down here talking 'bout whipping me. Man, I'll take that ol' crusty shoe of hers and throw it in the trashcan where it belongs." The infamous footwear I was referring to was more like a family heirloom, it had been passed down from one generation to the next for as far back as I could remember. It originally belonged to "Big Mama", my great great grandmother---a country girl who grew up on a farm in the heart of Mississippi. She was from a small, rustic community called "Midway"; the reason they called it that was because it was between Jackson, Mississippi and the middle of nowhere. Big Mama was a heavyset woman, but in most cases people who called her that were referring to her shoe size, not her weight. She had to have her shoes specially made to accommodate her peculiar feet; her left shoe---which was a men's size 13---was two sizes smaller than her right. Meaning that her right shoe was a men's size 15 extra wide! Whenever one of the LeCour children misbehaved, Big Mama would take off her size 15 shoe and use it for a paddle to spank whoever was acting up. The bloodcurdling screams that emanated from the poor unfortunate soul who was catching a whipping made the other children become like "sweet little angels" saying, "Yes ma'am" and "No ma'am".Historically, the shoe was given to the strongest woman in the family---the matriarch. The tradition certainly continued because the shoe was now in the hands of the woman standing at the top of the stairs.

"I'm not gon' call you again!" Mama warned, "If you not up these stairs when I count to three, I'mma blister yo' tail with this shoe! ONE! TWO! THR---"

"WAIT! I'M COMING UP RIGHT NOW!" I immediately shouted after remembering Jamal had gotten his ass whipped with the shoe just a few days earlier under similar circumstances. One thing was for sure, Mama didn't discriminate when it came to dispensing her brand of justice "Big Mama" style. As I slowly climbed the long spiral staircase, I glanced back and saw that Brandon, Jamal, and William were all laughing at me. I felt played but what could I do? Mama was already trippin' and I didn't wanna make matters worse by cussin' out "Willie" and the boys. So I sucked it up and took it like a man.

"Sometimes you make me so doggone mad I could just take this shoe and bust yo' brains out with it!" My mother was fuming mad waving Big Mama's size 15 in my face and threatening to whack me over the head with it.

"But I just came in the hous---"

"Shut up! I don't want to hear it," said the shoe-wielding warden of the LeCour State Penitentiary at Bocage. "I called you on the phone over twenty minutes ago and told you that Clemus and Joy was here and that they wanted to see you. Now take yo' narrow tail in there and speak!"I eased my way past her trying not to make eye contact, fearing that I might become paralyzed like when a mouse stares into the eyes of a cobra. I then went to the upstairs den where Clem' and Joy greeted me with hugs and smiles.

"Lord have mercy, Jesus," said Mama as she turned and headed back to the edge of the stairs. "These chur'n 'bout to run me crazy. They act like we still in the projects." Once she reached her destination all hell broke loose.

"Jamal Douchet LeCour! Bring yo' lil' black ass up these stairs right now! I know you don' done something you ain't got no business doing, so come here!"

Though he tried his best to sound innocent, Jamal wasn't fooling anyone when he said, "But Mama, I ain't even do nothing!" WHOP! WHOP! WHOP!...went the sound of Big Mama's shoe against Jamal's bare ass.

CHAPTER 23

FAMILY MATTERS

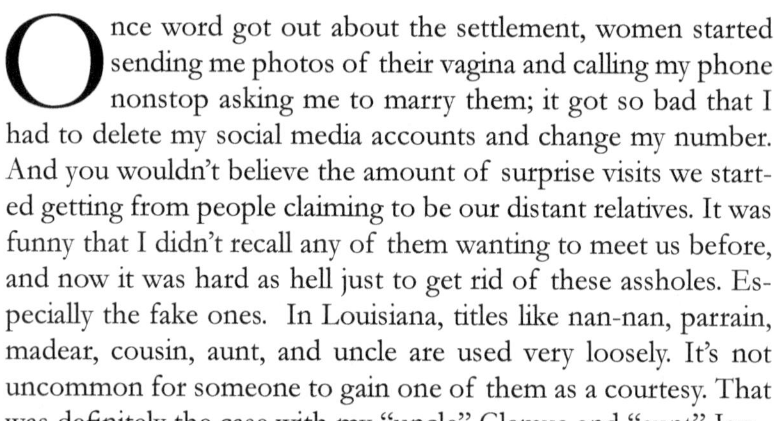

Once word got out about the settlement, women started sending me photos of their vagina and calling my phone nonstop asking me to marry them; it got so bad that I had to delete my social media accounts and change my number. And you wouldn't believe the amount of surprise visits we started getting from people claiming to be our distant relatives. It was funny that I didn't recall any of them wanting to meet us before, and now it was hard as hell just to get rid of these assholes. Especially the fake ones. In Louisiana, titles like nan-nan, parrain, madear, cousin, aunt, and uncle are used very loosely. It's not uncommon for someone to gain one of them as a courtesy. That was definitely the case with my "uncle" Clemus and "aunt" Joy.

"Hey guys! It's great to see you!" I said as I greeted them with false enthusiasm. "How was your trip from L.A.?" The obvious contempt in my voice earned me a menacing glare from my mother, who was standing in the doorway like a bouncer at a nightclub tightly gripping Big Mama's legendary footwear.

"The trip was absolutely marvelous," said Clem' with a broad smile on his face. "And the weather was perfect for sporting my snazzy new outfit. How do you like it, Trelly my boy?" I stood dumbfounded staring at the outfit not really understanding what would possess someone to dress that way. I knew that Clem' was somewhat of an oddball when it came to fashion, but this was ridiculous even for him. Here was a guy in his mid-fifties trying desperately to hold on to his youth by wearing colorful outfits that looked like a cross between Hip-Hop fashion and the stuff that's leftover after a rummage sale. Clem' always used the same word to describe his tacky outfits, he called them... "snazzy". Well, what wasn't so snazzy was his receding hairline, which Clemus tried to hide by wearing a ridiculous looking toupee that Joy purchased at a Mexican flea market in Houston for three dollars---she said it made him look foreign. The cheap hairpiece obviously had been made for a person of Spanish or Asian dissent. So when Clemus put it on, you could see his African American "buckshots" sticking out from underneath the damn thing making him look like a black Jackie Chan from the projects.

Clem's latest outfit featured a pair of purple and black argyle socks with pink giraffes covered in bright orange polka dots. He stylishly wore them pulled all the way up to just below his ashy kneecaps, making his scrawny legs look like two twigs wrapped in Halloween stockings. His "spooky" legs protruded downward out of a pair of checkered golf shorts made of polyester, and for reasons unbeknownst to mankind, Joy hemmed the shorts putting 6-inch cuffs at the end of each leg. So everywhere Clemus went, the giant cuffs would swing back and forth like 70's bell-bottoms and people would break out in hysterics at seeing such a spectacle. His fashion wreck was being held together by a pair of pink, fuzzy suspenders and a fake cowhide belt that had been dyed red, green, and lavender using Easter egg coloring. Attached to the front of the belt like an anchor, was a huge goldplated buckle that was shaped like a woman's uterus... hey, we haven't even gotten to the weird stuff yet. On this particular occasion,

Clemus showed up wearing purple and gold "alligator" slippers made of cheap patent leather---he called them "Now and Laters". And he claimed they were a big hit with the ladies out West.

Nigga, please!

"Well, what do you think Trelly my boy?" Clemus said with outstretched arms modeling the hideous outfit as if it had come from a famous designer. "It's pretty snazzy, huh?"Before I answered him, I glanced over toward the doorway where Mama had been standing moments earlier. She was no longer there but I figured why take any chances.

"Yeah Unc', that outfit is really something." I managed to say with a straight face. "The ladies down here are going to be all over you when they see you in those flashy threads. Aunt Joy had better watch out." I poured it on just a little too thick.

"You have good taste, Trelly, I knew you'd like it! That's why I insisted on getting you one as well. I left it in the car, let's go get it so you can try it on for size." Clemus was smiling so broadly that I couldn't find the heart to turn him down.

"Gee, thanks Unc'. I umm... don't know what to say."As I begrudgingly followed my fake "uncle" to the driveway where I was sure more embarrassment awaited, I thought to myself: "God, what did I do to deserve this?"

If you thought Clem's taste in fashion was strange, wait until you see what his taste in cars is like. I must warn you, this next part is not for the squeamish or the faint at heart. Parental discretion is advised.

Curious onlookers from the neighborhood, mostly children, had already begun gathering near our driveway. They stood gawking at the spectacle that was parked in our yard, some of the kids took snapshots with their smartphones and posted pictures of the car on social media telling others to take a look at the ghetto version of "Chitty-Chitty Bang-Bang".The car that Clemus and Joy drove up in was a Daimler Chrysler Sebring convertible that had been modified to look like a hearse. It was painted in psychedelic colors beginning with a bright "canary" yellow at the front and showcasing every other color of the rainbow thereafter. There were two huge elephant tusks mounted on the hood and they too sported the kind of illuminating colors that would have gone over big at Lollapalooza. At any moment, I thought the Beatles might jump out of the car singing, "We all live in a yellow submarine, a yellow submarine..."

Welded above the rear bumper of the car was a tire that had been stolen off a Continental LS, and sitting in the middle of it was a portable black and white TV with a broken antenna wrapped in aluminum foil. The TV was connected to an orange extension cord that ran along the outside of the car and disappeared beneath the hood near the place where the battery was located. The suspicious looking tire was decorated with colorful lights that blinked in sequence to the sound of music; I could hear RUN-DMC's famous holiday classic---"Christmas in Hollis Queens"---playing continuously on a tiny music box hidden amongst the lights. Clem's automotive nightmare was sitting on a set of mismatched tires that he purchased from crack-heads in his neighborhood. Not only were the stolen tires different sizes, each of them still had the original car's logo on the hubcap. One hubcap, in particular, was supposed to keep spinning whenever the car would stop moving, but all it did was make a loud ratchet noise that would scare the hell of pigeons every time Clemus drove near a park or playground. And when he drove too fast, the other hubcaps would start whistling as loud as the ratchet noise coming from the broken spinner. I could just imagine the look on our white neighbors' faces when Clem' came click-clacking and whistling up the boulevard in the jalopy from Christmas past.

My Aunt Joy, the copilot of the damn thing, made matters worse with her eccentric beehive hairdo and her bright, colorful makeup. She looked like she was riding a float in a Mardi Gras parade, and when kids would run up to the car shouting "Throw me something, lady!", Joy would reach into her purse and pull out handfuls of toiletries that she and Clem' had swiped from hotel bathrooms. Joy would ride shotgun in the front seat of the car wearing fake "ruby studded" sunglasses that made her look like Elton John in drag. And she had a body odor that smelled like a combination of eucalyptus balm and pickled pigs' feet. It was a pungent odor that reminded me of old people's slippers. But the most peculiar thing about Aunt Joy---besides the fact that she hung out with Clemus---was her odd facial expressions. You see, Joy shaved off her natural eyebrows long ago and now she draws new ones on every morning using a Marks-A-Lot. Sometimes she gets them perfect, but more often than not, she draws them too high upon her forehead and it makes it appear as though she's asking a question like, "huh?". Her odd facial expressions are absolutely hilarious. Even when engaged in conversations with her, people would often find themselves staring at Joy's conspicuous eyebrows rather than listening to whatever point she was trying to make. Then they too would end up mimicking her expression before asking the question, "huh?".

From their strange appearance to their tacky costume jewelry Clem' and Joy were the perfect "odd couple". The only problem I had with them was that they were always putting on airs, pretending to be well off when they knew they weren't. Some people call it acting "booshie", which is a loose interpretation of the French word "bourgeois". In other words they were frauds---especially Clemus. He had even gone to the extent of speaking with a false accent to try and get people to believe he was from Los Angeles, when in fact he had only been to California once in his entire life; and that was because he was admitted into a rehab center right outside of Fresno. Clemus and Joy are actually from St. Francisville, a small town about 45 minutes from Baton Rouge. Somehow, they were under the impression that we didn't know where they lived. To spare them some embarrassment, Mama would tell us not to say anything because she felt that it would be rude. So whenever Clem' and Joy would drop by, we would all pretend to believe that they had drove down from California for a visit. Well, all of us except for Jamal of course.My mother would always assign me the job of keeping Jamal away from the guests. She knew how much he hated when people pretended to be something they weren't. If given the opportunity to be alone with Clemus, my thuggish brother Jamal would definitely... well, you know.

"Your snazzy outfit is right here, Trelly my boy. You're going to love it," said Clem' using his most proper Caliphony-an accent. "Mine was all the rave, I received lots and lots of looks as me and Joy drove up the coast on the way here to visit with you all." I wanted so desperately to say, "But Unc', there are no coasts between here and St. Francisville.", instead, I just changed the subject.

"Unc', I'm surprised that no one has tried to steal this sweet ride of yours." I was sarcastically referring to the monstrosity parked in our driveway.

"Oh, that's because I've installed my very own car alarm. It's really snazzy, would you like to hear it?" Before I could say no, Clem' brushed up against the car and all hell broke loose.

"WOOFH! WOOFH! WOOFH! GGRRRR!" went the amplified sound of growling attack dogs blaring out of six large speakers that had been embedded in the trunk. The terrifying sound sent the neighborhood kids scurrying away in every direction. Then out of the trunk came a different sound: "CHIT-CHIT! BOOM! CHIT-CHIT! BOOM!" It was the sound of shotgun blasts ringing out so loudly I could feel the bass from the speakers ricocheting off my chest.

"AAAHH! SOMEBODY PLEASE HELP ME!" I couldn't fucking believe it. Clemus had a recording of a white woman in distress. "SHUT UP! WHERE IS MY MUTHAFUCKIN' MONEY, BITCH?!"

And that was her Black pimp.

"Uncle Clem'! Uncle Clem'!" I shouted, "Turn it off!"

"Trelly, you have to speak up I can't hear you," said Clemus while digging around in his pocket for the remote.

"Turn it off! Turn off the alar---" Tweep! Tweep! *Silence.*

"Unc', are you nuts?! We have neighbors!" I chided before making a break for the house hoping that no one had saw me standing next to Clem'. I ran so fast that I fell and skinned my knee on the pavement and then started dragging my leg like a wounded soldier trying to make it safely back inside the house. By the time Clemus finally turned off the alarm, all of our neighbors had come outside and were standing on their lawns shooting videos with their camera phones of the freak show taking place in our front yard.Looking on from an upstairs window, my mother was shaking her head saying, "Lord have mercy, I know them white folks saying to themselves, 'There goes the neighborhood.'" The hysterical scene reminded me of the time my uncle "Dub" came to the Calliope bragging about being a professional bass fisherman. He was our family's version of "Bernie Mac", whenever Uncle Dub would show up at a family function something hilarious was bound to happen. On this particular occasion, after telling everyone that he had just won a bass tournament down in Morgan City, uncle Dub talked my grandmother into letting me go on a fishing trip with him to prove it. The minute we left the projects, Dub started whining about opening his big mouth.

"Ooooh-Weeh! Ain't that a bitch!", he cried while fidgeting with his raggedy ol' Saints football cap that's been part of his wardrobe for as long as I've known him. "Shaggy, I don' laid there and got myself in a jam, ya heard me. I don't know what I'mma do, I ain't got no goddamn boat. Shit, this ain't even my car." My uncle Dub would always call me "Shaggy", which was never my nickname, it was just that he had so many nephews that it was hard for him to remember our names. So he called all of us by the same name, Shaggy. Since we didn't have a boat, my uncle and I ended up fishing off the Jackson Street Wharf. It took him nearly ten minutes just to bait his hook because he was so scared of the live worms we were using for bait. The worm that he settled on was smaller than the rest, but it was extremely feisty. Each time Dub tried to put it on the hook, the energetic nightcrawler would wrap itself around his finger like a snake and Dub would scream out loud as if he'd been bitten by a cottonmouth. Man, I laughed so hard that I almost had an asthma attack right there on the wharf.

After finally getting the worm to cooperate, my hilarious uncle grabbed hold of his rod and reel and then reared back as if he was going to cast the line clear across the Mississippi River. Unfortunately things didn't go as he planned. The brand new gear he had purchased from a sporting goods store on the way to the wharf slipped right out of his hands and sailed through the air before disappearing into the murky waters of the mighty Mississippi.

"Shaggy! You saw that?!"

"No Unc', what happened?" I said while pretending not to have seen him accidentally throw his rod and reel into the river. "You didn't see dat big ol' bass jump up out the water and snatch my pole right outta my hands?!"

"No Unc', I must've missed it. How big was it?" My uncle Dub's eyes grew wide as he twisted his ol' beat up Saints cap around to the back and showed me with his hands how large the fish was that got away.

"Shaggy, dat big bass like to took my whole arm off. It was at least 'bout 10 or 11 feet long," he exaggerated while rubbing his shoulder as though his arm had been jerked out of socket. I was trying my best not to laugh but my crazy uncle was carrying on like you wouldn't believe.

"Oh Lord! Shaggy, I ain't gon' be able to do no more fishing for a while, no cheah," he said while standing at the end of the wharf staring out over the river. He was desperately trying to figure out what he was going to tell everyone back in the Calliope, which he called the "Yo". Then I heard him shout, "Aaa-lah-bas!", and I knew right then that our little fishing trip was about to get way out of hand.

"Say lil' Shaggy, I don' figured out how we gon' get us a big ol' bass to take back to the Yo! I can't let them haters clown me, nephew---ya heard me." Uncle Dub started tossing the rest of our gear into the water: ice chest, tackle box, folding chairs, fish stringer, bait bucket, and even the extra worms he bought in case we ran out. The dysfunctional bass wrangler then removed his shoes and socks and threw them in the river too.

"Them niggas in the Yo gon' be waitin' on me to come back empty-handed, nephew, but I ain't going out like dat."Next thing I knew, we were sitting in front of a fish market on Tchoupitoulas Street where I insisted on waiting in the car while Dub, barefoot and all, went in to buy his "trophy bass". He intended to lie his way clear of being ridiculed by everyone he had bragged to about his pro bass experience and all the tournaments he supposedly won. Once inside the market, Uncle Dub began negotiating with the owner.

"Nah look here, cheah. I need you to hook me up with the biggest bass you got, ya dig?" A few minutes later my uncle came running out of the market carrying a large package wrapped in newspaper and tied with string. He tossed it on the backseat of the car and excitedly jumped into the driver's seat.

"Shaggy! I'mma 'bout to shine on them haters for real! You know them niggas holding they nuts wishing I ain't catch no fish, but I'mma 'bout to act a fool and show my natural black ass when we get to the Yo. Man, them haters ain't gon' liiike dat!" Uncle Dub was determined to show off in front of the people who had doubted him so fiercely. Though I tried to talk some sense into him, he insisted that he knew what he was doing. I pleaded with him all the way back to the projects to no avail. And when he jumped out of the car with the package tucked underneath his arm, I knew it was too late to save him. "Come nah! I say! Y'all ain't believe me when I told y'all I'mma pro fisherman. Well, whatcha' got to say nah?! Watch out cheah!" Dub boasted as he flung open the newspaper containing the big fish he had purchased from the market minutes earlier. But when his prize catch was revealed to everyone who had gathered around to see it, I heard my grandmother let out a loud whoop which was quickly followed by a chorus of contagious laughter. My poor uncle couldn't understand why they were laughing at him. He was expecting them to congratulate him for catching such a magnificent bass, Dub wanted his props but instead all he got was loud jeers from the mob around him that seemed to grow bigger by the minute. And just when I thought it couldn't get any worse, Uncle

Dub jumped on top of the table and started telling everyone how he had to battle the giant fish for over an hour just to get it in the boat, and how he had lost his shoes and socks---not to mention his rod and reel---during the fight. My grandmother laughed so hard that her dentures flew out of her mouth and landed on top of the fish causing an explosion of laughter that brought even more people running to see Uncle Dub's bass.

"Lord have mercy, Jesus!" said my grandmother while reaching for her teeth and trying to catch her breath. "This crazy lil' man gon' mess around and give me a heart attack!"

The reason that everyone was laughing at Dub was because the fish he purchased from the market wasn't a bass at all, it was a northern pike. The fish actually had been caught in the Great Lakes near Michigan.

After being exposed as a fraud and literally laughed out of the projects, Dub returned to the market on Tchoupitoulas Street and cussed out the Vietnamese store owner who had sold him what was supposedly "the biggest bass in Louisiana".

"But mark this: There will be trouble times in the last days. People will be lovers of themselves, lovers of money, boastful, proud, abusive, disobedient to their parents, ungrateful, unholy, without love, unforgiving, slanderous, without self-control, brutal, not lovers of the good, treacherous, rash, conceited lovers of pleasure rather than lovers of God---having a form of godliness but denying its power... They are the kind who worm their way into homes and gain control over weak-willed women, who are loaded down with sins and are swayed by all kinds of evil desires."

---2 Timothy 3:1-6

CHAPTER 24

EX LIBRIS MIRABILIA: FROM THE BOOKS OF MIRACLES

This sure is a nice house you've built for your mother, Trelly my boy." Clemus said when he returned back inside the house after making a spectacle of himself in front of our neighbors. "Bren' has told me that you've also purchased an estate in New Orleans, is that right?"

"Oh no!" I thought to myself. "I wonder what else has Mama discussed with this fool?"

"Yeah Unc', I bought a place on the beach overlooking Lake Ponchartrain. It's where I go when I want to spend time with my fiancée Azoria." I paused a moment and then asked, "Did Mama mention her at all?" (Azoria and I got engaged after a long courtship-I'm talking 36 months!)

Clemus smiled a glorious smile and then emphatically replied, "Yes! Yes of course, the little mermaid." He could hardly contain his laughter; it was times like this that I wished I hadn't said anything to Mama about my adventures on the Galactic Island. She insists that it's all in my mind, that I must have bumped my head during the explosion and dreamed the whole thing. But I didn't tell her everything. She doesn't know that I was shown a vision by the oracle where Azoria and I were together in New Orleans---just as we are now. I didn't tell her because I knew she would come up with an explanation for that too.

"So um..., Unc'. Mama told you about my little adventure, huh?" I said to Clemus who was still grinning for some reason. "Yes, but I don't believe a word of it. In fact, I think it's quite commendable that you're able to make light of such a traumatic experience," he said as if to sympathize with me.

"A black mermaid, indeed." Clem' chuckled, "Black women don't even like getting their hair wet."

"Well Unc', there's more to the story than just---"

"Trelly my boy," Clem' interrupted. "I'm sure there is. But let's stick to reality for a moment. Is your fiancée a real person?"

"Yes! Of course she's real!" I snapped at Clem' for questioning my sanity, "Do you think I just made her up?"

"Well, did you?" Clem' said while mumbling under his breath.

"Now listen Unc', Azoria and I met at the hospital where she works. She was my doctor for crying out loud." Clemus' unrelenting skepticism was getting the best of me---I could feel it. Yet I was determined to have a civil conversation with my dubious guest, so I took a deep breath, suppressed my anger, and moved on to the next matter at hand.

"Unc', I'd like to get your opinion on something if you don't mind." I now had Clem's undivided attention, "I recently asked Azoria to quit her job at the hospital so that the two of us could travel the world together, but instead of being excited about it, she got real upset with me. And she said that I had a lot of nerve to ask her to abandon her patients and go on a permanent vacation. Unc', do you think I was out of line?"

Clemus stood gazing up at the ceiling rubbing his chin as if he was a great scholar contemplating the meaning of life. He cleared his throat and then spoke in an authoritative manner saying, "Trelly my boy, I must give it to you straight. You see, a woman is like a fine wine... the longer you keep her down in the cellar the better she'll taste later once she's had time to fumigate."

I was thinking to myself, "What the hell is this nigga talking about?"

"What you really need, Trelly my boy, is a good ol' country girl, one who's never been off the farm before. Take your Aunt Joy for instance, she knows who wears the pants in our relationship." I looked down at Clemus' pants and had to refrain from making a snide remark. Aunt Joy's role in their relationship wasn't that of a companion, but more like that of "a sidekick". She's virtually a puppet who sits there grinning and nodding her head in agreement with every ridiculous thing that comes out of Clem's mouth. She's pitiful.

"Um... on second thought," I said to Clem after reassessing my position on the matter. "I believe I overreacted a bit, in fact, I should be glad that Azoria is capable of making her own decisions and speaking her mind when in comes to matters of great concern. She certainly doesn't need me dictating her every move." I was alluding to the fact that Joy doesn't leave Clem's side unless he tells her to.

"Yeah Unc', I think I'm pretty lucky to have a woman like Azoria in my life. She's smart, kindhearted, independent, and she doesn't take any crap off anyone---including me." I said while staring at Aunt Joy who sat there wearing that ridiculous expression on her face like, "huh?".

"Hey Unc', at least I convinced Azoria to come with me to the Super Bowl this weekend. Can you believe the game is in New Orleans this year, and the Saints are favored to win?" Clemus was only half listening to me talk about the big game. His mind was on trying to find a way to ask my mother could he and Joy stay for the weekend. As soon as Mama returned to the den with refreshments, Clem' sprung into action.

"Oh Bren'," he said with the utmost charm. "You wouldn't mind if Joy and I visited with you all for the weekend would you, hon'?"

"Well,---" said Mama.

"Oh, thank you Bren'!" Clemus hurriedly accepted before she could think of a reason to turn him down. "We won't be any bother," said Clem'. "In fact, Joy can help you with the cooking and the cleaning---you know, the women's work." Mama nearly came unglued at hearing the chauvinistic remark Clem' made. But for Joy's sake, she caged her anger and resisted the urge to bust Clem's brains out with Big Mama's size 15 billy club.

"Clemus! Me and Joy ain't doing no cooking and cleaning! We 'bout to hit the malls and shop till we drop! Ain't that right, Joy?" Aunt Joy was looking like someone had stuck her finger in an electrical outlet and turned the switch on. She was shocked at Mama's candor, and when she glanced over at Clemus as if asking his permission to go shopping, Mama grabbed her by the hand and said, "Come on here, Joy! You don't need no man's permission to go with me, we family, child. You, me, and the girls fitnah go out c'here and tear the malls down! You hear me?"

Mama was fuming mad, "Lord have mercy! Y'all lil' women sure is weak behind these men. That's why they treat y'all so bad." She said while glaring in Clemus' direction wishing he *would* say something. But he knew better. Not only that, he noticed Jamal standing near the doorway with his fists tightly clenched waiting for the opportunity to catch our fake uncle alone.

"Oh, Bren'?" Clemus cried out in near panic, "Who's going to stay behind and watch over me, I mean, spend time with me while you all are away?"

Mama paused at the door and said, "Trell, why don't you take Clemus to New Orleans with you this weekend?"

Oh, hell no! I thought to myself, but said, "I can't Mama! I promised Azoria we'd spend the weekend at the beach house, alone. Besides, I don't think Uncle Clem' would want to be away from Aunt Joy for two whole days. Especially not now, knowing she's about to get a makeover at the mall with you guys."

I turned to my befuddled uncle and said, "I'm telling you, Unc'. There are lots of smooth brothers down here in Baton

Rouge who'd love to hook up with a 'California girl', know what I'm saying?"

Clemus' eyes grew wide as he pictured Joy with another man. He quickly jumped up out of his seat and told Mama, "You know what, Bren'? I'd better stay put right here. You may need me to take care of something that comes up over the weekend and I don't want to let you down."

Mama just gritted her teeth and grunted. But then, like always, I came up with the perfect solution, "Hey, why not ask Pop to hang out with Uncle Clem' this weekend?" I offered while brandishing every tooth in my head.

"Baby, that's a great idea!" said Mama. "Willie can show Clemus around and introduce him to all his friends."

"He sure can, Mama. And I know Pop's friends will just looove meeting Uncle Clem'!"

That's what he gets for laughing at me.

The Saints had just won another Super Bowl and the entire city was celebrating in the streets. Azoria and I, after leaving the Superdome in a limo, joined the rowdy crowds and headed to the French Quarter where thousands of Saints fans were yelling "Who Dat!?" and tossing elaborate beads to beautiful women who were showing off their naked breasts like it was Mardi Gras. The nicer the breasts the more exquisite the beads, and let me tell you, Azoria received so many exquisite beads that I had to tell her to keep her damn shirt on---that girl was having the time of her life.

We soon headed to a little spot called Pat O'Brien's and had our picture taken while standing next to the "flaming water fountain" that the Irish pub was famous for. Azoria's radiant smile lit up the entire room, and people were staring as we began slow dancing our way onto Bourbon Street, oblivious to everything and everyone around us. We were deeply in love and it was a beautiful thing to see.

After our romantic interlude, Azoria and I went looking around inside every little gift shop on Bourbon Street. Some of them sold "kinky" sex toys and T-shirts with explicit images on front. I saw one shirt that had Wily Coyote getting a blowjob from the Roadrunner, and the caption at the bottom read, "Not so fast!!!!!".

Bourbon Street also had lots of exotic strip clubs, but you had to careful about which ones to visit. Some exclusively featured "she-males". They always say, "If you have to ask, then you really don't want to know". There was this one joint that featured a naked woman sitting on a swing that was gliding in and out of the roof where everyone standing down on Bourbon Street could see her. She served as "advertisement" to get horny guys to pay a ridiculous cover charge to get into the strip club. I thought to myself, "I wonder what her mother thinks of her daughter's career choice?"

I later found out that the exotic dancer's mother was "Booty-licious", a stripper who worked in the club next-door.

When Azoria and I made it to the end of Bourbon Street down by the Royal Sonesta Hotel, I began to experience déja vu. It happened the moment I laid eyes on the bookstore across the street from us. It looked the same as the one I saw in the vision that had been shown to me by the oracle.

"I've been down here many times and I've never seen that bookstore before," I said to Azoria, who said nothing in return. The little shop was dimly lit and there wasn't a sign anywhere on the building that showed the name of the store.

In accordance with the vision, Azoria led the way as we curiously approached the front window of the shop and looked inside.

"Can we go in?" she pleaded. "I'm sure we'll find all sorts of interesting things. It's on Bourbon Street, after all!"

There was a small table covered with a black cloth standing next to the entrance, and on top of it was a crystal ball with a note instructing patrons on how to gain entrance to the store. I read the note and then gently rubbed the glass orb, and like magic, the door to the shop opened up and Azoria and I walked inside. We began looking around at the thousands of books on the shelves and began wondering how could the shop be so large on the inside and look so tiny from the street.

"Wow! This place is enormous!" said Azoria from several aisles away.

"Yeah, but what's that smell?" I said after detecting a strange odor in the air. "It smells like death up in here."

"Trell, come check this out!" shouted Azoria. "You're not going to believe what I've found!"

I rushed over to see what all the excitement was about, and there was Azoria holding a large book with crude writing on the cover. The title of the book was written in Gothic letters, which seemed quite appropriate for the eerie atmosphere inside the bookstore. The cover was bound in a leathery material, but it wasn't leather.

"It feels like---Oh my god!" screamed Azoria as she ran her fingers over the strange material. "The cover is made of flesh! Human flesh!"

Azoria dropped the book and quickly backed away as it landed on the floor sending clouds of dust and cobwebs flying through the air. Once the dust settled, the flesh bound book revealed its full title: Ex Libris Mirabilia. A Latin phrase meaning, "from the books of miracles".

It was, in fact, a compilation of magic spells kept secret through the ages and entrusted to one immortal being.

"Can I help you find something in particular?" said the old woman who had suddenly appeared from behind the counter.

"Um... no ma'am. We were just looking around." Azoria said in a nervous voice while staring at the old witch.

"What about you, sir?" said the mysterious shopkeeper. "Perhaps I can interest you in a gift for your lady friend?"

I shook my head, no, and continued staring at the witch trying to figure out where she had come from. It was as if she had appeared out of thin air. She was wearing a tattered and torn black dress with long sleeves that flared out at the cuffs like bell-bottoms, covering her hands to where only the black tips of her razor sharp fingernails could be seen tapping on the countertop. Her hair was in dreadlocks, and sitting atop her head was a tall, pointed hat with a wide brim---the classic "witch's cap". And dangling from the front of the black Afghan she wore was a white, creepy broach shaped like a human skull.

"That can't be her!" I said to myself. "Mama Jo has been dead for years!"

The witch's face was hidden behind a long, dark veil hanging down from the hat's wide brim. Through the veil, her eyes pierced the darkness and she was watching our every move.

"Excuse me, ma'am," said Azoria, who stood trembling nervously in the aisle where the book had been dropped. "What type of bookstore is this, we missed the sign on the way in?"

"Sweet child," said the old witch to Azoria. "You have entered into a place that has many names." The witch spoke in a raspy voice and her breath was so foul that Azoria and I had to cover our faces.

"This can be the place of beginnings for some," the witch continued. "And for others, it can be the place where their journey ends."

Azoria glanced over at me, and I could see the terror in her eyes. We were both thinking the same thing---that the situation was becoming a virtual nightmare.

"Careful, my dear!" the witch warned Azoria. "The book lying in front of you guards many powerful secrets. Come now, give it to me."

Azoria's hands were shaking uncontrollably as she stooped down and picked up the Ex Libris Mirabilia. She then handed the enormous book back to the witch saying, "I'm sorry for taking it from the shelf, I was only curious."

"Come closer, child," said the witch while holding out her creepy hands to Azoria. "I want to show you something."

"No, Azoria!" I shouted. "Don't go near her! She's not what she seems!" I had sensed that something was wrong the moment we entered the bookstore. It felt like we had walked into a tomb that had been sealed for a thousand years.

"Azoria! Let's get the hell outta here!" I screamed, but she did not move. Azoria was frozen with fear. "C'mon! We have to leave this place!"

Tears started streaming down her face like tiny waterfalls, raining softly atop the dust-covered books scattered on the floor next to her. The witch grabbed the book out of Azoria's hands and said to her, "Though the Underworld has many doors there is but one key that unlocks them all."

She opened the gigantic book and removed a long wand that had been neatly tucked in the crease of one of the pages. The witch pointed the wand at a peculiar looking chart inside the book and said, "This, my child, is the Key of Adwah. Behold its powerful magic!" She then began to recite passages "from the books of miracles".

"Eik-nay lyoom nahnook sharporah!" chanted the witch who was now levitating off the floor and twirling around in midair. "It has begun!" she yelled out to the spirits of the Underworld.

It suddenly went dark inside the bookstore but the lucid witch remained visible. The temperature quickly fell to below freezing and I could now see a trailing mist with every breath I took. But nothing was coming from the mouth of the witch... because she wasn't breathing at all.

"Azoria! Where are you?" I shouted in the dark. "I'm over here!" she cried. "Over here by the wall!" I followed the sound of Azoria's voice and made my way through the darkened aisles knocking over several book shelves and a magazine rack as I went. But before I could reach her, the witch cornered me and began whispering in my ear. The foul stench from her awful breath made me gag, and it seemed to linger in my nostrils like a deadly poison as she delivered her ominous message with piss and vinegar: "You must again travel to the place that was once Abyssinia, there is soon to be trouble in paradise!" said the ire witch as she brandished a wicked smile. "I must warn you that the end is near, and though your name is on the tongue of every prophet who is spreading the news about the second coming of the great savior D'Shawn, I say to you, woe be unto those who cherish the light! For the great dragon has taken his place upon the golden throne and the world is his footstool!"

Being back home in New Orleans meant that I had no idea that a thousand years had gone by in Azoria's world. Atlantica, the most glorious kingdom under the sea, was about to feel the wrath of the devil. Its many citizens were praying for me to return to their world and do what I did the first time. But something was very different.

"The great beast is already gathering his armies and your new destiny has not yet been revealed to the seers," said the witch in a condescending sort of way. "Gaze into my eyes and you will see a future that is soon to come... unless you choose to tempt fate by returning to the Galactic Island and forging a brand new destiny that hasn't been foreseen by anyone."

I reluctantly looked into the witch's eyes and I saw a vision of Atlantica in ruins, the magnificent kingdom had been ravished by demons and goblins and by things that go bump in the night. Sapian had crawled out of the Abyss and was given the power of a thousand demigods. The infamous dragon gained dominion over the world and that was only the beginning... *The ocean had turned bitter and the sky had an ungodly look as it cast down an eerie light on the world below. But most disturbing of all was the Dark Forest and the evil things lurking inside the woods. Monsters so vile that nature refused to give them names. I saw myself in the witch's eyes standing silently on the beach in the pouring rain, my bare feet planted firmly in the soft white sand that glowed like burning coals along the water's edge. An unusual chill lingered in the salty breeze whisking swiftly across the acrid sea; a deadly storm was approaching, one that would bring an end to life on earth---Judgement Day had come at last. I dropped to my knees and wept copious tears on the endless sands encompassing the island. Watching. Wondering. Waiting on the inevitable. The concept of time in Azoria's world was frail at best it had no continuity, no order, no meaning. Which means a thousand years could have easily gone by since my beclouded exodus from the island of Cam where I vanished amid an ocean of blue vapors spewed from the nostrils of a mystic dragon that granted me a single wish. Now---according to the witch's apocalyptic version of things to come---my return to the Galactic Island would be a trial by fire. I would be struck by powerful bolts of lightning that would rip my flesh apart leaving grotesque wounds across my back like scars made by the cruel lashes of a slave master's whip. It was to be the result of being caught in a hellish storm, a paranormal event, a great reckoning.I looked and I saw thousands of biblical monsters spewing from the blackened clouds above me, they were being sent forth to terrorize the four corners of the earth. I saw fiery hailstones raining down from the heavens and watched the souls of men cast into burning lakes of fire after being expelled from the bodies of the dead. Those who survived the Apocalypse suffered a fate worse than death---they became an army of "undead" zombies after being exposed to caustic radiation spawned by the devil himself.In the vision, I was walking through the Dark Forest when I came upon a female elf who was sitting alone in the woods playing with a litter of cute little kittens. She---the same way the six-winged seraph had done in the beginning---greeted me with an encrypted message: "The thousand years has ended," said the elf in all her glorious nudeness. "Woe be unto the sons and daughters on man. A great demon has placed your world under his dominion. And now the only way that you can reclaim that which is rightfully yours is by returning that which never was."*

The light in the witch's eyes slowly began to fade, and so did the eerie vision that showed the world's end. But before the vision was totally gone, I caught a glimpse of the elf sitting beneath a large tree holding a crystal ball in her hands. There were icons floating above her head, a message written with the same symbols that had been used by the seraph in the flying restroom. I immediately noticed that the first word in the message was missing. And just as the vision ended, I spotted the missing symbol floating inside the crystal ball... it was the symbol for "love".

"Therefore, since the children share in flesh and blood, He Himself likewise also partook of the same, that through death He might render powerless him who had the power of death, that is, the devil."

--- Hebrews 2:14

CHAPTER 25

DEVIL'S ADVOCATE

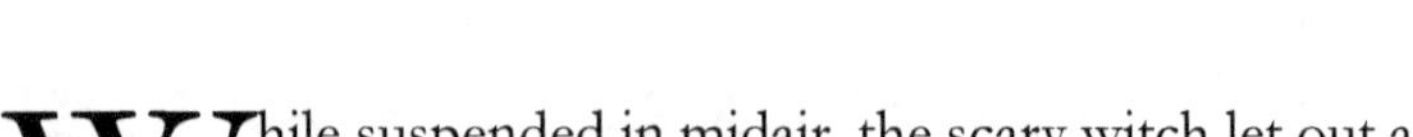

While suspended in midair, the scary witch let out a loud cackle and resumed her weird incantation speaking feverishly for minutes without pausing for a single breath. She soon began making animal noises such as grunts and growls, hoots and howls. And all the while the symbols from the Key of Adwah steadily rose into the air with each inaudible word uttered from the witch's mouth. Meanwhile, I took Azoria by the hand and we made a dash for the door.

"We're getting out of here! And we're not looking back!" I said to Azoria. But the moment my hand touched the doorknob I knew that something was wrong. The wooden knob had turned frail and brittle like a dry leaf in the dead of winter, and it crumbled inside my hand before falling to the floor and leaving a light layer of sawdust on the tips of my shoes.

"What happened?!" cried Azoria. "Stop playing around and open the door!"

"I'm not playing around, the doorknob just fell apart inside my hand."

Before I knew it, Azoria was standing beside me banging her fists against the large glass window at the front of the store. She was yelling, "Help! Help! Please, somebody help us! We're trapped inside!" People were walking on the sidewalk right outside the window going up and down Bourbon Street but no one stopped to help us. They didn't even look our way, it was like the bookstore wasn't there.

"What's the matter with you people?!" shouted Azoria. "Why won't you help us?!"

I reached for Azoria's hand in the dark and felt something brush up against my arm.

"Holy shit! Something just touched me!" I said to Azoria right before it happened to her too.

"Oh my God! What is it?!" she screamed. "Something's in here with us!"

A mysterious creature with scales for skin was roaming loose in the darkness---and it wasn't the witch. Things were definitely getting out of hand.

"Trell, I'm scared," said Azoria. "Please take me home now." I wanted to look brave in front of Azoria, but truth be told, I was just as scared as she was.

"Stay calm and let's look for another exit." I said over the loud chattering that was coming from my teeth hitting together. "There's got to be another way out of here, we just have to find---"

"AAAAAHHH!!!" A gut wrenching scream pierced the darkness as Azoria spotted the beast walking behind me headed in the direction of the witch. "Do you see it?!" she yelled, "Do you see the monster?!" I narrowed my vision and honed in on the beast moving through the shadows.

"Yes! Yes, I see it!" Slowly, the humongous dragon raised its head and focused its attention on the witch. She was still twirling in midair chanting and laughing like a crazy person, seemingly oblivious to the liquid fire now streaming down from the dragon's nostrils. The belly of the beast, meanwhile, was swelling to phenomenal proportions as it was being filled with air and combustible gases.

Without warning, whooosh!, a rush a fiery wind laced with bright yellow flames shot out of the dragon's mouth and roasted the witch like an evil marshmallow. But not before she could finish her incantation. She cast a spell, and bright symbols began to appear over the dragon's head revealing an ancient riddle that the beast had been guarding since the beginning of time---the riddle of a man.

I suddenly thought about what the oracle had said to me long ago:

"Study the markings well. Click! Click! Click!... You must first solve the riddle of a man if you are to defeat the red dragon at his own game - Yep! Yep! The dragon's riddle was also written in the book of Revelation, it was in fact the burning question surrounding the mystery of the number "666"---What does it actually mean? Revelation 13:18 says, "Here is wisdom: Let him who has understanding calculate the number of the beast, for the number is that of a man, and his number is six hundred and sixty-six."

I suddenly thought about the lecture I had once heard by a college professor on the campus of LSU in Baton Rouge. His oral presentation was open to the public, and took place in an outdoor coliseum style structure called "The Forum". He was a tall elderly professor with a shock of white hair who strangely resembled Albert Einstein by the face but had long limbs and a gangly strut that made the girls giggle when he walked past them on his way to the podium---his name was Dr. B. Ezel-bub.

Courtney Hill, a friend of mine at LSU, had invited me to join her so that we could listen to the professor's speech about mechanical engineering and the integration of biophysics with artificial intelligence on a molecular level and later discuss our views on what we learned. The lecture, however, took an awkward turn when someone from the audience asked the professor a question about the Bible. Dr. B. Ezel-bub had claimed to be a renowned mathematician and scholar who had traveled to some of the most remote regions on earth solving mysteries that involved numbers. And now, here he stood on the campus of LSU faced with the greatest numerical mystery of all time---the mystery of the number 666 in the book of Revelation. The question had been asked by a blonde-haired, blue-eyed cheerleader named Babylon, but everyone called her "Baby" for short. She was a real "valley girl" from Los Angeles, and she posed the question to the professor as only a valley girl could: "Like um, Professor, really. Since you're like this genius, or whatever, why don't you tell us the meaning of the triple sixes in the Bible? Like um, really. We wanna know."

Everyone turned and looked at the professor but instead of responding to the question that was asked by Baby, he went on a longwinded tirade about the "Singularity"---the theory that one day machines will take over the world because computers will have gotten much smarter than the people who created them. The professor, who was obviously trying to avoid the question, also brought up the subject of "Move 37". Which was a miraculous move made by a system of artificial intelligence while playing a match of "Go"---a 2,500-year-old game of strategy and intuition that makes chess look like checkers.

During its match against Lee Sedol, the best Go player in the world at the time, the artificial intelligence---which was named AlphaGo by its team of Google engineers---made a move on the 37th play of the game that changed everything. Move 37 showed that AlphaGo wasn't just regurgitating years of programming or foraging through predictive algorithms. It was actually thinking. Not only had AlphaGo mastered the game, it had used a form of intuition to defeat the best player our world had to offer.

The professor's stall tactics got undermined when a brave student stood up and shouted, "What about the question, professor? Are you going to weigh in on it or not?" Then another student chimed in saying, "Yeah professor, what's the deal with the triple 6's? Let us hear your theory on the subject." Echoing outbursts continued one after the other until finally the brainy professor felt compelled to appease the masses.

"Okay, very well." He conceded. "Since you all insist, I will share something with you that I have not shared with anyone. But before I begin, you must all agree that what you are about to hear goes no farther than this forum."

Everyone shook their head in agreement with the professor's request.

"Good. Now let us begin." The professor said with a sly grin. "To determine the meaning of the number 666 in Revelation---which, by the way, appeared as the number 616 in an earlier manuscript---one needs to acquire much knowledge in a number of areas: political science, religion, mythology, world history, mathematics, astronomy, and even witchcraft, just to name a few."

"What about the 'Da Vinci Code', professor," asked a student in the front row of the circular arena that had been modelled after the Roman Colosseum but on a much smaller scale. "Is the Illuminati real?"

"Poppycock! Pure rubbish!" shouted the professor. "Don't be ridiculous!" He took a deep breath and then reached into his vest pocket and pulled out a small pouch filled with pipe tobacco. He panned the audience with his eyes, all the while tapping the old tobacco out of his corn pipe and packing it tightly with a fresh pinch. He lit the pipe and took two quick puffs before reiterating his demands.

"If I am to enlighten you about such a controversial subject, it is imperative that you turn off all recording devices so we can speak privately amongst ourselves. That goes for you too, Mr. Le-Cour." The professor had obviously busted me using my smartphone to video record his lecture. I immediately turned it off and eased it back into my pocket.

"Now pay attention because I'm only going to explain this once, and you must never repeat this to anyone. Agreed?" Again, we shook our head in agreement that this would be kept between us, but surely the professor didn't believe that a group of eager minds like ours would be capable of keeping a secret. We would have agreed to any terms, because we were dying to hear the professor speak totally uncensored on the subject. Dr. B. Ezelbub had our undivided attention as he took us on a tour through history that we would never forget:

"Atop the U.S. Capitol Building in Washington, D.C., stands the statue called Freedom. But her historical name is Persephone, the Greco-Roman goddess of the psyche or soul. Her very name means 'she who destroyed the light'. Persephone was sculpted in Rome and placed atop the Capitol on the 47th anniversary of the death of America's first Roman Catholic bishop, John Carroll. The event was heralded by 47 gunshots, thirty-five from a field battery on Capitol Hill, and twelve from the surrounding forts. Incidentally, the Capitol was erected on property owned by Bishop Carroll's family. But we'll get to that later.

"All of you sitting here are aware that Roman Catholicism is a universal secular government domiciled at the Vatican City State in Rome. And that its sovereign ruler, the Pope, is deemed by worshipers to be infallible. In the political context, the Roman Catholic Church has been determined by the U.S. District Courts to be a foreign State (See U.S. Court of Appeals for the Third Circuit, case No. 85-1309), and required universal obedience to the decrees of its omnipotent ruler and his various councils.

"Vatican Council II's Constitutions on the church requires secular officials, whoever they are, to expend all their energy for the growth of the church and its continued sanctification. Most of you have studied early American History and know that Maryland was a Roman Catholic colony named for the Virgin Mary. And that it was founded by Lord Baltimore, Cecilius Calvert, whose father, George, had been converted to Catholicism in 1625, about the time that King Charles I came to the throne in England.

"Charles was the son of King James I, under whose direction the King James Bible was published. George Calvert was the Secretary of the State to Charles I. When Charles converted to Catholicism, he resigned his position because of difficulty in serving a Protestant king. Oddly, King Charles himself married a Roman Catholic princess named Henrietta Marie, known also as Mary, the sister of Louis XIII of France. He also promoted to the highest levels in the Church of England men who were sympathetic to the

Roman Catholic rituals and traditions, which greatly disturbed the Puritans and Calvinists.

"King Charles's pro-Catholic policies came to a head in November 1614, when Irish Catholics massacred thousands of Ulster Protestants. After that, many Protestants lost faith in him, asking how could he be trusted to protect them when he himself had a Catholic wife and had promoted pro-Catholic clergy. This, of course, led to the English Revolution where King Charles I was deposed and beheaded, and the monarchy abolished for a time. Now boys and girls, here's where the plot thickens!

"Even after George Calvert resigned as Secretary of State, King Charles gave him territory in the New World. Which, of course, is now the United States. Calvert died before he could make the trip, but his son, Cecilius Calvert (Lord Baltimore) did so.

"On November 22, 1633 Cecilius Calvert sailed for the New World with two ships: the Ark and the Dove. The ships carried three Jesuits, twenty Roman Catholics (including Cecilius's brother Leonard) and several hundred Protestant slaves and laborers. The voyage was spiritually directed by a Jesuit priest named Andrew White, remembered today as the 'Apostle to Maryland'. In fact, the White House was named after this fine gentleman.

"The property given to the Calverts by the late King Charles I was called 'Rock Creek Farm'. But in the 1663 property records it was named 'Rome', and was owned by a man called 'Pope'. Additionally, the branch of the Potomac River it was located on was called 'Tiber'. This information was published in the 1902 edition of the Catholic Encyclopedia under the article on John Carroll. It was later deleted in the 1967 edition to keep the public from finding out that Washington, D.C., which was carved out of Maryland, is actually owned by Rome.

"If you're wondering how all of this relates to the number 666 in Revelation, you must bear in mind this important fact. The main avenues in Washington, D.C. are laid out in the shape of the five-pointed star of Baphomet, the Satanic symbol of the goat. The layout of the streets was under the task of a French engineer by the name of Pierre-Charles L'Enfant. He got the job at the suggestion of John Carroll. Yes, BISHOP John Carroll."

Using a wand affixed with a laser beam, the professor directed our attention to a map of Washington, D.C. that had been superimposed on the large screen next to him. He began tracing the streets with the laser and explaining to the audience what we were looking at:

"The White House marks the place of the goat's mouth. The two ears on the sides are marked by Mt. Vernon Square and Washington Circle. The horns are marked by Logan Circle and DuPont Circle."

When he had finished connecting the points, a pentagram was formed. And none of us would ever look at our nation's Capitol the same.

❖　❖　❖

'When L' Enfant numbered the city blocks, the series ran from Q Street North through the Capitol grounds down to the mouth of James Creek. All the numbers between 600 and 900 are assigned to blocks within this area, except for the number 666. Which is missing. It stands to reason that the address must belong to the only section of blocks in the 600 series---the Capitol grounds."

A collective gasp rose from the audience, followed by an eerie silence because everyone had been left speechless. We were virtually in a state of shock and the professor could see it in our eyes.

"Okay boys and girls, let's not panic here. After all, this whole discussion started with a math question." The professor adjusted his Oxford tie and then set the stage for an unforgettable grand finale:

"To be fair, biblical scholars have debated this topic for a very long time and many believe that the mark of the beast, meaning the cryptic mark in Revelation which indicates allegiance to Satan, is best understood in the first-century context in which it was used, as a polemic against the Roman Empire.

"The Book of Revelation is a complicated text. Written toward the end of the first century by an author who calls himself John. He tells a story of an ongoing cosmic battle between good and evil with good triumphing eventually. In Revelation 13, John describes 'the beast' as having seven heads and 10 horns, a leopard's body, the feet of a bear and a lion's mouth. The beast in this text is powerful, Satanic and is the object of worship.

"John also mentions a second beast that promotes worship of the first. The most notable thing about the second beast is that it causes people to receive a mark on their forehead or right hand. Many biblical scholars maintain that the first beast is a symbolic representation of the first-century Roman emperors. Their position is that each head represents one emperor, and it is widely believed that Emperor Nero is one of them. This conclusion is drawn not only from other references to Nero in Revelation, but also from his reputation in the first century for persecuting Christians in Rome.

"In A.D. 64, when Nero was emperor, a great fire took hold in Rome and burned for nearly a week. Roman historians Suetonius, Cassius Dio and Tacitus claim that Nero himself was the one responsible for igniting the blaze, Tacitus adds that Nero attempted to free himself of blame by placing guilt on the Christians living in the city. John's description of one of the beast's heads being 'wounded' may be a reference to Nero's death, which Suetonius describes as a self-inflicted stab to the neck.

"But the clearest reference to Nero in Revelation, according to the scholars, is the number '666'. There is a well-known practice in the ancient world called 'gematria,' in which letters are assigned number values. This allows authors to refer to individuals by using 'the number of their name,' rather than their actual name. And biblical scholars have long noted that in Hebrew characters, the numerical value of Nero's formal title---Caesar Nero---is 666."

The crowd erupted with loud gasps and nervous chatter, it was the perfect opportunity for me to take out my phone and begin recording the professor's riveting speech:

"But enough about that," said Dr. B. Ezel-bub in reference to what the scholars believe.

"Here's what I know to be true. The prehistoric name for the city of Rome was STUR, from the word 'Satyr', which was short for Saturnia or Saturn. In the ancient Chaldean language, which used its letters for numbers because of gematria, S=60, T=400, U=6, and R=200, for a grand total of 666."

Again the group erupted with nervous chatter, but this time Dr. B. Ezel-bub stood basking in the glorious chaos he was creating---he knew the devil was in the details, and the details could not be refuted.

"On December 8, 1584, Pope Pius IX declared the 'Ineffabilis Deus', the decree defining the Immaculate Conception of the Virgin Mary. It declared that Mary had conceived free of original sin and remained so throughout her life. Within days, federal legislators in Washington became obsessed with expanding the Capitol dome. According to one official publication, 'Never before or since has an addition to the Capitol been so eagerly embraced by Congress'. Legislation was quickly passed which incorporated the new papal doctrine into the Capitol's brand new cupola. "

A week later, the goddess Persephone was ordained to surmount the legislative center of the free world, becoming the only government authorized symbol of American heritage. Turns out that Persephone was one of the Roman goddesses whose statues, in the 4th century A.D., was taken over by the Church and renamed the 'Virgin Mary'. Few realized that Proclus, head of the Platonic Academy in Athens in the 5th century, described Persephone as having an Immaculate Conception. Or that she was also known as 'Libera' (Liberty). It was for that reason that the sculptor, Thomas Crawford, called his statue atop the U.S. Capitol, 'Freedom'. She stands 19 feet 6 inches tall, which is equivalent to 6+6+6 feet, and 6+6+6 inches."

Chatter turned into mayhem.

Cameras flashed.

Text messages went out by the droves.

The forum was about to go live.

Dr. B. Ezel-bub took center stage and smiled as he stood next to the podium watching the circus from on high. Everyone in the audience was totally freaking out, and it was obvious that he was enjoying his role as ringmaster.

Let's continue, shall we," he said with the look of a sorcerer. *"Persephone was placed on the dome of the Capitol on December 2, 1863, in the middle of the Civil War. The event, as you recall, was marked by the salute of 47 gunshots as a tribute to John Carroll, the Jesuit bishop who had put Washington, D.C. under Mary's protection. The statue of Persephone (or Mary) was conspicuously placed on the dome 47 years after Carroll's death.*

"President Lincoln did not attend the ceremony, claiming that he had a 'fever'. He, and other masons, knew the truth behind what was going on but could do nothing to stop it from happening. Meanwhile, a guy by the name of Constantino Btumidi arrived to do the artwork for the dome of the Capitol. He painted what is called the 'Apotheosis of Washington', or 'the deification of George Washington'."

I went on my phone and Googled the phrase, and an image of the painting popped up on the screen.

"Between the deified Washington and the earth flies the Virgin with the Roman eagle at her side. Her position between heaven and earth was meant to identify her as the Mediatrix, the most prominent role of the Roman goddess Minerva (or Venus). The eagle at her side is the mascot of Jupiter, the ruling god of Rome. It represents Roman justice. In fact, the motto of the Justice Department is 'Qui Pro Domina Justita Sequitur' (He Who Follows the Goddess Justice). The Justice Department's motto encircles the eagle, of course, which was said to follow Justica... into the pits of Hades.

"Other details of the painting are far too many to discuss in the time we have remaining, so I'll focus solely upon the one young man in the painting who is called 'Young America'. He wears a liberty cap, also known as a 'Phrygian cap'. They were given to freed slaves to show their liberated status. However, Roman law stated that this freedom could be revoked at any time and for any cause. In other words, their liberty was given as a privilege, not as an inherent right."

Dr. B. Ezel-bub placed a new image on the screen behind him, and then continued speaking with a British accent that was as fishy as the story he was telling:

"The most significant fact of all comes when we look at the famous Black Obelisk of Shalumaneser III, King of Assyria, which stands today in the British Museum. It depicts King Jehu of Israel kneeling before the king of Assyria, paying tribute. In fact, this is the only ancient monument that portrays art wise, a character in the bible who was alive at the time of the portrait. Jehu is pictured wearing a Phrygian cap in order to show that he is free only because the king of Assyria has given him the privilege of freedom in exchange for tribute. Jehu, you recall, is the one who fufilled the prophetic word of Elijah that Ahab's next generation would cease to rule Israel. This prophecy was given after Ahab and Jezebel killed Naboth and his sons, and stole his vineyard. Jehu is also the one who destroyed Baal worship out of Israel (2 Kings 10:29). His destruction of Baal worship eliminated a denominational competitor for the religious devotion of the Israelites and inadvertently solidified the golden calf as the national religion of Israel.

'Now, let us move to the 21st century: On January 29, 2002, the Catholic Church and U.S. Government secretly issued a 'divine decree' to overthrow the golden calf. They did so with little knowledge of what this signified in the world. Though millions had watched then President George W. Bush refer to Iran, Iraq, and North Korea as the 'axis of evil' during his State of the Union address, they remained blissfully unaware that America herself was considered by many nations of the world to be home to the Anti-Christ.

"You who are in possession of a Strong's Concordance, look up the word translated from 'calf'. It is numbered 5695 in Strong's; it's the Hebrew word 'egel', which is pronounced the same as the English word 'eagle'. You're probably not aware of this, but the American bald eagle was not the original choice when selecting the national bird. It was first suggested that the turkey---in tribute to the Pilgrims' Thanksgiving feast with the Indians---be named America's mascot, but because of those who were part of the secret society that chose the American bald eagle instead, the turkey lost its bid. The men responsible for the change in national birds knowingly borrowed the concept from the Roman Egel (or golden calf), and they made it palatable to the public by saying that it was because the eagle was a majestic symbol of American freedom. People back then, just as people today, were

unaware that the real power brokers behind the scenes were well versed in the mystic Jewish doctrines known as the Cabala. Consequently, America has worshipped the golden calf from the time of the bald eagle's inception as the U.S. mascot to its pontifical overthrow on January 29th. Its being dethroned was only through spiritual decree, no one knows when it will manifest in the world. But what is certain is that the golden calf was the lawful basis for the Prince of Persia's petition to enter into America. Those lawful grounds were removed by decree in order to deny the prince the right to enter here.

"History has shown that America can be quite nasty when dealing with those she deems intolerable, and in recent decades the White House has revealed its true nature. It began with Bush's War in Iraq, which was waged under false pretense, accusing the Iraqis of being in possession of weapons of mass destruction and saying that Saddam Hussein was planning to use them against the U.S. So at the behest of the Bush Administration, Saddam's tyrannical reign ended with him being hanged for crimes against humanity. And that, boys and girls, marked the beginning of the end."

✦ 285 ✦

"The relativity of moral ideas is proved anew every time there is a war. Whatever the enemy does, however gallant or reasonable, is denounced as immoral, and what the home boys do, however brutal or dishonorable, is praised as heroic."
---H. L. Mencken

"Patriotism is the last refuge of a scoundrel."
---Samuel Johnson

CHAPTER 26

THE GREAT EPIPHANY

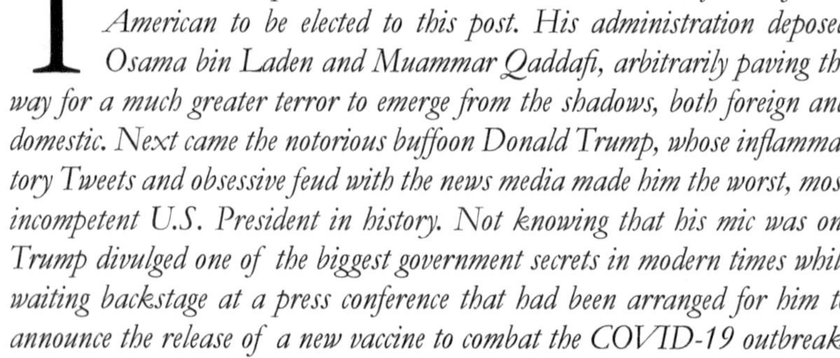

The next U.S. president was Barrack Obama, the first African American to be elected to this post. His administration deposed Osama bin Laden and Muammar Qaddafi, arbitrarily paving the way for a much greater terror to emerge from the shadows, both foreign and domestic. Next came the notorious buffoon Donald Trump, whose inflammatory Tweets and obsessive feud with the news media made him the worst, most incompetent U.S. President in history. Not knowing that his mic was on, Trump divulged one of the biggest government secrets in modern times while waiting backstage at a press conference that had been arranged for him to announce the release of a new vaccine to combat the COVID-19 outbreak. An audience of millions heard only a snippet of what he said before someone realized his mic was on and cut the transmission to the networks. But the entire conversation was recorded by a staffer who was working for Mitch McConnell, the person to whom Trump was speaking. The recording ended up on the dark web, and in it, you could clearly hear Trump bragging about a secret session that was held by Republican members of Congress prior to the insurrection at the U.S. Capitol. A bill was introduced by then Louisiana Senator John Kennedy, and was secretly rushed through the Republican controlled House and Senate before Democrats could figure out what was going

on. The ambiguous legislation was then signed into law by the president. It decrees that no one will be allowed to legally buy, sell, or trade commercial goods without the expressed written consent of the President of the United States---whoever he or she may be from that day forward. This tyrannical power now belongs to whoever sits in the Oval Office and controls the Capitol with the missing address 666.

"As you all remember, the coronavirus---along with its many variants---ravaged the nation and the world in the early 2020's. But what has been kept secret all these years since, is that the U.S. Government modified and then mandated subcutaneous inoculations (flu shots) along with vaccinations against COVID-19. For years, hospitals and clinics throughout the country and the world have been unknowingly vaccinating people with a government sanctioned tracking serum disguised as vaccines from Pfizer and other major vaccine makers. This was all part of the Trump Administration's plan toward world dominance, but there was one problem---he lost his bid for reelection and did not get the opportunity to wield the newly ordained power afforded to the President of the United States.

"Now getting back to how all of this ties together. The secret serum developed during Donald Trump's term as President introduced cybernetic probes into the bloodstreams of every person who received a flu shot and/or got vaccinated in the years since Trump left the White House. The microscopic probes were designed to attach themselves to veins in the forehead and the right hand, and to transmit a unique signal to satellites orbiting the earth. The highly intelligent probes are also capable of mapping a person's genetic code and predicting social behavior very accurately. "

I'm sure that most of you, if not all, have been vaccinated. Which means that an alarming amount of your 'personal data' has already been transmitted into space. Everything about you has been recorded and stored in a government database that's reportedly located in a top secret military installation somewhere in New Mexico. I have it on good authority that the U.S. Department of Homeland Security uses the data to keep tabs on high profile targets and domestic terrorists, which often turn out to be suburban white females who become radicalized after being seduced by propaganda videos made in the Middle East and posted online as a recruitment tool by groups like al-Qaeda. So you see, boys and girls, the Office of the President not only holds the power to control many aspects of one's personal life, it aspires to control the lives of everyone on earth through global spending. For he who controls the global economy owns the world.

"It has already begun imposing economic embargoes and strict sanctions on foreign nations that are not fully vaccinated with the serum, which high ranking officials refer to as 'GRI's' (Global Registration Inoculations). The White House plans to loan its power to the World Health Organization (WHO) and vaccinate everyone worldwide: young and old, rich and poor, free and incarcerated. Sound familiar? "

According to classified documents that were posted on a government website by mistake, participation in the GRI's protocol---once fully implemented---will become a prerequisite for all businesses, corporations, and individuals wanting to engage in commerce of any kind. This insidious plot was prophesied by the apostle John during his exile on the island of Patmos. His prediction on the matter appears in Revelation 13:16-17 where he says in reference to the second beast, 'He also forced everyone, small and great, rich and poor, free and slave, to receive a mark on his right hand or his forehead (the two areas where the probes attach themselves to veins, creating painful blisters on the forehead and hands in order to mimic symptoms related to the virus known as "Monkeypox"), so that no one could buy or sell unless he had the mark, which is the name of the beast or the number of his name.' "So there you have it, ladies and gentlemen, boys and girls. The infamous beast referenced in the book of Revelation by the apostle John stands right there on Capitol Hill today. And the number of his name is the missing address 666."

Babylon, the girl who had originally asked the professor to explain the triple 6's, suddenly fainted and had to be carried to the infirmary. Meanwhile, Dr. B. Ezel-bub gave further proof to substantiate the claims made during the lecture.

"In Strong's you'll find that in ancient times whenever three like numbers appeared together in a series, the first number was multiplied by 1. The product of the equation was subsequently multiplied by 10, as were the products of the second and third equations. The number 666 would have been described this way: (6x1=6)+(6x10=60)+(60x10=600). Keep in mind that the ancient Chaldean language used letters for numbers, so let's break down the number 666 and see what letters we get: 6=U, 60=S, and 600=A (USA). Class dismissed."

No one in the audience attempted to leave, we had become like living monuments blankly staring at the professor and waiting for him to admit that it was only a joke. But Dr. B. Ezel-bub did no such thing. He stood mulling over our faces and seeing the irreversible damage that had been done to our subconscious mind. If what the professor said was true, then how could we---in good faith---trust the government to protect us from the evils of the world when the Capitol itself was the lair of the beast?

"Excuse me, professor." I said with my hand in the air like a fifth grader, "In your opinion, will the good have to suffer for bad when judgement comes?"

"Mr. LeCour," said Dr. B. Ezel-bub. "You need only visit the parable in the book of Matthew 13:24-30 to find the answer you seek."

The parable he referred to basically said that when The Judgement comes, the wheat will be separated from the weeds but only after being harvested as one collective crop. And while I was deciphering the text's allegorical meaning, it suddenly dawned on me that I hadn't told the professor my name.

"Excuse me, but how did you know my---" Before I could finish my statement, a loud, thunderous boom sounded in the clouds directly above us. I looked and I saw dark, angry clouds gathering together to create a heavy rainstorm on the campus of LSU. And as the students started picking up their books and personal belongings, the professor again took out his wand with the laser tip and pointed it toward the large screen saying, "Take heed to the five things that are listed here. Research them and you will discover the truth about the world you live in."

Everyone joined me in taking snapshots of the list provided by the mysterious professor. We were at a lost for words---all of us---but here are the enormous breadcrumbs he left for us to follow:

1.) America is a British colony; because the United States is a "corporation", not a land mass, and it existed before the Revolutionary War. British troops didn't leave until 1796 (Republican v

Sweers 1Dallas 43, Treaty of Commerce 8 Stat 116 IRS Publication 6209, Articles of Association October 20, 1774).

2.) The Pope can abolish any law in the United States. (Elements of Ecclesiastical Law Vol. 1, 53-54).

3.) You own no property in the United States. Read the fine print on the deed to the property you think is yours. You will find that you're listed as a " tenant". (Senate Document 43, 73rd Congress 1st Session).

4.) Britain is owned by the Vatican. (Treaty of 1213).

5.) Your 1040 Form is for tribute paid to Britain. (IRS Publication 6209 IMF decoding manual). IMF stands for International Monetary Fund.

The professor had disappeared amid the torrential downpour that finally came and sent everyone running for cover. The large group that had attended the lecture broke into several smaller groups, all setting out to research the information that was on the screen. A few hours later, the group reassembled at the Student Union and discussed what we found. After everyone spoke their mind, the overwhelming consensus was that the professor was right on the money... about everything. Holy shit!

Meanwhile, back inside the pitch black bookstore, I stepped to the dragon and attempted to answer the riddle floating above its head written with the symbols from the Key of Adwah:

"The number 666 in Revelation is not much of a mystery at all," I said to the dragon, who stared at me as though contemplation whether or not to set me ablaze. "The apostle John experienced a vision while exiled on the island of Patmos that revealed to him that a great beast would one day deceive the inhabitants of earth. It would force them to worship its image (Democracy), and those who refused would be severely punished. The infernal beast that John mentions in Revelation is the government of the most powerful nation in the world today, the United States of America."

A tremendous roar leapt from the dragon's throat and the beast began spewing long streams of fiery liquid from its mouth and nostrils. The inside of the bookstore lit up like a bonfire, and the luminous symbols above the dragon's head took on the brightness of starlight. They began to slowly rearrange themselves into a glorious message from God, which came to me like a great epiphany:

"Trell, what's going on?" said Azoria. "Who were you talking to?"

"I was talking to the dragon," I replied.

"What dragon? What are you talking about?" I looked over my shoulder and the dragon was no longer there.

"You're scaring me," Azoria cried. "Have you gone completely mad?"

"No!, of course not! The thing that moved past us in the dark was a dragon. It came into the bookstore through the portal that was opened by the witch and she did some kind of spell that made a riddle appear above the dragon's head. And when I answered the riddle, that's when the dragon got upset."

Azoria was staring at me like she didn't know who I was anymore. She said nothing, and then started backing away from me.

"What's wrong, Azoria? Why are you acting that way? You don't think I have anything to do with this, do you?"

"I just want to go home. Take me home, Trell."

Before I could explain to Azoria that I didn't have anything to do with the strange things taking place inside the bookstore, the dragon reappeared out of nowhere and whisked her away without a trace.

"Noooo!" I screamed while running after her. "Come back! Come back! Come back!" But it was no use, Azoria was gone. I aimlessly wandered around in the dark for what seemed like an eternity, hoping to stumble upon a clue that would lead me to the dragon and to Azoria. But the farther I walked the closer I came to being back where I started from, I was stuck in a time warp it seemed. Then suddenly I saw a flickering light and immediately I knew where it was coming from: it was dragon's fire! The beast that had taken Azoria away was now in my sights, and I intended to free her at all cost.

"Where is Azoria, you son-of-a-bitch?!" I yelled as I ran toward the dragon with a heart full of rage. "If you've harmed her in any way I'm going to kill you right where you stand!"

"She hasss been transssported back to her rightful place in time," the dragon said as the words slithered out of its mouth and tumbled into the darkness. "She isss of no interessst to me. Her presence will only disssstract you from your dessstiny, which now liesss beyond the cosmos. No other mortal hasss ever possessed the wisdom to solve man's riddle, because the answer did not exissst until now. You have amazzzed even I---the Gatekeeper of Worldsss."

Upon hearing what the dragon said, I again thought back to the lecture that was given by Dr. B. Ezel-bub. It had taken place on a rainy Friday afternoon at the LSU Greek Theatre, which was the outdoor theater also known as "The Forum". All of us who had attended the lecture that day returned the following Monday hoping to share our findings with the professor, but he never showed up. Instead, there was a lady professor there by the name of Marsha Billingsley who claimed she'd never heard of Dr. B. Ezel-bub. In fact, several students from the group said the university had no record of him ever being on campus. And all I had was the grainy video which never clearly showed the professor's face because of some type of electrical interference that was coming from the wand with the laser on it. I thought it was pretty strange at the time, but now it seemed even weirder.

"You anssswered my riddle," said the dragon. "Therefore I must grant you safe passsage across the Great Void which leads to Elysium, the Realm of Realmsss. But first you must sssuffer the death of a mortal before your élan vital---your sssoul---can transcend this world and enter the next."

There I was, caught between Scylla and Charybdis---a rock and a hard place---and I had no idea what the beast was talking about. Before I knew it, the mystic dragon snatched me up with its deadly claws and tightly wrapped its leathery wings around me. It was like being trapped inside a fleshy, foul smelling cocoon with no way out. I could see bright lights flashing through the skin covering the dragon's wings but could not hear the tremendous explosions going off all around me as the battle for my soul raged on between the angels of light and the angels of darkness.

Suddenly the fighting stopped, and up-up-up I went as I felt myself being carried by someone more powerful than all the angels and demons combined. Someone who had made the ultimate sacrifice to save me---I knew this person... and he knew me.

We travelled toward a brilliant light, and inside the light I heard a familiar sound---it was the sound of the ocean. I was again returning to a place that was beyond my world. A place where anything was possible. A place called, the Galactic Island.

"All this visible universe is not unique in nature and we must believe that there are, in other regions of space, other worlds, other beings, and other men."

---Lucretius

CHAPTER 27

EZEKIEL'S WHEEL

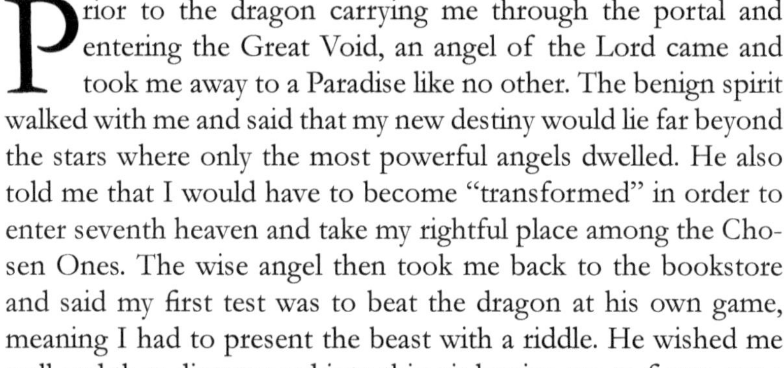

Prior to the dragon carrying me through the portal and entering the Great Void, an angel of the Lord came and took me away to a Paradise like no other. The benign spirit walked with me and said that my new destiny would lie far beyond the stars where only the most powerful angels dwelled. He also told me that I would have to become "transformed" in order to enter seventh heaven and take my rightful place among the Chosen Ones. The wise angel then took me back to the bookstore and said my first test was to beat the dragon at his own game, meaning I had to present the beast with a riddle. He wished me well and then disappeared into thin air leaving me to figure out a way to pass the test I was given. That angel was my father.

"Hey dragon! Let's play a game!" I said as I startled the beast by popping up out of nowhere. "Here's the deal. Instead of you wrapping me in that funky smelling cocoon, let's make a bet that I can come up with a riddle that you can't solve. And afterwards, you have to take me across the Great Void in style. I'm talking first-class all the way." The dragon was a master at solving riddles, so my challenge really intrigued him to no end. Now the question was, would he take the bait?

"What am I to gain by sssolving the riddle?" the dragon said with a nasty snarl and I knew I had him.

"Well, what do you want?" I said.

"I want your sssoul!"

"Okay, it's a bet! Now all you have to do is tell me what can be described this way," I said with all the gall I could muster. "You ready? Here we go." I wrote the riddle in a thick layer of dust covering the huge glass mirror that stood next to me, and the dragon read it aloud word for word:

"THE BEGINNING OF ETERNITY, THE END OF TIME AND SPACE, THE BEGINNING OF EVERY END, THE END OF EVERY PLACE."

The dragon repeated the riddle to himself several times, and then I saw that look in his eyes, the one you get when you know you've lost the game.

"What's wrong riddle master?" I said to the fuming dragon. "Cat got your tongue?"

The Gatekeeper of Worlds had been stumped by a riddle that was told to me in third grade. The simplicity of the riddle was the key, I knew the dragon would have trouble thinking on a remedial level after spending eons guarding the grandest riddle of all time. Immediately, the beast went into a violent rage and started ripping shelves off the walls and setting books ablaze with his fiery breath.

"Tell me the anssswer! Tell it to me now or you will buuurn!" the dragon shouted.

"I'll tell you the answer, but only after you calm down." I said, and the dragon did as I asked.

"It's very simple, the answer is the letter 'E'. Here, let me show you." I stepped to the mirror and placed parentheses around each letter "E" that the riddle described...

THE BEGINNING OF (E)TERNITY, THE END OF TIM(E) AND SPAC(E), THE BEGINNING OF EVERY (E) ND, THE END OF EVERY PLAC(E).

Without further adieu, the dragon handed me a small golden egg covered with brilliant stones of every kind, along with a clear glass case containing a slender key made of pure ivory and laced with ribbons of silver. There was a keyhole near the egg's midsection, so I inserted the key into the opening and gently turned it to the right. Instantly, the bejeweled egg became a luxurious carriage built for one. Inside the cabin of this "royal" ride were all the amenities one might expect to find in a plush limousine: expensive champagne neatly arranged in ice buckets made of pure gold, several boxes of Cohiba cigars, velvet drapes, decorative lamps on the walls, a mini bar filled with miniature bottles of Hennessey and rum, white leather seats with built-in temperature control, tinted windows, latest smartTV with voice command remote, classical music playing in the background, and the list goes on. The egg-shaped carriage was attached to a giant herringbone chain that hung from the dragon's neck. And when the beast raised his head, the golden carriage slid along the chain like a flashy medallion.

Through the tinted windows of my gilded cage I could see absolutely nothing. Still, there was a sense that evil spirits were gathering in the darkness nearby. I began to envision frightful creatures lurking outside my window, monsters that were responsible for stealing the innocent souls of children while they slept. They were the bogeymen in our closet, and the hobgoblins that hid beneath our bed. They were the creepy things making noises in the middle of the night, the ones our parents said weren't real. But we know better---don't we?

After entering the portal, I glanced back at the desolation of the doorway to my world and totally freaked out. There was a guy lying on the floor of the bookstore who looked just like me. We even had on the same clothes! What the *hell*?!

My mind began spinning out of control and I couldn't seem to get a grip on reality. "Is this really happening?" I said out loud as I sat back and allowed myself to sink into the soft leather interior of my ride and tried to relax. "Oh well! It is what it is." I kicked back in my G7 egg smoking Cohibas and sipping Hennessey while listening to Stravinsky's "Firebird" playing softly in the background. The miniature bottles of Hennessey and rum were more than I could handle, and before long I was totally wasted. All I remember was being facedown on the floor listening to the rhythmic sounds of the dragon's gigantic wings as they propelled me across the Great Void like mighty oars powering a Viking ship bound for war... Whoosh! Whoosh! Whoosh! I didn't believe that anything could ever top flying over the ocean in a flaming toilet. Boy!, was I wrong.

After fading in and out of consciousness for a while, I finally succumbed to the eerie lullaby being played by the dragon's wings and fell into a deep sleep. I don't know how long the lullaby lasted, but the moment it stopped playing, my eyes popped open and I discovered that both the dragon and the egg had vanished. I once again found myself alone and stranded on a beautiful island. But little did I know, things had drastically changed since the last time I set foot on her alabaster shores. Something had altered the mystical energy that once flowed abundantly on the Galactic Island. It now felt tamed and diminished, lacking any strength to loan itself to the living things in need of it. What an awful thing to happen to such a magical place.

I walked along the beach until I came across a grassy knoll near the base of the giant cliff that stood towering over the Dark Forest. From this vantage point, I spotted a series of majestic waterfalls that came together and formed a placid lake filled with crystal clear water. A golden pond where exotic birds flourished and fields of dreams came to life. I saw sanctimonious swans and egotistical egrets, proud peacocks and mischievous macaws aplenty. I saw fields of black roses dancing joyously with white dandelions in the tropical breeze blowing swiftly across the rolling meadows. The picturesque landscape was immensely beautiful and I wanted to spend the rest of my life staring at it. But low and behold, my attention was suddenly drawn by strange sounds coming from beyond the tall trees on the opposite side of the lake---it almost sounded like a rocket was preparing to launch.

I followed a fresh game trail along the perimeter of the lake and it soon led me to the area where the disturbance was coming from. When I finally saw what was making the weird sounds, I couldn't believe my eyes. Sitting on a patch of scorched earth the size of a baseball diamond was an intergalactic spacecraft with gleaming wheels and dark tinted windows. The metallic ship had a triangular shaped hull and there were four large creatures---one at each corner and another up top---standing motionless like British sentries in front of Buckingham Palace. The strange craft was parked behind a powerful energy field that was making a subtle humming sound, and every now and then I could feel the energy being drawn out of my body ever so slightly.

"So that's what's draining the life out of this place," I said as I stood behind a tree watching the miraculous feats now being performed by the creatures. They were moving large boulders and heavy debris through the air using telekinesis, the power of the mind, and making it look as easy as tossing Frisbees. The largest creature in the group---which I assumed was the alpha male---made a series of clicking noises and grunts with its throat, prompting the other creatures to leap from the hull and take up defensive positions along the edge of the woods. Then, with the precision of a black ops military team, they disappeared into the forest without a trace.

Their appearance was out of this world, literally. Each had multiple faces depicting a variety of living things such as lions, oxen, eagles, and even the faces of men. Unlike the six-winged seraph, the creatures had four transparent wings that were genetically enhanced to be part of a nuclear powered propulsion system. I know this because inside the wings I saw several components related to such a system: thermal coverings, biological shields, cores of fuel elements, control rods, cooling systems, neutron moderators.

"DO NOT VENTURE ANY CLOSER! FOR YOU WILL BE JUDGED!" shouted the creatures in unison after reappearing out of nowhere. "YOU ARE NOW STANDING AT THE PRECIPICE OF ETERNAL DAMNATION!"

The four living creatures closed ranks and formed a line directly in front of me, as if to make certain I saw the breadth of their grandeur. Each of them was about the size of a semi, and attached to their cloven hooves was a set of gleaming wheels that intersected one another like the intricate workings of an expensive timepiece. Wheels intersecting wheels. Now where have I heard that before?

Holy shit!, ...Ezekiel.

The thought suddenly occurred to me that in the book of Ezekiel 1:4-21, the prophet himself gave a detailed description of the craft and creatures I had just encountered:

"I looked and I saw a windstorm coming out of the north---an immense cloud with flashing lightning and surrounded by brilliant light. The center of the fire looked like glowing metal, and in the fire was what looked like four living creatures... each of them had four faces and four wings. Their legs were straight, their feet were like those of a calf and gleamed like burnished bronze... and their wings touched one another... Fire moved back and forth among the creatures, it was bright, and lightning flashed out of it... I saw a wheel on the ground beside each creature... they sparkled like Chrysolite, and all four looked alike. Each appeared to be made like a wheel intersecting a wheel... and when the creatures rose from the ground, the wheels rose along with them, because the spirit of the creatures was in the wheels."

The four living creatures addressed me in unison saying, "Welcome back, D'Shawn. We've been waiting for you."

"How do you know that name?" I said.

"We know everything there is to know about everything. For we are the watchers and seers of all living things in the universe," said the creatures in random order this time. "Princess Azoria sent us to protect you on your journey to Elysium, we are your guardians."

"First it was Gemini, now you guys?!" I said before beginning my interrogation. "Hey listen, I thought the dragon was supposed to take me to Elysium, what happened to that plan?"

"Dragons are deceitful creatures and pathological liars. The beast never intended to take you to Elysium, his kind cannot enter any of the holy realms---and the creature knows it is forbidden. His plan all along was to lull you to sleep and deliver you into the hands of the one he serves. The dragon's trap was in fact the golden egg in which you traveled. Fortunately, we rescued you from your eternal nap and placed you safely on the shores of the Galactic Island," said the creatures. "Princess Azoria now waits in Elysium, the Realm of Realms. We must go to her at once." The majestic creatures then raised their giant cybernetic wings toward heaven, spreading them so wide that they touched one another... Ezekiel was right on the money.

"So when do we leave for Elysium?" I asked the four living creatures. "I can hardly wait to see Azoria again."

"Although you have travelled across the Great Void, you've not yet become transformed," explained the guardians in unison again. "The Gates of Elysium will not open for you as you are now. But soon you will not be who you are, and the world around you will look much different when you view it through the true windows of your soul."

"Well, how does one actually become transformed?" I said.

"You must discover that on your own. But know this: Your world is ending, and soon everyone you know and love will be vanquished and erased from the face of the earth."

"What the hell are you talking about?!" I shouted. "Why would you say such a thing?"

"Mankind's obsession with technology and artificial intelligence has marked the end of his reign on earth. The one chance he has for redemption lies with you reaching Elysium, great D'Shawn. Azoria will show you the way."

At that very moment, bright flashes of lightning struck the alpha male and began ricocheting throughout the rest of the group, energizing them like small nuclear reactors. Thick clouds of white smoke was pouring from the ship's engines as they began firing up, and I was again reminded of what the prophet Ezekiel had said:

"I looked and I saw a windstorm coming out of the north---an immense cloud with flashing lightning and surrounded by brilliant light..."

✦

"Blessed is he who reads and those who hear the words of the prophecy, and heed the things which are written in it, for the time is near."

---Revelation 1:3

"The interpretation of dreams is the royal road to knowledge of the unconscious activities of the mind."

---Sigmund Freud

CHAPTER 28

UNTIL THE END OF TIME

Azoria's sweet voice came to me for the first time since my return to the Galactic Island, it was like an amazing dream.

"Hello my love," she said telepathically from a distant realm called Elysium. "I have missed you tremendously." "I've missed you too, Azoria. What have you been doing since I've been away?"

"I've been preparing a place for us, away from prying eyes and eavesdropping ears. A private command base where we can develop strategies and educate our people on the particulars of war."

"I thought the fighting was over." I said to the warrior princess.

"There is always a war somewhere, D'Shawn," she replied. "I'll brief you when you get here. But first you must board the Chariot of Fire and align the cherubim with their adjacent stars in the Constellation Orion."

"Chariot of Fire? You mean that contraption over there with Ezekiel's rims on it? I'm not getting in that thing!"

"What are you talking about?" said Azoria. "You say the strangest things."

"What I'm talking about is, ain't no way I---"

"We don't have time for one of your episodes, D'Shawn. So put your 'big boy' pants on and get your ass on the ship."

"You think I'm having an episode?" I was taken aback by Azoria's comment. She had hurt my feelings a little.

"Listen my love, there's no need to get defensive. I just need you to understand the seriousness of what is about to happen. No mortal has ever entered the Chariot of Fire and lived to tell about it. The ship is capable of many amazing things, some of which you won't believe. So I must prepare you because you're about bear witness to wonders beyond your wildest dreams."

"What if I don't want to bear witness to wonders beyond my wildest dreams? You ever thought about that?" I said while still in my feelings about her snide remark.

"Yes, I have. And that's why I've instructed the cherubim to encourage you." I turned around and there were the four living creatures licking out their tongues as if preparing to eat me alive.

"Okay! Let's get this show on the road!" I said with newfound enthusiasm. But in the back of my mind I was thinking, "Oh my god! I'm about to get on an alien spaceship that has big shiny rims and four talking weirdos on the roof."

"I heard that," said Azoria with an attitude.

"Dammit!" I said after getting busted. Again.

"Now make a fist with your right hand and press it firmly against the fuselage." Azoria instructed, "Do you feel that?"

"Yes! I feel it! It feels tingly!" I said.

"Good, it means the ship is responding to your bioelectrical rhythm. Now brace yourself!"

"What?" Suddenly, a bolt of lightning struck my hand and a small U-shaped handle appeared out of nowhere and started doing the "Ricky Bobby" dance to a dope-ass trap beat. The dancing handle was a sophisticated hologram, a three-dimensional image created by invisible laser beams, and was accompanied by holographic woofers with a sound quality comparable to Bose speakers. The bass sounded so good that I joined the little handle and started doing the Ricky Bobby too.

"D'Shawn! Stop dancing and pay attention," chided Azoria. "You haven't even entered the ship and already you're out of control!"

"Yeah well, the handle started it." I said before realizing how ridiculous it sounded.

"Are you done?" said Azoria. "Because we can say to hell with saving the universe and just shake our asses to a funky beat." Her sarcasm was a bit over the top but I got the message.

"Sorry, Your Majesty. It won't happen again."

"Lose the attitude, D'Shawn, and just grab the damn handle," she chided. "Turn it counterclockwise till you hear a metallic click. Are you listening to me?"

"Roger that, Boss," I said to myself forgetting that she could hear my every thought.

"You're right, I AM the boss! And don't you forget it!" she shouted loud and clear just to let me know that I had once again put my foot in my mouth.

Dammit!

Assuming the handle wasn't real, I didn't expect to physically touch anything when I reached out my hand. But the little handle, which was still dancing its ass off, was as real as can be. I had to again remind myself that I was in a world where anything was possible. So I grabbed little "Ricky Bobby" and turned him to the left until I heard a metallic click, and like magic, a hidden compartment opened up on the underbelly of the ship and a crystal staircase came spiraling down to the ground.

"What are you waiting for, an invitation?" said Azoria. "Head for the stairs and go inside." I placed my feet on the stairs and immediately felt myself being lifted toward the cockpit as if riding an escalator in a Macy's department store.

I entered the cockpit and it was like walking into a planetarium and seeing trillions of holographic stars floating all around me. There were quasars and asteroids hurling past my face and giant vortexes projected onto the gigantic dome-shaped ceiling which was several times larger than the ship itself. This three-dimensional star map showed the location of every planet, galaxy, constellation, and extragalactic civilization in the universe. I stood gazing in disbelief, solemnly thinking about the message that was sent into space on the Voyager spacecraft back in 1977. The intuitive message was sent on a gold record affixed to the exterior of Voyager, it was signed by then President Jimmy Carter, and the message was this:

"We are a community of 240 million human beings among the more than 4 billion who inhabit the planet Earth. We human beings are still divided into nation states, but these states are rapidly becoming a single global civilization. We cast this message into the cosmos. It is likely to survive a billion years into our future, when our civilization is profoundly altered and the surface of Earth may be vastly changed. Of the 200 billion stars in the Milky Way, some---perhaps many---may have inhabited planets and space faring civilizations. If one such civilization intercepts Voyager and can understand these recorded contents, here is our message: This is a present from a small distant world, a token of our sounds, our science, our images, our music, our thoughts and our feelings. We are attempting to survive our time so we may live into yours. We hope someday, having solved the problems we face, to form a community of galactic civilizations. This record represents our hope and our determination, and our good will in a vast and awesome universe."

"On the star map above you," said Azoria. "Locate the Constellation Orion. You must travel there and wait at the 'armpit of the giant' until the seventh Moon rises over Sagittarius. Only then will the Orbital Sphinx awaken and show you the way to Elysium."

Studying astronomy and astrology was one of my favorite pastimes. So I knew exactly what Azoria meant when she referred to the "armpit of the giant". It's the traditional body part that represents the brightest star in the Constellation Orion called Betelgeuse (Beetle juice), which is also known as the Alpha

Orionis---the first star of Orion. But if memory serves me right, Betelgeuse is about 527 light years away.

As for the seventh Moon rising over Sagittarius, I'm sure she was alluding to the Moon in Sagittarius that takes on a brightness that it does not have in other signs of the zodiac. Sagittarius is the astrological sign of higher learning and breadth of vision. There the Moon's influence loses its passivity and comes to life. If you have the Moon in Sagittarius you are noted for your quick, sharp mind, extraordinary insights, and an ability to get things done in a flash. Your clear-thinking intelligence sifts through sensory impressions swiftly and with startling lucidity, allowing your mind to elevate to optimum levels of consciousness.

For me, Azoria's ode to astrological phenomena held connotations of Scripture. I immediately thought about the book of Luke 21:25-27, "There will be signs in sun and moon and stars, and on earth dismay among nations, in perplexity at the roaring of the sea and the waves, men fainting from fear and the expectation of the things which are coming upon the world. For the powers of the heavens will be shaken. Then they will see THE SON of MAN COMING IN A CLOUD with power and great glory."

"Azoria, I'm afraid it's going to take more than a spaceship to reach Betelgeuse," I said. "What we really need is a time machine." Azoria ignored me and continued issuing out instructions at a frantic pace.

"Head over to the navigation panel at the center of the cockpit, it's the one with the symbols on it. I want you to place your left hand on the symbol for sigma, which represents a thousandth of a second. Then place your other hand on the symbol for infinity. Simultaneously press down on the symbols and try not to make a mess."

I did as she instructed, and the next thing I knew I was floating around inside the cockpit like one of those kids in Stephen

King's scary classic "IT". All that was missing was the evil clown "Pennywise". Pressing on the symbols at the same time activated the antigravity system, and Azoria knew what would happen---she set me up. Being in zero gravity was something I wasn't prepared for. I had been seasick before but this was much, much worse. At least when you're on a boat you know which direction the vomit is going, but in zero gravity the shit you throw up stays right there in your face floating around in nasty chunks of wobbly liquid. I mean it was gross as hell! And the worst part was hearing Azoria laughing her ass off while I nearly heaved up my lower intestine from puking so hard.

"You think that's funny, huh?" I chided. "Well let's see how you like this!"

"I know you're upset, D'Shawn, but don't do anything foolish."

"Oh, I'm not upset." I said in a nonchalant way that made her even more nervous. "Just be cool, I have an idea that's going to blow your mind."

After deactivating the antigravity system, I began making modifications to the navigation panel where the launch mechanism was located.

"Don't play around with that!" Azoria complained. "Chill out, lil' momma. I know what I'm doing." The idea was to rearrange the controls on the panel to match the buttons on my game controller back home. Needless to say, my plan backfired in a major way, and Azoria got so mad when I set the forest on fire while testing the engine boosters that she kicked my ass from like a gazillion miles away. That's not a metaphor, she metaphysically kicked me in my ass from the other side of the cosmos! Dammit!

Following the mishap with the engines I felt the need to redeem myself, so while Azoria was recuperating from expending so much energy chastising me, I secretly installed a manual override switch in the navigation panel so that I could gain access to the ship's main power source---the four living creatures that Azoria called cherubim.

"What are you doing?" said the princess after reestablishing the telepathic link between us.

"I was just checking the instruments in preparation for the test flight."

"What test flight?" she asked.

"The one that you're about to instruct me on." I said as if we had discussed the topic before. Azoria didn't respond right away, she took a few moments to ponder my suggestion before deciding that a test flight might not be such a bad idea. Especially considering the unprecedented journey ahead.

"Alright D'Shawn, but only if you promise to follow my instructions to the letter. That means no fooling around."

"Of course I promise." Azoria knew from past experience that when it comes to getting into sticky situations, I was the best in the business. Nevertheless, she began calling out launch commands as if she worked for NASA, going on and on about turning off switches and calibrating oxygen levels and checking cabin pressure and blah, blah, blah.

"Azoria, I just want to fly the damn thing not learn how to build one." I said after getting bored listening to her rambling instructions. Then, as you might've expected, I did a very foolish thing.

"D'Shawn, what did you just do?" I heard Azoria say inside my mind. But I was too busy trying to stop the ship from lifting off the ground.

"Did you disengaged the autopilot?" asked Azoria.

"Umm... yep! That is an affirmative!" The alien ship lifted off the ground and I watched helplessly as its powerful energy field set the forest ablaze yet again.

"Azoria, I just wanted to show you that I could---"

"Don't say another word! Just pull down on the lever that's next to you and be quiet."

I knew I had screwed up big this time, there was nothing I could say to smooth things over, so I did what she asked and kept quiet for a while.

When I pulled down on the lever beside me, the four living creatures leapt from the ship and began extinguishing the burning forest using the supercooled air from their breath which also produced an electrified mist that was capable of regenerating living matter. The sentinels restored the forest using a mysterious life force that lied within each of them. There was more to these beings than met the eye, and I was beginning to wonder what else were they capable of.

Once the blaze was out and the forest restored, Azoria began venting her anger in response to my reckless behavior in the cockpit. She cussed and fussed for several long minutes until I finally broke my silence and said, "What are you gonna do about it?!" There was a brief pause... then I felt the painful sting of a metaphysical foot kicking me in my ass again.

It took a bit of practice, but I was soon piloting the extragalactic spaceship like a pro. Even Azoria was impressed with how quickly I learned to fly.

"Very nice," she said after seeing my perfectly executed bank and roll, a nifty maneuver I learned from playing video games in my dorm room back in college. I was feeling pretty confident about the inaugural flight, but as the ship left orbit and entered outer space, my confidence went out the window. The vastness of the universe blew my mind in such a way that I could not move, I was frozen in place gazing at the world I had left behind, watching it grow smaller and smaller in the window through which I stared. Meanwhile, I reengaged the autopilot prompting the four living creatures to begin initiating the preprogrammed flight plan that Azoria had given them prior to my arrival. They set a course for a destination beyond the solar system but by the time the ship reached Jupiter, a magnificent comet with a long fiery tail came roaring across the galaxy heading straight for us. The comet was so bright that it caused the ship's thermal shields to engaged at full power.

"What's going on?" said Azoria. "Why did the shields go up?"

"There's a burning rock outside the windshield the size of Manhattan. That's why!"

"Oh no!" cried Azoria, "D'Shawn, it's the Hale-Bopp comet! I forgot to account for its return when I made the flight plan. If it damages the ship even in the slightest way, the entire mission could be put in jeopardy!"

"How do you know about Comet Hale-Bopp?" I asked Azoria. But as usual, she ignored the question because it had something to do with the prophecy.

Comet Hale-Bopp was one of the most widely observed comets of the 20th century and one of the brightest seen for many decades. It had an apparent magnitude of 10.5 and lay near the globular cluster M70 in the constellation of Sagittarius. It's hard to predict the maximum brightness of comets with any degree of certainty, but Hale-Bopp met and exceeded most predictions when it passed perihelion---the nearest point of a body's direct orbit around the sun---on April 1, 1997. It's believed that the comet made its pervious perihelion 4,200 years ago, in July 2215 BC, when its approach to Earth was observed in ancient Egypt during the 6th dynasty reign of the Pharaoh Pepi II. Inside Pepi's pyramid at Saqqara is a text referring to an "nhh-star" as a companion of the pharaoh in the heavens, where "nhh" is the hieroglyphic for long hair---a reference to Hale-Bopp's luminous tail.

Moments later, the ship lost all power and the cockpit went completely dark. I glanced out of the window and saw that the ship was still on a collision course with the comet, then I turned to see if the sentinels were going to change course. Unfortunately, the four of them had fallen into a deep sleep and could not be awakened, or so it seemed.

"That's just great." I thought to myself when seeing the guardians of the galaxy laying down on the job. It's a good thing I installed the manual override switch as a backup plan for situations such as the one at hand. "Here goes nothing."

Suddenly, as if by magic, the sentinels snapped to attention and took up new positions along the outer hull. They began extending their wings upward and outward forming a giant pyramid atop Ezekiel's extragalactic space shuttle. Every dimension of the four-sided pyramid was symmetrically precise, and engraved on each side was the stoic face of an Egyptian pharaoh---Amenhotep III, Xerxes, Khufu, and Pepi II.

A brand new chapter in this never ending odyssey of mine was beginning to unfold. Little did I know it would lead to something so spectacular that not even Azoria in all her wisdom would be able to explain it.

An immeasurable amount of cosmic energy came bursting out of the pyramid, I could feel it pulsating through my very soul as it enveloped the ship and ignited the four living creatures like never before. The engines roared to life causing the extragalactic vessel's velocity to exceed the speed of light. For a brief moment I felt like "Han Solo" flying through the galaxy in the Millennium Falcon while "Chewey" engages the ship's hyperdrive. I always suspected the sentinels were part of an advanced propulsion system, but in this situation I don't think that even they knew what was going on. The phenomenal energy emanating from the pyramid was greater than that of a thousand supernovas, making the event awesome as hell to watch. Needless to say, the ship's control panel was going crazy and everywhere I turned I saw flashing red warnings saying "critical overload". The gauges that monitored the ship's speed caught fire and exploded, but not before showing that the ship was travelling at five times the speed of light.

During this incredible flight, I witnessed firsthand the relationship between time, energy, and mass as explained in Einstein's Theory of Relativity. What I discovered was that even when considering Heisenberg's uncertainty principle, where certain pairs of observable quantities like energy and time or position and momentum cannot be measured with complete accuracy simultaneously (because an object cannot exist in two places at once),

Einstein got it right. I understand that quantum physics is a strange animal, a virtual unicorn in the realm of logical thinking, but I also believe that this guy Einstein was something other than a theoretical physicist. I believe he was a goddamn alien.

Nevertheless, while travelling at such a high rate of speed, extremely weird shit started happening in the cockpit that scared the living daylights out of me. Keep in mind that the manual override switch I had installed involved a crude form of nuclear fusion. Though it boosted the ship's thrusters, it also opened up a doorway into "the unknown", inviting an evil presence that cosmologists refer to as dark energy---a mysterious, undefined energy leading to a repulsive force pervading all of space-time---to enter the cockpit and torture my mind. I looked and I saw a window next to me that wasn't there before, and right away I knew I was in deep shit.

"Where did that come from?" I said aloud while fearfully staring at the anomaly. "I must be trippin'!... I must be trippin'!... I must be trippin'!" At first I thought there was an echo in the cockpit, but soon realized that my words were being repeated back to me in the same voice by someone standing on the other side of the window looking in. The hairs on the back of my neck stood straight up and goosebumps rippled down my arms because the person on the other side of the window looked exactly like me---but wasn't me.

"Azoria! Some really weird shit is going on!" I said in a telepathic message laced with panic. "There's someone pretending to be me standing outside of a window that wasn't there before!" When Azoria didn't respond to my cry for help it confirmed to me that the ship was travelling too fast for there to be a telepathic link between us. I was literally on my own... and the dark energy somehow knew it.Suddenly, out of nowhere comes this bright red balloon floating towards me with a tiny piece of string attached to it as if it had broken free from a child's grip and took flight inside the cockpit. I was again reminded of the movie "IT" where the kid went down into the basement and ran into the evil clown Pennywise whose smiling face appeared from behind a red balloon and brandished a mouth full of pointy teeth. The dark energy had obviously searched my innermost thoughts and discovered my fear of clowns, which is called coulrophobia. I stood frozen and watched the creepy balloon come closer and closer until it was only a few inches away. I can't remember whether I lost consciousness at that point but I do recall thinking back to the witch in the bookstore and how eerily similar the atmosphere inside the spooky cockpit was beginning to feel. All it took was one mistake and the dark energy used my memory of that experience and conjured up a host of images to accommodate me in the worst way.

Standing outside the mysterious window in place of my Doppelganger was the wicked witch from Bourbon Street. She was reading from the books of miracles, Ex Libris Mirabilia, and chanting strange words that brought forth hordes of ghoulish looking nymphs called harpies. These treacherous creatures were all females and had long flowing hair, slender arms, jagged wings, and razor sharp claws which made them extremely dangerous.

The demonic creatures came rushing into the cockpit through the imaginary window like bats out of hell. The witch had conjured them out of the abyss and I could tell by the awful stench, which smelled like rotten eggs and dead fish, that the creatures were made of dark energy. They started paying homage to the witch by kissing her warts and licking her in places I'd rather not mention---but trust me, the shit was gross. The lascivious demons then disappeared into a swirling vortex that opened near the center of the cockpit. Still, I could hear them laughing and breaking things like unruly ghosts wreaking havoc inside a kitchen filled with fine China.

I figured the best way to put a stop to the madness was to go after the witch but as soon as I tried to approach her, the harpies returned and started attacking me from every direction. They looked like demonic fireflies glowing in the dark with an eerie green light coming from their frail, slender bodies. The harpies began slashing and clawing and biting me with tremendous force, causing excruciating pain with every lick thrown my way. I laid on the floor in a fetal position and covered my head to guard against getting my eyes ripped out by a glancing blow from one of the harpies' sharp claws. The witch spoke in a strange language and the harpies immediately responded by tearing off their skin and revealing their true form.

"Holy shit!" The witch had actually summoned a group of fire demons known as Drachens and disguised them as harpies. The Drachens looked like balls of fire with glistening white teeth and razor like claws that hung down to the floor. A rancid smell of sulphur, similar to the stench of rotten eggs trailed them everywhere they went. Drachens are vile and disgusting spirits that love to torment humans, they have a hostile temperament and the ability to breathe fire but would much rather drive their victims insane to the point of committing suicide. Then the Drachens drag the condemned souls into the burning catacombs of Hades and tortures them for all eternity.

I looked and I saw the Drachens burst into flames creating a mystic firestorm at the center of the cockpit. That's when the vortex increased in size and I could feel myself being drawn into oblivion by a powerful spirit being.

"Oh, no! Azoria h-e-e-e-l-p!"

Ezekiel's spaceship disengaged its warp drive and returned to its normal speed. It was then that I heard Azoria's voice calling out to me.

"D'Shawn! Where have you been? I've been trying to reach you for hours!" I wanted to answer her but I wasn't sure if it was actually her or just my imagination running wild. I had to keep reminding myself that while in the throes of the demons' firestorm, anything was possible. My thoughts were already in shambles and I didn't want to risk the dark energy tricking me again. But little did I know the telepathic connection between Azoria and I had been restored due to the ship coming out of warp speed. By this time, she had decided to break the rules of space-time travel and release her essence in metaphysical form so that it could appear inside the cockpit as a frightening apparition. Azoria loaned her likeness to a dark and ominous cloud of pure energy. Woe be unto the minions of the Devil, for a greater power had been loosed inside the cockpit.

"Demons be gone!" She roared at the Drachens who coward in fear when seeing the apparition she had become. "Or I will rip you from existence!"

The fury in her eyes and the thunder in her voice convinced the fire demons to crawl back into the abyss, leaving the witch to fend for herself. Azoria told me to dispatch the old hag by using a spell from the Ex Libris Mirabilia, so I snatched the book and spoke these words: "Tuuliah bezalee octuk raksha!"

The witch's body snapped in two and was quickly sucked into the vortex at the center of the ship. I thought that was the end of it, but there was one more entity I had to face.

"Azoria, before you get mad, let me explain what happened." I said to the apparition bearing her likeness. "I made one little tweak to the engines' boosters and then all of sudden some guy was standing outside the window. But hey, you should've seen how I handled those fire demons. I had their scary asses ducking and hiding and---."

"First of all, I saw the whole thing." Azoria interrupted, "And if I hadn't done what I did your ass would still be on the floor curled up like a little baby waiting to get your diaper changed. Secondly, you should not have tampered with the controls in the first place. What if you had gotten yourself killed?!" I could tell that Azoria was angry, but I also detected an air of sadness in her voice as she berated me for disobeying her...

"D'Shawn, my beloved, you must understand that this journey of ours began long before we met. According to the Holy Spirit and the prophecy, we were destined to travel this path together because God has a plan for us that is bigger than anything we can imagine... so if there is any consolation of love, if there is any fellowship of the Spirit, if any affection and compassion, make my joy complete by being of the same mind, maintaining the same love, united in spirit, intent on one purpose... becoming obedient to God's will to the point of death."

The words she spoke were so powerful they moved me to tears. I humbled myself before God and all the angels in heaven as Azoria continued speaking from the book of Philippians and reminding me of why I was chosen for this journey.

"Then God said, 'Let there be lights in the expanse of the heavens to separate the day from the night, and let them be for signs and for seasons and for days and years."
   ---Genesis 1:14

CHAPTER 29

FINAL DESTINATION: THE WAY TO ELYSIUM

As Azoria's ghostly personification disappeared, in its wake a brand new anomaly began to take shape outside near the starboard bow. I quickly made my way across the bridge of the ship and peered through the octagonal shaped porthole in the wall that was adjacent to the anomaly. And as I looked through the 8-inch thick glass window my eyes were drawn to the strange clouds directly in front of me. The rolling mist pitched to and fro and was as perplexing to watch as the swirling vortex that swallowed the witch. Deep in my soul I felt that something amazing was about to unfold before my very eyes, and the space anomaly didn't disappoint me. It crept slowly up the sides of the giant pyramid that had been formed by the sentinels and put on a spectacular light show. The brightly colored dust particles inside the cosmic cloud bank were spontaneously changing from red to pink to lime to fuchsia to every other color of the rainbow. It was like seeing a psychedelic strobe light reflecting off the metal pyramid turning it into a cosmic "Christmas tree" surrounded by cotton candy and decorated with dust covered lightbulbs from the 70s.

I had suspected that the culprit behind the strange clouds and colorful lights was cosmic radiation. But it didn't explain the ghost in the machine that hacked the ship's computers and changed the coordinates in the flight plan without my knowledge or consent, causing the ship to take a sharp right turn and head straight into a fierce lightning storm. Powerful bolts of electricity from the lightning forced the sentinels back to their original positions along the outer hull. Collectively the four living creatures became a set of highly efficient conductors, creating an electromagnet of phenomenal strength. It wiped out every electrical device on board, casting me back into a pitch dark environment as black as space itself. But there was one instrument aboard the ship that never stopped working---the extragalactic spectroscope.

This powerful device was built using alien technology from an undisclosed planet that was home to an advanced alien civilization of time travelers. Its primary function was to take spectroscopic measurements of stars no matter where they were located in the universe. The data collected by the spectroscope showed that the source of the anomaly was more than 171 trillion miles away. It was the bright star Capella (the Goat) in the constellation of the Charioteer. Capella---a yellow star with golden rays like our Sun---was a paradox in itself. Its mass was 18 times the mass of the sun, but its parallax showed that it was 128 times brighter than the sun, which meant that Capella's great brilliancy produced enormous amounts of radiation that caused large swaths of cosmic dust to become energized to the point where weird occurrences were bound to happen. At first, the spectroscope showed the anomaly as being a blurry little smug, but the electrified clouds of space dust grew expeditiously and soon took up an area the size of Jupiter---and then came the weird noises.

"What was that?" I said to myself before hurrying back to the window and looking outside. "You've got to be kidding me!"

A large portion of the ship's hull and two of the sentinels were suddenly missing. All that remained was shooting stars and distant quasars sparkling like "pixie dust" in the black expanse of outer space.

"Azoria, do you see what's happening outside the ship?"

"Yes, my love. And you must prepare yourself for what is about to happen next."

"What do you mean? I don't understand what you're talk---" There was suddenly someone standing in the cockpit staring at me with eyes as bright as starlight. The mysterious figure wasn't a man of flesh and bones but a "spirit man" partially hidden behind a veil of white smoke seeping into the cockpit through a small crack that had opened in the ceiling.

"Who are you?" I said to the angelic spirit standing before me. "Where did you come from?"

He turned to me and said, "I am The Way."

"The way to what?" I said while taking up a defensive position next to the navigation panel with the symbols on it.

"The Way to Elysium," said the spirit. "Do you not know who I am?"

"I know who you want me to believe you are." I said with a clumsy tongue and nervous tone. "If you are truly Him, then tell me about Elysium."

"I will tell you more than that," said the spirit, sounding more and more like a false prophet as he slowly continued to move towards me. "You have already been to Elysium," the spirit said in a puzzling way. "You're from New Orleans, are you not? A city where there lies an eccentric neighborhood called Elysian Fields, and yet you say you want to learn about Elysium? The names are one in the same. Have you not seen the play 'A Streetcar Named Desire'? Stella! Stella!"

I was both surprised and confused by what the spirit said. In a sense he was right, Elysian Fields is a neighborhood in New Orleans made famous in 'A Streetcar Named Desire' equivalent to déclassé purgatory where Stanley, Stella Kowalski, and Blanche Dubois lived. But the Elysian Fields was also a concept of the afterlife, separate from the realms of Hades. Admission to this

Paradise was reserved for mortals likened to gods... wait a damn minute!

"Yes, young D'Shawn, one has to be 'chosen' to see The Way to Elysium... it is like a dragnet cast into the sea, and gathering fish of every kind, and when it is full, I draw it up on the beach, and I sit down and gather the good fish into containers, but the bad I throw away.

"So it will be at the end of the age. The angels will come forth and take out the wicked from among the righteous, and will throw them into the furnace fire, in that place there will be weeping and gnashing of teeth. Have you understood all these things?" I wasn't certain whether the spirit knew that he was reciting Matthew 13: 47-51. Nevertheless, it didn't prove a thing because even the devil knows what is written in the Bible.

"Hey listen, dude. You're going to have to do a lot better than that, my friend." I said half jokingly. "Show me a sign, and then maybe I'll believe you."

The ambiguous spirit rose into the air and commanded the clouds to follow him, and then all at once he sent them to collect me. I immediately ducked out of sight, but when the rolling mist settled atop the navigation panel next to me, its symbols and gauges slowly started disappearing into the anomaly. The panel itself disappeared next, followed by the holographic star map that I had grown accustomed to staring at on the ceiling. Everything inside the cockpit was soon engulfed by the strange clouds---including me.

"I can't believe this is happening," I said while staring at my hands. Or should I say staring at the empty place where my hands should've been. "Who would've ever thought that becoming invisible would be so terrifying?" I watched as my hands became like clear water, then like glass, and finally turning solid crystal before disintegrating into tiny particles of light.

"Oh no! Not those too!" I screamed as the clouds started creeping up my legs threatening to turn my "family jewels" into sparkling chandelier ornaments.

I suddenly heard a loud sound that scared the bejesus out of me.

"What now?!" I cried, "Have the angels started blowing their trumpets?" It turned out that the noise was coming from an alarm system ran by artificial intelligence. It signaled that the ship was approaching the designated coordinates that had been programmed into the navigation computers. In the recesses of my mind, I could hear faint laughter. It was Azoria, she was laughing her ass off about something totally oblivious to me. She apparently knew that I would experience severe hallucinations on the trip to Orion, and had played along with my delusions in order to teach me a lesson. Everything from the clown to the witch to the Drachens to the ambiguous spirit was part of the psychosis I suffered as a result of the extragalactic spaceship jumping time and passing through a region of space known as the "Underverse". Azoria had been there before, so she was well aware of how the astronomical "Twilight Zone" would affect me, and that lil' heifer didn't say a word.

"Serves you right," she had the nerve to tell me after the fact. "Next time you'll know not to go tampering with things that are beyond your understanding."

I started thinking about all the crazy shit that happened during my hallucination and realized that, "Man, my nerves way too bad to be flying around in outer space. All I want to do right now is find me some good weed and get high as a motherfucker, ya heard me. I'll deal with her ass later."

Upon arriving at the destination set by the new coordinates, I thought about what Azoria had said to me back when I first stepped foot in the cockpit and gazed up at the three-dimensional map projected on the ceiling:

"...use the star map above you to locate the Constellation Orion. You must go there and wait at the 'armpit of the giant' until the seventh Moon rises in Sagittarius. Only then will the Orbital Sphinx awaken and show you the way to Elysium."

"It makes perfect sense now," I said to myself, "I'm right where she wanted me to be- the Alpha Orionis. The brightest star in the Constellation Orion." The extragalactic spaceship was now caught in the gravitational field of the massive star and was being pulled towards its super hot surface. It didn't matter whether the ship could withstand extreme temperatures, there was always the chance that a gravitational red shift might occur. A shift toward longer wavelengths of electromagnetic radiation produced by a massive star's molten surface. Fortunately, because of the seventh Moon rising in Sagittarius, the four living creatures took action to safeguard the mission. They rejoined as one, forming an even more spectacular pyramid than the original one. The magnificent creatures lent themselves to the cosmos and then harnessed the positive energy which returned to them tenfold, turning the giant pyramid into a superconductor of electricity. The next thing I saw was lightning flashing beneath the mighty pyramid, creating an electrical storm the size of Mars. The pyramid suddenly cracked open from the top and I saw the four living creatures standing with their body facing inward and their eyes gazing down at a magnificent orb sitting at the center of the cockpit looking like a gigantic crystal ball filled with pure starlight.

"Great D'Shawn!" shouted the four living creatures in one harmonious voice. "The Orbital Sphinx has been awakened! It is time for the Judgment to begin!" They then turned and stared at me saying, "Do not attempt to deceive the Sphinx! For if you do, you cannot be redeemed! And your soul will suffer eternal damnation!"

Getting to Elysium was turning out to be more than I had bargained for.

"Hey listen, I think you guys forgot to mention this part before we left the Galactic Island, because it seems there are some things being stipulated now that weren't discussed prior to our agreement. You see, I sort of have a problem with following rules."

"Once the Judgment befalls you, Great D'Shawn, you will be introduced to your élan vital---the unique life force within you that makes you who you are---and the universe will be at your beck and call."

"What in heaven's name are you guys talking about?" I said to the sentinels. "In fact, where's Azoria?"

"I am here, my love," Azoria's sweet voice came to me like in a dream. "You must listen to the guardians as you would me, they are here on your behalf and have sacrificed greatly to protect the mission and you as well."

"Okay, I'll hear them out. But only because you've asked me to."

"Thank you, my love."

While the sentinels continued to explain the rules of the game, I listened closely to ever word they spoke.

"...soon you will experience the dreams of immortals and discover that the Alpha Orionis is not only 'the Light which is in heaven' but a doorway that leads to the Truth. Beyond it are two golden gates standing open in heaven, and stationed in front of them are the cherubim and the flaming sword. Collectively, they are responsible for executing the Judgment. But it is the Sphinx alone who will decide the fate of your physical self, whereas the cherubim and the sword will decide the fate of your élan vital, your living soul."

The mentioning of the cherubim and the flaming sword stirred my thoughts and I was reminded of the verse from Genesis 3:24.

"...He drove the man out, and at the east of the garden of Eden He stationed the cherubim and the flaming sword which turned every direction to guard the way to the tree of life."

"Great D'Shawn," the sentinels said in unison. "There are but two paths to eternal life. The first path is guarded by God's second highest ranking angels, we, the cherubim. The second path is guarded by the Sylph---a dark and evil spirit that lives inside the flames of the sword. Be warned! The Sylph is not alone! It is accompanied by a deadly siren with flaming red hair and big yellow eyes. She is called the 'Nothingness'... the 'Nothingness'... the 'Nothingness'."

I suddenly fell into a trance and was shown a vision that frightened me tremendously. The vision took me back into the Dark Forest: I was standing nude in the brush talking to a gorgeous nymph who was playing with a litter of kittens under the shade of a massive weeping willow. Then suddenly the nymph turned into a hideous monster with seven heads and four huge feet like a bear.

"Woe be unto the sons and daughters of man!" the beast roared. "A great demon is coming to place your world under his dominion! Only those who are anointed with the Blood of the Lamb will go unharmed! Those who are without Christ will surely perish and their souls shall belong to the Nothingness and the sword! That is the Covenant! So shall it be!"

I awoke from the premonition and immediately noticed that my hands were shaking like crazy. The sense that I got from the eerie vision was that no matter what lengths I was willing to go through to save my world, it was still doomed. But the sentinels had a different perspective of what the future of my world would be. They believed that I possessed the power to save my world and defeat the devil in the process. But in order for me to unleash this awesome power I would have to be born again, I would have to become transformed.

I channeled my energy, summoned my courage and challenged the Orbital Sphinx to find fault in me. I stood before the giant orb with a calm spirit, asking God to please send His angels to watch over me during this important trial in my life. As the pulsating orb began testing me, I could hear the words of Victor Hugo's poem "Ecstasy" relaying the details of my experiences in vivid colors:

"I was alone on the waves, on a starry night, not a cloud in the sky, not a sail in sight. My eyes pierced beyond the natural world... And the woods, and the hills, and the voice of Nature seemed to question in a confused murmur, the waves of the sea, and heaven's fires. And the golden stars in infinite legion, sang loudly, and softly, in glad recognition, including their crowns of fire,... And the waves that's naught can check nor arrest sang, bowing the foam of their haughty crest... Behold the Lord God---Jehovah!"

"D'Shawn, my love," said Azoria in a kind and loving voice. "Relax your mind and search only for the cherished moments of your childhood that brought you great joy. When you're ready to begin, place your hands on the orb and let your spirit be your guide." I took in a deep breath and then prepared my mind for a brand new experience.

"I'm ready, Azoria." I said as I pressed my hands firmly against the cool glass surface of the glowing orb and started thinking about the fun I used to have as a kid. I thought about Christmas mornings hopping out of bed and racing to the living room anxious to open presents waiting under the tree. I thought about pool parties with friends from Elysian Fields and trips to Pontchartrain Beach during the summer. I remembered the festive times on the Lakefront having crawfish boils and barbecues with family and friends. I thought about the times my brothers and I would go down to the Riverfront Mall and play on the escalators before having hilarious caricatures drawn of our faces to take home and show Mama. I even thought about the time Mama took us all on vacation to Panama City Beach, Florida, where it was the first time in my life that I saw the ocean. I went running out into the water after spotting a family of dolphins swimming in the surf, but less than a minute later I got stung by a jellyfish and thought it was a shark attack. You should've seen the commotion I caused at the beach that day, people for miles were running and screaming and trying to get out of the water because I had yelled "Shaaark!!!". I thought for sure Mama was going to whoop my behind, but instead, she put meat tenderizer on the area of my leg where I had gotten stung and the pain instantly went away. Then she took me and the rest of the family to the biggest amusement park we had ever seen, and we completely lost our minds. That day I vowed to never go back into the ocean... well, I guess the old saying is true. Some promises were meant to be broken.

I would have to say the most memorable time of my young life was the weekend I first fell in love. It was at the annual Shrimp and Petroleum Festival in Morgan City, and she was the most beautiful Creole girl I had ever laid eyes on. Her name was Marche' Piquc, but everyone called her "Cutie Pie" or simply "Pie" for short. She reminds me of "Lyric", the down south honey played by Jada Pinkett Smith in the movie "Jason's Lyric" --not the "bald" Jada from the Oscars who prompted Will Smith to slap the living shit out of Chris Rock, I'm talking about the "young, sexy" Jada with short hair and a smile that could light up the whole world. Pie and Lyric could easily have past for twins. Both are petit and fine as hell, and they share the exact same skin color---caramel with a hint of chestnut and a dab of olive, for good measure. And just like Lyric, Pie has light brown eyes and cute dimples that soften when she smiles, giving off that warm and fuzzy feeling like being home again.

The Shrimp and Petroleum Festival in Morgan City takes place every year during Labor Day Weekend, and that particular year my family shared a camping area at Lake End Park with Pie's family. It was a spectacular campground on the banks of Lake Palourde, and from the moment I first saw Pie sitting with my mom under the canopy of a beautiful camper laughing and talking and showing off pictures of the fish she had caught the day before, I knew the weekend was going to be one to remember. She looked so gorgeous in her yellow sundress and straw hat with matching sunflowers on the brim. Pie was the "life of the party", and everywhere she went she made people smile.

Later that night while the two of us sat next to the campfire roasting marshmallows, Pie told me a frightening story about the strange creature that was said to roam the bayous near Morgan City.

"People from around here are afraid that the 'Rougarou' will go hunting tonight because there's a full moon over the bayou," said Pie with a serious expression that made it seem like every word she spoke was true. "No one would dare go into the woods tonight, not when the moon is this full and bright."

I, too, had heard stories about the werewolf on the bayou called the *Rougarou*, but that night was all about getting to know Pie. So I told her that if the Rougarou showed its ugly face around here, I'd go get my brother Jamal and we'd bring that smoke to his ass. Needless to say, I never saw anyone laugh so hard before.

We spent the rest of the evening fishing along the canal that extended from the lake and ran adjacent to Brownell Holmes subdivision. Pie showed me some of her special techniques for catching everything from black crappies to brem to sac-a-lait to catfish to perch to bass and even taught me how to catch alligators. Not saying that I actually tried to catch any. I'll leave that to my lil' cousin Jacie who moved to Pierre Part and opened her own restaurant that features fresh alligator gumbo.

You go girl!

It was still evening of the first day, and I remember Pie taking me on a long pier that led out over the lake to a huge two-story pavilion. The entire structure was surrounded by a chain link fence and there were rows of picnic tables and benches on both floors to accommodate large gatherings. She said it was the best place to watch the speedboat races on the lake. We stood next to each other looking up at the stars while the moon's sallow light shined down on the placid waters of Lake Palourde. I remember how the tall cypress trees rose out of the lake's dark green water, their moss covered limbs stretching freakishly outward as though teasing the less fortunate trees that were stuck on land and could not venture out into the water. Nor could the other trees flaunt the exclusive moss attire worn by the cypress trees, which according to the pelicans and egrets that frequent the lake is a really big deal.

"Wow! This place is a paradise," I said to Pie. "How long have you lived here?"

"I've been here my whole life," she answered with a beaming smile. "And if you think this is something, wait till you see what I've planned for us tomorrow."

We returned to the campground where we rejoined our families and turned in for the night. But truth be told, I didn't sleep a wink, because every time I closed my eyes I saw visions of Pie smiling at me with that look of hers. I remember pacing back and forth all night pausing only to check the time, which seemed to be moving slower than molasses. When morning finally arrived, Pie came over and asked my mom for permission to take me around the city to see all the sights. Of course Mama said "yes", but Jamal stood his crazy ass up and told Pie that if she didn't hook him up with one of her potnahs, he was going to punch her in the throat. Well, as you can imagine, we started brawling right there in front of everybody. And Mama got so mad with Jamal that she went and got Big Mama's shoe out the trunk of her car. She came marching back towards us like she had a drako in her hand.

"Baby, you and Pie have fun today, okay," she said as she walked past Pie and me on her way to tearing Jamal's ass up in front of all them white folks at the lake. WHOP! WHOP! WHOP! went the sound of the shoe.

With Mama's blessing, Pie and I set out to paint the whole town red---well, at least as red as a couple of twelve-year-olds were allowed to paint it. Our first stop was at the riverfront in downtown Morgan City where we saw dozens of shrimp boats parading up and down the Atchafalaya River. They were decorated like Mardi Gras floats and had colorful flags streaming from bow to stern in an array of beautiful patterns. The reason why the shrimp boats were all dressed up was because it was part of a local ritual called the Blessing of the Fleet. The boats blew their horns and sprayed water from high-pressure hoses straight in the air making huge arching patterns that produced rainbows when the sun hit the mist beneath the main jets of water. The ceremony began with the introduction of a priest from the local diocese who stood on a high platform and blessed the fleet of shrimp boats and prayed for the boat captains to have a safe and bountiful shrimping season.

From there we headed over to Lawrence Park where there was live music and plenty of activities going on. I saw people dancing to zydeco and blues songs played by musicians with all sorts of instruments I'd never seen before. It was the kind of music made for dub stepping, and Pie wasted no time grabbing me by the hand and leading me to the dancefloor. Man, we cut up so bad and had so much fun while dancing that the old people started clapping for us. That down home Cajun music had me so hyped that I spun Pie around and then pulled off a Michael Jackson-style lean move that surprised everyone in the crowd, including me. Pie couldn't get over how well I danced that day, and I couldn't get over the fact that I was with the most gorgeous girl I had ever seen. The weekend was becoming more magical by the hour.

Before leaving the concert in the park, Pie and I sampled every kind of shrimp there was to eat. We must have visited nearly 30 different food courts set up in and around the park that were giving out free samples. We tasted everything from boiled shrimp to fried shrimp to barbeque shrimp to stewed shrimp to puréed shrimp to shrimp shish kebab to popcorn shrimp to shrimp Clemenceau, and we even tried shrimp popsicles. I ate so much shrimp that day that I nearly came down with a case of iodine poisoning.

After stuffing our faces with every Cajun delicacy imaginable, we joined the throngs of jubilant revelers headed toward the New Bridge, which is right next to the Old Bridge connecting Morgan City with the town of Berwick, to watch the big parade that was just about to start. The parade was supposed to begin at the corner of Onstead Street and Federal Avenue, then go down Second Street cross Brashear Avenue and Greenwood Street before turning left on Everett and then making a left on Sixth Street before ending at Frerett. But thanks to Pie, the parade took a brand new route that year, straight through the hood.

At first we were just watching the floats roll by with riders tossing beads and doubloons to the masses like hundred dollar bills at a strip club. But when Pie heard the unmistakable sound of the "Human Jukebox" marching towards us, she completely lost her mind and went running out into the middle of the street and started dancing like a "Wild Tchoupitoulas". That girl kicked off a second line by herself, and when Southern's drum major saw how she was getting down, he blew his whistle three times and the drummers started playing a New Orleans second line cadence.

"Aww shit! It's on now!" I heard a huge Black woman say before charging out into the street and buck jumping like her big butt was on fire.

Hundreds and hundreds of people poured into the streets of Morgan City forming the largest second line in the world. Pie had the whole city jumping to the rhythm and sounds of Southern Band. The massive second line started in Cleansville by Julia B. Maitland Elementary and traveled down Willow Street before turning right on Sixth and making its way to Margarette before pausing in front of Morgan City Jr. High. From there we travelled through the hoods of Back O' Town, Cross the Tracks, and the Coal Chute before reaching the fairgrounds at the Municipal Auditorium where thousands of people were now dancing and enjoying themselves at the second line. It didn't matter your race, color, creed, or the gender you claimed, Pie's party included people of all colors and ethnicities. It was like watching Dr. King's dream come to life right before my eyes... beautiful. It was simply beautiful.

It was evening of the third and final day, and I noticed the sky above Morgan City had a weird tangerine glow about it.

"Pie, have you ever seen the sky that color before?" She ignored the question, and instead grabbed my hand and led me toward the bright lights down on Front Street where I saw the most amazing street fair ever! There were literally thousands of people enjoying the rides and festivities at this mega event which had just as many attractions and rides as a major theme park. I saw dozens of clowns in funny costumes making the little kids laugh at their crazy antics. There were Go Karts and bumper cars and roller coasters galore! I remember going inside the "Wacky Funhouse" and this guy dressed in a Dracula outfit jumped out from behind a dark curtain and scared the shit out of me. I wanted to kick his ass, but Pie was having a great time and I didn't want to ruin it.

The main attraction at the fair that year was a ten story tall gondola which carried riders across the Atchafalaya River from Morgan City to Berwick and back again. The gondola was as tall as the two bridges on either side of it, and I counted at least 12 cable cars gliding high above us on steel cables being towed by powerful pulleys. From where we were standing, me and Pie could see people with their feet dangling beneath the chairs on the ride, enjoying a bird's eye view of the quaint little towns on both sides of the Atchafalaya. I sensed that Pie was waiting for me to ask her to go on the ride together, but I was deathly afraid of heights. So I quickly steered her attention toward the gaming booths to our immediate right.

"Wow! I can't believe it!" I shouted with false enthusiasm. "That's my favorite game!"

We headed over to the booth and was greeted by a chubby white guy wearing red suspenders and a dinghy T-shirt with the name "Bubba" written on it with a permanent marker.

"Step right up!," he hollered in a loud and country manner. "Make a basket and win a prize! Step right up, sir!" I gave Bubba three dollars and he handed me a miniature basketball and said, "Good luck!" There was a disingenuous tone in his voice like he wasn't being sincere when he wished me luck. I had three shots and three chances to get the ball through the hoop and win a prize for my beautiful date. But it wouldn't be as easy as I thought.

The goal appeared to be closer than it actually was, some sort of optical illusion had been created by the red and black lines running along the side walls leading to the rim. I failed miserably on the first try. My shot hit the front of the rim and ricocheted over the top of the backboard."Dammit!" I cried out in frustration after missing the shot. "I need to put more spin on the ball." So I stepped into the next shot with confidence, placing my hands on the ball in the proper position and spreading my fingers for absolute control of the shot.

BLAM! "Ooooohhhh!"

My second shot was a total "brick". The ball slammed into the backboard so hard it made a sound like someone hit it with an actual brick. I tried to play it off by holding my wrist and acting like it was hurt but the mob behind me wasn't buying any of my shenanigans. They already had their cameras rolling hoping to record a viral video or capture a TMZ moment, and so they egged me on to take another shot.

My third and final shot was perfect, the ball went straight through the hoop and I started celebrating right away. But little did I know the ball had popped out of the rim and hit an old lady in the face knocking her dentures clean out of her mouth. It was as if somebody had goal tended the shot by punching the ball out of the net on the way down. I was furious as I marched up to Bubba's fat ass and said, "The game is rigged! Gimme my money back!"

Bubba smiled and showed every fake gold tooth in his head while he stuffed my three dollars into his greasy trousers and told me to have a nice day. Man, I felt played. And in the midst of the huge argument that broke out between me and Bubba, I heard Pie's sweet voice intervene:

"Excuse me, sir." She said to Bubba who was still wearing a shitty grin while tucking my money deep down in his pocket. "Mind if I give it a try?"

"Step right on up, miss! And give it your best shot!" There was that disingenuous tone again. But this time Bubba---and his gang of video vigilantes---was in for a big surprise. It just so happened that Pie was the star point guard on the basketball team at her school, she held the title for "Best All-American 3-point Shooter" in the state. She leaned in close to me and whispered, "Watch and learn."

Pie walked up to the counter, handed Bubba three more dollars and then winked at me before scoring three straight baskets. She won her choice of cool prizes which included matching charm bracelets, a pair of glow-in-the-dark eyeglasses, and a huge stuffed crawfish that giggled whenever its tail was pinched. The crowd behind us cheered Pie's triumphant victory and then slowly melted into the sea of bodies moving to and fro like ants in a colony.

Everywhere I looked I saw couples holding hands and cuddling close together to stay warm in the brisk wind coming off the Atchafalaya River. I glanced to my left and Pie was staring at me with those enchanting eyes of hers, and just like that, I lost my fear of heights.

"So umm... would you like to ride the gondola with me?" I said with a smile.

"Yes, of course. I thought you'd never ask," Pie said with a twinkle in her eye. "I've been saving these all night hoping we'd get a chance to use them." Pie reached into her pocket and pulled out two golden tickets labeled "V.I.P.", they were exclusively for riding the gondola. She had won the tickets by calling in the correct answer during a radio trivia contest promoting the Shrimp and Petroleum Festival that year. The question was "What is the easternmost state of the United States?", and it seemed that no one knew the answer. The callers basically named just about every state on the eastern coast from Maine to Massachusetts to Connecticut all the way down to Virginia and the Carolinas, and still, no one got it right. Then Pie called the station and gave the correct answer, which shocked the other listeners and made the announcer say, "Damn girl, you're like a walking encyclopedia!" Her winning answer to the trivia contest was Alaska. Specifically, Semisopochnol Island, which is part of the Aleutian Islands that make up Alaska and extends across the 180th meridian, the line that separates the eastern hemisphere from the west. Ironically making Alaska the westernmost, northernmost, and yes, easternmost state in the country.

With the golden tickets in hand, we approached the ride and was given the Royal Treatment by a guy wearing mint green slacks with matching suspenders and white spats over his polished black shoes. His oversized shirt was aqua blue and had a butterfly collar that was so big that I thought he might lift off at the next gust of wind that came through. The oddly dressed man was in charge of operating the gondola, and when we handed him our tickets he asked our names and then made an announcement on the PA system that the gondola was now closed to all passengers "except for the Royal Couple---Prince Trell and Princess Pie." The glowing aura that surrounded Pie was growing brighter and becoming more alluring by the minute. I felt myself being drawn to her, falling for her in ways that I never experienced with anyone before.

"The stars sure are plentiful tonight," I said in an attempt to let her know that I was acutely aware of the magical atmosphere she helped conjure and was somehow deeply connected to. "I've never seen the moon this bright before, or this close." Pie simply smiled and kept nudging me with her shoulder, signaling that she was cold and wanted to share my jacket. I obliged her, of course, as any gentleman would. I removed my jacket and draped it around her shoulders making sure the wind couldn't get in from either side. We then stepped onto a tall platform leading to the open chariot waiting to take us among the stars. Once we were in our seats, the guy who was operating the ride carefully closed the safety bar across our lap and shook it, checking to make sure we were secure. I heard the engine rev up and then felt a slight tug on the cables, and soon the ride slowly began lifting us toward the night sky. Pie scooted closer, then leaned over and put her arms around my waist before gently laying her head upon my chest. I could suddenly smell the sweet, bewitching scent of fresh strawberries and French vanilla ice cream as it rose from her scented hair and awakened my soul from its slumber. I was beginning to feel like she could actually be the one.

"Trell, isn't this romantic?" said Pie.

"Yeah. This is pretty nice." I was trying to remain cool, but things were heating up fast. The closer Pie pressed her body next to mine the faster my heart would beat against my chest. It was our last night together... the thought of never seeing me again weighed heavily upon Pie's mind.

"Will you miss me?" she said with tears starting to form in the wells of her eyes.

"Of course I'm going to miss you, Pie" I said with a sincere heart. "I'm missing you already and I haven't even left yet."

"Don't tease me, Trell. I'm trying to be serious right now." To my surprise, Pie reached in her pocket and took out a gold chain necklace with a small locket attached to it.

"I want you to have this to remember me by," she said as she placed the gold chain around my neck and fastened the clamp in back. I looked down at the beautiful locket and was speechless. It was the most thoughtful gift I had ever received, and it was given to me by a girl who stole my heart the moment I saw her.

"Go 'head and open it," said Pie while flashing that gorgeous smile of hers. "I made it just for you."The locket looked very expensive, and judging by the weight, I could tell it was real gold. I opened it slightly and a song began playing on a tiny music box inside. It was our song!---"Do Whatcha Wana, Pt. 2" by Rebirth Brass Band---the one we danced to in the park where I did my Michael Jackson move. Me and Pie started jamming right there in our seats on the gondola while hanging high over the Atchafalaya having ourselves a ball. We laughed and reminisced about the "Smooth Criminal" dance lean I pulled off that had everyone cheering. It was good to see her laughing and having a great time. I adored this girl in ways I never thought possible, and when I pushed the locket door all the way open... there was Pie looking like a dream come true.

On the inside of the gold locket was a photo of Pie wearing a short red dress with matching shoes and dazzling earrings that sparkled like exquisite jewels. I was mesmerized by her beauty right off, it had a paralyzing effect on my mind to the point where I could barely think, and that made me very nervous. I had heard stories about how Creole girls would use charms and amulets to "voodoo" guys into falling in love with them. I could almost feel myself becoming "zombitized" by Pie's photo. The longer I stared at it the deeper it drew me into the bottomless ocean that lay beyond those mysterious light brown eyes of hers.Thankfully, after realizing how ridiculous I was being, the blank stare and rigid scowl I had cultivated out of fear and superstition melted into a natural smile and I was able to laugh at myself for acting so silly.

"Wow! That's a lovely picture," I said to Pie, who was smiling broadly. "Red is definitely your color. You look absolutely stunning in that dress."

"Thank you," she said with a twinkle in her eye. "The dress once belonged to my mother, it was her favorite. And now it's my favorite. I wore it to remind you of our time together, so that whenever you're feeling lonely, all you have to do is open the locket and I will be right there to cheer you up. I want you to know, Trell, that you've made a lasting impression on me. One that I can't describe. And this past weekend has been the most wonderful time of my entire life."

Her words touched my heart in such a way that I had no choice but to open up and tell her how I felt as well.

"Dear sweet Pie, from the moment we first met I have been beside myself with grief because I didn't know how to express the feelings in my heart whenever you're near me. I have adored you from the start, and now that I've come to know your heart, I am convinced beyond a doubt that I'm in love with you. So I want to say 'thank you' for bringing so much joy into my ordinary life, and thank you for the quiet moments when your eyes told me all I wanted to know about the world. You have shown me your compassion and spirit, and have taught me to live beyond expectations, beyond fear. Because of you, in a place where there was nothing before, in the deepest part of my heart... there is *love*."

Tears started streaming down her face as I professed my love to her under the stars and the moon and the heavens above. "Pie, I love you more than you could ever imagine and I wish I could be with you forever."

"You know, Trell, you should be careful what you wish for," Pie said as she closed the locket and gently kissed me on the cheek. "Wishes have a way of coming true around here."

And with that said, she laid her head upon my chest and began singing a soulful hymn that moved me to tears. Her melodic voice was so beautiful that it seemed to sway the wind and the trees to begin a courtship while making a joyful noise that only angels could make. It was during her heavenly rendition of "Precious Lord, Take My Hand" that the gondola stopped midway the Atchafalaya and Pie sang her heart out for all the world to hear:

"Precious Lord, take my hand, Lead me on, let me stand, I am tired, I am weak, I am worn. Through the storm, through the night, Lead me on to the light: Take my hand, precious Lord, Lead me home..."

I sat mesmerized wondering how in the world did I get so lucky. It was the most amazing experience of my young life and things were just getting started. I looked down and saw a parade of shrimp boats on the river, and there were bands on deck playing music for Pie and me as we sat high in the air clapping our hands to the beat. We could see people on the boats raising their glasses to us offering a toast that we may live long, prosperous lives in honor of God. While Pie continue waving back to the people on the boats, I suddenly noticed there were crowds standing on both sides of the river cheering and calling out my name.

"Pie, do you hear them? They're calling my name!" Little did I know, Pie had been born a "clairvoyant", a person blessed with extraordinary abilities beyond what most people could sense or perceive. And that night while sitting above the Atchafalaya, she revealed something to me that completely blew my twelve-year-old mind. No! Not *that,* you pervs! She revealed to me that one day I would go on a dangerous journey that would take me far from home where my loved ones could not follow. And because of this journey, I would become transformed by God into a fierce and mighty sword, the very kind He would use to kill the dragon who lives in the sea. And lastly, she explained that my coming to Morgan City wasn't a coincidence, that everyone was already expecting me to show up because it was my *homecoming,* and that's why the crowds were cheering my name. It was a lot for me to take in at such a young age, and Pie could see that I was struggling to comprehend the meaning of it all.

"I feel sad when someone I care about, like you Trell, has to face such a difficult trial. You don't deserve to go through such a thing, and there's no easy way around it. You just have to live through it. As time goes by, you'll grow stronger and rise above it, I know this, because I know you. I have seen the warrior you will become, he's not one to trifle with. There's a meaning in what the future will bring for you, a meaning that will have a purpose in your life you can't even imagine right now. But until then, hold on to God's unchanging hands and know that those who truly love you will always be by your side."

We rode the gondola to Berwick and was treated to a marvelous tour through town by horse drawn carriage, people lined the streets waving and cheering as me and Pie greeted them with smiles, hugs, and handshakes. I remembered Berwick from the romantic scene in the movie "The Yellow Handkerchief," starring John Hurt and Kristen Stewart, the girl who played "Bella" in the "Twilight" series. They were crossing the bridge from Morgan City to Berwick when suddenly they spotted a yellow handkerchief tied to the mass of one of the shrimp boats moored to the docks. It had been placed there as a sign from the guy's long lost wife letting him know she was still waiting for him. A happy ending to a beautiful story.

We later returned to the sky ride and traveled back across the Atchafalaya to Morgan City where we were immediately accosted by the mayor, who presented us with the "Key to the City". I was enjoying all the attention we were getting, but Pie was ready to get away from the lights and cameras and find a quiet place where the two of us could say our goodbyes. She asked the mayor for a favor, and the next thing you know, police on horseback were clearing an area of Downtown like the conclusion of Mardi Gras. There wasn't a soul in sight for three square blocks. Pie then took my hand and led me to the riverfront where I saw a huge cement structure that separated Downtown from the docks along the Atchafalaya. She called it the "Seawall", and said it protected the businesses on Front Street from flooding whenever the river would rise over the docks. I was amazed at seeing the beautiful images that were carved in the wall, each scene exemplified the spirit of the people who lived in and around the area. The carvings showed hunters and fishermen wearing camouflage gear and rubber boots surrounded by a collage of deer, rabbits, ducks, raccoons, crawfish, shrimp, crabs, and of course, alligators. There was also images of boats hauling huge catches of fish and shrimp while their nets and pulleys strained to bring them in. But the carving I found most compelling was the one that showed a gigantic oil rig in the Gulf of Mexico with giant waves rolling onto its lower decks. The scene struck a familiar chord in the recesses of my mind, but at the time it was only a premonition... *Weird, right?*

As we ascended the stairs beside the massive Seawall, I noticed the tantalizing aroma of Creole gumbo coming from one of the food courts around the corner. I was tempted to turn around and go back over to Lawrence Park for a sample of delicious seafood, but I abandoned the thought once I saw the expression on Pie's face and realized she had no intentions of delaying her quest to be alone with me. So onward and upward we went with unwavering determination, and once I saw the magnificent view from the top of the wall, I knew something magical was bound to happen.

"Pie, I can't believe how beautiful the view is from up here! Hey, look over there!" I said while pointing toward the majestic bayous west of the Atchafalaya. "Wow! This is so amazing!" The immaculate horizon was like something out of a movie. There were beams of light emanating from the brightest full moon I'd ever seen. It looked like the roof of the Superdome was sitting over the bayou shining its incandescent light on the ancient bald cypress trees standing in the enchanted woods rumored to be the last place the legendary Rougarou was spotted.

Pie turned to me and said, "Would you like to go for a walk in the woods?" And before I could say anything she made a spooky face and yelled, "GGrrrooaarrr!!!", catching me off guard and scaring me half to death. I nearly jumped right off the wall thinking that the Rougarou had snuck up on us. Pie laughed until she was out of breath, then offered an apology for the prank and promised not to scare me like that again. I have to admit, she got me good that time.

The stage was now set for our final moments together, we couldn't have asked for a more romantic place to share an interlude: plumes of misty fog from the swamps and bayous were rolling over the levees nearby while the moonlight settled on the murky waters of the Atchafalaya creating a dreamscape like no other. When the fog reached the docks, it made the shrimp boats look like lonely ghost ships waiting in the night. In the distance, I heard owls hooting their hearts out above the rest of the critters trying to have their voices heard in the gentle wind blowing through the woods... Meanwhile, me and Pie stood atop the great Seawall gazing at the horizon and listening to the music of the waves splashing against the ramparts beneath us, and I remember thinking about all the fun we had that weekend. From the impromptu second line parade to the enchanting ride on the gondola to the magical atmosphere atop the Seawall, everything that happened during these amazing three days in Morgan City will forever be my most cherished memories of my youth. I will never forget the soft touch of Pie's caramel skin next to mine and the twinkle in her gorgeous brown eyes as she gazed up at the fireworks exploding overhead. And just when I thought life couldn't get any better, Pie leaned over and pressed her sweet, luscious lips to my mouth and gave me a passionate kiss. I remember tasting the delicious strawberry flavored lip gloss she was wearing that night, and when I felt her warm tongue inside my mouth---Oh my god!---I passed out right there on top of the Seawall in front of God and all His angels.

All I remember thinking to myself was, "Oh my god! Is this really happening? Am I tongue kissing this amazing girl right now?" The next thing I knew, Pie was standing over me wearing a broad smile that showed her dimples in the most alluring way.

"Are you okay?" she asked while holding back a laugh. "I tried to catch you but it happened so fast that there wasn't any time."

Yep! I fainted right in front of her, but she was real cool about the whole thing. We started laughing and then she sat next to me and we continued cuddling and kissing like two hot lovers reunited after spending a long time apart... it was beautiful.

I remember hearing sea gulls singing whimsical songs of romance and mischief while whisking by on the wings of love. I remember the soft, majestic light of the full moon reflecting in the shimmering waters of the Atchafalaya, and the extravagant street carnival behind us in full swing with the promiscuous sights and sounds of Bourbon Street on Mardi Gras day. I remember the spectacular midnight sky alit with colorful fireworks and the misty rain blowing gently against my skin while I remained entangled in a passionate kiss with the most beautiful girl I'd ever seen, me and Pie remained lost in our own little world, caught up in the rapture of love. Even the stars above recognized that we were kindred spirits, and they began twinkling in celebration of our love. How could anyone forget something like that?

Thank you Pie, for giving me the best moments of my life.

"Uhh-HHmmm!" I didn't realize Azoria was listening to my thoughts about Pie until I heard her make a loud, obnoxious sound as if clearing her throat.

"Are you done reminiscing about that girl?" she said with an attitude. "Your little soliloquy is running a bit long, don't you think?"

Despite her indignation toward my memories of Pie, Azoria knew that the immense joy I experienced when falling in love for the first time was exactly what the Sphinx needed to see in me if I was to have any chance of reaching Elysium.

"As much as it pains me to say this," she begrudgingly admitted. "Your memories of being with that girl should be offered to the orb."

"Thank you, Azoria. I know how awkward this all seems but you asked me for my most cherised memories, and that's what I gave you."

"You're right, my love. Now focus your mind and project the memories into the center of the Sphinx, along with the joyous feelings they invoke within your spirit."I followed her instructions and gathered my thoughts about that magical weekend in

Morgan City, then telepathically introduced them into the giant orb sitting at the helm of "Ezekiel's Wheel". The orb immediately sensed the great joy in my heart and in my spirit, and it began to hum and sing as its light grew brighter and brighter until the brilliancy exceeded that of the Alpha Orionis itself... And that's when it happened.

The Spirit of God came upon me like a rushing wind, and I was so overcome with joy that tears started falling from my eyes. Every struggle, every disappointment, every heartache I had ever endured in my life was pouring out through the copious tears I shed before the Lord. The presence of His Holy Spirit was everywhere, I could feel Him building me up where I was torn down and nourishing my spirit with His love. He opened my eyes to the wonders I could achieve if only I put Him first in my life. I witnessed His awesome power and saw that it was greater than all the demons in hell combined.

Jesus wrapped His loving aura around me and lifted me up, and as we ascended toward Elysium I noticed the wounds in His hands and feet and was reminded of 1 Peter 1:3-5...

"Blessed be the God and Father of our Lord Jesus Christ, who according to His great mercy has caused us to be born again to a living hope through the resurrection of Jesus Christ from the dead, to obtain an inheritance which is imperishable and undefiled and will not fade away, reserved in heaven for you, who are protected by the power of God through faith for a salvation ready to be revealed in the last days."

Through my faith in God and because I was anointed by the Blood of the Lamb, the doors of heaven were opened for me and I became... *transformed.*

I was carried toward a brilliant light wherein I heard angels singing God's name in harmony. "Come!," the angels sang. "Come unto the Elysian Fields! O Lord God, the Almighty!"

I looked and I saw Azoria waving and gesturing for me to join her. She was standing atop a fiery enclave and she had huge angel wings extending outward from her body, they were alit with white flames so beautiful that I could not look away from their enchanting light.

"I have dreamed of this moment a thousand times," said Azoria. "And now that you are here, I cannot find the words to express the enormous joy I'm feeling right now. I've really missed you, D'Shawn."

"I've really missed you too, Azoria. But why have you summoned me so far from the Galactic Island? I thought the island was like, 'our spot'. You know, the place we built together."

"You are the Chosen One, my love. Chosen by God to lead His most powerful arcangels into battle against the dark forces threatening to destroy all that is good. There is a war coming, a great reckoning of souls on earth and in heaven. And God has placed you in command of His armies to defend the greatest kingdom in all of heaven... the KINGDOM OF ZION."

"And He said to him... today you shall be with Me in Paradise."---Luke 23:43

ABOUT THE AUTHOR

The pseudonym "Parish V. Damone" is an artistic expression of the author's real name (Victor Damone McClendon) and his stage name (M. C. Parish) of the 1990's hip-hop duo "Surrender" on Mobo Records in New Orleans. He also went by the name "M. C. V8" on his solo debut album entitled "Big Tyme" on Regal Records in Baton Rouge.

He was born in Milwaukee, Wisconsin, but later moved with his mother to Louisiana and graduated from Morgan City High School in 1984, which was the same year he entered college at Southern University in Baton Rouge. He studied at Southern from 1984 to 1987 and was a star performer in the marching band there known around the world as the "Human Jukebox."

Mr. McClendon is a U.S. veteran who received an honorable discharge in 1995 after serving eight years in the army. In the year 2000, he graduated ITI Technical College and began a lucrative career in designing and building control panels used in the control rooms of major oil plants throughout the Gulf region. Tragically, due to false testimony brought against him, he is now a first time offender at Angola serving life. He thanks you for all the encouragement and prayers he's received and wishes to convey a message of deep appreciation to his many loyal readers.

Translation Table

Page	Encryption	Translation
6		Fear not, for you are the chosen one.
119		Walk by faith, not by sight.
131		Come touch the ball, and then enter into the bookstore.
162		Witches wail while warlocks watch, ten goblins steal the tick and tock; move with haste you must not wait, to cross the gate with leap of faith; brooms and wands go round and round, moons collide and stars fall down; then is now and now has passed, the door is open for you at last.
271		Love is the key.
291		"Behold, I am coming soon... My reward is with me... I am the Alpha and the Omega, the First and the Last, the Beginning and the End." (Revelation 22:12-13) "He who believes in me will live, even though he dies." (John 11:25)

"When the thousand years are over, Satan will be released from his prison and go out to deceive the nations in the four corners of the earth… to gather them for battle. In number they are like the sand on the seashore."
------Revelation 20:7-8

www.ingramcontent.com/pod-product-compliance
Lightning Source LLC
Chambersburg PA
CBHW060318100726
47907CB00002B/455